DR SWEET AND HIS

Peter Bradshaw is the film critic for the *Guardian* and writes regularly for the *Evening Standard*. He has also contributed to the *Modern Review*, the *New Statesman*, *Tribune* and the *London Review of Books*. His first novel, *Lucky Baby Jesus*, was published in 1999 to critical acclaim. He lives in London.

Praise for Peter Bradshaw's first novel
Lucky Baby Jesus:

'Tender in the romantic moments, with a great supporting cast, this is a fine and funny piece of work'
Susan Jeffreys, *Independent*

'Wickedly funny debut novel'
Alex Clark, *Guardian*

'The funniest novel of the year'
Stephen Pollard, *Daily Express*

'Focused, literate, intelligent, nicely observed, humane, funny'
Phil Baker, *Sunday Times*

'A comic treat'
Sebastian Shakespeare, *Tatler*

'Fresh, impressive and . . . unexpectedly moving'
Jason Cowley, *The Times*

Also by Peter Bradshaw

LUCKY BABY JESUS

PETER BRADSHAW

Dr Sweet and his daughter

Peter Bradshaw (signature)

PICADOR

First published 2003 by Picador
an imprint of Pan Macmillan Ltd
Pan Macmillan, 20 New Wharf Road, London N1 9RR
Basingstoke and Oxford
Associated companies throughout the world
www.panmacmillan.com

ISBN 0 330 49216 0

1 3 5 7 9 8 6 4 2

A CIP catalogue record for this book is available from
the British Library.

Typeset by Intype London Ltd
Printed and bound in Great Britain by
Mackays of Chatham plc, Chatham, Kent

For

Albert Desmond Bradshaw

and

Mollie Bradshaw

'A Last Judgement is Necessary
because Fools Flourish'

William Blake

PART ONE

1

Nothing in Dr Sweet's life until that moment would hint he was capable of killing anyone, still less capable of enjoying it. Yet on one sharp winter night, with his physical capabilities drifting back on the ebb tide of middle age and at the limit of his professional career, Dr Sweet found that he could indeed kill someone, and that his life had begun again.

2

'Cordie!'

'Cordie!'

Dr Sweet's elderly parents, John and Rosemary, were trying to engage the attention of their only grandchild. An exhausting car journey to London from Carlisle had not diminished their enthusiasm for this. They stood in the kitchen, sensible coats still on, talking brightly yet fiercely to a five-year-old girl in a fairy tiara, who was rearranging her beanie babies in military rank and precedence on a chair near the hissing gas fire.

'Cordie!'

'Hello, Cordie!'

Dr Sweet came into the kitchen with the intention of asking his parents if he could take their coats and if they wanted a sherry, but he found they ignored him quite as intently as Cordie was ignoring them. John and Rosemary's faces were made pink and hot by the kitchen fug after the bitter cold, and by their exasperation at Cordie airily declining to acknowledge them.

'Let's play a game, Cordie.'

'Yes, let's play Fizzbuzz!'

Dr Sweet's heart sank. Many was the birthday party

of his own boyhood that had been dampened and soured by his parents' insistence on Fizzbuzz.

'Fizzbuzz is a numbers game, Cordie. And numbers are *fun*, aren't they?'

John and Rosemary, retired maths teachers, left a tiny pause for Cordie to drop what she was doing and give a gleeful confirmation of this; when none was forthcoming, they pressed on.

'It's a numbers game,' Rosemary repeated. 'You take turns counting up from one to a hundred!'

John interjected, 'Only when you reach a number divisible by, say, three you say, "Fizz," instead of the number!'

'Yes,' said Rosemary eagerly, 'and instead of a number divisible by, say, five, you say "Buzz!"'

'And when you reach a number divisible by both three *and* five, you say, "Fizzbuzz!"'

Again, they left a beat for little Cordie to whoop with excitement.

'So, Grandma and I will show you,' said John, unable to abandon Fizzbuzz now, the pedagogic severity of a lifetime forcing him to continue. They hadn't even got their coats off.

'One!'

'Two!' returned Rosemary.

'Fizz!'

'Four!'

'Buzz!'

'Fizz!'

'Seven!'

'Eight!'

'Fizz!'

'Buzz!'

'Eleven!'

'Fizz!'

'Thirteen!'

'Fourteen!'

'Fizzbuzz!'

'Fuck off!'

This last was Cordie, who had turned from her beanies and was solemnly pointing her fairy wand at them.

For a fleeting moment, Dr Sweet remembered his father standing on the green Subbuteo football field on his ninth birthday to enforce a game of Fizzbuzz, crunching a player with his brogue and giving his son a misjudged, hearty cuff round the ear when he tried to object. Dr Sweet thought he saw John's hand flex and stiffen again now as he turned towards him, as if quite ready to mete out this punishment again. Dr Sweet could remember it, the flat of his hand coming off the side of his head with a quick, clean impact, like a skimming stone.

In the appalled silence, Dr Sweet scooped up Cordie and her toys and carried her out of the room, while she continued to point her wand at her grandparents over his shoulder.

'She's been poorly,' he called out. 'She's had a lot of Calpol. In fact, she's got a bit of a Calpol hangover. She's got the beginnings of a Calpol abuse problem. I'm going to get her into a twelve-step programme. *Now* then, Miss Cordie,' he said, as he entered the small dining room, hoisting Cordie round and putting her down with a bump on a chair by the big round table on which she had been drawing. '*Now* then. *Now* then.' Dr Sweet was puffing a little. Cordie had allowed herself to be sat, and rested her wand on top of her crayons, looking down at them meditatively, fine chestnut hair a little ruffled under her tiara, downy chin doubling slightly.

Dr Sweet shifted the chair so that he could look directly at Cordie; he took both her little hands between the finger and thumb of his own and whispered, 'Cordie, you remember what we said about saying bad words, especially to your grandma and grandpa?'

Cordie's eyes met his own briefly, evasively; she raised her eyebrows a little and nodded, the tiny pouch of fat under her chin appearing once. Dr Sweet didn't want to press the point. Actually, *he* was the one that said bad words. Dr Sweet ferried her around in the car, with Cordie strapped uncomplainingly in the child seat in the back, and naturally, she'd learned from the way he spoke at the wheel, so whenever he had to brake sharply, little Cordie would squeak, 'Fuck!' but remain entirely impassive and go back to singing how the wheels on the bus go round and round. Having established a consensus on the bad-language issue, Dr Sweet released her hands and patted his own decisively on his thighs.

'So, what do you want to do? Play something on your typewriter xylophone?'

'*Jungle Book.*'

'Do some drawing?'

'*Jungle Book.*'

'Come into the kitchen and sing "Away In A Manger" for your grandma and grandpa?'

'*Jungle Book.*'

'Watch *The Jungle Book* on video over and over again?'

'Yes.'

'Allow *The Jungle Book* video to become your primary care giver?'

'Yes,' sang out Cordie again, oblivious to the irony, responding only to the magic title itself.

Dr Sweet sighed with his mouth closed, nostrils flaring. He peered out into the corridor and guessed that his parents would by now have taken their coats off, laid them over one of the chairs, and be feeling a bit restless. A few minutes more and they would be side by side at the sink, washing up the dirty mugs. He looked back at Cordie, who was tapping expectantly on the video box with her wand. Could there be a single scene of Walt Disney's *The Jungle Book* that she didn't have off by heart? Couldn't Cordie simply close her eyes and recreate any still from this film effortlessly, down to every jungle leaf, every nuance of bafflement on Baloo's face, every banana-leaf frond on his skirts?

Dr Sweet placed the video in the slot and began the slow rewind back to the beginning.

'Have you had enough to eat, Cordie?' he asked, glancing at the half-eaten banana on her little plate.

To this question, and many plaintive equivalents, Cordie tended to parrot the answer that would be given by Ana, her Portuguese child-minder and occasional baby-sitter before Cordie started school. Ana thought that 'too much' meant 'a lot'. Had Cordie played with other children today, Ana? Too much. Had she had any juice? Too much. And what about her 'quiet time' nap? Too much.

The VCR's whirring got higher and faster and then gave a thunk. Leaning forward, Cordie pointed imploringly at the remote. Dr Sweet picked it up and gave it to her, and she pressed Play and settled back as the credit sequence began. 'You like Dumbo,' she said accusingly as he went back out to the kitchen.

'No I don't,' he said.

'Yes you are,' said Cordie bafflingly, and looked back at the screen.

*

Back in the kitchen, John was remembering the Subbuteo incident. It was on his son's ninth birthday, and he and Rosemary had invited a lot of his friends, some from the village, some from his new prep school. It was the homespun 3.30-till-6 children's party that you seemed to be able to get away with in those days, not the expensive bashes that he and Rosemary saw being laid on for Cordie and her little cousins. Games were pass the parcel and Ring-a-ring-a-roses, get them all tuckered out and a bit of an appetite up for tea, and then afterwards the parents would come and pick them up, but in the lull, they'd often scratch together a game of their own. That was when some of the boys suggested Subbuteo and started behaving really quite badly, messing with the little plastic players, throwing the ball about; his son was on the verge of tears, and the day might have been quite spoiled. John took control of the situation by standing in the middle of the room, one foot on a corner of the green baize, and firmly suggesting a round of Fizzbuzz.

Dr Sweet had gratefully agreed and John had tousled his hair, a manly tousle, the sort of physical contact licensed between father and son in his day and his own father's day. It was the last time he did it though: after that, Dr Sweet had got a bit precious about having his head touched. Sometimes, when Dr Sweet was in his teens, John would wake him up in the morning by running a hand across his hair, and his son would lurch up with a convulsive shiver, brushing him away.

'Well, not a bad run, eh?' said John to Rosemary.

'No, not at all,' she replied, glancing at her watch and the kitchen clock. 'Six and a half hours, door to door.'

'Got in before the rain came on, too.' John was looking out of the window at the dank back garden, with its climbing frame and tricycle, and ducking a little so he could squint up at the sugary sky.

'Shall we have a crack at these mugs then, Rose?'

'Rather.'

'You wash, I'll dry.'

'Mum, Dad.'

Dr Sweet came back into the kitchen and forcibly removed the mug from his mother's grasp with one hand and with the other grasped the tea towel John had put over his shoulder, whisking it off with a loud whiplash crack. 'Don't worry about doing that. We'll put those things in the dishwasher with everything else after dinner tonight.'

Reluctantly, John and Rosemary nodded and settled back down into their chairs.

'Sherry?'

'Mm,' they said together without enthusiasm. Sherry was what they were always offered by their son, as a testament to the good cheer he felt he ought to provide at Christmas. Really they would have preferred a cup of tea, but felt that declining sherry would be unsporting and construed as some kind of disapproving comment, although having just been told to fuck off by their only grandchild, they were surely entitled to a few of those?

'David, is Cordie quite . . .'

'Oh, Mum, I'm sorry,' said Dr Sweet, putting his own small, sticky sherry down and clutching his head in a pantomime of anguish and self-reproach. 'I'm sorry. Cordie's very naughty. I really told her off just now and she's very sorry.' There was a pause while the three of them reviewed the patent untruth of this last sentence. 'The thing is, she's *been* poorly, she's *had* Calpol—'

'If I'd have spoken that way to my father . . .' said John, in a low voice, shaking his head.

'Dad—'

'I'd have got a clip round the ear, me or my sister. And if I'd spoken to my grandfather like that in front of my father . . .'

'. . . he'd have got his heavy service revolver out of the attic and shot you through the heart.'

With this last weary and belligerent pleasantry, the thin crust of diplomacy broke. John looked out of the window again, the corners of his mouth turned down, while Rosemary put her mug down on the kitchen table.

'David, we are not going to stay here and be spoken to like that.'

Dr Sweet raised both palms but was not yet ready to offer an apology.

'We are not going to stay here,' concluded Rosemary and made a great show of getting up, removing three brightly wrapped parcels from her bag and walking over to the door.

'I have left presents for you, Alice and Cordie there on the table, but now John and I will have to go.'

'Rose.'

'Mum.'

'No, I'm sorry. I'm sorry. We won't be spoken to like this again.'

'I've made up the bed and everything. Please, Mum.'

'Rose,' repeated John, on a sad, falling note. Slowly, with the dignified air she had used for thirty years as a non-stipendiary magistrate, Rosemary resumed her seat, as if willing provisionally to suspend judgement in the light of new evidence or extenuating circumstances.

'Mum, I'm sorry; I really am. I've been under a lot of stress. Cordie hasn't been well and she's anxious about seeing Alice again tonight.'

Dr Sweet judged that a reminder of his ex-wife's planned arrival that evening, exactly one year after their divorce had gone through, would re-establish the sober atmosphere of crisis management handy for keeping his parents in check. At the word 'anxious' his mother's face creased itself into a constellation of tender concern.

'Is she? Is Cordie upset?'

Dr Sweet paused, cunningly conveying the sense of some awful truth withheld.

'Well, Alice coming back like this at Christmas has stirred up quite a lot of nerves. There've been broken nights, thumb-sucking, sleepwalking and bed-wetting. And Cordie's not too happy, either.'

'David, for heaven's sake, if you can't—'

'Mum, look I'm just – I don't know. I'm just saying that both Cordie and I are quite stressed.' But Dr Sweet saw instantly that this emphasis on stress was misjudged; John and Rosemary were from a generation that didn't see 'stress' as an occasion for leniency. 'What I'm saying is that it's a difficult time for Cordie and she needs her grandma and grandpa to provide *stability* and *continuity*.'

John and Rosemary were mollified.

'And love,' said John quietly, looking down at his hands folded in his lap.

Before Dr Sweet could reply, the doorbell rang. He went out into the gloomy corridor where the green-and-red coloured glass in the front door, backlit by the street lamp, glowed with cathedral calm. He saw a silhouette, off centre, like a film poster for a psychological thriller. This couldn't be Alice, could it? It was a quarter to six and she was expected at half past seven.

'David?'

He turned back to face the kitchen.

'It's all right, Mum, I'm just going to answer it.'

No, it wasn't Alice. Hang on, yes it was. She'd had her hair cut.

'David.'

'Alice! How are you? It's only, you're early.'

Her hair was short. While they were married it was shoulder length, now it was in a severe bob, razored up the nape of her neck, perhaps because of the new strands of silver in the chestnut brown. For the very first time he realized that throughout their married life he'd had no clear sense of the shape of her face: the clear hazel eyes, the straight nose and wide, thin mouth were set in a round, almost plumply boyish face.

'I'm fine, how are you? Are you all right?'

'Fine, why?'

Because he was staring at her in a very odd way. Dr Sweet had expected to be upset by seeing his ex-wife again. He had anticipated having to master feelings of depression and wary dislike, but her new short haircut made her look so startlingly like Cordie, or rather, brought out Cordie's startling resemblance to her mother, that he was assailed by a quite different feeling. He saw again how her irises were flecked with black, like petals, from the pupil stem, and that the bridge of her nose lengthened and narrowed emphatically, as if drawn with two light strokes of a 3B pencil. Soon, he thought, Cordie's little button nose would begin to break through and grow to resemble her mother's. Dr Sweet felt a brief electric pang of gentleness and tenderness for them both.

'Because you were staring at me in a very odd way.'

'Was I? Sorry.'

'Don't apologize, but could you give me a hand with one of these?'

In a great fluster, and after almost knocking his head against Alice's as they both went for her bags, Dr Sweet followed his ex-wife into the house. Without waiting for her ex-husband, she dropped her case by the stairs and walked straight into the kitchen where she found John hovering by the sink, experimentally testing the weight of a short, squat bottle of Fairy Liquid in his right hand.

'Alice,' he said with a guilty start, putting it down on the draining board.

'John,' she said, with a brilliant professional-person smile that none of them could remember her ever using before. 'How are you?'

'I'm well,' John beamed. 'Very well, and *you're* looking very well.'

'Thank you. Rosemary,' Alice turned to face a cooler welcome from Dr Sweet's mother.

'Alice.'

Alice gently, experimentally, angled her cheek toward Rosemary's, to see whether a kiss would be proffered. It was not, and Alice had to convert her lean into a sort of absent-minded neck movement, which segued into stretching her eyes open wide, and touching the side of her right eye with a fingertip, as if steadying a contact lens. For a moment they all gazed at the three glasses of sherry.

'Mummy.' That small, light voice acted like a cattle prod.

'*Cordie*. Cordie.' Alice scooped the little girl up and did a little jiggling dance round and round the kitchen while the rest looked on.

'Hello, Miss Cordie,' said Alice placing her nose directly against her daughter's. 'How are you? How has daddy been treating you? What have you been doing?'

'Don't eat the prickly pear with the paw, When you eat the pear try to use the claw!' said Cordie, waving the remote about. Alice gave Dr Sweet a withering glance.

'It's all she wants to do,' Dr Sweet semi-mouthed, semi-whispered with a shrug. Alice put Cordie down and she scampered off into the other room, returning with all her beanie babies crammed in a single adult's slipper.

'My goodness, Cordie, what are those?' said Rosemary with the extra 20 per cent volume adults use to address small children.

Alice motioned Cordie to show them to her grandmother.

'They're beanies,' said Cordie with a patient sigh, taking them out of the slipper and arranging them on a chair with her back to Rosemary. Rosemary got up and tried leading Cordie back to where she was sitting by taking her by the hand and pulling her. But Cordie stayed where she was. Her arm was yanked in its socket.

'Ow!'

'Easy now, Mum,' said Dr Sweet. 'She won't move if you tug her; she's like a seat belt in that regard, aren't you, Miss Cordie?'

Cordie, with an air of martyred dignity, started arranging her beanies in a conga-line. Rosemary was a little abashed, conscious of having lost her usual moral high ground. Quietly, she came up and sat next to Cordie and asked her what their names were. Cordie answered; Rosemary guessed that they were presents and Cordie agreed they were. So far, so good, though a tiny emergency alarm was tripped in Dr Sweet's mind by her next question.

'And how much do these dollies cost?' Both Cordie and Dr Sweet winced at that grotesque solecism. Hadn't she just been told they're called *beanies*?

'Four pounds ninety-nine,' said Cordie accurately.

'And how many of them have you got?'

'Six.'

'So how much money do they cost in total?'

Just as Cordie turned to her grandmother, top row of teeth pressed against lower lip and little cheeks slightly inflated, Dr Sweet whisked her away.

'That's enough for now, Miss Cordie,' he said, picking her up by her waist and carrying her under his arm. 'Do you want to watch some more *Jungle Book*?'

'Yes,' said Cordie simply in her horizontal position. They went out and there was quiet, and John and Rosemary's mood passed from mild resentment at being forced to indulge this little girl so uncritically to a stab of regret that she had gone and they now had to concentrate on each other's company without her palliative distraction.

'Vodka and tonic?' Dr Sweet asked his ex-wife as he came back into the room.

'Just a fruit juice,' said Alice, settling herself on the third seat near the gas fire. 'Or maybe I could get a soda?'

Soda, thought Dr Sweet with a silent sniff of scorn. *Get* a soda? She might be able to *have* a soda.

'I don't think we've got any soda water,' said Dr Sweet insolently. 'Will something like Coca-cola or Sprite do?'

'Fine, yes, Coke,' said Alice sweetly, with a tight little smile that indicated her refusal to be drawn into hostilities while registering a formal complaint at the provocation.

'We didn't expect you until half past seven, Alice,' said Rosemary, by way of making conversation.

'Oh really? I e-mailed David saying half past six or so.'

'E-mailed? At home or work?' said David from a crouching position, the voice bottled because his head was inside the fridge.

'Work.'

'Ah. I was at home.'

Still searching for the Coke, Dr Sweet removed a plate of chicken legs intended for that evening's dinner, each big enough to kill a thief.

'You said to e-mail you at work.'

'No I didn't. You know I didn't.'

There was a pause in which all four of them assessed the possibility of a row. Dr Sweet's head throbbed with irritability and dismay, Then he said, 'Do you know, we haven't got any Coke. I'll just nip down to the shop and get some.'

Instantly there was uproar.

'No, no, David, don't do that, I'm fine with anything.'

'Oh, darling, do you have to go out now?'

'No, that's fine. We need some more milk and coffee anyway. I won't be more than a quarter of an hour.'

Desperate to disperse the white noise of his ill humour, Dr Sweet dashed out into the hall, shrugged on his coat and ducked into the next room. There, as he calculated, was Cordie, entranced by the scene in which Kaa, the boa constrictor, is hypnotizing Mowgli. Under her arm was a plump Santa beanie which she squeezed like an accordion. Her pupils, like Mowgli's, seemed to radiate unwholesome kaleidoscopic circles.

'Just off out, Cordie,' he said, and then knelt down and took her little hands between his fingers and thumbs. He noticed that, quite unbidden, Cordie had put on her cardigan and buttoned it up by herself – the bright pink and green cardigan with A for Apple and B for Bed on it. It must be too cold in here. 'How much do you love me, Cordie?' he asked plaintively. 'How much do you love your poor old dad?' Cordie stirred like an unquiet sleeper and her opaque eyes briefly met his.

'Too much.'

3

Once outside, Dr Sweet's head released its pain potential. The fine mist of London rain and darkness augmented the sheen of cold sweat on his forehead. He looked at his watch; it was quarter past six. Better get moving. Dr Sweet removed the pain-wash by closing his eyes, tilting his head back slightly and rotating it in a small figure-of-eight movement. His brain cleared like a touch on the FM tuning dial.

The dismal truth about his relationship with his parents and his ex-wife had returned, and any hopes he'd entertained for a miraculous Christmas of good cheer had fled like dreams. Grimly, he marched on towards the convenience store on the next corner, briefly executing the Napoleonic tic of checking his wallet was in place.

The pavements of the Archway Road, which led up from the mighty confluence of Junction Road, Holloway Road and Highgate Hill to the great reaches of the North Circular, were bleached and sparkling yellow under the sodium lights from much rain and a recent freeze, which had removed the murk yet appeared to have inscribed into the concrete various flotsam: a brown leaf and a cigarette packet, flattened out with all its tabs and sections. One flagstone lay marginally below the others, making a dark rectangle where Dr Sweet briefly tripped, smacking the palm of his hand unpleasantly on the ground, a sensation that returned him to the experience of childhood and the playground in a way nothing else could.

Straightening up, and in his discomfort and mortification quite forgetting what he was supposed to be doing, Dr Sweet paused and looked in the window of the martial arts shop that neighboured a terrace of deserted short-lease commercial premises, each with its compost-mound of unregarded mail and yellowing flyers. There, next to photographs of people in pyjama-like outfits demonstrating ju-jitsu moves, was a display of replica Lugers and Smith & Wessons. But these took second place to the crossbows with their heavy mahogany-looking butts, taut parallelograms of cord, and the firing mechanisms that discharged thin, carbon-coloured steel bolts. The shop's opening hours, he noticed with astonishment and awe, were Monday to Friday, ten till six, and within these hours there was nothing to stop him popping in here and buying a crossbow, a weapon as lethal as any gun. With this, he could kill someone, or himself. But what was this? What was that strange oval with two ungainly wings on either side? Some strange new nunchuck perhaps, some hideous object suspended from a short, brutal chain? Or perhaps a thin metal disc with a mortally sharp edge and a cunning arrangement of wings to facilitate its flight through the air?

Adjusting the focus of his eyes, Dr Sweet saw the truth. Jesus, it was his head. His own head, reflected in the glass. And one of his ears was bigger than the other. Much bigger. Actually, both of them seemed big. Jesus, that was it. He *was like* Dumbo. He had middle-aged-man big ears.

Thunderstruck by this revelation, Dr Sweet put his hands up to his ears, touching them gingerly as if for the very first time. He tried gathering each ear in the palm of each hand and crushing them back, then releasing them, silk kerchiefs in a conjuror's palms.

Middle-aged men suffer from subtle but inexorable ear growth. Not only does your face get fatter and your stomach bigger, but your ears get larger, too. Not your penis, oh no. Your ears. They would continue to grow after his death, thought Dr Sweet, and his coffin lid would bulge and pop out with the pressure of the great pink, fleshy shroud swarming all over his decaying body. Or was it that his head was getting smaller?

It was twenty-five past six. He trudged on and reached the PriceBest supermarket, where a rack for black bananas and liquid avocados stayed outside twenty-four hours a day. Dr Sweet stepped into the shop just as a mother was leaving with her tiny son strapped into a pushchair. The boy, holding a giant bag of cheesy snacks in his right hand, one small snack in his left, so vividly coloured it was almost glowing, was immobile, contemplative, staring straight ahead.

Ears. Big Ears, thought Dr Sweet. Noddy's unattractive friend. Unattractive even given the low standards of sexiness in Noddy's milieu.

'Hello, David. Hellooo.' Kamil, the proprietor of PriceBest, gave his strange crooning greeting; Dr Sweet smiled back and for a second they looked together at the Turkish cable programme on the wall-mounted TV opposite. A tall blonde woman with the tanned, equine face of a transsexual was standing on a podium in an electric-blue stage-set. Opposite her was a panel of casually dressed middle-aged men, comporting themselves with gravity; the woman directed their attention to a low perspex table, on which were a set of mugs, a cocktail shaker and a pair of secateurs. Dr Sweet's eyes wandered to a smaller black-and-white television, showing a silent four-way split-screen composition: top left, a small dark-haired girl of Cordie's age walked briskly out of frame carrying a box; top right, a still life of a refrigerator cabinet; bottom left, the small girl again, this time shot from above; and bottom right, a man with prominent ears looked up into some distant corner. Suddenly a figure appeared in front of the refrigerator cabinet still life: a swarthy, grinning man of indeterminate age who looked directly into the camera. From the other screen came a burst of studio applause: the blonde woman had her arm around one of the men on the panel, who was holding up the secateurs.

When Dr Sweet turned back to Kamil, the dark-haired girl had arrived with a box of chewing gum. She started to decant the little packs into a similar box, cut open to form a kind of rudimentary display case.

'How are you, David?' asked Kamil politely. His bearing was ramrod straight, bolt upright, his right hand resting on the glass counter, his left positioned in the small of his back. He held a lighted cigarette between his left forefinger and thumb which he conscientiously kept hidden from his customers.

'I'm fine, Kamil, thank you. And you?'

'Oh,' exclaimed Kamil brightly, inclining his head with a sad smile and leaving it at that.

'Have you any Coke?'

Kamil pointed to the refrigerator cabinet at the back and proffered the same sad smile. With a nod, Dr Sweet set off for the cabinet, stepping over a puddle of extra virgin olive oil that was seeping into the aisle from a broken bottle. He arrived at the cold cabinet and reached through a fringe of transparent strips which enclosed the contents in a kind of climate-controlled bower. He took two big bottles, put one under his armpit, and reached for a can of Spanish olives.

When he turned round, something was very wrong. The pool of olive oil in the aisle seemed to have grown larger and even a little deeper, a shallow viscous mound of oil whose surface curvature reflected the neon lights in fluent stripes. And there was a splodgy, splashy trail of oil leading to the front of the store by the till. The floor's incline meant that secondary rivulets ran around a triangular piece of glass a little further on.

And standing by the till, the broken olive oil bottle in his hand, was the man he had seen on the TV monitor. The man held the bottle by the neck so that the triangular hole, drooling oil, was facing outwards in an unpleasantly sharp spike.

Kamil was not there. Some time between directing Dr Sweet to the cold cabinet and Dr Sweet turning round he must have disappeared to the storeroom, leaving his six-year-old daughter in charge of the premises, and it was towards her that the man's sharp bottle weapon was now pointing.

'What's this, what's this?' he jeered, waving the broken glass very close to the little girl's eyes. 'What's this?'

Dr Sweet silently replaced the can of olives and the two Coke bottles and got ready to move. An unnecessary precaution, because the noise from the television made everything he did quite inaudible.

Where was Kamil?

Slowly, very slowly, Dr Sweet moved towards the counter. Outside, people were passing by, quite heedless. But was there anything to be heedful of? He could walk out briskly now, turn right, go home, and this would just have been an altercation at the till that he hadn't noticed.

'I'm gonna c'ya,' said the man to the little girl, his teeth clenched in an odd way, his jaws working.

Catch you, did he say? Keep you?

'I'm gonna cut ya,' repeated the man.

Oh, I see. Cut you. He was going to cut a six-year-old girl with a broken bottle.

The little girl's hands were clasped together in a paradigm of submissive anxiety on her little pinafore dress. She said not a word. From the storeroom, Dr Sweet could hear what sounded like Kamil dropping a heavy cardboard box and making a puffed-out 'oof' noise. Here was a window of opportunity. Dr Sweet could say something audible which would bring Kamil running; something loud, which conveyed the seriousness of what was happening. Kamil would come out and deal with this man using his special shopkeeper's training – a mixture, perhaps, of diplomacy and unarmed combat – and Dr Sweet need neither shoulder responsibility for the situation, nor admit that he had wished to avoid it. He could say in a loud clear voice, 'Look here, leave her alone.' But if Kamil didn't hear him, Dr Sweet would be very much in the frame.

'What ya,' the man seemed to say to the girl, who was looking somewhere past him and Dr Sweet. She was in some sort of shock.

'Ha'ya,' said the man, banging the bottle down on the counter. The little girl had tears in her eyes. Oh Christ.

'Look, leave her. Can you just leave her alone?' Dr Sweet's question was entirely obliterated by a burst of laughter from the TV game show. The man continued to look at the girl. For a long time nothing happened. He looked at her and she looked down at the floor; Dr Sweet looked at both of them and listened to a heavy scraping sound from the stockroom, where Kamil was propelling a box across the floor by shoving it with his knees.

'Ya. Ya,' said the man, and gestured with the bottle, from which a small triangular fragment of glass fell, enclosed in an olive-oil teardrop.

Dr Sweet stepped forward and extended his hand into the man's peripheral field of vision. 'Look, could you just—' he said as quietly and indistinctly as if he were talking in his sleep. There was a great ripping sound from the storeroom as Kamil wrenched off the strip of brown sticky tape that secured the lid of his cardboard box. Another hiatus. The man started to wave the bottle rhythmically back and forth.

Dr Sweet leant forward and gently, diffidently, touched the man on the elbow, in the same way that he might attract the attention of an elderly lady who had taken his seat at the theatre. The man was wearing a jacket of what appeared to be a green tweed rendered dark and shiny with age; touching it was like laying his fingertips on seawater-slippery rock.

Physical contact changed everything. Instantly the man flinched away, clutching his elbow with his free hand, evidently pained and aggrieved. The little girl looked up for the first time, now at Dr Sweet, then at the bottle man.

'Wha?' he said. 'Wha?'

For a fraction of a second Dr Sweet wondered if he could get away with suggesting that he wanted to pay for something, and that the man was holding up the queue, but he had put his olives and Coke bottles down at the other end of the shop.

'I was just—'

'Wha?'

'Just—'

'Ya. Ah ya. Wha.'

Dr Sweet mentally urged the little girl to understand that this diversion he had dearly purchased on her behalf had placed her out of physical danger. She was free to fetch her father, so that Kamil could come and place *him* out of physical danger, but she was obviously more interested in this encounter.

'Wha ya? Why ya.' Bottle Man could not have made it clearer that his anger had been smoothly transferred to Dr Sweet and, like all bullies, he found the experience of being stood up to an intoxicating stimulus, producing enormous reserves of courage and physical strength.

Dr Sweet gulped – an audible cartoon gulp – and his Adam's apple travelled from his chin to his knees and back. He tried a conciliatory smile, in which unconquerable fear and horror were visible.

'I think we might all need to calm down here,' he said, attempting a little laugh. But if Dr Sweet thought his use of the first-person plural would be emollient, if he hoped to suggest that this situation was just a bit of rough-housing between two good-natured equals that had gone

a little bit too far, and that Bottle Man should not there-
fore take amiss any request to stop, he was sadly mistaken.

'Kya,' grunted the man. 'Kya. Fa. Kya.'

Perhaps he could take his Underground season ticket
out, flourish it in the man's face like a warrant card and
pretend to be an off-duty policeman. He had seen that
done dozens of times on television, but only now did he
have a full sense of its fatuous impossibility.

'Look. Please. Put the bottle down. Put the broken
bottle down,' he added with more volume, still hoping to
attract the proprietor's attention. Couldn't he just walk
past the man, out of the door, and pretend this had never
happened?

The answer to this question was no. As if sensing his
craven thought, the man positioned himself away from
the till, between Dr Sweet and the exit, past which people
outside continued to wander. Perhaps he should scream
for help, but that might just cause everyone to hurry on
by and pretend they'd heard nothing. Or they would rush
in and the situation would immediately subside; the man
would turn out to be a well-known local eccentric who
raises thousands with charity walks and skydiving and
who wouldn't hurt a fly, and Dr Sweet would look really
stupid. He had read somewhere that the only alarm call
that really galvanizes people is 'Fire!'

'Fire,' said Dr Sweet in a tiny, throttled squeak.
'Fire.'

No-one heard, except for the bottle man, who
appeared to interpret it as an intolerable insult. Very deliberately, he took one step towards Dr Sweet, holding up
the bottle. Equally deliberately, Dr Sweet took one step
back, raising both palms. The bottle man took another

step, and Dr Sweet matched him with a one-step retreat of his own.

At this stage the man paused, perhaps reviewing his strategy. Dr Sweet himself felt the weird, dull coldness of fear in his bone marrow. This man was going to smash a broken bottle in his face. He would be scarred for life, or blinded, or both. Unless he could say something, or do something, to avert the crisis.

For the first time, the bottle man came up with an intelligible sentence.

'What ya want?'

Gratefully, Dr Sweet responded at once. 'I want us to calm down' – still that craven and mendacious 'us' – 'and we can sit down and have a drink or something, before someone gets hurt.' *Someone* gets hurt.

The little girl had gone. She had disappeared. She had gone to get her father. How long had she been gone?

The bottle man's face had creased into a grimace of derision and disgust. How old was he? Thirty? Sixty? He made a few more ill-coordinated steps towards Dr Sweet.

Who made a run for it. Heart pounding, and with a feeling of numb faintness tingling up his legs, he turned around and ran up to the refrigerator cabinet at the back, skidding ninety degrees to the right, with every intention of running back down the opposite aisle, out of the door to freedom.

Something made him pause, though, at the top. He hadn't done enough to lure the bottle man up the left-hand aisle. All the man needed to do was fall back to the till, dodge across to the right, and wait for him as he came charging down the right-hand side. But then *he* could double back, couldn't he? They could go on doing this all evening, and sooner or later someone would have to come and rescue him.

There was something else, though. What made Dr Sweet stop was the sound of the bottle man saying, 'Whaa? Aaaagh?' He turned round and this is what he saw: the bottle man had run onto the oil slick. A memory swam fleetingly into Dr Sweet's head: when he was a boy, he'd had a Dinky car model of the old Aston Martin that James Bond drove in *Thunderball*. It had an oil-slick gadget for deterring pursuers. Or was it tin tacks?

For a fraction of a second, the bottle man seemed almost to be running on the spot, his feet making that slithery, swooshy *slap, slap* sound on the rippling oily floor, but he was beginning to slow and steady himself. The time had come for a bold and decisive move, and in his madness, Dr Sweet knew what it was.

'Ha!' said Dr Sweet, and made a lunging childish feint towards his aggressor, immediately jumping back into a tense, static position. The idea was that the man would lunge towards him, lose his balance and fall over, giving Dr Sweet more than enough time to make his escape – and, naturally, call the police when he was far away from PriceBest.

But that isn't what happened. The bottle man yelped with fury and his right foot made a final swipe forwards through the oil, shooting a spray ahead of him. For a fraction of a second, his whole body lifted off the ground, then he measured his length on the floor of the shop. Every millimetre hit the ground at the same time, from his ankles to the back of his head. This it did with a single, thin sharp report, like a castanet. There was a slight puff of flour dust from a bag torn in the mêlée.

In the next few seconds, Dr Sweet realized something else: the man's head was not actually on the floor; it had hit the bottom shelf of the central island, where the bags of flour were. Dr Sweet knew at once that he was dead.

Time stood still. The throbbing cold-hot sensation of fear receded, and for the first time he felt a warm, wet sensation down his right trouser leg. He realized that the TV monitor had been switched off and Kamil had reappeared. He was shouting at his little girl, who ran away crying. Then he started shouting again, with an edge of panic and hysteria, at someone else, in the stockroom. Then he started yelling at Dr Sweet, holding his hands up to his head and pulling his hair back behind his ears in anguish.

Dr Sweet didn't know what to do. He couldn't understand what Kamil was saying. His voice sounded far away or under water; then it sounded very loud and clear, as if he was right by his head. The feeling of faintness disappeared, but then Dr Sweet felt his brain begin to overheat in some physiological way, like the beginning of meningitis.

'Out. Get out,' shouted Kamil. 'Out.'

Dr Sweet righted himself. He tried to ask where the little girl was and if she was all right, but no words would come out.

'Out,' repeated Kamil harshly.

Dr Sweet wondered if he should try to buy the Coke and the olives.

He thought not.

The temperature in his head was just outside the red zone at the end of the dial.

He had killed someone.

No – there had been an altercation in a convenience store between a disturbed homeless person and the young store attendant, which had ended in a tragedy, but which he had not witnessed and in which he was not involved.

But what about the video monitors?

'Out.'

And his footsteps in the oil?

'Out. Out.'

Kamil, the manager and licensee of PriceBest Continental Foods, Archway Road, was ordering him to leave, exempting him from responsibility. That was good enough for Dr Sweet.

4

Cordie climbed precariously up onto Baloo, grabbing fistfuls of brown, shaggy hair. This close, Cordie could see each strand reflect a kind of rainbow-sheen in the sunlight. She scrambled perilously up the sheer face of Baloo's enormous behind, so vast its curvature was almost non-existent, cheekily gripping his thin tail for extra purchase, and then heaved herself further up onto the more level ground of his back, in constant danger of falling – especially as Baloo suddenly reared up, all thirteen feet of him, around four times Cordie's height. She shrieked with wild excitement as the ground plummeted away beneath her and she was borne up high, high, high. She was right at the back of Baloo's big head now, hanging on by the scruff of his neck. What a view of the jungle she had from this height! What a wonderful view! All those greens and browns and blues. There was the clearing; there was the dense forest over to the east, above them the hot sun (it was just past midday) and behind them – Cordie chanced twisting around a little – was the rocky incline, and there was the tree on which Bagheera was reclining, glowering at Baloo resentfully. What a grump he was sometimes!

Cordie found that she could steer silly old Baloo by holding her hand over his head to shield his right eye from the sun, which made him veer off to the left, and then she could shield his left eye, which made him veer right. And yanking hard on his scruff with both hands made him slow down. What fun! Of course, it meant changing her grip on his fur, and we all know how Baloo reacts to *that*.

'Aw no, no, no.' He chuckled. 'Now you're *tickling*.'

Cordie squealed with corroborative laughter.

'Now we don't do that. Nope! I can't stand it,' howled poor Baloo, and started to shake her madly. He shook her to the left; he shook her to the right; he bent his great bear body right over so Cordie found herself almost upside down and staring directly at the forest floor with its twigs and grass far, far, below her. But she never cried or let on she was afraid, even though, to be truthful, she really was, and boisterous Baloo didn't realize that he had gone a little bit too far with this rough game.

Before she could come to grief, Baloo tumbled her over into the safety of his paws and she found herself staring right at his great black snout and into his humorous brown eyes. In a moment, she forgot she ever felt like crying.

'You know somethin'?' he asked in that great rumbling bass voice.

Cordie shook her head, grinning, her eyes shining.

'You're all right, kid.'

Cordie felt as if her heart would burst with happiness.

'Say,' he asked, 'what do they call you?'

'Cordie,' said Cordie, getting that odd mouth-twisty feeling of self-consciousness that all children feel when a grown-up asks them to say their first name.

Baloo smiled and raised his eyebrows; he'd never heard of anyone called that.

'Cordie, huh?' he said. 'Well, that's a swell name.'

Cordie suspected that Bagheera would not allow this conversation to continue unchallenged. Nor did he.

'She's going back to the man-village with me right now,' he said severely from his branch. Cordie guessed that Bagheera wanted to get down from the tree, pull her away and square up to Baloo, but that would concede the advantage of height.

'But they'll ruin her,' said Baloo with dismay. 'They'll make a woman of her.'

Bagheera shrugged, as if to say, 'What of it?' or 'What's it to you?'

Baloo placed a paw on her shoulder, and this protective gesture exasperated Bagheera.

'How else is she going to survive?' he snapped.

'She's with me, ain't she?' said Baloo indignantly, scooping her up, and Cordie could feel the hard black pads of his paw under her legs, not furry, but even hotter than fur. 'I'll learn her all I know.'

'That shouldn't take very long,' said Bagheera dryly.

At that moment, all three of them heard the front door slam loudly. Baloo and Bagheera looked at each other, perplexed. Cordie scrambled down from Baloo's hand, expertly put the video on pause, and opened the door that led out into the hall.

What she saw was her dad with his back to her, standing still, facing the front door he'd just slammed. When *she* or any of *her* friends slammed the door in her mum's house she got told off. He looked hot and sweaty, as if he'd been running. He was panting, and he looked sad. Cordie sniffed: it smelt like the boys at school when they wet themselves.

'Dad,' she said.

He turned round.

'Hello darling,' he said.

'David,' said her granny from the kitchen.

'David, is that you?' said Mummy. 'Where on earth have you been? Did you get the Coke, or what?'

'Just coming. I just have to change.'

'Change? Why?' said her mum.

'It came on to rain for a bit just as I was walking home,' her dad shouted as he ran up the stairs.

'Did it?' said her mum, walking into the hall as her dad vanished into the upstairs bathroom.

'Daddy's wet his pants,' said Cordie to her mummy.

'Is he soaked through?' asked her mum. 'But it's stopped raining.'

'No, he's wet his pants,' said Cordie.

'Just coming,' her dad shouted from the bathroom in a high voice.

Cordie started to run the head of her Barbie along the skirting board in the hallway. The head fitted exactly into the off-white ridge, and she knew that there was an all-but-invisible lump that would make Barbie's head bump. Bump – there it was. She could run Barbie's head back and it would make it bump again. Bump. Doing it that way made her head catch on a teeny little nobbly bit that tangled up her pink hair. Tsk.

'Do you want to have some supper with us now, Cordie?'

Cordie shook her head and tried to get back into the playroom.

'You can watch *The Jungle Book* any time,' said her

mum and tried to guide her back to the kitchen. Cordie held up her arms.

'No, Cordie, you're a big girl now and big girls don't need to be carried.'

Cordie kept her arms in the carry-me position and shook them insistently.

'Cordie, no. *No.*'

'Oh-h,' said Cordie plaintively on a rising two-tone, and her face crumpled.

'Oh all right then,' sighed her mum, and gathered Cordie up, who calmly started picking pink strands of nylon hair out of Barbie's face.

In the kitchen, the table had been set. Cordie guessed that her granny and her mum had done it, but not Grandad. When Granny and Grandad were there with Dad, but not Mum, Granny made her help set the table, carrying in the salt and pepper and table-mats, but not the knives and forks, in case she fell over and poked her eye out. Grandad was there, pulling a cork out of a bottle between his legs, and now *he* looked like he had wet himself too. Cordie giggled madly as her mummy put her down, and instead of sitting in her special chair between Mummy and Grandad, she just stood there.

Her dad came in, wearing a very clean pair of pale blue jeans that the cleaning lady ironed so they had a crease down the front of each leg which just looked stupid. He was smiling and laughing a lot in a loud voice.

'Did you get what you wanted, dear?' said Granny.

'Where's the Coke?' asked her mummy in a funny, cross way, even though Cordie knew she really didn't want Coke that much.

'They didn't have any,' said Daddy and took a handful

of crisps from the bowl on the kitchen cabinet and started eating them.

'Didn't have any *Coke*? Then what took you so long?'

'I had to go down to the supermarket at the top, and they didn't have any either.'

'But why were you so long? And will you for Christ's sake stop eating crisps?'

Both Granny and Grandad looked up crossly at Mummy for saying this. Cordie tried saying it in her head. Christ's sake. Christ's sake. Christ's sake. She paced some laps around the table, heel to toe, saying the rude phrase in her head as she walked. Grandad had got the cork out. Christ's sake. Christ's sake. Christ's sake.

'Walking took longer than I thought. And then there was the rain.'

'You were away for *thirty-five minutes*,' said her mum, and actually slapped her dad's wrist when he reached out for more crisps. Cordie could see that he wanted to go all quiet the way Cordie did when her mum once slapped her hand, but he had to keep talking because she wanted to know things.

'I had to duck into a doorway to get out of the rain,' said her dad in a small voice.

'What rain?' said her mum. 'There hasn't been any rain.' It was exactly the way they'd talked before they began to live apart. Cordie went for another lap. Christ's sake. Cer–ista's *sake*.

'David. David, old boy,' said Grandad, and came over and put his hand on Daddy's arm. Daddy was sad and Grandad knew it, and he wanted her mum and Granny to stop ganging up on him. 'Is anything the matter?'

He didn't say anything, but just nodded. Cordie went back to pacing and didn't look up.

'Yes,' said her dad, and he sat down and poured himself a great big glass of wine and drank it all in one go and some of it spilt. 'Something is the matter.'

Cordie kept very still. Very, very still. She knew that if she made too much noise she wouldn't be allowed to stay and listen. But she also knew that if she went completely quiet, the grown-ups would think she was upset and make her go out, when really *they* were upset, not her. So she took her Barbie and started to attend to her pink nylon hair with a tiny comb, while quietly telling her how nice she looked.

Her mummy hung back now and Cordie could tell that she was sorry she had smacked his hand. Granny went round to her dad's other side and asked, 'What is the matter, David? What's wrong?'

His voice went low and slightly gurgly.

'I – I saw something horrible in the shop. In PriceBest. It was really horrible, what I . . . witnessed. I've never been so shocked; I thought I was going to throw up.'

Grandad said nothing, but Granny said, 'Oh, David, what was it?'

'I saw someone fall over.'

Cordie did not risk looking up. She knew that sometimes her dad had come home late in the evening and said stupid things that made her mum cross and then she hadn't been allowed to see him. She continued to brush Barbie's hair.

'What do you mean, you saw someone falling over?' That was Mummy, Cordie could tell, she had almost decided to be cross again.

'No, no, you don't understand; there was this man, this aggressive man, like an aggressive beggar or something. He was in the shop and he had a broken bottle and he was threatening everyone.'

'He was threatening you with a broken bottle?' asked her mum, and Grandad and Granny were quiet.

'Not really me. Not just me. He was threatening everyone. He was threatening Kamil, the owner, and his daughter.'

'His *daughter*?'

Cordie sensed her mum was now upset and that it would not be long before they would remember she was there and she would not be allowed to stay.

'Yes, his daughter. It was – it was sort of general. But it wasn't very nice. He was sort of shouting and charging about.'

'Charging about?'

'Yes. Yes.'

'So what happened? What did you do?'

'I didn't really do anything I just sort of witnessed it. It was just kind of going on as I walked into the shop.'

'Cordie,' said Granny, 'perhaps you'd better go and play now.'

'Oh yes,' said her mum with a funny little jump. 'Cordie. I think you'd better go and play outside for a bit. I mean outside this room.'

'But Mum, I wanted to have something to eat,' said Cordie with tremendous cunning, pointing at the wholesome plate of mini pasta shells and toast that Granny had placed on her special Peter Rabbit plate. 'I'm hungry.'

Persuading Cordie to eat was a continuous domestic

crisis and she knew that almost anything would be sacrificed to her caprice in this matter: Granny and Grandad and her mum and dad all knew that. She could decide to close this precious window of opportunity at any time. To maximize her advantage, Cordie quietly seated herself at the table and unassumingly forked some pasta shells into her mouth, austerely contenting herself with some sips of water – not even juice. There was a pause and Cordie triumphantly sensed that all four adults had tacitly agreed to let her stay while they spoke in hushed voices.

'*What* did you witness?' said Mummy.

'What was it, David?'

'Well, the man fell over. I saw him fall over.'

'And?'

'Well, it looked like I'd . . . it looked like he'd sort of banged his head.'

'Banged his *head*? What do you mean?'

Cordie watched her daddy pour himself another glass and hold it up to his lips while his left hand held his right wrist.

'Well, he'd banged his head and it looked like he was . . .'

He lowered his voice and they all leaned in to hear him, and Cordie guessed that he'd said 'dead'.

'And did you call an ambulance? Or the police?'

'No. What's the point? I mean, I don't know for sure what happened. It's nothing to do with me.'

'Nothing to do with you?' This was Granny talking now. 'David, of course it had something to do with you. You were there, you should have made sure that the appropriate authorities were contacted.'

'I *did*. I mean they were.'

'Were they?' That was Grandad.

'Yes. What I mean is that Kamil would have contacted them. In fact, he was very keen to get rid of me so that he could take over the whole thing.'

With her little knife and fork, Cordie dexterously cut up her half slice of toast into a sub-set of small triangles, then placed a single ketchupy pasta shell on top of one of them, and prepared to spear the whole top-heavy arrangement from above.

'How much of all this did you actually see, David?' said Granny.

And that was the moment at which the grown-ups decided Cordie had to go. She saw that she had made a strategic error by eating too much. She should have held back, should have asked for one of the grown-ups to help her, should have kept them guessing. But that might have made them stop talking. She saw that deciding to be hungry was a calculated risk which had paid off to the fullest extent possible, but now the game was over.

'Cordie, shall we take our suppers and go and watch the video for a bit?' She could hardly believe that Granny, a notorious disciplinarian on the subject of sitting up properly at the table to eat, was advocating slopping around in front of the television like the childminder.

'Cordie, you and Granny are going to go and eat some supper in the playroom and watch the video, *and then you can have a Creme Egg*,' said her mummy, raising her voice in a crescendo to match and override the sobbing.

Cordie was at her most disobliging to Granny while in the playroom. She knew it wasn't right to be eating her supper in there, but took no pleasure in this infringement of the rules. She was silent and didn't respond to any of Granny's sallies. Cordie sensed that any rude words would get her into trouble, even the Christ's-sake ones she had just learned from Mummy. But eating anything was out of the question.

5

By eleven, with Cordie just persuaded to go to bed and Dr Sweet's parents having retired long before, Alice was completely exhausted. Her ex-husband, however, was still wide awake, his shock and disquiet having been transmuted by some bodily alchemy into a jumpy, hyper-alert energy. Alice was semi-prostrate on the sofa with a Scotch that Dr Sweet had pressed on her, and he was in the armchair opposite with a cup of black coffee. Always vigilant for changes in his ex-wife's behaviour, he was counting the number of times she prefigured any simple declaration with 'you know what?' – another Americanism she had picked up. Not an affectation exactly, as it was obviously second nature to her.

'You know what?' she yawned, draining the last of her whisky. 'I'm going to go to bed.'

'What do you think of Cordie?' said Dr Sweet quickly, pouring her another drink.

'Nothing. I mean, why?'

'Don't you think she's slightly different?'

'Well, she's still very difficult to calm down and getting her to concentrate, even with the video, is almost impossible. But how do you mean, different?'

'Well, I think she *is* calmer. But more responsive to stimuli.'

'More responsive to *stimuli*? She doesn't need to be more responsive to stimuli, David. As it is, when I take her out for a walk and someone across the street takes out a shiny candy wrapper, she runs towards it shouting.'

Candy wrapper?

'You know what I mean,' said Dr Sweet, raising his eyebrows. 'She's responsive in the sense that she responds meaningfully. She makes sense of the stimuli.'

Alice made no reply, but took another sip of her charged glass, always receptive to praise for Cordie.

'How's her swearing been here?' she asked.

'Well,' he said, remembering the incident with John and Rosemary, 'it's stabilizing.'

'You mean she's already told your parents to fuck off?' asked Alice shrewdly, taking another sip. It was a retrograde step for Cordie, and yet Dr Sweet was nettled to notice that Alice had a tiny smile, and he suspected that she was not altogether displeased at this proof that Dr Sweet's mother and father were still not very good with their granddaughter.

'What I'm saying is that it's under control. She doesn't do it any more than any other moderately naughty little girl. Children are much more grown up these days, anyway. Swearing isn't the catastrophic thing it was when we were growing up. What I mean is, I think I can see evidence of Cordie thinking more analytically about things.'

'Such as?'

'Well for instance, she saw me brush my hair this morning, and about five minutes after I'd finished I felt a little cold, so I was about to put on my jumper and Cordie said: 'Wrong order, Daddy. Jumper, then brush.' She meant there's no point in putting your sweater on after brushing your hair, because you'll just have to brush it all over again.'

'So what's your point?'

What's your point? That was another belligerent phrase Americans loved using in any sort of debate – irritating, but effective, he had to admit, because replying to the question automatically conceded that you hadn't been sharp enough to give a clear, concise argument. Lots of his colleagues used it, yet Dr Sweet always shrank from doing the same thing for fear of seeming rude.

'My point, Alice darling, my point is obvious. Being with me for some of the time is not the optional extra you and the courts seem to think.'

'Oh really?' said Alice, instead of proffering the coldly sceptical rebuttal he had expected: a précis of the argument her solicitor had prepared eighteen months before. She just smiled and continued to sip. Was Dr Sweet imagining it, or was there something a little flirtatious about her?

'Yes, really,' he said, for the moment not responding to the change of mood. 'Really. Staying with me gives Cordie a chance to—'

There was a sound from upstairs, from Cordie's bedroom. Both of them looked up sharply, and Dr Sweet made a point of half rising from his chair, to underline his parental prerogative in this house. They'd had a baby monitor when Cordie was very little, but had to get rid of it because it picked up transmissions from every other baby monitor in the street, and the speaker was always cracklingly sobbing and crying, a nonstop Mayday signal of tiny infant suffering. From then on, they had trusted to their highly tuned parent hearing.

'It's OK, David,' said Alice. 'She's just singing.'

'Is she? Yes, yes, of course she is,' said Dr Sweet, settling back. Cordie habitually spent about an hour singing or talking to herself after going to bed, or acting out conversations between Barbie and the plump, grey furry hippo she took to bed with her. 'I suppose I'm just a little freaked out after what happened today,' he added, combing his hair back from his forehead with his fingers. Subtly, inexorably, he was beginning to believe his own story about having 'witnessed' the event at PriceBest.

'Oh darling, yes of course,' said Alice, completely sympathetic now, reaching forward and touching his hand, rubbing her fingers briefly against his. Dr Sweet was dismayed to feel an electric charge of possibility. Cordie murmured on and relapsed into quiet; for a moment all they listened to was the wash of traffic.

'You were saying?' Alice asked at last, taking a bigger sip.

Dr Sweet looked puzzled.

'Staying with you gives Cordie a chance to . . .?'

'Oh yes. *Yes*. Staying with me gives Cordie a chance to get in touch with her masculine side!' Dr Sweet gave the last few words a little rising note of provocative triumph. Alice snorted, but kept that flirtatious smile in position.

'What do you mean, get in touch with—'

'Her masculine side. Yes, what's wrong with that?'

'What the hell does that mean?'

'Her rational, problem-solving side; the side that enables her to surmount obstacles . . .'

Alice's mouth was a round O of astonishment, very similar, Dr Sweet remembered with a now distinct charge, to the expression of open-mouthed rapture she used to have when they were making love and he penetrated her. He would be on top and she would have both her legs up over his shoulders. What was she saying?

'. . . completely grotesque! Completely bloody grotesque! How dare you?'

She was keeping unblinking eye contact with him, too, just like during sex.

'What's wrong with that?'

'What's *wrong* with it?'

'You were always telling me to get in touch with my feminine side, weren't you? You and your new bloody boyfriend both said it. And what did that mean?'

There was a tiny pause while Alice realized it wasn't a rhetorical question.

'It meant stop being an emotional cripple. It meant getting in touch with your emotions and feelings.'

'Ha!' said Dr Sweet triumphantly. 'Emotions and feelings. The "feminine" side . . .'

'Well, that's not entirely—'

'Nevertheless, that's what you said; that's what everybody says: feminine side. So logically there must be a masculine side, that's the implication, a side of rational analysis . . .'

'Are you saying women are incapable of that?'

'No, that's what *you're* saying—'

'You like.' This last was Cordie, quite audibly from her bedroom. Particularly loud words and phrases were not an uncommon part of her bedtime soliloquy, but they knew her noises would soon rouse Dr Sweet's parents, who were very possibly wide awake and listening to them. Dr Sweet raised a forefinger and went up the stairs, tiptoeing up to the little room Cordie slept in, and looked in. She was lying on her back, arms thrown dramatically back onto the pillow on either side of her head, face to one side, apparently fast asleep. Dr Sweet tiptoed across to the door of his parents' bedroom, the spare bedroom, and checked the light wasn't on.

Back downstairs, there was something subtly different about Alice's position. She had resumed the languorous sprawl abandoned during their argument, but her feet were pulled up a little, allowing him – was he imagining this? – room to sit next to her on the sofa. Dr Sweet thought about this for a moment and then sat down on the armchair as before.

'I like your hair,' said Alice.

'Why?' asked Dr Sweet, baffled.

'I think it's because you're grey.'

'I am *not* grey,' he spluttered, 'I have *some* grey hairs.'

'David, darling, you're as grey as a badger.' Dr Sweet weighed the emotional import of 'darling' and 'badger' on opposite scales. He knew that a humorous, self-deprecatory display of mock vanity was called for at this point, but was genuinely shocked to hear that he was now thought of as grey. Perhaps, he wondered, his hair had actually turned grey during the PriceBest incident.

'No,' he said.

Alice leaned forward and, pressing her fingers on the side of his head, turned him to profile. With a secret thrill, he felt her fingertips stroke his temple. This was turning into a Bad Idea. They had only been divorced twelve months. How much time was supposed to go past before divorced couples could have sex again without it being a stupid, messy fiasco? How long did Richard Burton and Liz Taylor leave it?

'There's actually not much grey close to the scalp,' said Alice. 'You should get your hair cut.'

'That's exactly what my mother said this afternoon.'

'No, I mean it would look better. It would just be a few flecks of grey then.'

She released him and they both took some more sips.

'I was going to say how much I liked *your* hair,' said Dr Sweet shyly.

Alice looked up at him sharply. 'You mean the fact that I've had it coloured?'

'No, no,' said Dr Sweet, alarmed and baffled. 'I didn't mean that. *Have* you had it coloured? It doesn't matter. I meant the length. It makes Cordie look like you. I mean it makes you look like Cordie.'

'Oh,' said Alice, mollified. 'Yes, well I suppose it does. I didn't think of that.'

'Your hair was short like that when we . . . when we started going out. Do you remember?'

Alice smiled at him with real tenderness. She had forgotten how 'started going out' was their private, genteel code for 'first slept together', an intimacy that pre-dated any of the 'going out' business. Alice had slept with Dr Sweet within a couple of weeks of meeting him, when he was a post-doctoral research fellow at the Department of Biochemistry at Oxford and she was an undergraduate economist at Hertford. He was twenty-seven and she was twenty, and whenever they considered these ages – as they did now, silently – it seemed incredible that they had got old enough to think of twenty as almost a child's age. When Dr Sweet saw the undergraduates that occasionally came through his lab, their youth looked painful, not desirable; they were raw, peeled and unripe, like adult foetuses. Could Alice really have looked like that when they first met, with her shapeless Oxfam coat and pale yellow canvas bag?

It was incredible. Some students carry with them the recipe for their later, adult selves; their sophistication, their capacity for commerce with the world, is unobtrusively present like a bud. Not Alice, though. She was an occasional participant in the intercollegiate Christian Union; she rowed; she chattered about her siblings to people she'd just met and she was a saucer-eyed respecter of other students' reputations and the exam results they had achieved the summer before. When Dr Sweet met her, *he* was the grown-up one, rather than the cowed simpleton Alice effortlessly made him feel like these days.

They first laid eyes on each other in the meeting hall of a Methodist association that allowed their premises to be used, free of charge, by Lifeline: a voluntary organization that provided a 24-hour listening service on the phone during term time for students who were depressed, unhappy or suicidal. At the beginning of every academic year, Lifeline would audition potential counsellors by asking them to act out various roles: the depressed person calling up and the Lifeline operative taking the call. There were lots of people there, mainly student actors who were intrigued by the improvisation and showing off demanded in the screening process itself. Alice had a fierce, high colour in her cheeks from having cycled there in the bitter wind, and she held her detachable white and red bike lights while she looked for somewhere to sit. Her face had a pinched, perky prettiness, plumply framed by an unassuming short hairstyle, too flat to be called a bob, which she had attended to by a local hairdresser each vacation. Dr Sweet liked her.

He was, incidentally, the oldest person there by some years, and that included the president of Lifeline and the Methodist church member who was there notionally to superintend proceedings. He could not join in with the bright, concerted optimism and friendliness of the others. On the contrary, Dr Sweet was morose. He was depressed and lonely. But instead of calling Lifeline, he had decided to respond to their audition notice for volunteers, on the grounds that it might help him meet new people. At the time, he had congratulated himself on fudging the issue of his depression so ingeniously. The lexicon of adulthood, hard won over the next fifteen years, would call this *denial*.

The president called for quiet, and after a short speech outlining the work of Lifeline both in the university and wider community – everyone nodded soberly at this pious invocation of the non-student population's well-being – she asked everyone present to split up into pairs and prepare improvised encounter scenarios, assigning themselves the roles of caller and listener. In about fifteen minutes she would come around to each couple in turn and ask them to play out their little scene in front of her, though it was stressed that she didn't want some scripted play, just an animated account of the kind of issues and feelings they expected to encounter.

The crowd started to hook up and went away to

various corners and stairwells. Alice ambitiously headed for a tall, fair-haired boy her own age who she recognized from her college's entertainments committee, but was chagrined to find Dr Sweet standing in her way.

'Hi, I wondered if you . . . er . . .'

'Well, I . . . yes, OK, that would be fine,' said Alice, seeing over Dr Sweet's shoulder that the fair-haired boy had already found someone else, and her natural good manners, in any case, forbidding a ruthless refusal, and aware, moreover, that it was precisely this kind of snub that made people suicidally depressed.

They went over to an unoccupied bench at the side of the room and silently listened to the buzz of creative, exploratory talk all around them.

'Hi,' said Dr Sweet with a smile, 'I'm David.'

'I'm Alice.'

'Right.'

'Are you some sort of mature student?'

'I'm a post-grad,' was his miffed reply.

'How old are you?'

'I'm twenty-seven. I'm a post-grad. Post-*doc* actually. I'm a member of the university.'

'So you're not actually a student?'

'Not as such, no. Can we get on?'

'Yes, yes, absolutely,' said Alice guiltily. 'Would you like to be the caller or the listener?'

'Could you be the suicidal one?' asked Dr Sweet.

The president of Lifeline appeared from nowhere.

'Actually, we don't like using words like 'suicidal' in these discussions,' she said firmly. 'It's unhelpful and tracks the discussion in a negative way.'

'Could you not listen in to our discussions until we're

ready to present them?' replied Dr Sweet with deadpan insolence.

'No, OK,' said the president uncertainly, 'but if you could avoid focusing on—'

'Thank you,' said Dr Sweet with a peremptory nod, turning back to Alice.

'I'll be the caller if you like,' she said in a quiet voice.

'Fine,' said Dr Sweet. 'Fire away.'

There was a pause while Alice looked at the backs of her hands, which she had placed face-down on an earnest student notepad.

'I find this sort of thing very difficult,' she said at last.

'Mmm yes, that's OK,' said Dr Sweet, his head on one side, lower lip pushed out thoughtfully, 'but the caller wouldn't necessarily be that kind of picked-on, pissed-on victim type.'

'I haven't started yet.'

'Oh sorry. Are you ready now?'

Alice was wondering if she should pretend to go to the lavatory, go down the stairs, out into the street and just not come back.

'Yes, OK. Shall we just feel our way into it?'

After a while, the president invited them each to present their improvisation, starting with Alice and Dr Sweet.

'Ring, ring! Ring, ring!' said Dr Sweet loudly, and the president and Methodist gave a little jump. 'Hello, yes?' Dr Sweet mimed holding a phone up to his ear by extending his thumb and little finger.

Alice thought about doing the same thing but just said, 'Hello. I'm calling because I need someone to talk to.'

'And why is that, my love?' asked Dr Sweet, deadpan.

'Well, I find talking to people difficult.'

'And what is the reason for that, do you suppose?'

'I think I'm a bit shy.'

'Shy?' Dr Sweet mimed covering the mouthpiece of his phone and mouthed the words 'She's a bit shy' to the president and the Methodist. 'Shy I don't like, darling,' he said, returning to the conversation. 'Shy is the great non-problem. Shy is all right if you're under eight or a puppy, but a grown-up being shy is just being rubbish and not making the effort.'

Alice made a noise like a nervous giggle, and the president and the Methodist briefly transferred their cold gaze to her.

'I sometimes wonder whether I might just kill myself,' she ventured, now simply curious as to what he would say.

'Ha,' said Dr Sweet, and from this moment utter quiet descended on the whole room. 'You mean play the Roman fool and fall on your own sword? Well let me tell you, you have to be pretty fat and heavy to make that work. Or else you need some sort of clip arrangement to keep the blade pointing upwards. Have you?'

'No.'

'Well there you are.'

'Sometimes I think I might be better off dead.'

'Dead? There's nothing wrong with being dead. Some of the world's greatest men and women are dead.'

'If I could just interrupt,' said the president forcefully, 'I think we need to listen to some of the other pairs.'

Dr Sweet listened equably while the others falteringly tried out their versions. Alice just sat there, stunned and amazed that she had participated in this debacle. When the time came for the four successful applicants to be invited back, Alice and Dr Sweet were not among them, and they soon found themselves back on the street outside.

'I rather think I buggered up your chances there,' he said to her as they ambled away.

Alice thought about it for a bit and smiled.

'That's all right. I wasn't sure about it anyway. Would you like a cup of coffee?'

In later years, in the conventions and regulations of adult dating, this was, of course, a coded sexual invitation. Back then coffee meant little more than that. However, the fact that Alice had made the invitation – which Dr Sweet, for all his anarchy and smirking bravado, would never have dared initiate – signalled the first sign of Alice's upper hand. They had coffee. They agreed to go to a concert the next weekend; the weekend after that they slept together and by the end of Alice's third year they were married.

And now look at them; Dr Sweet in science, Alice in the City, negotiating her career in a series of quantum leaps, having a baby, apparently differing from her colleagues only in allowing her hair to grow longer. Dr Sweet's progress in research science was becalmed, but Alice's life blossomed. Now they were divorced, after Alice's adultery on a business trip to Arizona. It was a liaison Dr Sweet could not bring himself to condemn, on account of his own infidelity. His gift for belligerent facetiousness, which had miraculously won her heart eighteen years ago, had faded. But it remained strong enough to stymie opportunities for advancement, and alienated potential allies in whose gift it was to recommend Dr Sweet for committee places, appointments or labs in prestigious institutes. And as for becoming a Fellow of the Royal Society – a distinction already being conferred on some of his contemporaries – he had about as much chance of being invited to join the Sadler's Wells Ballet.

'When we started going out,' said Alice wonderingly.

'Yep.' Dr Sweet sighed with a little sighing laugh.

'I never knew you were going to get so plump,' she said.

'No,' he said. 'I never knew you were going to get so . . .'

'What?'

'I don't know. Sleek.'

For once in his life, Dr Sweet had said precisely the right thing. Alice at once assessed sleek as a complimentary remark that could plausibly be made to someone of her age, and stretched with pleasure, like a cat. Then she patted the place next to her on the couch.

Dr Sweet knew that to accept this invitation would be a drunken error of judgement that could shatter the uneasy emotional truce they had negotiated for the sake of their daughter. He decided not to; he decided to finesse some adroit manoeuvre where he could get up to clear away the cups, and then, from a neutral standing position, yawn, stretch, say he was tired and wanted to go to bed. This would keep them both out of trouble.

Having arrived at this decision, Dr Sweet felt a deep sense of peace and maturity. Then he went over and sat next to her, very close, with a banging heart.

Alice again inspected his greying hair by turning his head this way and that, allowing her fingers to linger, and Dr Sweet happily submitted to the manipulation.

'Yes,' she said. 'Definitely a Grecian 2000 job. And what exactly do you mean by "sleek"?'

'Well,' said Dr Sweet, his forefinger idly tracing circles round the buttons on her blouse, near her belt. 'Prosperous. Well-heeled. At home in the world.' He had pulled up her blouse, and laid the fingertips of his left hand on her tummy which was creamy and pale, and somehow discreetly convex in a way it hadn't been when they'd first gone to bed. With an inaudible grunt of effort, he turned onto his right buttock and slipped his right hand under her left armpit, let it remain there for a little, and then caressed her breast, feeling the crinkly little *bas-relief* details of her bra under the blouse.

Alice turned to him and they kissed, deeply, wetly and drunkly, for the first time in years. Their marriage was nowhere near the end the last time they'd kissed like this. Alice undid the other buttons on her blouse while Dr Sweet looked on dumbly. The gas-effect coal fire made its continuous hissing sound, together with the odd click. Her bra turned out to be black and silky. Dr Sweet wondered if her pants were the same colour and fabric, matching bra and pants being the nearest thing to formal eroticism in married life. With a smile, Alice indicated that it did up with a catch at the front, between the two cups, rather than from the back, which always defeated the hopeless Dr Sweet.

So Dr Sweet undid it, cupped her large, heavy breasts in his hands and sucked on her left nipple, then the right, until they rose up glistening and hard, to Alice's breathy *mmm*s. How often had he done this when they were married? Actually, not all that often. In fact, hardly ever. Oddly, she'd never really liked it that much. Was this something she had learned to like from another lover? Something about the thought excited him profoundly, and he reached down, loosened her belt and felt inside her pants, without waiting to check the colour. Alice gasped and writhed, and tried to pull his shirt off. Then Dr Sweet paused and glanced up the stairs.

'Let's go to bed,' he whispered urgently. 'My bed.' They'd planned that Alice would sleep in his bed while he slept on the sofa downstairs.

'No,' moaned Alice, perceptibly louder. 'Let's do it on the sofa; I'll bend over the arm and you can do me from behind.'

'Ally, darling,' he said with a quiet laugh, 'Cordie might come down the stairs and see us; she sometimes comes down to the kitchen when she can't sleep. Or Mum and Dad might come down.'

'OK,' said Alice, getting up, and with a nervous, skittering haste, they hurried up the stairs and into Dr Sweet's bedroom.

Almost at once, things weren't quite as good. Out of force of habit, Dr Sweet snapped on the light as they entered his room, so they were suddenly deprived of the soft, romantic, tactfully muted glow of the downstairs fire. And they certainly didn't have its toasty warmth, the central heating having gone off hours ago.

Despite the fact that this was supposed to have been Alice's guest room, Dr Sweet had left the bed covered with papers, and he quickly started taking them off and placing them on the floor, not, to Alice's irritation, just sweeping them away in a blaze of passion.

'Come *on*,' said Alice, pulling the duvet back, sending notebooks flying and then switching off the overhead light.

They got in together, Dr Sweet unhappily aware that they were both treading on documents and slides he'd been working on.

It was like ice. The electric blanket had not been on.

'Jesus!' hissed Alice.

'Let's cuddle up,' said Dr Sweet.

They did, with much kissing and fondling, and Dr Sweet was hard in no time.

'Oh, David, please now, come on!' said Alice.

Dr Sweet entered her and, obeying the sexual drill of a lifetime, immediately started to think about something unerotic to delay his orgasm. He couldn't think about anything too unpleasant or he'd lose his erection completely: this mental operation was as delicate as the treatment of a clinically dead donor body for a kidney transplant. It has to be dead enough for the relatives to consent to the procedure, but with enough residual vital signs maintained for the organ to be viable.

These were idle thoughts. With a terrible inevitability, Dr Sweet knew exactly what unerotic thought was going to come into his head: a homeless person in PriceBest, lying on the floor in a pool of olive oil, stone dead. There, that should keep ejaculation at bay.

'David. David?'

'What?'

'Is anything the matter?'

'No. Why?'

'You've stopped moving and your whole body seems to have gone as stiff as a board.'

'Has it?'

'Yes. Now just . . . just relax.'

A violent homeless person, down on his luck, and now dead in a convenience store.

'Jesus. Did I say your *whole* body?'

'Sorry?'

'David. What the fucking hell has happened to your erection?'

'I'm . . . It's . . .'

The man's arm. Reaching out to touch him on the arm, and feeling the material dark and slippery and rank. Kamil in the stockroom moving boxes about with his knees. The little girl scared, and then gone.

'David, look. It's OK.' She was stroking his hair. 'I know this is weird, but it's OK. Work with me. Just relax. Whenever this happened before, I just stroked it back to life, didn't I? I just stroked it, and . . . Jesus where *is* it?'

Dr Sweet's body on top of her seemed to have tripled in weight and his penis had reduced to the size and consistency of a lark's tongue.

With an effort, Alice twisted out from underneath him to turn on a little side light on the table by the bed, and as she did so, both Alice and Dr Sweet realized that his hand was resting on quite a large mole under Alice's left armpit. It was a mole that Dr Sweet had always been persuading her to do something about; she had irritably waved his concerns away.

'Yes, well,' said Alice in a quiet, cold voice after a long silence. '*That's* still there. And yes, I know I should do something about it. But I never thought it was *that* unattractive.'

Flicking the duvet back she climbed out of the bed and started pulling her underwear on. Her bra and pants did match. Desperately, Dr Sweet rallied.

'No. Jesus, no, Ally it's not that, you *know* it's not that.'

'No. Fine. Whatever.'

'It's just that I'm still upset about that man in PriceBest today.'

'What man?'

'The homeless man in PriceBest.'

'Oh yeah, right, David, the homeless man who you didn't help but who made you all upset and who you're now using as a pathetic excuse.'

'It's not an excuse,' said Dr Sweet angrily, but, like Alice, keeping his voice down to a hiss.

'No, you're an excuse, David,' said Alice, wrenching on her skirt. 'You are an excuse for a man and a human being.'

'Yes. Yes. Hm,' said Dr Sweet, his mouth pulled into a thin line of hurt and dismay.

'I can't *believe* I got into this situation again with you. I can't *believe* I threw away months and months of self-esteem rebuilding just so you could make me feel like shit again about my body.'

'That's not true.'

The pleasant drunk feeling in both of them had turned into a hard, bright, dry throbbing in the head.

'Jesus, I can't believe I wasted all those years with you. Do you know that?'

'Let's not get into this again.'

'I can't believe I chucked away all those chances just to nurture you. Just to send all my energy and attention into that great big black stupid hole that is you.'

'Oh well, that's great.'

'Yeah, wasn't it?' snapped Alice on a rising tone that

can only be approximated in an American accent. '*Wasn't* it, though?'

'Yes, well, we've been through this; we've been through it with our solicitors. And your accountants.'

'Jesus, what a train-wreck you are, David. Do you know that? What a train-wreck.'

'Do you mean train *crash*?'

'What? What the hell are you talking about now?'

'You're doing your unconvincing impression of an American.'

'Jesus, I *work* for an American company, and . . . and I might be spending a lot more time in the States as well.'

For the first time, Alice had stopped pulling her clothes on and her voice had faltered, lost its certainty.

'What do you mean?'

Alice opened her lips to speak, making a dry smacking sound. She exhaled heavily and began again.

'I wasn't going to say anything about this until after Christmas, but I've kind of been offered that job in New York City.'

'In New York?'

'In New York City, yes. It would mean being out there for about two years. Or maybe three.'

'Two years? Three years? Have you thought about this, Alice? What are we going to do about Cordie? How is she going to live both in America and here . . .'

Even as he began this last sentence, Dr Sweet realized the truth, but felt impelled to carry on until the end.

'Well, she wouldn't be living here in London, David,' said Alice quietly. 'We would have to . . . reassess the arrangements we have at the moment.'

'You mean she'd be living in New York with you.'

'You would of course have visitation ri— You would be able to visit whenever you wanted.'

'Visit. Oh yes.'

A delirious moment passed in which Dr Sweet was actually grateful for this intelligence, as it appeared to give him back the moral high ground he had lost during his display of impotence. In the next second, he remembered that he was not to blame for his impotence, on the grounds that it was caused by the incident at the convenience store and not Alice's mole. And the moment after that, he realized that his daughter was being taken away.

'And I'm supposed to accept it just like that, am I?'

'This isn't the way I was going to tell you, David.'

'Have you told Cordie yet?'

'No. I was hoping we could tell her together, after Christmas.'

Silence reigned, in which they could hear stirring and indistinct sounds coming from Cordie's bedroom: rustling, talking in her sleep. How loud had they been talking?

'And supposing I want to contest this?'

'Jesus, David, don't make this hard. It doesn't have to be hard.'

'When are you leaving?'

'It's not fixed yet. And it's not for ever.'

'You say that,' said Dr Sweet, shrugging, from his prone position, and then sitting up and huddling his knees under his chin. 'But supposing you meet someone out there? Some American guy?'

Something about the way Alice averted her glance at this remark, something about the redundant way she fiddled with buttons she'd already done up, caused a chill to settle on him, as if from an opened window.

'Alice?' he said. 'Is Richard going to be out there?' Richard was the American executive at her bank who she'd been seeing, but not very seriously, or so Dr Sweet had thought. He was a New Yorker, come to think of it. Alice turned to look directly at him, brazening it out.

'Yes, he might be. Sure. In fact, yes he is.'

'I see.'

Alice decided to regain the initiative.

'Oh you see? Well what I see is that I have been offered the chance to develop my career out there and I would be very stupid not to take it.'

'Right.'

'Well what am I supposed to do? Turn everything down? Give everything up?'

'Oh don't be so queeny.'

'Oh grow the fuck up.' Alice moved towards the door.

'Where are you going?' said Dr Sweet. 'Don't go.' If Alice thought this was a last-second flash of tenderness, she couldn't have been more wrong. Dr Sweet was getting up and putting on his clothes.

'This is your room. Don't you remember? You're sleeping here tonight. I'm sleeping on the sofa.'

With extraordinary speed, Dr Sweet was dressed and on his way down the stairs. Alice could hear Cordie talking in her sleep a little louder as he opened the door, and then muffled again as he closed it.

6

'Everything all right, David?'

While the Director of Research looked on impassively, Dr Sweet hurriedly attempted to close down his computer, having apparently sent a message to someone on a Hotmail account, not via the standard office e-mail.

'I can come back later. When you're less busy.'

'No, no, Jonathan. Hah!' Dr Sweet laughed mirthlessly. 'I was just looking something up on PubMed. There.'

The screen was blank.

'I wonder if you're free for a quick chat about The Situation.'

'Mmm. I mean, yes.'

The Director of Research turned away sharply, his habitual signal to subordinates that they should follow, and Dr Sweet was presented with his immaculately bald head, framed with a perfectly shaped horseshoe fringe of grey hair. The skin on his pate was gleamingly taut, evidently in the process of being pulled forward from the front. The Director of Research was frowning.

He led Dr Sweet out of his lab, past his German postdoc Heinrich and his Australian graduate student Hattie. But instead of turning left and heading for the Director's own lab, they went right, towards his officially constituted administrative office: a large pale room with a giant picture window that overlooked Queen Square, in which post-operative patients from the National Hospital for Nervous Diseases, often clad in stripy pyjamas, were being gingerly walked about. The Director's pate was so taut you could bounce coins on it.

Once in the office, Dr Sweet found himself not being expansively invited to sit on the plump cream sofa that formed a little suite at one end of the room with two matching armchairs. He was motioned instead to sit on the single uncomfortable chair opposite the colossal mahogany desk, behind which the Director levered himself by placing the flats of his palms on its surface and transferring most of his bodyweight onto them while wincingly lowering his lumbar region. His forehead was as creased as a bulldog's.

'Oof,' he said.

Dr Sweet saw that some Christmas decorations had been put up, tasteful green hollyish conceits without the vulgar gold and silver in evidence in his own home, and these partially concealed the painting of the institution's founder, Max Ruzowitsky. He was depicted in the classic tradition of portraiture, with his wife and two sons: his left hand on her shoulder, a proprietorial gesture duplicated in reverse for the son in front of him.

Ruzowitsky had made his substantial fortune from Florida retirement homes. A decade-long investigation by the Internal Revenue Service had culminated, in 1982, in an ambiguous and hotly disputed stand-off outside this Philadelphia house between armed police officers and Ruzowitsky, who appeared to be gesturing out of an upstairs window with a hunting rifle. The encounter was resolved only when Ruzowitsky's attorney was allowed in – an event adduced in subsequent court proceedings to counter police claims that the house was barricaded – and the final settlement had resulted in the substantial diminution of his personal wealth. One tax avoidance scheme, however, remained unchallenged: his foundation for research into cancer, which had spawned laboratories in almost every European capital city, as well as a number on both seaboards of the United States. Ruzowitsky himself had become a recluse, having long since left his wife and sons, who had themselves published agonizing memoirs of his abusive behaviour. Reputedly living in a cardboard box, Ruzowitsky restricted his communications with the outside world to writing letters to the *Philadelphia Enquirer* about various numerological codes in the Bible.

'So David, how's it going?' asked the Director.

Dr Sweet removed his gaze from the portrait.

'Well, it's fine, you know, I'm looking forward to Christmas. Got the family over. You?'

'I really meant the research situation,' said the Director thinly. Dr Sweet knew very well what he meant. 'Your paper about *BAD*.'

BAD was a gene responsible for producing a particular protein that allegedly reduced *apoptosis* or cell death; when this natural death failed to occur, aberrant cell growth was the result, which led to cancer. Dr Sweet had tanks full of zebrafish bred without this *BAD* gene to assess the effect of its absence. But these glittering creatures were in the pink. It was Dr Sweet's lab members, and especially Dr Sweet himself, that looked rough.

'Your paper is in press at the moment, is it not?' said the Director, turning over the pages of a file he had brought out of a drawer.

'N–no,' said Dr Sweet. '*Molecular Cell* sent it back and we are working on revising some of the experiments.'

'Yes I have the referees' reports here,' said the Director blandly.

'Have you?' asked Dr Sweet with a start of alarm. 'How did you . . .?'

' "The work is merely preliminary," says Referee One, "transparently derived from work done by the Imamura lab in Tokyo." '

The Director left a pause, apparently for Dr Sweet to offer his own comments, but the minute he tried to speak he was interrupted.

'That—'

'Referee Two is no kinder. "Abish and Sweet's paper is purely artefactual, riddled with errors, lacking in controls and in any case cannot match the rigour and originality of the work published by the Imamura lab." '

'What happened was that—'

'There is no comfort, moreover, in Referee 3: "The work proffered by Abish and Sweet is simple effrontery, especially when compared to the—" '

'We got scooped,' said Dr Sweet flatly.

The Director paused.

'Imamura published in *Genes and Development* in November. It's not exactly our work, but it's close enough to make our publication very difficult.' Dr Sweet gave another of his mirthless laughs. 'Hah! Bloody Imamuram—' closing off his competitor's name with an extra 'm' was the result of trying to gulp it back into his mouth, and that was the result of realizing, too late, that he and the Director were close personal friends and Imamura was the godfather of the Director's first son. The Director raised a playful forefinger.

'Aki Imamura is a formidable man and a formidable scientist.' Wretchedly, Dr Sweet noted the Director's familiar contraction of his enemy's first name, plus the use of his surname as well, to remind him of his superior status. 'When he was your age, he had published five first-author *Cell* papers. He now publishes three a year and is a dollar millionaire many times over from his company GenomeTech.'

The Director's supercilious rehearsal of Imamura's accomplishments would be dismaying under any circumstances, but Dr Sweet sensed something more serious: that he was using it to delay something even worse.

'David, am I right in thinking that you have received a job offer from the University of Douglas in the Isle of Man?'

Dr Sweet's blood ran cold. Yes, he had had an offer from Douglas of a lecturing position. And he had turned it down. Teaching at the University of Douglas in the Isle of Man was a scenario he would expect to read about in Solzhenitsyn, not experience in real life.

'Well, I turned that down,' said Dr Sweet. 'It was eighteen months ago.'

'It was ten months ago, David. And I happen to know that the offer is still open. It still stands.'

'But . . . I turned it down,' said Dr Sweet faintly. 'I didn't want it. I have my research group here.'

This was the signal for the Director to rise from his chair, after an eloquent preamble of wincing, come round to Dr Sweet's side of the desk and perch athletically on the edge of it, a posture that clearly occasioned him intense physical discomfort, jabbed the corner of the desk into his crotch and stretched the material of his trousers across the tops of his thighs to breaking point.

'David, a teaching position can sometimes be the most rewarding, the most *organic*, part of a man's career. Staying in pure research, especially where, in terms of publication, one is, ah, underperforming, can be counter-productive. Why not return to the wellspring of intellectual inspiration – teaching?'

'Because I have my research project here. I am directing the work of post-graduate and post-doctoral scientists. And I have pastoral responsibilities for fifteen students at the University of London.'

Dr Sweet's prompt answer, with its edge of obstinacy, disconcerted the Director, who had finished his last question by bunching up both fists against his chest and assuming a smile of priestly persuasiveness and certainty. Now that seraphic smile faded and was replaced with something grimmer.

'David, you know the situation with your contract here. I can only justify it to the governors on the basis of a real publication record. Without it, I am placed in a difficult position. Space is at a premium.'

'I admit that the Imamura paper was a setback, but we can regroup and re-submit the paper, perhaps to *Journal of Biological Chemistry* . . .'

'David, I beg you to consider how exciting the teaching position would be at the University of Douglas in the Isle of Man; I am certain that you would find passing on your knowledge to young adults academically and spiritually rewarding. What was it Thucydides said? To know a thing and not express it – it is all one as if one knew it not.'

' . . . and that will form the platform for a screen we're doing for binding partners for *BAD* which my lab can carry out *in vitro* . . .'

'David, you are out at the end of this year.'

' . . . and that will shed real light on the problem of – what?'

'Out. You are out at the end of this academic year.'

'The problem of what *BAD* is actually doing,' Dr Sweet persisted, and in fact went pointlessly on with a description of his work for about a minute, gamely continuing like a riderless horse while the Director tactfully nodded.

'David, this is never easy for me,' said the Director quietly, while Dr Sweet reflected that, like a surgeon or concert pianist, he perhaps just made it look easy. 'The space is required for an expansion of the mass spectroscopy lab. All your zebrafish are taking up too much room.'

There was a silence while Dr Sweet fancied he could hear the distant squeak of wheelchairs in Queen Square.

'I'd like you to make an appointment to see Roger Dalton,' said the Director suddenly, with an air of energy and decision, while placing an arm across Dr Sweet's shoulder and guiding him to the door. 'He's our new outplacement counsellor. Outplacement *consultant*, rather. I mean, in case you feel the Douglas position is not for you. I'll get Jenny to fix it up. Jenny,' he shouted, as loudly as if he had seen his secretary drowning or being robbed. The outer office was deserted. 'Where *is* she? Well anyway, call her up this afternoon, and she'll sort it out. Thanks, David!'

The Director turned and Dr Sweet saw the skin on the top of his head relax. Then the door closed.

Dr Sweet reflected on the opening of Max Ruzowitsky's 1979 memoir, *The Way I Succeeded*:

> Friedrich Nietzsche once said, 'That which does not destroy you makes you stronger'. But my experience of hurting my business competitors has taught me something different. That which does not destroy you makes you weaker and considerably more likely to be destroyed in the future. If I get in my car and run over an old lady and she doesn't die, is she stronger? Maybe I should put it in Reverse and back over her, and then put it in Drive and run her over again, back and forth, back and forth, bumping over her bones until she's as strong as Superwoman.

But Ruzowitsky went on to concede that setbacks and failures, properly understood and filleted for their life lessons, can be character building.

> When I was twenty-seven, I was refused permission to build a retirement home in La Jolla, California, and even now I hurt at the memory of it. But I channelled that negative energy into building up a real-estate portfolio elsewhere. I bounced back, and at twenty-seven I was no spring chicken.

Dr Sweet was forty-one. All at once he felt those years on him, a patchwork quilt of time draped around his shoulders like a homeless person's blanket, as he traipsed back down the corridor. The second left was his lab, but the first was the zebrafish room and it was there that he decided to turn for comfort.

His fish were not brilliantly lit, as in an aquarium, but in a cold dark tank and had to be viewed largely from above. They really were exquisite creatures, fish that looked like zebras. Zebras were a marvel as well; unglamorous, but still wonderful animals. And here were their fishy equivalents, bred without the *BAD* gene which Dr Sweet considered might have the cure for cancer. But these fish, his tiny marine subordinates and colleagues, were superb specimens of health. Dr Sweet pushed back his sleeve and put his hand into the cold water, simply for the pleasure of feeling them slithering up against his skin.

'David.'

'Mmm?'

It was Hattie.

'David, I've got an interesting result,' she said in a loud, clear voice.

'Uh-huh?' replied Dr Sweet in a similar voice. 'How interesting?'

'I think that experiment we were talking about has worked.'

'Oh yeah? Well come in here and tell me about it, I've got to see to the zebrafish.'

This stilted exchange came to an end and Hattie closed the door. A tall young woman with close-cropped dark hair and deeply tanned olive skin, attractively set off by a Persil-white T-shirt, she grinningly walked up to Dr Sweet, who allowed her arms to snake around his neck. They kissed, but Dr Sweet felt, as never before, that this affair with a graduate student was not a thrilling adventure but a terrifying domestic burden, a complex and intimate undertaking in which sex played a very small part. Dr Sweet wasn't married any more, but it was an affair in the sense that Hattie had a boyfriend back in Sydney to whom she was disloyal in ethical tandem with Dr Sweet's flouting of the rules about sexual congress with one's own graduate students. But now a third element of betrayal and deception had entered into the 'affair': Dr Sweet was about to betray Hattie by not having the older man's power and seniority on which he believed her affections for him were founded. He was about to lose his job. He was about to be exiled to the University of Douglas in the Isle of Man. She was having sex with an older man who was also a loser. On what were about to become the falsest of false pretences, he was enjoying sex with a young woman in her twenties.

'Hey,' said Hattie softly after the kiss. 'Hey,' again, on a rising note, as if she wanted something, or wanted to know something. But Dr Sweet knew it was just her style.

'How are you, Harriet?' he asked, and this playful use of her much-loathed Christian name earned him a little smack on the chest from the back of her hand, a physical gesture he returned by placing his fingers on her silver belly-button ring and turning her round so he could embrace her waist from behind.

'I'm OK.'

'Do you really have a good result?'

'Of course I really do,' said Hattie with a touch of asperity. 'I always do.'

'Not always,' said Dr Sweet. 'In fact, I was beginning to wonder if you were saving them up for me for some reason, maybe to present them on Christmas Eve.'

'Are we going to the Rylands today?'

The Rylands was a hotel. Dr Sweet would have been quite content to meet later at Hattie's flat in South London, but conceded that the daytime assignations at the Rylands obviated the need to find a babysitter for Cordie when she came to stay. On the other hand, taking an expensive suite at the Rylands – and they had to be disproportionately expensive not to be depressing – was becoming a real problem. Not a problem for someone with a prestigious and secure job at the Ruzowitsky Cancer Research Institute though, surely? Dr Sweet's interview with the Director came back to him with a queasy twinge.

'Sure,' said Dr Sweet, suppressing an internal clamour of dissent. 'I think I could get away about one thirty.'

'Mmm,' said Hattie, and with her right thumb scuffed the material of what appeared to be a black thong riding up just above the limit of her jeans. Men of Dr Sweet's generation were nonplussed by women's underwear this century. For their underwear to be visible this way was not, as far as he could determine, as forward or overtly sexual as he assumed. It was simply empowered, though it would be grotesquely offensive of him to refer to it directly, at any level of raillery. And yet it would be quite in order to displace this observation into a general complimentary remark about her top or her jeans, and it was his intuition of this – a droll but astute congratulation on her choice of earrings – that broke the ice at their first meeting when Hattie came to his lab.

'What time do you have to get back?'

'Early. Around six thirty. Alice and my parents are taking Cordie for a day out today and I need to be home when they get back.'

'Oh. I was hoping for a little early evening sojourn, but lunchtime is OK. Are you all right?'

Mentioning Cordie and Alice in the same sentence had brought back her decision to go away to America, something Dr Sweet had been suppressing all day. The reappearance of this fact in his mind suddenly made him dizzy with defeat.

'Yes, I'm . . . I'm fine,' he said curtly. 'Perhaps we'd better get back to work,' he added, meaning that Hattie should go back to the lab, and he would arrive there later, after a discreet and plausible interval. As it was, their secluded interview had lasted a little too long.

Hattie turned and walked away without another word, banging the door behind her. Dr Sweet turned and looked at his zebrafish moving darkly in the obscure tank.

When he returned to the lab, he found Hattie at work in her little bay and Heinrich at work in his, each studiously oblivious of the other. The other members of his team, Olwen from Wales, Bela from Hungary and Michiko from Japan, were downstairs availing themselves of elevenses, something which he had rashly implied was a custom in his lab, and which they now enforced as strictly as a union break, as well as lunch, tea and the obligatory early evening drink. They were in the canteen right now, he thought, talking about him, maybe even talking about him and Hattie. It was the only extra-curricular subject they could possibly have in common; conversation on any other subject was simply inconceivable.

Dr Sweet walked into the little screened-off office in the corner of the lab and awoke his computer screen from its doze with a keystroke. An e-mail awaited him from Roger Dalton. Nothing else. Dr Sweet looked out at his lab, at the shelves, the bays, the equipment. Soon, very soon, all this would be gone. Dismantled for a giant mass spectroscopy machine, the partition walls that defined the space of his lab, and his little office in the corner, would all be gone. It would be just a warehouse, a holding tank for a great big hunk of hardware. And all his team would be dispersed to the four corners of the globe. Perhaps poor Heinrich, Hattie, Bela, Olwen and Michiko would return to their native lands and rebuild their careers with the help of their own national governments. Either way he, Dr Sweet would have failed them. He would have to tell them, and very soon, that they should now be looking for other jobs, that their decision to take this one had been a major and damaging disruption to their careers.

Dr Sweet placed his elbows on his desk and his fingertips on his eye sockets for their cooling properties.

'What the bloody hell am I going to do?'

7

'Now Cordie, you don't have to *do* anything. Don't be naughty. You just have to play, and you don't have to do that if you don't want to.'

Cordie held her big bag of beanies and dolls to her chest defensively, and perhaps also for the warmth, twisting back and forth from left to right, the big red handle-loops of her bag framing her field of vision. Hugging the bag pressed the toggles of her boxy old-fashioned dufflecoat – a present from her grandparents – further into her chest. She had only been to this play-ground once before, when she was eighteen months old. Everything about it was unfamiliar. The big red-and-yellow slide; the climbing frame with black bars striped with peeling yellow paint; the big wooden pirate ship that she could already tell was going to be boring to climb in and out of; the tightly sprung see-saw that, at rest, stayed fully horizontal; the swings positioned against a delimiting wall of young trees, and with a shallow raised perimeter-line at the front, showing the danger zone. She looked at her feet and watched her milky indistinct shadow become clean and sharp across the tarmac and grass as the sun came out. She said, ''Choo!' because she had what is known as a photic sneeze, a reaction to sunlight or any bright light.

Now the sun was out, she tried to jump onto her shadow. But as always, it was much too quick for her. So then Cordie released one hand from hugging and held it up for her mother, who had taken her to the new Waterlow Park children's playground, along with Dr Sweet's parents, who were notionally there to look after Cordie as well. But really they had been taken out at least partly to be looked after, or rather entertained, by Cordie, from whom a faithful undertaking had been extracted not to say any more rude and nasty words. She was already in breach of this promise.

The four of them went round to sit on a dry bench next to a big rubbish bin. John and Rosemary positioned themselves in their beautifully tailored coats and hats. Alice was wearing a white windcheater with zips all over it; she was going to wear it skiing next month.

'Do you want to play on the pirate ship, Cordie?' said Rosemary brightly.

'No,' said Cordie promptly, and took Ken and Barbie out of her bag, twisted their arms forward into the Superman flying position and, angling them forward, flew them at a run over to the roundabout while Rosemary followed, puffing.

Cordie climbed aboard as the great drum wobbled and imperceptibly began to move. Rosemary settled herself on the seat as well, and set Cordie a good example by grasping the safety bars as tightly as she could. They were beginning to wheel round so as to be able to see Alice and John. Without holding on tight, Cordie twisted Ken and Barbie's arms back down to their sides. Rosemary wondered if she should relinquish her own hold to grab on to Cordie. The roundabout was slowing down.

'Do you like the roundabout, Cordie? Is it as good as the roundabout at the fair?'

Cordie did not dignify this with a reply. She pushed Ken and Barbie's heads along the graffiti-artist grooves in the woodwork. Ken and Barbie's heads were making the grooves; their little skulls were creating waves of energy which were buzzing through the wood, blazing a trail, parting the wood and paint like Moses and the Red Sea. They made patterns. Cordie stared at them and closed her eyes suddenly so she had a mental freeze-frame of them. Then she opened her eyes and looked at her granny, and took a mental, shutting-eyes snapshot of her face, which turned out not to be of her smiling, but looking away seriously towards her mum and grandad.

Then Cordie unceremoniously thrust Ken and Barbie into Granny's hands and climbed down to the round-about's skirt, its protruding running board. She remembered this from the last roundabout she had been on. Holding on to the bar and keeping her left foot on the board, she brought its clockwise movement to a skittering halt by jamming her right foot on the ground, and felt the shuddering all the way through her body. Then she started scootering the roundabout in the opposite direction, slowly at first, then really quite fast.

Granny started saying, 'Cordie!' as if she was scared, but as she pushed the ground away from under her, Cordie felt that the roundabout was quite still and it was the world that was going round and round; that she was turning the world with her great steel fulcrum.

When she scrambled back up, Granny had retreated

to the middle, as near as possible to the theoretically still centre of the turning circle, where the six safety rails converged by a great metal globe. She held on tight at either side, with Ken and Barbie in her lap. Cordie looked up at the spinning sky. Cloud formations blended into the blue. Like Granny on earth, Cordie sought out the dead centre in the sky. Then she sat up and watched the revolutions at their whizzing equatorial velocity, images distended through speed: slide, swings, climbing frame, Mum and Grandad on the bench; slide, swings, climbing frame, Mum and Grandad on the bench; slide, swings, frame, Mum on the bench; slide, swings – oof.

Grandad had stopped the roundabout. And just as Cordie thought, like a lot of grown-ups without playground roundabout experience, he thought he could stop it by keeping his feet planted in position, and just grabbing the bars and stopping it dead. But it wasn't as easy as that. The roundabout's momentum jolted him off his feet and he had to pretend that jogging beside it was what he'd wanted to do all along. Cordie waited until Grandad got aboard, and established that he wanted to play on the roundabout with her and Granny, then she grabbed Ken and Barbie, scrambled off and ran over to where her mum was. She knew that Granny and Grandad would have to pretend they wanted to stay on the roundabout for a bit.

John and Rosemary did indeed stay on it, because a bit of a breather was what they both needed. Rosemary felt hot and dizzy – dizzy in a bad way, a high-blood-pressure almost-going-to-faint way – and the jolt John had sustained while stopping the rotation had ignited his arthritis. Both knew exactly what the other was feeling, down to the discomfiture and anxiety of not admitting it and not needing to admit it. Forty-five years together had taken them beyond mere telepathy. They were computer terminals attached to the marriage mainframe.

'All right?' said John softly after a while.

'Mmm,' said Rosemary, extracting a folded Handy Andy from her sleeve and blowing her nose. When she was a little girl in Lincolnshire in the last century, there were no play areas, no swings, no municipal enclosures of this sort. She and her two brothers played in fields and hedgerows and on other people's property: they roamed for miles and miles, with as sure and complete a sense of the landscape as if they had been photographing it from a light aircraft. They roamed from the earliest morning in the summer and on into the evening half light. *Roaming* was something narrow roads and footpaths seemed to facilitate; she couldn't imagine anyone roaming in the suburban new towns that had obliterated this area since the war, and certainly not in London. Going somewhere meant driving or getting the Tube, and it was always disproportionately exhausting. As children, Rosemary and her friends could run and play and swim and pretend-swordfight without the need of an afternoon nap. And also – and this was one of the things that periodically astonished Rosemary about the past – without alcohol. Just think. From her infanthood until she was twenty, she got through day after day after day without a drink, without even thinking about it. When was the last time she went for twenty-four hours without a sherry or a gin and tonic or a glass of white wine?

John was thinking about his bones. His elbows hurt and his ankles made a funny clicking or snapping sound when he walked. His doctor ascribed it to the attrition or crepitude of these bones – a word tactlessly close to decrepitude. Some years ago, he'd heard a CD of his son's, playing a song called 'Everybody hurts', and for a moment he'd thought that it was the only pop song he had ever heard that could appeal to his generation, so long as everyone understood that it was physical pain the lyrics referred to. Everybody hurts – the old people at the bus stop, the old people in their front rooms, the old people trying to climb the stairs or get in and out of the bath. The twinges, pangs, nips and snips of pain in the joints, heart, arms, feet or head. Everybody in the day centre hurts. Everybody hurts; everybody cries. Perhaps there should be a special cover version by Max Bygraves – pictured on the sleeve with a lumbago-wince – that they could all sing along to on Saga holidays.

Alice was thinking how very strange her parents-in-law looked sitting serenely on the roundabout, holding hands, going round and round like figures in some giant and faintly heartless art installation. They must be cold, surely? Alice felt cold. She huddled into her great white windcheater with its many zips and fussed with Cordie's dufflecoat, pulling up the hood as Cordie pulled it back down again. What on earth were they all doing? It was December; it was too cold to be out in the park. Soon it would be time for lunch. What *was* the time? When was David going to call? She checked her mobile just as the sun came back out again, and instinctively she raised her face to be warmed.

' 'Choo!'

Cordie was watching Barbie sitting on Ken and hitting him. 'Ow, ow, ow,' said Ken. 'Stop, stop.'

'I shan't,' said Barbie, a serene intergalactic Princess

with superpowers that no boys had. 'I won't stop, because you are stupid and I can fly.'

'I grow out of your feet, but you can't jump on my tummy,' said her shadow.

Cordie felt a tiny piece of gravel in her shoe. Placing Ken and Barbie on the ground, she sat back down on the bench next to her mum and, frowning ferociously, untied the blue laces on her red canvas shoe and shook out the stone. Then she looked at her shoe, howling with pain with its great open mouth and its many insect eyelets. Aah! it said. Not like her sandals, whose mouths were laugh-shaped as if she had told them a very funny joke. Hahahaha! Aah!

Cordie silenced her shoe with her foot – Aah-ghlmph – and held her foot up for her mum to tie. Then she saw a small boy, perhaps a year older than she was, being led up to the see-saw by his parents, the only other family group in the playground. The little boy was conventionally dressed in a tiny pale grey sweatshirt with a Lilliputian 'Lonsdale' legend and dark blue jeans with white stitching that stood out with unnatural sharpness. But he also wore a dark-blue cape, and a loose Batman mask with pointy ears which flopped out sideways like an old cat.

Cordie thought Batman was a wanker.

John remembered taking his son to a playground when he was seven, and watching him play on a see-saw with another boy – one of the old-fashioned see-saws, a long section of timber with a bit of old tyre cushion at each end, and small handles. They see-sawed with a will, their bottoms lifting clear off the wood with each ascent, but after a few minutes, when Dr Sweet had been high, the other boy at ground level suddenly decided to stop playing and jumped off to join someone else, letting Dr Sweet descend with a terrible, unimpeded crash. There were a few gulping tears, but it was an accepted occupational hazard with see-saws in those days. The other boy didn't feel he'd done anything badly wrong, nor did anyone else. Up and down, old chap, John had said to his little boy, one minute you're up and then you're down – that's life.

*

'See-saw, Marjory-daw, Johnny shall have a new master,' said the little boy on the safe, modern see-saw as his father grasped the other end and pumped it up and down. If John tried that, he considered, his elbows would feel like two pieces of smoking sulphur. 'Johnny shall have a new master.' What century did that sentence come from?

'Come down,' ordered Cordie, pointing Ken at this little boy, but holding the doll in such a way that it might have been Ken she was addressing. She had appeared by the see-saw without anyone noticing. Alice smiled uncertainly over at the parents, who smiled gamely back. Then they looked at their little boy, whose name was Scott.

'You've got a new friend here,' said his father heartily.

'Nao,' said Scott, pushing his chin into his chest and letting his toes, which had been tensed upwards with see-saw enjoyment, go limp.

'Come down and play,' ordered Cordie.

'Don't you want to play with the little girl?' said Scott's mother, her voice betraying a hint that if the answer was no, she would understand.

'Nao,' he repeated.

'Oh come on, Scott, be a sport,' said the father, lifting poor Scott off the see-saw. Evidently the time for Scott enjoying himself quietly in his Batman mask and cape was at an end.

Cordie gave Ken to Scott and held on to Barbie herself. But Scott's father felt that preparatory civilities had not been satisfactorily completed.

'What's your name?' he said to Cordie.

'Cordie,' said Cordie self-consciously.

'This is Scott. Say hello to Cordie, Scott.'

'Nao.'

'Hold Ken like this,' said Cordie, demonstrating her fencer's grip on Barbie's feet. Silently, Scott complied. Then Cordie bashed Barbie's head against Ken's for about a minute. Alice wandered up to chat with Scott's parents, and John and Rosemary were coming over. Soon it would be time to go anyway.

Ken was being beaten by Barbie in a fight, but Barbie loved Ken; Barbie was beating Ken, but Ken loved Barbie.

'Do you want to go on the swings?' said Cordie suddenly.

'Nao.'

'Let's go on the swings,' she said insistently. Keeping her hold on Barbie with one hand, Cordie took hold of Scott's hand, the one without Ken, and led him over to the swings, stepping over the raised perimeter lip. The knot of grown-ups followed warily.

There were two swings, both vacant.

'Do you want to go on that one?' asked Cordie, pointing to the swing on the right.

'Nao.'

Civilly, Cordie nodded and took that swing herself

with a quiet, 'OK,' and gestured to Scott to take the one on the left.

Scott hesitated, but Cordie impatiently repeated her gesture, and then demonstrated how he should sit, with one hand holding onto the chain on her left and the other mirroring this grip, holding of Barbie with right thumb and forefinger. Scott followed suit and soon they were off, swinging.

The grown-ups made to go round behind, to give them both a bit of a push. Cordie quelled them with a look.

Swinging was fun. Swinging was the best thing in the playground. You bent your legs backwards to go backwards and then stuck your feet forwards to go forwards. Cordie could feel herself flying up with Barbie flying through the air. Scott was flying back and forth, too, his cape billowing dramatically behind him as he swung out, then clinging to his shoulders with a rippling slap on the way back. Whoosh, slap. Whoosh, slap.

Cordie looked at the trees' sighing branches as she went up; she felt she and Barbie could float to the top of them. These were the trees she dreamt about when she dreamt she could fly, and she was *always* dreaming she could fly. And *up* to the top of the trees. *Up* to the top of the trees. She and Barbie could fly *up* to the top of the trees.

Scott was swinging as well, but he had got out of synch: he and Ken were swinging back when she and Barbie were swinging forward. With a minute adjustment, Cordie slowed a little and within two and half swings they were back in step again. Obediently, Scott held Ken in just the way she had shown him. Cordie switched her gaze and established that the knot of grown-ups had rashly retreated to the bench far away from the swings and taken their eyes off them. Now Cordie felt it was time to go to the next stage.

Holding the left-hand chain in the crook of her elbow instead of her fist, she shifted her bottom back so her thighs were on the seat, and relinquished her grip on the right-hand chain entirely, so she could point Barbie forward in a bold gesture without losing balance.

'Do like this,' she ordered Scott.

'Nao,' he said.

'Do like this,' she insisted – and Scott did like that.

The rate of swing slowed, the height diminished and the asymmetry of their new position caused their swings to wobble and yaw as they went back and forth. But they soon grew accustomed to this new mode, picking up confidence and speed and thrusting out Ken and Barbie like some Fascist salute each time they swung forward.

'Now,' shouted Cordie. 'Fly!'

Scott's parents turned around in time to see Scott leave his seat at the swing's apex, fly through the air with his arms out like Ken, who flew with him, and land on the ground, palms making contact first, the right hand twisted round backwards and his right elbow making a noise very similar to John's crepitude-clicking sound.

Cordie skidded her feet on the ground to stop her swing and ran forward to check Ken was all right. She snatched him up and dusted him off, making a 'tsk' sound, then she went forward to where Scott was lying, howling in agony, and surrounded by the grown-ups. Scott's parents were closest to him, occasionally glancing sternly at Cordie's mortified mother and grandparents, clearly blaming them for this appalling disaster. Alice had her mobile out and was talking at great length to the nurse at her local general practice, unsure if the mishap merited a 999 call. The nurse was telling her not to move Scott.

'Are you all right, Scott?' asked his father.

'Nao,' said Scott.

'Only Superman can fly,' explained Cordie pertly, showing a little Superman 'S' badge she had pinned on her duffle coat, an 'S' that she had been practising drawing with the funny swoopy-shaped forms inside its fat shield outline, 'or Supergirl.' Then she walked off to the bench where she was chagrined to see the grown-ups had left her big toy bag where just anyone could get at it.

Truth to tell, Cordie was very worried. But she didn't know why. She left the group behind and went over to the bag, which contained the materials for a very important new game.

'Cordie you will come back here this instant,' said Rosemary, but Cordie was deaf to her.

Ken was now her daddy, and Barbie was Barbie, and she rummaged around in the bag for someone she needed. Here he is. From the bag she produced the toy with the most obvious authority, the Grenadier Bear. A big stuffed bear dressed up as a Buckingham Palace grenadier guard, with red tunic, and big black bearskin.

Grenadier Bear was cross. Grenadier Bear was cross with Daddy. And Barbie was cross with Daddy. Barbie was hitting Daddy and jumping on him and sitting on him and hitting him.

Some spots of rain landed on Daddy and Barbie's hard pink skin, staying there as droplets; on Grenadier Bear they just made damp patches. Cordie pulled up her duffle hood.

Barbie hit Daddy for a bit and then Daddy got away. But then Grenadier Bear marched up and put his paw on Daddy's shoulder. Barbie couldn't do anything but watch; it wasn't up to Barbie to do anything else. Grenadier Bear poked Daddy with the fixed bayonet on his rifle. Daddy accepted it stoically as Barbie looked on.

It got darker and rained harder. There was a funny feeling in the air, a stormy, muggy feeling, and Cordie had a funny feeling as well. The smell of damp earth and damp grass rose up past her nose like a water level. Ken, Barbie and Grenadier Bear hunched together in a shivering, rained-on clump, awaiting permission to go back in the big toy bag. Over by the swings, her mum and granny and grandad and Scott's mum and dad were hunched over in a similar knot, Scott now sitting up, his batmask still on, but cape scrunched around his left shoulder, right arm bent across his chest at the elbow and supported limply at the wrist by his left hand. Her mum was standing up, trying to talk to someone on her mobile phone, occasionally walking away and ducking down a bit, and doing little half turns this way and that, so that she could hear the other person better. The tarmac was so speckled with dark raindrops that they were joining up in lattice pattern, and the grass all around the playground was dark and sloping and wet, like seaweed. Across from the park she could see that people in their houses had turned on their lights, and she could see their Christmas trees and their decorations. The air felt squashed and tight.

At any other time Mummy would rush over and get her indoors out of the wet, and it was well past lunchtime. But Mummy was still over there with Scott, looking at her every so often. Everyone else had left the playground and the park. Then there was a great flash somewhere on the horizon and Cordie shut her eyes, stuck her tongue out to taste some rain, and started to count.

8

'Christ. David. David? *David*!'

'What, darling? What is it?'

'What is it? You've stopped moving and your whole body seems to have gone stiff as a board, that's what it is. And could you open your eyes?'

Hattie was astride him, naked apart from her glasses, a touch Dr Sweet usually found deeply sexy, but now her schoolmarmish vexation did not belong to the realm of the erotic. Dr Sweet opened his eyes to find Hattie's face at the bottom of his field of vision, and the rest occupied by the blank cream of the ceiling in this ordinary double room at the Rylands Hotel – all the suites had been taken. It was an ill omen, as was the fact that Dr Sweet had asked Hattie if he might have a glass of wine in the bar before they went up.

'Are you OK?' asked Hattie, and then, consciously lifting her mood, she leaned down with a smile and stroked his cheek: 'Are you OK, baby?'

'Yes, I'm fine.'

'You wanna carry on?'

'Mmm.'

'Mmm meaning yes or mmm meaning if you insist?'

'Yes, mmm meaning mmm-*mmm*, yes.'

They carried on, with Dr Sweet smoothing his hands over Hattie's breasts and cupping them, then letting his palms trail back down her sides. Usually they made love with her on top, but facing in the opposite direction so that she could see herself in the large wall mirror, and then, towards climax, allow him to get up into a kneeling position and penetrate her from behind. This was something he and Alice had liked to do from their honeymoon onwards, and were so adept at it that the manoeuvre was almost smooth enough to defeat gravity: everything from her splayed descent onto his straining lap to the final horizontal path of his left hand along her spine, and his right along the underside of her thigh. A decade of marriage had worked and planed and varnished it down to a comfortable continuum. With Hattie it had gone back to being rough timber, jolting, angular, sweaty, full of impact and uncertainty. The sumo aspect of sex had been reintroduced.

There wasn't, however, a mirror in the right position in the standard double room. This had added to both their senses of unease: an unnervingly *marital* sense of unease. A suspicion that things were going wrong and gritty little dust-clouds of recrimination were whipping up. Hattie carried on, earnestly fucking him, until Dr Sweet's body suddenly slid down the bed a little and his head bumped infinitesimally on the TV remote hidden in the sheets.

Was that what the man in the convenience store had felt when he hit the back of his head? Did the proximity of death simply dwarf the pain, rob it of mass and substance? Was it like soldiers getting their arm blown off and not realizing it because of the sheer adrenalin tidal wave? Did his life flash before his eyes before he died?

What did he feel like when he died? How old was he when he died? Was this the end of Dr Sweet's career in research science? What was the moment of death like?

'Jesus, if you're just going to lie there, this isn't going to work out.'

'Darling, I'm sorry. Let's . . . let's go on.'

'Yes, well, you're going to have to give me the tools before I can finish *that* job.'

Dr Sweet had comprehensively lost his erection. Was this becoming a regular thing, he wondered with a shiver of fear – a hint of future ruin, like twinges in the back or not being able to remember names?

In a moment Hattie was in the shower, and in another moment she was out, towelling herself down matter-of-factly. There was no question of Dr Sweet languorously joining her in the shower stall for a post-pre-coital mutual soaping. Hattie shrugged on a T-shirt, which paradoxically made her navel-ring more conspicuous. Remaining naked from the waist down, she slumped onto the side of the bed, and removed the long wooden toothpick from the club sandwich they'd ordered beforehand. She put it to her mouth, and then put it down again.

Dr Sweet clicked on the TV with the remote and BBC News 24 suddenly sprang into life, with a spruce young man standing in front of a building saying into a microphone, '. . . children aged *five*.' He turned it off.

Hattie had got her knickers on and was rummaging in a bag. She found her phone, frowned at it and put it back. She sighed. For the second or third time that day, Dr Sweet wondered whether to tell her about the man in the shop.

'It's OK,' she said suddenly, stroking his hair. 'It happens, don't worry.' And with that, Dr Sweet realized

Hattie had dealt with his sexual failure with efficiency and despatch. There was something very disquieting about the way Hattie was so unconcerned about it. He was about to make some self-deprecatory reply in order tentatively to re-open the subject when Hattie started again.

'How long are you going to be away over Christmas?'

'Well, I don't know about *away*. I've got my parents, my daughter and my ex-wife here; I'm going to take about a week off.'

'. . .'cause I think I'm going to be away an extra week. Two more weeks actually.'

Hattie unwrapped some chewing gum. Dr Sweet stirred irritably: he didn't care for one of his subordinates absenting herself so casually from the lab like this. Of course, objecting was out of the question under the circumstances, but in the next second, Dr Sweet could see there was something else to it.

'I got an e-mail from Arlen. I mean, we've been sort of corresponding. He wants to go hiking with me.'

'Arlen? Oh, *Arlen*.'

Oh yes, Arlen. Hattie's boyfriend. A man with a stupid name that Hattie unaccountably liked to go hiking with in the Australian wilderness. They would be 'coptered out into the middle of nowhere, left out to wander around, camping, defecating alfresco and running away from animals. Then Arlen would make chillingly competent use of some Global Positioning System device to get them back to a pre-ordained spot where they would be picked up again. Hattie had shown him a photo of Arlen once: they were out in the wilds together, both wearing stout longish shorts that are the cosmic antithesis of sex: Arlen was blond, and Dr Sweet guessed there was a fine down of blond hair covering his legs and arms. Arlen had the longest head he'd ever seen, with a chin as big and sharp as a shovel.

'Oh, right,' said Dr Sweet, his voice too quiet to be convincingly casual.

'Yeah, well, it's something he's been keen on since last Christmas,' said Hattie, pointedly referring to a time before their relationship began.

'Right,' he said again, blinking.

Hattie settled back on the bed, resting against the headboard, and then turned towards him with an expression of determination. Hattie being fully clothed and Dr Sweet being naked made it seem like she was visiting him in some very expensive private psychiatric hospital.

'David, listen.'

Dr Sweet felt a terrible coldness. He feared, more than anything in the world, four terrible words. He saw them galloping over the horizon like the horses of the apocalypse.

'We need to talk.'

'Do we?'

'Yes. Yes we do. When I get back from Australia next year, I think we need to cool our relationship.'

'Why?'

'Because it's distorting our friendship and our professional relationship. Our scientific relationship.'

'I wasn't aware that we had much of a friendship and professional relationship before this' – he waved vaguely at the hotel room – 'all started.'

That had come out wrong, especially the over-formal, pompous 'I wasn't aware' formulation. He knew he was right to suspect that she had prepared this little sentence, and yet somehow he had put himself in the wrong by objecting to it. Hattie went a little pale and swallowed. Dr Sweet pressed on, 'I mean, I'm not sure there was that much there to distort, anything that was different and separate from our – relationship. Yet.'

'Well I want, I wanted there to be something,' said Hattie. 'Something different. Don't you? Didn't you?'

'Of course I did. Do. But since when has *this* been something we had to discuss? Shouldn't we first discuss the end of our pre-friendship relationship? If it is in fact ending . . .?'

Hattie was silent, as if to assure him that it was indeed ending, but also to concede that she had been insensitive in passing over it so easily.

'Why?' asked Dr Sweet at last. 'Why do you want to end it? *Do* you want to end it?'

'It's obvious, isn't it?'

'I don't know. I want to hear it from you.'

Hattie sighed. 'I think our relationship has run its natural course.'

'Oh really? Is there something wrong with me? What's wrong with me? Tell me what's wrong with me.'

'When do we have to check out of this room?' asked Hattie after a pause.

'Oh great, I see. You're going to need about an hour to tell me, are you?'

'Jeez, David, don't be a baby, that's not what I mean. I mean we need to think about when we're going to get back to the lab – separately. I wanted to arrive first; there are things I need to do this afternoon.'

'What, apart from dump me?'

Hattie sighed and was quiet for a while.

'David,' she said, stroking his shoulder, 'it was never supposed to go on for ever, was it?'

Dr Sweet was utterly immobile. He didn't offer an opinion.

'It's just ended. It had to end and it has. I think our relationship has to move away from being a sexual one.'

'Yes, well, it's already moved away from that, hasn't it? It moved away from that in the last half hour.'

Now Hattie hardly knew what to do. He was the older man, the sophisticate. He was the one who was supposed to teach *her* the love lessons, harshly or otherwise. How was she supposed to play this? Tentatively, she reached out to touch his shoulder again, but he snapped away as if from an electrified fence.

'And I'm not crazy about this extra two weeks off you say you want,' he snapped coldly, stirring from the bed and starting to put his clothes on. 'What about your experimental work?'

'I've told you, Arlen and I are going hiking.'

'Yeah, yeah, for one week. One week. So what do you need the second week for?'

'The second week is when Arlen and I are getting married.'

Some big spots of rain came splatting on the window that looked out over Russell Square. Down on the street a bagpiper, who had been droning a yuletide carol medley, packed up and went home. The traffic sounded heavy and sluggish, buses and cars braking hard in the wet, pedestrians wheeling round and waving rolled-up newspapers on street corners, suddenly unable to find cabs.

'Well, actually, that's happening the first week. It's, um, the second week we're going hiking.'

Dr Sweet had got most of his clothes on and was standing at the window with his back to Hattie, buttoning his shirt with a fierce, emphatic, one-handed movement. Some swallows swept across the skyline and changed course in exactly the direction he was looking, dwindling to black dots. He tucked his shirt in all around. His belt had missed one of the loops. The sky was now getting really quite dark. Hattie reached down to the switch at the side of the bed and turned on the light. Instantly, Russell Square was extinguished and all Dr Sweet could see was his own reflection in the glass: a tired-looking man with crow's-feet and elephant ears. He had never looked more like his father.

'It was really a sudden thing,' said Hattie, with a forced attempt at gaiety and amazement. 'I guess it's taken us both by surprise. It was something we thought was kind of way ahead.'

He had enough self-possession to hope very fervently indeed that Hattie wouldn't express the wish that he and Arlen should get to know and like each other. He need not have worried on that score. A constant theme of Arlen's long daily e-mails to Hattie was his genial dislike and derision of Dr Sweet, who he had met the previous summer and with whom he had disagreed, in a fractious, ill-tempered way, about the importance of daily exercise.

Dr Sweet was now fully dressed and was putting some things into his bag. One of them, she was pained to see, was a little talisman of their relationship: a talisman she had always brought to these meetings. It was the programme of a conference organized by the European

Academy of Molecular Biology last August, where they had spent their first night together – a deliciously clandestine meeting in her campus-style room. In one of the very few gestures of ordinary affection he had ever made to her, Dr Sweet had taken Hattie's copy of the little booklet and written his initials, DLKS, and hers, HMcB, together on the flyleaf in his distinctive looping handwriting and surrounded them with a little heart. She had kept it and placed it by the bed in the hotel every time they had sex – like a sort of erotic Gideon Bible – to recapture that sense of anonymity and adventure.

Now he was taking it back, confiscating it, cancelling it. He was clearly getting ready to walk out. The room had already been paid for.

'Jesus, David, we don't plan all the things that happen in our lives, sometimes they just happen. This is, I don't know, a little bit messy, sure. I didn't mean it to be like this. I'm *sorry*.'

'No, no,' snapped Dr Sweet, who had been waiting for a forced apology of this sort, 'congratulations. Many congratulations to you and Arlo.'

Hattie knew that Dr Sweet knew what his name was.

'There's just one thing.'

'What?' asked Hattie.

'I expect you'll be asking him for a blood test, to make sure the long-head thing isn't geneticary!'

'What?' said Hattie again, baffled, as Dr Sweet swept out of the room and down the hotel corridor with the most horrifically unsuccessful exit line of his life ringing in his head. He had tried to mock Arlen's long head, implying it might be 'genetic' or perhaps 'hereditary', but had only managed to jumble up the two words. Dr Sweet blushed so fiercely that he felt the blood actually humming in his cheeks and forehead as he marched down the passage. It was perhaps the most grotesquely embarrassing and undignified thing he could have done. He had entirely forfeited whatever respect or sympathy was his due.

'Oh Christ,' he wailed as he reached the cul-de-sac. He had come the wrong way; the lifts were in the other direction. Now he would have to turn back and walk past their room. As he did so, Hattie was standing at the open door, her expression conveying that she had, though it had taken her a moment, understood his bungled jibe, that she was offended, but also that she felt pity and anxiety on his behalf.

'Are you OK?' she said as he stalked past.

'Yes,' he said quietly, 'I'll see you back there.'

It was raining hard out on the street and Dr Sweet luxuriated in the misery of walking round in the wet with no umbrella. He turned the collar of his coat up in the traditional way that makes no difference whatever, and walked clockwise round the square. What an idiot. Surely he could have seen what was coming. It was just a little fling, a little affair. She didn't take it too seriously; neither did he. Neither *should* he. It was a just a sex thing.

But this final mental shrug, intended to calm himself, or comfort himself, had precisely the opposite effect. *Just* a sex thing? The sex thing hadn't exactly worked out just then. Maybe if the sex had been wonderful, or even just as good as last time, Hattie would have delayed telling him. Or maybe she would have delayed the marriage. Maybe if they had been blissfully happy in bed, Hattie would have eventually given Arlen and his long head the heave-ho. But he had failed, and so the deluge had begun.

CHILDREN AGED 5 read a part of the newspaper headline that he could see. Children aged five . . . what? Children aged five . . . lead happy, healthy lives? Children aged five . . . have something nice happen to them? Dr Sweet looked around, but could see no children in the square. The rain had made them disappear, as in Vulgaria. There were only ex-children about. From the other side of the square he could see Hattie leave the Rylands under her yellow umbrella, heading back to the Ruzowitsky. He would give it fifteen minutes or so and then saunter back himself. Sauntering was what he used to do anyway. Now a defeated trudge was more in order.

Almost everyone was cowering in doorways and shop-fronts; whole bus queues had decamped, and informally maintained their queue precedence under shelter. Dr Sweet was quite alone in the rain.

What was he going to do now? His job was about to vanish and he was alone. Were his best years behind him? From his earliest childhood, Dr Sweet had assessed every-thing that happened to him on the basis that it was all right, but that there was more and better to come. But perhaps now there was no more to come, or nothing of any consequence. Life was like a stick of chewing gum, with all the flavour gone, and now he had to just keep chewing for three or four more decades.

He turned the corner into the street leading to the institute. Soon he would have to summon up the energy to exchange badinage with Arthur, the security porter, who he suspected was aware of his lunchtime assignations. Both Hattie and he had to sign in every time they re-entered the building, writing down the time. Arthur would have noticed the repeat patterns. 'Had a good *meal*?' was the impertinent way he phrased his daily greeting, smiling brightly, his gingery eyebrows at their fullest elevation.

'Yes, thank you, Arthur,' was Dr Sweet's habitual clenched reply. He had always meant to ask Hattie if Arthur's comments to her were as loaded, but that was something he didn't really feel like asking now.

How many lunchtimes had he spent like this in his life, wandering about, looking into shops, reading the paper, reading a book. How many lunchtimes had he had in his life? How many had he got left? The rain was easing up a bit. There was a beautiful young woman in an ad hoarding directly ahead of him, on the glass siding to a bus shelter, wearing a bikini, but with her thumb hooked lubriciously into her minuscule pants, pulling on the waistband, while chewing sensually on her lip. What was she selling? Insurance? Telecommunications? Was it a council ad reminding people to register to vote?

There was someone talking to himself. Dr Sweet didn't need to wonder if he was talking to someone on a hands-free cellphone: people doing that always looked relatively relaxed, focused. This person was looking down and a little to the side, talking animatedly, silently, with a touch of inebriation colouring the triumphant smile of someone winning an argument. He was a well-dressed middle-aged man wearing a hat.

Geneticary. Oh, very cool. Very Oscar Wilde. He couldn't have made his pathetic, bitter *loserness* more obvious if he'd tried. Perhaps he should have said, 'You know what they say about long heads, don't you? Short pennies.' Penis! Christ, he'd cocked it up again. Even in his head he cocked it up. He couldn't even do *esprit d'escalier.* Even in his own imaginary world he made a fool of himself. It's penis, penis, penis you *wanker.*

The well-dressed middle-aged man in the hat was staring at him. He realized he had been emphatically mouthing the words, 'Penis, penis, penis, you wanker.'

When Alice and he broke up, she had said, 'I think we need to be apart for a while,' and he had agreed. It was a dignified, civilized exchange, perhaps the most thrillingly direct and emotive moment of communication in their entire marriage. He almost misted up now thinking about it. Would Arlen and Hattie split up? Or would they stay together for ever? Was their wedding going to be a modest civil ceremony or a big church affair? If the latter, Dr Sweet thought with a pang, then she and her mother must have been preparing it for months. Maybe for over half the total length of their affair.

He and Alice had married at Oxford Town Hall: a register office event, one of many scheduled for each day, at which you could very clearly hear the guests for the next wedding assembling in the corridor outside. She had worn a cream-coloured suit, not a dress, he'd noticed: the first hint of her tough womanhood emerging from the girlie chrysalis. Dr Sweet smiled now, as he always did, remembering how the registrar had called him by his full name:

'Do you, David Leonard Kingdom Sweet . . .?'

He had told Alice his middle name was Leonard, but he hadn't told her about Kingdom, his father's tribute to the greatness of Isambard Kingdom Brunel. He never used it; never expected to hear it again in his life. When the registrar said it, Alice had burst out laughing; so did he and so did all the guests as well!

Here was another strange shop. It was the health-food centre where Alice had asked him to pick up another pack of a certain type of herbal tea she liked. Entering the store, Dr Sweet felt very strongly that there was something deeply unhealthy about the whole place. The lighting was oddly pallid, like the inside of a warehouse or goods depot, making everyone there, customers and staff, look like they'd just come round from an operation under general anaesthetic.

The brand Alice wanted was called Serenitea, a special bagged herbal blend of hawthorne and lime flowers, naturally caffeine free and calculated to induce an organic sense of stillness. The assistant told him they were all out. He would have to make do with the alternative Alice had authorized him to purchase, Equanimitea, in which chives and wild thyme were used instead of lime. Dr Sweet browsed a little, thoughtfully picked up a packet of Magnanimitea as well and took them to the cash desk.

Outside again, Dr Sweet did a balletic body swerve to avoid a despatch cyclist who leapt up onto the pavement, rocketed past him, cruised into a bus lane and shot a red light. He remembered his mother once actually standing in front of a young man riding on the pavement and insisting he dismount. Nowadays, objecting to this was quaint as well as dangerously futile. In London, riding your bike on the pavement was like soft drugs or the incorrect use of the word 'disinterested'. There was *de facto* decriminalization.

And here was the Ruzowitsky, a building distinguished by the vainglorious banner hanging down announcing its identity in the manner of an art museum in an American city. How vividly he remembered arriving here six years ago, with every intention of becoming a world-class player in molecular biology, the great scientific adventure of the twenty-first century, as he was wont to say to his colleagues, the adventure which would be to his age what physics was to the last. And now his career was doomed to peter out into dullness and banality.

Dr Sweet rustlingly transferred the health-food carrier bag to his right hand and checked his watch. Hattie would have had ample time now. Time to punch the clock for the afternoon. He had papers to write, correspondence to settle; he had to see to the zebrafish, he had to fix a time to meet his outplacement counsellor. Such a lot to do. He felt for his security Cryptag which activated the entrance doors.

But when he walked in, Dr Sweet saw that something was very strange indeed. Normally the entrance lobby was deserted, except for Arthur, who sat reading the paper and affected to be unaware of your presence until you were leaning over his desk. But now Arthur was standing, gazing at him, lips slightly parted, and next to him, but on the other side of the desk, was the Director – the Director himself was standing there, his arms crossed, causing the vents of his jackets to fan out. Like Arthur, he was staring at Dr Sweet but with his characteristic ferocious concentration, coloured by some non-specific air of rebuke. It was the way he would look at Dr Sweet while he gave a conference paper.

Then he became aware of the third and fourth persons there: two men who stood up and turned round with a professional air of deliberative heaviness that intimidated Dr Sweet more than anything he had ever experienced in his life. The first was a man in a suit, but no tie, and a light mackintosh. With elaborate formality, he took up a position directly opposite Dr Sweet, while his companion, a younger man in jeans and a sort of brown leather jacket with a faded tartan lining, took up a stance at an angle to Dr Sweet, fixing him with a similar stare.

The first man said, 'Sir, are you David Leonard Kingdom Sweet?'

Dr Sweet felt all the dust motes in the air stop moving. Everything was quite still. He felt the tendons in his legs begin to weaken.

'Oh Christ, is it Cordie?' he whispered.

The first man gave a tiny shake of his head, as if to say that, no, it wasn't, but that it was not his job to give reassurances on that or any other subject.

'Are you David Leonard Kingdom Sweet?' he repeated, taking half a step forward.

'Yes,' he replied, his voice high and light.

At this, the man placed his hand lightly but firmly on Dr Sweet's shoulder. 'Sir, my name is Detective Sergeant Cole from East Holloway Police Station CID, and this is Detective Constable McCready. I am arresting you on suspicion of the murder of John Patrick O'Rourke on the twenty-second of December at PriceBest Supermarket, four hundred and thirty-five Archway Road, London, North nineteen. You do not have to say anything, but it may harm your defence if you do not mention when questioned something which you later rely on in court. Anything you do say may be used in evidence. Do you understand?'

Detective Sergeant Cole's face was taut and strained with procedural gravitas as he and his colleague showed their ID. His gaze locked unforgivingly onto Dr Sweet's, who could now see that Cole's sandy fringe matched a wiry and unattractive moustache. Behind him he could see that the Director was awestruck by this moment and Arthur was simply spellbound, like a boy on Christmas morning.

'Sir, do you understand?'

Dr Sweet swallowed and said, 'Yes, I think so.'

'I am now going to escort you to East Holloway police station where you will be interviewed. Is there anything you need to do before we go?'

Dr Sweet thought of his computer monitor and lab, soon to be dismantled; he thought of Heinrich, Hattie, Bela, Olwen and Michiko making unsupervised messes of their projects, like five spoilt cakes, and above all he thought of his zebrafish, shifting like wheat in the cold unlit tank. Dr Sweet realized that Detective Sergeant Cole's hand was still on his shoulder when he felt it shaking.

'Sir, are you all right? Do you need anything?'

'No,' he replied in a quiet, wondering little voice, almost to himself.

Cole gave a nod to McCready and they guided the unresisting Dr Sweet back up the little flight of stairs. As in a dream, he accompanied the arresting officers to an unmarked car. In a dream, he stood by while Cole unlocked it and got into the driver's seat, while McCready ushered him round to the passenger door. And in a dream, the sort of dream where everything is expected, Dr Sweet felt the palm of Cole's hand settle on the crown of his head.

9

'I can't fucking believe this,' said Detective Sergeant Cole, pounding on the steering wheel with the flat of his hand. 'I could have explained this to a chimp by now.'

'Yes, well I'm sorry,' said Detective Constable McCready sullenly, refusing to meet Cole's glance when he turned round to look at him at the lights. 'But I don't see the difference.'

'The difference is – Jesus, the difference is with the bookmaker you're just betting. With spread betting you're participating in a market. You're *making* a market, it's just that it's not in gold futures or derivatives, but in the number of, I don't know, the number of runs England make against Pakistan.'

'Well,' said Detective Constable McCready with a derisive little snort, 'I can bet on that. I can bet on how many runs at Ladbrokes.'

'Oh yes,' sneered Cole. 'You can do that if you *like*. You can go down to your nasty little bookmaker with his instant coffee and his free pens. I mean if you like you can use an old steam engine to travel to work in, and go to the toilet in a trench. I mean if you want to go abroad for your holidays, you don't have to go by plane, you can go by fucking hot air balloon wearing goatskins. The point about spread betting is that it's modern and efficient. You keep betting after the match has started. Change your position in the market. Take profit or restrict your loss. Look at this cunt.'

They came to a halt while a young man holding a poodle walked diagonally across a zebra crossing, insolently not keeping to the proper black-and-white path. Almost as soon as Dr Sweet had entered the car, the ill-tempered debate about spread betting had kicked off, or resumed, and continued all the way up Eversholt Street. The solemnity they'd showed while they apprehended him had vanished entirely.

Cole and McCready thoughtfully watched the poodle man walk off, both aware that if they didn't have a murder suspect in the car with them, he would have been highly eligible for a bit of a talking-to. McCready looked at Dr Sweet directly for the first time and repeated his little snort, this time with a touch of amusement.

'What a time we had finding you, sir,' he smiled. There was a corroborative grin from Cole in the driver's mirror. 'What a time. What a high old time.'

Dr Sweet said nothing, and after a moment McCready continued.

'Mr Kamil Yildiz was able to give us your address because he does deliveries for you.'

That was it. Kamil used to deliver vegetables until Dr Sweet stopped asking about three months ago.

'But he gave us the wrong address, so we had to go back this morning, and then we had to ask door-to-door, and then your cleaner gave us the address of your workplace.'

McCready gave a little off-centre smile, a smile that

didn't invite praise or congratulation; it was more a concluding gesture to punctuate this matter-of-fact demonstration of efficient police work to a member of the public.

'What is it you do for a living, sir?' Cole suddenly asked.

'I'm a scientist. I work in cancer research.'

'So you're a doctor? A cancer doctor?'

'Well, yes, I suppose you could say so. Yes.'

Dr Sweet knew what was coming. Every taxi driver who'd ever asked him what he did for a living, or why he was knocking off work so late, reacted the same way: with a deeply troubled need to confide about his own experiences of cancer. As Dr Sweet got older, the status and prestige factor of his job in casual conversation at parties got higher virtually by the day. When he was in his late teens and twenties, he would tell people he was a scientist, a molecular biologist, and the trendy arts crowd would look blank or sneer to his face. Nowadays these same types, all of them in their late thirties and early forties and discovering lumps, or knowing people who'd discovered lumps, reacted very differently indeed. Sometimes, just as an experiment at dinner parties, Dr Sweet said his work touched on human fertility. The information would always electrify at least one childless professional couple, and they would solicit his views on a range of issues, respectfully, humbly, almost on bended knee. But mainly, Dr Sweet just said cancer research, and those words, repeated so casually every day, starting at a time in his youth when he had no fear of the disease, did not horrify him the way it did civilians. One evening, coming back from the lab, Dr Sweet had hailed a taxi, told the driver what he did for a living, and the man had simply pulled over, switched off the engine and sobbed with his face in his hands for ten minutes.

But the expressions of humble respect, mixed with panicky confessional, were not forthcoming.

'So it's your job to help people? People who are ill?' Dr Sweet sensed that this was not going well, and he was right. His bag of Equanimitea and Magnanimitea rustled on his lap, and his palms, holding the handles, felt sticky.

'You're a trusted member of the community and here you are.'

Evidently Cole and McCready felt they had a modern-day Crippen in the car with them, or one of those disturbed nurses that deliberately poison children to keep them in their care. Dr Sweet felt his breathing grow shallower. Surely now was the moment to explain himself?

'Look, I have to say, all this is just a mistake. That man, I can explain ev—'

But Detective Constable McCready held up a warning palm, pushed the corners of his mouth down and averted his face while squinting severely up at him, as if to say that raising the subject was in very poor taste, but maybe they too had been at fault for having alluded to it themselves.

'No, sir. None of that. We'll have time for all of that at the station.'

At that moment, East Holloway Police Station came into view, and they swept past it and went in the back entrance.

Until now, in the unmarked car and with plain-clothed officers, it had been possible not to think about what was happening. But now, the word 'police' was everywhere, a word that worked on him in a similar way to the word 'cancer' at dinner parties.

Cole and McCready got out of the car, and some of their grimness briefly returned for the fifteen seconds it took them to escort him from the car to the rear entrance door to the station.

Once inside, Dr Sweet's first thought was that the whole place had been taken over by some sort of gang in an Assault On Precinct 13 situation. In so far as he had thought about it at all, he was expecting frowning people walking about. Instead, disorderly shouts exploded right and left. The three of them chanced upon a group of officers going off shift.

'Oy! You *caaant*.'

'*Caaant!*'

'*Caaaaaant!*'

Dr Sweet was marched through a long corridor, round to the right, down some steps, through a double door and up to a big desk, at which a man Dr Sweet was later able to identify as the custody sergeant sat like a Dickensian beadle. He was lantern-jawed, bespectacled and appreciably older than anyone else.

Cole and McCready presented themselves while the sergeant said, 'Number, please?'

'1084,' said Cole, as the sergeant started clackingly typing up a report with two fingers.

'Reasons for arrest?'

Cole and McCready exchanged glances, savouring the moment.

'Murder.'

The word, used only for the second time since Dr Sweet's arrest and caution, made him feel feverish, as if he had bitten through a thermometer and swallowed the mercury. Oh Christ, he thought, I've got someone else's life by mistake. Surely they can see that?

The custody sergeant went, 'Ooh,' on a cheery rise-and-fall tone, and Cole and McCready smiled, as if accepting a tribute. He continued typing, to Cole's dictation:

'Subject entered PriceBest supermarket on 22 December and attacked victim by striking him with bottle.'

Dr Sweet tried to say the word 'What?' but it came out as a tiny inaudible gasp.

'Reason for detention: to be interviewed to obtain evidence re: the alleged offence and to allow him an opportunity to give his account.'

An opportunity to give his account? An account of how he murdered someone by hitting them over the head with a bottle?

Mutely, Dr Sweet looked at the sheet of paper the custody sergeant handed him, detailing his rights in this matter.

'Sir, do you wish to call your lawyer, or do you want us to appoint a solicitor on your behalf?' was the custody sergeant's next question, and it was now that Dr Sweet decided it was time to pull himself together. He was a professional middle-class person with money in the bank. Everyone knew that court-appointed lawyers were for no-hopers and petty thieves who couldn't afford to go private at this vital moment in their lives. Weren't they?

'I shall call my *own* lawyer,' said Dr Sweet grandly, taking out his Psion Organiser and, with sweaty, trembling fingers, typing in the name of Janet Wilding, the nice lady who had done the conveyancing for his house. Even as he did this, and aware of the stone gazes of the three policemen incuriously looking at their murder suspect, he felt like an amateur yachtsman losing sight of land. 'I shall call my *own* lawyer,' he heard echoing in his head, 'I shall call my *own* lawyer.' Dr Sweet typed the number into his mobile phone and after a few rings heard, 'This is Janet Wilding and Associates, the office is closed until 7th January. If you wish to leave a message, do so after the beep.'

Dr Sweet said, 'Janet, I'm . . .' and then, after a thoughtful pause, hung up.

'Janet not there, sir?' asked the custody sergeant with a wintry smile.

'No, not at the moment,' said Dr Sweet in a hoarse, defeated whisper. The sergeant, Cole and McCready were then expectantly silent.

'I, erm, I think I will have your solicitor. Please,' said Dr Sweet.

'Very good, sir,' said the custody sergeant briskly. 'Now I have to take possession of your property, please.'

Meekly, Dr Sweet handed it all over, starting with the Psion Organiser which the sergeant smacked down smartly on the desk in such a way as to cause the screen to go blank. Everything was painstakingly logged, including his Equanimitea and Magnanimitea.

'Is there anyone you wish to telephone?' he asked.

Dr Sweet's cellphone being now officially impounded, he used the phone on the sergeant's desk to try, firstly, his home number. He heard his recorded voice. Then he tried Alice and got her voicemail.

He said, quaveringly, 'Janet, I mean Alice, I'm in hospital, I mean prison. I mean I'm in, I'm at the police station, East Holloway Police Station. Please come and pick me up or talk to the policemen here.' He replaced the receiver, which felt as heavy as a dumb-bell.

'Right, sir, the duty solicitor will be about an hour.'

'Is there anywhere I can wait?' asked Dr Sweet humbly, every smidgen of independent defiance or self-possession utterly extinguished. But this got the biggest laugh of the afternoon.

'Yes, there is, sir,' said Cole after all three of them had stopped chortling, guiding him away from the desk and down another corridor. At the end of the passage, another officer unlocked a door with an observation slit and pushed it open with the flat of his hand, leaning back to allow Dr Sweet an unimpeded view, like a hotel proprietor.

'There you go, sir, it won't be too long,' said Cole, and with that he left.

The prisoner lingered at the cell's threshold.

'What if . . . what if I want to go to the toilet?' asked Dr Sweet, and was answered by this new officer directing his view back into the cell where, in the middle of the back wall was a lavatory, a brutally unenclosed lavatory with its seat up.

The prisoner looked at this for a while and started to inhale the cell's smell: sweat and cigarettes, with a top note of faeces. Beyond fear, beyond astonishment, Dr Sweet said out loud the first thing that came into his head.

'Are prison cells like this?' he asked.

The officer considered it. 'You've got this one to yourself, sir,' he said thoughtfully. 'Now, as my colleague says, it won't be too long, though I do have to say the duty solicitor is probably in the middle of his lunch.'

Clang.

PART TWO

PART TWO

10

Dr Sweet tried standing in his cell and he tried sitting. For the benefit of anyone looking in at the spyhole, he tried walking back and forth in an emphatic dumb show of astonishment that he should be incarcerated like this. He tried hunching down on the single-bed ledge affair and reclining against the wall, feeling its harsh texture against his back, and then getting up again. He tried looking directly at the lavatory; he tried looking away from it. He tried casually taking it in, in the course of a 360-degree visual sweep of his surroundings. He tried standing reasonably close to the lavatory so that it wasn't entirely in his ocular field. He tried standing at the opposite corner of the room. Eventually he just sat on the bed-ledge, on the very edge, perched so his feet and the periphery of his buttocks were taking the weight, like an exercise for building up his thigh muscles.

All the time he looked at his naked wrist. Obsessively, repeatedly, he shot his left cuff and looked at where his watch had been. What's the time? Wrist. Wonder what the time is? Wrist. How long have I been in here now? Wrist. Walls. Door. Lavatory. Floor. Lavatory. Door. Spyhole. How long am I going to be in here? Wrist. Floor. Walls. Ceiling.

Dr Sweet wondered if there was a way to measure the time naturally, organically, without his watch. Perhaps he could count his pulse, with his fingers on his neck. Or if there was a weak gleam of sunlight through a high barred window, maybe he could use his thumb as a sundial? But there was no high window. Just a single strip light. What about a distant church bell tolling the quarter hours?

After sixty-five uncounted minutes, Dr Sweet jumped, physically jumped, at the sound of a tannoy so close to his cell he thought there must be some speaker system in there with him: 'DS Cole, report to custody, please.'

Detective Sergeant Cole. One of his arresting officers. Dr Sweet dared to hope this meant the duty solicitor had arrived back from his lunch and an interview was now imminent. After a few minutes more his cell door clanged open and a policewoman appeared, framed in the doorway, her uniform enlivened with a sprig of tinsel playfully inserted into one of the buttonholes in her blouse. Distantly, a carol was playing. Behind her was a very young-looking man wearing a very rumpled suit and glasses; he held a kind of document wallet under his arm.

'Mr Sweet, your solicitor is here. Could you come into the interview room, please?'

So ended the great epochal moment in Dr Sweet's life. But imprisonment hadn't cowed him, or not as much as he thought. He felt a strange urgency thrill through his nerve endings. His middle-class horror of being in trouble with the police had distinctly abated now that his solicitor was here. Surely now this whole ridiculous misunderstanding would be cleared up? But it was only as he was following his solicitor and the WPC down the corridor that Dr Sweet permitted himself to think about the actual event itself: an event that he'd had an hour's solitary confinement to consider. Now it came back in his mind in a sequence of three or four subliminal mental flashes. The man, the little girl, the pool of olive oil, the man lying there. *Had* he killed him after all? Could his actions be construed as murder? *Was* he guilty?

Dr Sweet and his solicitor went alone into the interview room, drably carpeted in industrial grey and still smelling of cigarettes but without the residual hint of human waste. Dr Sweet sat on one side of a Formica-topped table but the solicitor remained standing opposite him, threw his file down on the table with a bang that made him jump for the second time, and then disconcertingly clapped his hands once with a hollow, resounding noise, like a flamenco dancer.

'So, Mr Sweet. Dr Sweet. My name is David Martin of Goodge and Company, representing you as your solicitor. And I have to say that at first blush it looks like you are up to here' – he tapped his nose with the side of his hand – 'in the brown stuff.'

Dr Sweet swallowed, and realized that now at last was the time to speak. 'It's a complete lie. I mean, it's a complete mistake. I didn't kill that man. I never laid a finger on him. It was an accident.'

He paused. Martin sat down heavily, and removed a pad and pen from his file. 'I must say, none of that sounds particularly compelling, Dr Sweet. And can I incidentally counsel you against beginning sentences with the phrase: "I never . . ."? It's the grammatical construction of choice for the criminal classes. We have eyewitness testimony from the proprietor of the shop that you came up to this man, had a fierce, enraged argument with him, smacked him with a bottle and left the shop. By the time the police arrived the man was dead. I can tell you now' – he leafed through some papers – 'that they don't have definitive CCTV pictures. Which is something. But the proprietor knows you well and says you hit this man with a bottle. They don't even have to put you in an identity parade. Now what have you got to say?'

'Well, I was there but that isn't what happened.'

'So you were there.'

'Yes, but Kamil wasn't. The proprietor wasn't.'

'He wasn't?'

'No. He was in the back room.'

'The stockroom?'

'I don't know, I've never been there; I don't know what it is. Yes, I suppose so, the stockroom.' Now Dr Sweet's voice receded a little from its pitch of exasperation and panic. 'But he wasn't there when I . . . when I encountered that man.'

'Well, suppose you tell me what *did* happen.'

Dr Sweet gulped. 'This man, this Mr O'Rourke, he was behaving in a threatening way. He was waving a broken bottle in Kamil's little girl's face. I felt I had to intervene.'

'So you did have an altercation?'

'No, not really. Well . . .'

Martin widened his eyes a little as if to say *I'm listening*.

'I put my hand on his arm. Very gently.'

Martin exhaled through flaring nostrils. 'Just now you said you never laid a finger on him.' There was silence. 'Go on.'

'Well, I touched his arm, very gently, to attract his

attention. I just wanted to calm things down. But *he* was the one behaving in an aggressive way; *he* was the one with the bottle.'

'And then what?'

'And then he slipped and banged his head on the floor.'

'Which killed him?'

'Yes. Yes.'

'And that's when the proprietor came back into the shop?'

'Yes. Yes. That's when he told me to go.'

'He did? He said that?'

'Yes. Look, are you sure Kamil said I hit him? Are you sure the police haven't just misunderstood him?'

Martin sighed again. 'No, Dr Sweet, I'm not sure. After our conversation is over, I could ask them if they might want to reinterview Mr Yildiz. But I have to say that if he sticks to his story, then we have a problem.'

There was silence.

'Dr Sweet,' he said at last. Dr Sweet, who had not moved, or shifted his gaze from Martin's throughout the conversation, did not prompt him. 'Dr Sweet, if what you're saying – and I'm not saying you are – but if what you're saying is that you might have attacked this man because he was about to attack a child, then I am happy to advise you we would be in an excellent position to plead guilty to manslaughter. At the very least, we would have strong extenuating circumstances.'

Dr Sweet considered this. Was that, in fact, a reasonably fair approximation, a *legal* approximation of what actually happened?

'Tell me, Mr Martin,' he said quietly. 'How much of a prison sentence might that mean?'

'I really don't think we should get into that now.'

'Please, just tell me. How long?'

'Well,' said Martin hesitantly, 'perhaps two or three years.'

'And murder?'

'I have to say all that would be contingent on a possible, erm, psychiatric assessment. But that would be nearer fifteen years.'

Dr Sweet got up, and pressed a tissue to his mouth, as if to wipe away the remains of a gluttonous meal. He walked a few steps away from the table, then a few steps back.

'Two or three years,' he repeated, 'or fifteen years.'

Martin said nothing.

'Well, Mr Martin,' he said. 'I think the University of Douglas in the Isle of Man might be happy to wait two to three years. But fifteen years is a bit of a long time to keep my position open.'

Dr Sweet shoved his chin onto his chest and made a long, ambiguous chuckling sound. Martin looked at him. Most of his clients were sullen and stoic, and more or less kept their cool. Was this one having some sort of breakdown? Had he been too brisk with him? If he was, that could be good news. It would be an excuse to delay the interview. Maybe he could claim some sort of claustrophobic reaction to the cell. But then Dr Sweet looked up again and Martin realized that this line of thought was idle.

'Listen,' Martin said, tapping out a stuttering line of dots on the pad with his pen. 'To be quite honest, one way you could go with this, is just not admit you were there.'

For the first time Dr Sweet felt sure of himself, felt relieved; he felt he knew what to do.

'No,' he said firmly. 'No. No, I'm going to go in there and tell the police the complete truth.'

Martin reacted with the silent incredulity of a NASA official at a flat-earth convention.

'And that's what you want to do?'

'Yes.'

'OK.'

Martin pressed a button on the wall which produced a startling buzz. As the crackling voice said, 'Yes?' he leaned in and said, 'We're ready now.'

11

Detective Constable McCready and Detective Sergeant Cole had their faces set in an entirely new expression as they sat opposite him and Martin, belonging neither to the genial tone they had affected in the car, nor to the tough blankness at the time of his arrest. This was a new mode, studiedly neutral, yet with an air of quizzical, faintly ironic cordiality. A mode which could be tilted towards aggression, or the other way, towards the sympathetic elicitation of a confession.

'Could you state your name and address for the tape, please?'

'David Leonard Sweet, 53 Munich Road, London, N19.'

DS Cole said, 'Present in the room are Detective Constable McCready, Detective Sergeant Cole, Mr David Martin of Goodge and Company and the suspect, Mr Sweet.'

'So Mr Sweet,' said McCready, perusing a typewritten sheet of paper in front of him. 'Perhaps you could tell me what happened last night?'

Last *night*? Was it really last night?

'I went into the shop. PriceBest supermarket on the Archway Road.'

'When was that?'

'At six-thirtyish. I wanted to get some Diet Coke.'

'Yes?'

'And that's when I saw the man.'

'The murder victim?' said McCready coolly.

Dr Sweet flinched. He looked across at Martin, who was already leaning forward.

'I think we should refer to Mr O'Rourke as the 'victim', Detective Constable, if that's all right.'

McCready fixed him with a level gaze of ostentatious inscrutability and then looked back at Dr Sweet.

'The dead man. The victim. The man who was dead when you left the shop, Mr Sweet. That man. Could you explain the circumstances of your encounter with him?'

Dr Sweet gulped. 'I was shopping. I saw this man there. We were the only customers in the shop. He had a broken bottle in his hand and he was waving it in the face of Mr Yildiz's little daughter. He was being threatening.'

'I see,' said Cole, speaking for the first time, rising from his seat, walking round behind his chair and then gripping its back. 'And that's why you assaulted him with a bottle?'

'No,' said Dr Sweet in a petrified, high voice. 'That's not why. I mean, that's not what happened.'

'Perhaps you will let Dr Sweet explain without interruption,' said Martin.

Now Cole did the ostentatious blank look. Hesitantly, the suspect continued.

'I tapped him on the shoulder and asked him to calm down. Then he turned on me. He walked towards me in a menacing way and I backed away, then he slipped and hit his head as he went down.'

'I see,' said Cole, still standing over him. 'Mr Yildiz says you cut in the queue ahead of him, you got into a furious row and you hit him with the bottle.'

'That's not true,' gasped Dr Sweet, his blood beating in his temples like drums, his breathing fast and shallow. He cleared his throat and licked his lips as he felt his mouth becoming very dry. 'Mr Yildiz wasn't there. Mr Yildiz wasn't there. It was just his little girl. It was just his daughter.'

'Dr Sweet, I put it to you that you are lying. You struck this man very hard with a bottle and he is now dead as a result of your actions. Now what have you got to say?'

'I nev— I didn't. It isn't true. Mr Yildiz wasn't there; he doesn't know what happened.'

'Mr Sweet,' broke in McCready, his face breaking into the most lenient, forgiving smile possible. 'What possible motive could Mr Yildiz have for lying to us about this?'

'What possible motive could I have for murdering a complete stranger?' he snapped back, not aggressively but with a note of despair and dismay.

Both Cole's and McCready's face darkened at the inexcusable solecism of Dr Sweet failing to answer the question, not with 'no reply' or 'no comment', the suspect's well-understood obstructionist tactics, but insolently presuming to ask *them* questions.

'You will have to tell *us* that, Mr Sweet,' said McCready, frigid with scorn. 'You will have to put us in the picture, *vis-à-vis*' – McCready's mouth snapped into a tight wince for this Gallicism – 'your *motive*.'

'Could we just—?' began Martin, raising his green Pentel pen, but McCready ploughed on.

'I mean, your motive could be any number of things. A man at your time of life. Some sort of breakdown. Some sort of rush of blood to the head. We've seen it time and time again. A middle-aged man with various troubles – marital, financial, bankruptcy, CCJs, who knows what else – picks a fight for no reason, takes his trousers down in Trafalgar Square, provokes a crisis, gets out of hand. Plenty of men like you in their mid- to late-forties end up in a mess just like this.'

Cole glanced over at McCready. They both knew very well that Dr Sweet was forty-one. Pretending suspects looked older and careworn than they were was a technique generally used on vulnerable women suspects, accused, say, of thieving or harming their children, the purpose of which was to plunge them into a crisis of anxiety and depression, the better to secure their sobbing co-operation. But this electro-shock baton of covert psychological cruelty had to be deployed later on, in a considerably more belligerent interview, and it had to be accompanied by a change of mood, a specious gesture of tenderness and concern. Had McCready miscalculated?

He had. Dr Sweet was well used to people thinking he was older than he was, and in certain professional circumstances this air of maturity had served him well. Slowly but surely, he was ceasing to be intimidated by Cole and McCready. Doggedly, he stuck to his story. And doggedly, he reminded himself that it was an easy story to stick to because it was the *truth*.

'Could we just bear in mind that my client has bent over backwards to be of assistance?' said Martin again, in apparent rebuke to this tough line of questioning.

'We'll bear it in mind, Mr Martin,' said McCready,

resuming his seat. 'Naturally we shall bear it in mind, though being of assistance to us is nothing more nor less than Mr Sweet's duty as a citizen.' The three of them could not withhold, for a fraction of a second, a tiny complicit smirk.

'So let's start again, Mr Sweet. You get into the queue for the till ahead of the victim. You become involved in an altercation, you hit him with the bottle. Now are you claiming self-defence? Are you claiming provocation?'

'No, no,' said Dr Sweet, his voice rising again in shrill dismay. 'That isn't what happened. I tapped him on the shoulder and I got him to follow me away from the till, away from the little girl that he was threatening.'

'*Away* from the till?'

'Yes.'

'Not *near* the till?'

'No.'

'And that's where you let him have it?'

'No, that isn't how he hit his head.'

'Oh so you're claiming he hit his own head? Suddenly consumed with suicidal self-loathing, he grabs a bottle off the shelf and smashes himself over the head with it?'

'No, *no*. I've already told you. He slipped. And Mr Yildiz wasn't there; he didn't see any of this.'

'Now really, Mr Sweet, how on earth could Mr Yildiz have got this wrong?'

'He got *my address* wrong, didn't he? Why shouldn't he get something else wrong?'

'Come now, Mr Sweet,' said Cole, asserting a sort of injured professional pride. 'You say he wasn't there, he says he was. Now who am I to believe?'

Martin leant forward again. 'Now really, Detective

Constable. That is not a permissible question. My client says that Mr Yildiz wasn't there, and he can do no more than that. This could very well be a mistake. Perhaps Mr Yildiz's English is not very good? Or he became overexcited? Perhaps it was possible that a *junior officer took his statement?*'

Another silence reigned. The two men looked disconcerted and Dr Sweet wondered if Martin had made a shrewd guess, or if this was some inside knowledge he had been saving up for an opportune moment.

'It's not beyond the bounds of possibility,' said McCready ponderously, 'that we will be re-interviewing Mr Yildiz in the course of clarifying certain details. But pending this, Mr Sweet, I must ask you again: did you or did you not hit this man with a bottle?'

'No.'

McCready made a fly-swatting gesture with his hand, as if contemptuously waving away some casuistry, some absurd evasion.

'I put it to you that you and the victim, Mr O'Rourke, became involved in a face-to-face, head-to-head argument, and that you hit him fatally with that bottle.'

'I'm sorry, did you say *face-to-face*? I mean, is that what Mr Yildiz is saying?'

Once again, the suspect had presumed to ask them a question.

'You heard what I said,' scowled McCready, after a beat.

'Because if it was supposed to be face-to-face,' said Dr Sweet, 'then the wound would be on the front of his head, his forehead, or on the top of his head, wouldn't it?'

'Well possibly . . .'

'Possibly nothing,' said Dr Sweet, amazing himself now with his brazen confidence, 'it would be. But you can see for yourself that that man's wound was on the *back* of his head, consistent with having fallen over backwards!'

Since when did Dr Sweet use words like 'consistent', wondered Martin? At that moment the door opened and the WPC entered with the most cursory tap on the door, her face flushed, and two sprigs of tinsel in her hair. Along the corridor, the sound of a Christmas party could be heard in full swing.

'Your suspect's wife and family are upstairs,' she said, suppressing a snort of laughter at the sound of a man beginning to sing just behind her. She moved a little to the side to reveal the custody sergeant in a high good humour, resplendent in a Santa outfit with padding. Spreading his hands, his feet planted wide apart and apparently addressing himself to the five people in the interview room, he began to sing in a beautifully rich, trembling tenor:

> *The holly and the ivy,*
> *The eagle and the hawk;*
> *Of all the female officers,*
> *You're the one I'd like to pork*

Cole and McCready looked at him, dumbstruck. But custody sergeant Santa simply walked in through the door, beaming with beatific good-will, snaked his arm round the WPC's waist and carried on singing, his voice now astonishingly loud in the enclosed space. DS Cole's eyes flashed to the tape machine, the six little teeth on each recording head still ploughing doggedly round.

'Oh Keith, for fuck's only sake. Interview suspended

at 7:17pm,' Cole said, ducking close to the machine and snapping it off.

It was then that Dr Sweet noticed the object in Santa's hand was not a can of lager, as he had supposed, but a charity-collection tin, bearing the logo of the Ruzowitsky Institute for Cancer Research.

12

Murderer. Murderer. Murderer. The word contracted to two syllables as John got closer to his son's house. Murdra. Murdra. Murdra. Animal rights campaigners had gathered outside, shouting. They were going to break in; they were going to hold David and Cordie – his grandchild – hostage. Murdra. Murdra. Torchra. Murdra.

There was his car, the car he had taught David to drive in when he was eighteen, sold years and years ago. What was it doing here? David had told him and his mother that the Ruzowitsky Institute had given him a special mirror for checking under the car for animal-rights bombs. It was a compact-sized mirror on the end of a long stick, the sort of arrangement John had for digging the garden without bending down: four curved blades in the shape of a corkscrew twist on the end of a four-foot pole, with a T-shaped handle at the top end. An excellent, practical idea.

David had told them he checked underneath the car every morning. He did a job that made people want to kill him. His son was in danger. Why did he have to tell them that? Why did he have to worry his mother? Why did he have to worry his *father*?

They were gathering round the car, pounding on its

roof. Murdra. They were releasing the animals. They were liberating eels and spiders and slugs, and these were swarming along his eyebrows.

John woke by consciously wrenching his head up and sideways from his pillow. Kneeling on his chest was little Cordie, wearing a warm and stoutly knitted sweater and a Scottish kilt with a huge metal safety-pin feature, a Christmas present from her grandmother. She was combing his eyebrows with her new Pooh Bear electric toothbrush, an expression of rapt concentration on her moonlike face which loomed over him like a dentist's. The toothbrush buzzed with a high whine, which lowered a semi-tone as Cordie pushed it through his eyebrows with the conscientious vigour of a stable groom.

John gave a startled cry, 'Argh!' This awoke Rosemary, who turned over and assessed the situation in a blink. Cordie scrambled backwards off the bed and just stood there, her toothbrush buzzing.

'Cordie, love, what are you doing?' she asked gently.

'Combing Grandad's eyebrows,' said Cordie, her face crumpling into tears as she ran out.

With as much speed as she could muster, Rosemary got out of bed, shrugged a long pale-blue dressing gown over her nightie, and went out into the corridor, where Cordie was trying the handle of the main bedroom, in which Alice was perhaps still sleeping. The door was either locked or jammed, and Cordie was obviously wondering whether she should escalate the seriousness of the situation by crying out for her or just go downstairs and forget all about it.

'Cordie, darling, it's all right,' said Rosemary, kneeling down, putting her face very close to Cordie's plump and teary profile. 'Grandad was just a bit startled when he woke up, that's all. It's all right. Come and say hello to him. It's all right.' Rosemary noticed from Cordie's Pooh Bear watch that it was 8.20a.m.

Back in the guest bedroom, John had struggled into a sitting-up position. He reached across to Rosemary's side of the bed and retrieved an ornate handmirror that she took travelling with her, a mirror that belonged in a fairy-story. Wonderingly, he looked at his eyebrows which had been turned from wayward iron-grey caterpillars into sleek unitary strokes. Cordie had smartened up his entire face; he looked younger.

Rosemary led Cordie back into the room, holding her hand, and John smartly laid the mirror face down on the scarred old blanket box that served for a bedside table on his side. Cordie's electric toothbrush had been turned off.

'Here you are, Cordie,' said Rosemary. 'Here's Grandad.'

'Hello, Cordie,' said John, smiling. 'Thank you for combing my eyebrows.'

Cordie approached her grandad and looked at his funny old face. When he smiled, as he did now, only one side of his mouth smiled; the other side of his face stayed more or less still, and the eye on the still side of his face was always a tiny bit watery. Quite without shyness now, she placed her hand on the immobile half; she thought for some reason that she mustn't stroke it, but just let her hand remain there. She had drawn lots of pictures of her grandad and grandma for school and home, on drawing paper and on the backs of junk-mail correspon-dence: stick-drawings of Grandad and Grandma holding hands in front of their house. Grandma was smiling in a perfect crescent-moon red-crayon smile, but Grandad's mouth, though curled up on one side, was flattened into a curt horizontal line on the other. There was another picture of Grandma and Grandad on Alice's fridge in her flat, showing them both in the rain, for no other reason than an ingenious variation: to show Grandma looking fully and symmetrically sad about the weather, and just half of Grandad's mouth turned down.

'Would you like me to read you a story, Cordie? Would you like to get into my side of the bed?'

Cordie thought about this for a moment and then nodded, scampering out, to return a minute later with some large laminated illustrated books and her big toy bag. Her absence was long enough for John to get up, put on *his* dressing gown and head for the bathroom with his clothes under his arm. Cordie seemed to be behaving well enough, better than when they first arrived, but he had never liked his grandchild's habit of bursting into their room first thing in the morning and had once even suggested inventing a pretext so they could stay at a local hotel on their Christmas visits and the like. Rosemary, horrified, had squashed this idea. She had always been profoundly touched and moved that Cordie had wanted to come to see them first thing in the morning, and it reminded her of David doing the same thing when he was a boy. While Cordie snuggled down for her story, Barbie alertly at her side, John washed, showered, changed and went downstairs, to where he guessed his son would be in the kitchen.

But he wasn't. Leaving his steaming mug of tea on the kitchen table, Dr Sweet had wandered out into the hall, looking at his reflection in the big, gaunt mirror. Since she had arrived for Christmas, Cordie had commented tactlessly on the fact that Dr Sweet's eyebrows seemed to be growing out of control, and it was true. They had become bushier and bristlier, a sign of encroaching middle age, along with the strands of wiry hair that had appeared around his nipples and the pale sag of skin around his waist which no amount of dieting or visits to the gym could diminish, of a piece with the cargo of heaviness he was carrying in his heart these days.

For the past week or so, all through Christmas, the cataclysm of his arrest had burned itself into his soul. It had cast a gloom over the Christmas meals with their paper hats and the flaming pudding and brandy butter. It was his first thought in the morning on waking and his last on going to bed; before sleep he mentally intoned all its circumstances, an orison of anxiety. And he kept the letter with him all the time, transferring it from his pyjama pocket to his dressing gown to his trousers, and finally, with the lowering of the sun, from his trousers to his dressing gown and back to his pyjamas. It was the letter from East Holloway Police Station, informing he was a BTR: Bailed To Return. He was allowed out on police bail, which didn't mean the temporary surrender of a cash sum – an inconvenience which would have caused his prudent parents to die with mortification and shame – but merely the undertaking to remain at his primary residence and check in periodically.

Bailed To Return. Not having to stay in a police cell was actually a stunning victory, and one for which Dr Sweet's duty solicitor crowingly claimed credit. The police evidence had been rubbish, he claimed, patchy and inconsistent, and he, the duty solicitor, had exposed it. Dr Sweet rather considered that *he* had exposed it.

Now he was at home, waiting. Waiting for the outcome of the police's re-interviewing Mr Kamil Yildiz of the PriceBest convenience store.

Alice had been due to leave today, taking Cordie with her. But he had asked her to stay, just for a while, until this was cleared up, and Alice unhesitatingly agreed, although she suspected it wasn't *her* moral support he wanted, but Cordie's. This was her first week back at the office, and working there and living at her ex-husband's house for the duration of this crisis had meant a wearisome and disagreeable trip back to her flat, getting changes of clothes, and some of Cordie's toys which she'd pined for, despite the armfuls of new playthings her parents and grandparents had bought her.

Alice had had a long telephone conversation with Richard just before the weekend. She got his call at the office and, for privacy, went out to call him back from the payphone in the chilly, deserted emergency stairwell. Richard was calling from Manhattan. She was delighted to hear from him, drinking in his voice like nectar.

'Oh, baby, I'm really looking forward to seeing you in New York,' she said. There was a minuscule pause. Was she imagining it? Was it a time delay on the line?

'Yeah, that should be . . . that's gonna be great. That could be . . . yeah.'

'Do you have a start date for me yet?'

There was another whistling silence on the line.

'Listen, Alice, there've been a few changes further up the chain of command here and I can't exactly nail that one down yet. You remember I told you about that. But, you know, we're working on it.'

We're working on it. Alice registered that distant, corporate pronoun.

'So tell me, Alice, how're you doing? How's that Coopers account?'

The question made Alice flinch like a paper cut. The Coopers account was a long-term project which was the sole responsibility of the London office, and on which she had been working before the idea of New York had been held out to her. Why was he harping on about that?

'Well,' she said, 'it's fine. I mean, I guess it's . . .' Alice realized that sounding casual or distant about the Coopers account looked unprofessional. '. . . I mean I know it's great.'

'That's great. Good work!'

Good *work*? But it wasn't her department now, was it?

'And how about Cordie?' Richard went on swiftly.

That was even worse. It was a question to which she genuinely didn't know the answer.

'Oh, I reckon she's fine. She's been a bit subdued recently actually.' Saying that last sentence out loud, a sentence unformed in the back of her mind for some time, forced her to think about it for the first time, and there was a tiny, panicky gulp in her voice as she suppressed tears. Had Richard heard them? It wasn't clear from what he said next.

'Hey, listen, I won't keep you, Ally. I know you've got to run, and I do too. I'll call you, OK?'

'OK.'

'Bye.'

Alice had stood for a while in the grim concrete stairwell after this thoroughly disappointing and unsatisfactory conversation. This wasn't the conversation she'd wanted to have, but she supposed Richard was busy.

As for John and Rosemary, they too had decided, simply decided, that they should stay on at Dr Sweet's house, and their son had agreed. It was tacitly held that for them to leave would be a sort of abandonment, and in any case, though they would never have admitted it, they were being competitive with Alice. Once it was clear that Cordie was staying over at Dr Sweet's house while this affair was being settled, then there should be no doubt in the child's mind that her grandparents were still there for her at this uniquely stressful time.

So for the first time in his life Dr Sweet was presiding over an old-fashioned extended family. It was the sort of household arrangement undreamt of when he was married, with all the unhappy negotiations about weekend visits to his parents or her parents. He woke in the morning and heard people busying themselves all over the house. One day between Christmas and the New Year, his parents had been to the local garden centre, of whose location and indeed existence he had been utterly unaware, bought herbs and plants, and re-potted them, a process as mysterious as alchemy as far as Dr Sweet was concerned, transferring them from oblong styrofoam packs into terracotta-style vessels. Cordie had actually helped them with all this, watering the plants with a little green can, also bought from the centre. Rosemary had pointedly marvelled that she'd never seen Cordie so calm and happy, an observation she saved for when Alice was in the room. And Dr Sweet heard the washing machine throbbing away almost continually, the ever-beating heart of any happy, bustling family home.

'Good morning, David.'

'Morning, Dad,' replied Dr Sweet, suddenly aware his father was fully dressed and he was still in his dressing gown. 'Would you like a cup of tea?'

'Yes, thank you, that would be nice.'

They trooped into the kitchen together, Dr Sweet pausing momentarily to place his fingers on his mug to check it was still warm. He put the kettle back on, but as he and his father sat down, Dr Sweet found himself doing a horribly loud morning belch of the sort he remembered his father doing when he was a boy: semi-liquid, wholly unapologetic, coloured with intestinal discomfort and audible, pre-emptive irritation that someone – his mother – would complain about it.

Silence reigned. The kettle boiled and Dr Sweet made John a cup with the tea-bag in a mug – if his mother had been there he would have used the teapot, and warmed it, too – adding milk and two sugars. John sipped and grimaced politely.

'What's the matter?' he asked.

'Well, I . . .' returned John uncertainly.

Dr Sweet clapped his hand to his forehead.

'Oh Dad, I've given you Equanimitea by mistake. It's a herbal preparation, supposed to make you calm.'

John diplomatically nodded, took another sip and snorted explosively.

'Oh Christ. Sorry. Sorry, Dad,' said Dr Sweet, mopping ineffectually at the table with a J-cloth. 'I'll make you another. Ah. Actually, we only have Equanimitea. Or would you like some Magnanimitea?' John said nothing. 'I'll make some coffee, what about that?'

'Coffee would be fine,' said John, rising slightly from his seat, and dabbing at his trouser-legs.

Alice came down, in sweats. She had a sports bag which contained big vivid red and blue towels and swimming costumes: hers, Cordie's and Dr Sweet's.

'Hi,' said Dr Sweet and Alice to each other simultaneously. What was the form for greeting in this new situation, the divorced spouses compelled to live together? Perhaps a kiss on the cheek, which could attain a more formal air, like the meeting of two Russian men? Alice placed her bag on the table, which Dr Sweet saw in an instant made his father uncomfortable.

'We're off, aren't we?' said Alice brightly. 'I mean after we've had a quick cup of tea.'

'I think Cordie's reading with Rosie,' said John blandly. Dr Sweet saw how Alice bridled at the way John put that. Cordie *reading with* Rosie? Maybe his mother was reading Cordie a story. Or maybe Cordie was reading aloud to Dr Sweet's mother. But *reading with* made it sound like some kind of remedial class for learning-impaired children from broken homes. And they were just in *bed*, weren't they?

'Well, I think we need her up and about. No, John, don't you get up,' said Alice brightly, moving over to the kitchen counter, pouring out John's coffee and bringing it over to him, thus simultaneously playing the parental discipline anti-laziness card and ostentatiously waiting on Dr Sweet's father hand and foot – neglecting, moreover, to remove her bag from the table. Beginning to squirm

with embarrassment, Dr Sweet saw how disconcerted his
father was.

'Come on, David,' continued Alice. 'Weren't you
coming swimming with us?'

'Was I? Am I?' said Dr Sweet, wide-eyed with dismay.
Wasn't this the sort of thing they would do with their
daughter if they weren't divorced? He suspected some
obscure sort of impropriety but couldn't quite put his
finger on it.

'Morning,' said Rosemary, entering the kitchen briskly,
carrying a large-ish soft white object in her hand.

'I thought you were reading with – to – Cordie, Mum,'
said Dr Sweet.

'Oh that,' said Rosemary, smiling tolerantly at this
absurd whimsy. 'That was just for a little while. We want
you up and about, don't we?' This last was to Cordie,
who had trailed grumpily into the kitchen, with her big
toy bag and some books under one arm. These she placed
on the table, along with Alice's bag and John's coffee, and
began to read.

'Come on, Cordie, you've got to get up and dressed;
we're going swimming.'

'Oh that modern swimming pool is so loud,' said Rosemary, busily taking a seat at the table herself. 'So much
noise and distraction, children rushing around madly. And
that sweet machine selling chocolate right by the water; no
wonder children nowadays have attention deficit disorder.
Now, Alice, I think Cordie might need this.'

She gave Alice the white object which turned out to
be a soft travel pack of Kleenex tissues, much larger than
the usual size, almost as big as a regular box. 'I think
she's got a little sniffle. Oh let me do that,' she added,

superfluously, getting up, as if Alice were going to get her a cup of coffee.

Cordie considered her book minutely and Dr Sweet saw Alice's grip clench on the pack of tissues behind Rosemary's back. The implication that Alice would let Cordie swim with a cold descended on her consciousness like a depth charge. Cordie didn't have a sniffle. Did she? The usual lattice of tensions between his parents and Alice and him had intensified and become muted all at once, as if they were unconsciously pulling together for Dr Sweet, but doing so under house arrest.

Just then the letterbox coughed some correspondence onto the mat and it was all any of them could do not to rush out into the hall and fight over it. This used to be Cordie's job; she loved the postman, and famously once recognized him in the street without his uniform. She would shout, 'Post! Post! Post!' and fanatically arrange the letters for each parent in order of size on the breakfast table: letters addressed to both of them conscientiously positioned equidistantly. But now she just sat reading, while all four grown-ups trooped grimly into the corridor, trying not to accelerate into a gallop.

There in front of them, among the white envelopes large and small, they saw it, the small brown envelope. Nobody sends letters in cheap brown envelopes any more, only hospitals with scan appointments and test results, and the East Holloway CID with curt updates on Dr Sweet's Bailed To Return status. Each of them, his father, mother and ex-wife, considered that he or she alone had the authority to snatch the envelope up and open it. Reluctantly, they stood back and let Dr Sweet squeeze through, and bend down to the mat.

It was only a circular from the local Pentecostal church. Dr Sweet held it up wordlessly, like a referee with a yellow card. The other three heads dipped fractionally and they made their way back to the kitchen.

Cordie had stopped reading her book. She had placed Barbie on top of Dougal, a shaggy sausage dog with a big black nose and a tongue that lolled out, but which was now coming off, and Barbie was driving him like a car. Vroom, vroom, vroom. The Dougal car bashed into Mummy's bag. It was a big obstacle that Barbie and her car had to get past. Bash, bash. Rearing up on Dougal like a Rodeo rider, Barbie pushed his nose down under the bottom of the bag to get some leverage. Vroom, bash, push, lift. Vroom, bash, push, lift. Hup!

Alice came back in to see her bag fall off the table, spilling out the towels and a big bottle of still orange juice with a loose cap, which started glugging over the floor.

'Oh, Cordie!'

'Oh no, Cordie.'

'Cordie.'

Cordie's lower lip puckered. Barbie and Dougal idled in neutral, unsure where next to go. Alice picked up the towels and the bottle and Dr Sweet rushed forward decisively to put his arms around Cordie.

'It's all right, Miss Cordie, perfectly all right – now why don't we go upstairs to get you dr—'

But Cordie pushed him aside and ran to her grandfather, hugging him round the shins, an astonishing gesture, considering she'd never willingly hugged him before, and generally shrank from his bedtime kiss as from a tarantula. She stayed immobile in this position, facing resolutely away from the grown-ups, sensing that they would be unwilling to cancel this rare and precious bestowal of favour.

Then the telephone rang. Cordie instantaneously released John's legs and ran for it.

'*Ye* – llo?' she twanged into the receiver. Dr Sweet stood frozen while Cordie did this, then Cordie began speaking again.

'Blah, blah, blah, blah,' she sang out, evidently interrupting the person on the other end. 'Blah, bleah, bleah, bleah. BLEAH, BLEAH, BLEAH, BLAH, BLEAH.' Then she hung up and ran up the stairs, shouting, 'Bleah, bleah.' Alice ran grimly after her. From her room there were raised voices and tears.

'Oh, Cordie,' sighed Dr Sweet and picked up the phone to hear the dialling tone. Whoever it was must have hung up, assuming they had a wrong number. He dialled 1471 but the number was unfamiliar. Who could it have been? The police? Then he remembered the spilt juice and raced into the kitchen.

Too late. His mother had already got the mop and bucket out from under the stairs and was engaged in an elaborate and entirely unnecessary mopping process, while his father had invented an ancillary role for himself by standing by with a roll of kitchen paper, ready to dry the floor.

'Mum, Dad, it's all right. *It's all right*. I mean that's great, but you really don't have to mop it all up. That's fine. Really.' Dr Sweet forcibly removed the mop and bucket from Rosemary and carried it back. Alice returned with Cordie, sucking her thumb.

'Now, Miss Cordie, we know we shouldn't do that,' he said, shooting a querulous glance at Alice for allowing it. 'You know you're a big girl now.' He plucked the thumb out of her mouth and Cordie was taken out to the hall. Bailed To Return, he heard in his head. Bailed To Return. Bailed To Return. Sometimes the tom-tom of those words receded almost to silence; sometimes they came back thuddingly into his head for no reason and he had to just pretend it didn't bother him. He was *in trouble with the police*. He had been *arrested for murder*. He had been *Bailed To Return*. Cordie had to put her coat on and he and Alice were going to take her swimming. Everything was going to continue as normal, for all the world as if he wasn't a criminal, a desperado, the sort of person who has spent some time in a police cell. He and his ex-wife were going out now with their little girl – and his BTR letter rustling in his pocket.

Cordie tugged at Dr Sweet's trouser leg.

'Is our trip to the swimming pool today?' she asked.

'*Yes, today*,' said Dr Sweet, exasperated.

'Well, if it's yes-terday then I've missed it. Hee-hee,' Cordie finished on a triumphant, sing-song note and capered out of the room.

'I'm sure she hasn't got a cold you know,' said Alice suddenly to Rosemary, who managed a thin smile in return. Both women knew that Rosemary had used the far less loaded word 'sniffle', and amplifying this to 'cold' was a challenge Alice knew Rosemary would not rise to, now that Cordie had her coat on and going swimming was an obvious *fait accompli*.

'I only had a bit of a sniffle because I was sad,' said Cordie calmly, coming back into the room, her first serious words of the day, apart from the ones about combing Grandad's eyebrows.

'It's all right, Cordie,' said Alice with a little laugh, 'there's no need to be scared of your grandma and grandad in the mornings!'

Dr Sweet groaned inwardly. There was no need for that. Cordie had already given Alice her little victory over the 'sniffle' thing. Did Alice have to go too far with that remark about Cordie being scared of John and Rosemary? Did she have to upset them like that? Now Dr Sweet felt himself bridling on his parents' behalf. Bailed To Return. Bailed To Return.

As he got his own jacket down, Dr Sweet switched on his cellphone, which showed one message pending. Was it Hattie? he thought, his heart leaping. No, he remembered, with a chill. Of course it wasn't. Hattie had broken up with him. Hattie was going home to marry Arlen with his four-foot head. He listened to the message, which was just a tiny period of silence followed by the metallic voice confirming when it had been recorded.

Hattie didn't care about him any more. And in any case, Hattie wouldn't want to have anything to do with a psychotic criminal, would she? A man who kills strangers in convenience stores? All through Christmas Day, Boxing Day and beyond, Dr Sweet had checked his phone for messages from Hattie, but there was nothing. Well, she had enough to worry about: the bridesmaids, the venue, the flowers; liaising with the vicar, the caterer, Arlen's best man. Jesus, what sort of a man did Arlen consider the 'best'? Somebody with an even more freakishly long head than himself? Doubtless this man would make the tables roar at the reception with his amusing speech about Hattie's ex-boyfriends, including a jailbird scientist – correction, *unemployed* jailbird scientist. And then there was the honeymoon. The Australian hotel room where their 'hiking' trip was to begin, perfumed with honeysuckle or Bougainvillea, perhaps, carried by the night breezes and distant wash of the moonlight-dappled strand, a room where the millpond calm of their crisp bedlinen would be churned into surf as Arlen transformed Hattie into a squealing, yodelling—

'Daddy, Mummy's talking and you're just staring and you're not even listening!' shouted Cordie, punching Dr Sweet on the kneecap.

'Sorry, darling,' gasped Dr Sweet to his daughter and ex-wife equally, clicking his phone off.

'I said shall we take the *car* or do you want to *walk*?'

'Oh cork. I mean, walk. I mean let's walk to the car, and then take the car.'

Alice looked at him closely.

'Are you sure you're feeling all right?'

'Shine. I mean fine. I'm sure I'm fine.'

Alice sighed.

'Mum, Dad,' said Dr Sweet to his parents. 'Are you sure you don't want to come?'

'No thank you, David, that's fine. We're fine here for this morning,' said Rosemary, and Dr Sweet caught her glance straying to the cupboard under the stairs where he'd put the mop.

'All right then, we'll be back soon.'

Once outside, as the front door swung shut, Dr Sweet could hear the telephone again, and mastered an impulse to get his key out, go back in and answer it. Just one ring. His mother must have got it instead of leaving it for the machine. Dr Sweet stood by the door. Would it be Hattie – calling the house?

'Dad-dy,' said Cordie, pulling at his jacket.

The drive to the pool unmanned Dr Sweet more than he thought possible. For a start, Cordie announced that she had to ride in the front passenger seat or she would be carsick. So he took the child's position in the back of Alice's Mercedes, which was really only designed for two people: there was no *room* in the back.

'Are you good at swimming now, Cordie?' asked Alice, wearing her modishly slimline driving glasses.

'I'm really brilliant,' said Cordie, hugging her knees.

'Which way is the pool from here, actually . . .?' Alice asked with a frown.

'It's the second on the left,' said Dr Sweet.

'Down *there*,' said Cordie, pointing to the first turning on the right. Unhesitatingly following Cordie's instructions, Alice took the first right and they were at the Tufnell Park Leisure Centre in no time. 'I thought that was still a no through road,' explained Dr Sweet lamely as he clambered out in the car park.

Inside, Dr Sweet had expected to have an ill-tempered dispute with Alice about whether Cordie should go with her mother to the women's changing rooms or with him into the men's. The women's was the obvious favourite, and yet hadn't Dr Sweet taken Cordie to this pool far more often than Alice? Didn't he, as father, have equal rights in this? Wasn't Cordie under his care? In his house?

He cleared his throat. 'Alice, Cordie could come with me if she—'

Both Cordie and her mother looked at him, baffled at his stupidity.

'Dad-dy. Family booths.'

'Family booths,' repeated Alice, pointing.

How was it that Dr Sweet had never seen the family booths before? There was a row of about seven or eight: the new booths which allowed one- or two-parent families to get changed together in a bigger area, the size of a disabled people's lavatory. No more of the Victorian steam-bath/work-house insistence on separating the patrons into men and women, with the inevitable embarrassment for the modern family and its needs. How absurd! So Dr Sweet, Alice and Cordie found one and started to change, Dr Sweet feeling as embarrassed and vulnerable as if he were eleven years old again.

Soon he was there in his floppy shorts, still feeling like a gawky child. Cordie, frowning with concentration and with minimal help from either parent, wriggled into her costume, vivid orange bathing cap and inflatable arm-bands, feistily puffed up like Popeye's muscles.

The extraordinary thing was Alice. Without wanting to gawp, Dr Sweet saw that she was wearing matching bra and pants again, quite sexy underwear, and that she'd simply never looked better. Had he *noticed* that the other night? Her stomach was utterly flat, with traces of musculature just visible like athletes' bodies – not swimmers, but runners, the ones with streamlined Lycra outfits. His ex-wife really did look fantastic. Soon she and Cordie would be *en famille* with some other man in some other family booth somewhere in the United States. That thought entered his head like an ice-pick, and he sat down and fiddled disconsolately with his tote bag while Alice casually stripped entirely naked – she really did look magnificent – and shrugged on an elegant black one-piece. There was a time, at the very end of their marriage, when Alice's breasts were as unerotic as those exposed in advertisements for cosmetic enhancement. But now she was gorgeous. Cordie, sitting next to him, swung her legs and sang a little song to herself.

The ex-family wandered out onto the distinctive terrace area that bordered the water's edge. Like the seaside, this was infinitesimally shallow at its lip, deepening out towards the far reach, where there were eddies and whirlpools, fountains and waterfalls, and over everything was the bending pipe of the flume, which swimmers of all ages shivered up the stairs to slide down. The café, which his mother had complained sold caffeine-rich soft drinks to parents and children, was right at the water's edge, just like at the beach, and there Dr Sweet and Alice put their bags down on chairs, where the kindly attendant promised to keep an eye on them.

Alice got glances from everyone, Dr Sweet was sure. The men admired her superb body and confident, sexy walk; the women seemed to pay a silent, awestruck respect to her empowerment, her radiant self-confidence. And as she strode along, hand-in-hand with Cordie, who looked sidelong up at her, other children seemed to pine for her to be their mummy too.

Dr Sweet's own pigeon-toed walk across the clammy floor behind them attracted no notice at all. He was invisible, just another stooping, chubby bloke, desexed and infantilized by the children's pool.

Alice and Cordie stopped and Alice turned round.

'Do you think we should go for a quick swim now or should we have a go in the jacuzzi?' she asked.

'The jacuzzi, I think,' said Dr Sweet thoughtfully, a fraction of a second before realizing that it was Cordie's opinion that was being canvassed and that his views were neither here nor there.

'Swim,' said Cordie smartly and waded out into the water with Alice behind her. Even at its deepest, at the other end, the pool only went up to just above Dr Sweet's waist. Where Cordie was, it rose halfway up his calves. Alice was sitting down in the water and Cordie was gigglingly swimming across her lap. She bumped into a tall man and Alice genially apologized to him: a handsome and athletic man, with longish blond hair tied behind in a ponytail with a red elastic band, who *helped her up*. It looked like Cordie had got a bit of water in her eyes and they were going rather red. Hand-in-hand, Alice and Cordie followed the man to the whirlpool section where swimmers were carried round a small island by the powerful, artificial current. He explained that he was here with his nephews.

Dr Sweet went off by himself. Heaving himself out of the pool at the waist-high deep end, disdaining the steps – one show of virility he could muster, at least – he headed for the flume queue.

The flume was the most remarkable leveller of modern family life. Everybody queued equally; men of forty-five, children of eight, preening adolescents of seventeen. And even if the adults were with their children, they couldn't pretend essential detachment, as they could with a movie or fairground ride, because each flume ride had to be taken singly: small children couldn't take their elders along for protection. Everyone had the same experience.

Dr Sweet joined the queue halfway up the stairs. From out of the great glass pane that made up this side of the building, he looked out onto the car park, the main road, the buses and a traffic calming speed bump which took newcomers by surprise and caused the concussed drivers to pull over and stagger out of their vehicles, clutching their heads. This part of London was one giant kebab shop, he thought – takeaway kebabs accounted for ninety percent of the local trade: Mr Kebab, Kebab World, The Kebabberie, Kebabz, and so on down to Kebab Heaven on the Kentish Town Road. Around here, people loved kebabs, and not just after closing time either. And there was no danger that their kebab culture would be taken over by some soulless globalized chain, either – Kebab Republic, selling kebabs and cappuccino with sofas and the Sunday newspapers. On the contrary, the kebab economy favoured the squalid, harshly lit premises, the photographs above the counter depicting the various kebabs and burgers in idealized form, and the slow vertical spit of the sweating flesh-log.

There they all were, shopping, working, going out for a cigarette or a kebab, worried about their careers, their mortgages, their children. And, of course, worried about cancer, worried as hell, losing sleep over it – everyone was. Dr Sweet wondered what they thought when they looked at the line of shivering swimmers visible through the glass up here, the sills and connecting struts between the panes painting cruciform shapes on their plump, unclothed, sunlit bodies: a row of pudgy naked hedonists waiting in line like children to go 'wheeeee' down a funfair-type ride. Perhaps, from the utter lack of fun on their faces, they resembled some hospital group undergoing a novel North London form of hydrotherapy. From where he was standing, Dr Sweet could see a young bike despatch rider leave an office building, unsling the bag he carried *banderillero*-style across his shoulders, open it in front of his waist as he walked along and awkwardly grope inside, but then drop it and, in trying to grab it with a downward swoop of his right fist, punch himself in the groin. From the little *hmph*s of laughter along the line, Dr Sweet knew that two or three other people had seen it as well.

The line advanced, perceptibly picking up speed, and it was time for Dr Sweet to turn away from the view, round 180 degrees up another flight of stairs towards the mouth of the flume itself. Small children raced up past him and joined little knots of pre-schoolers further up the line. Should he complain about queue-jumping? Apart from children, Dr Sweet's fellow flumers were mainly young men. Were these people really the fathers of sons and daughters, he wondered. They seemed so young in their plump bodies, enlivened with garish tattoos. He seemed to be the only one in shorts: the rest of them wore impossibly brief slips, little strips of silvery, black, red and gold material, encasing their bulbous genitalia with the detail of a plaster-cast mould. And each of them wore blank expressions, different from any they could have worn in the pub or at work. They were the same big, pale moon faces they'd had as children, waiting to get an injection from the school nurse. The man next to Dr Sweet was egregiously overweight and about twenty-five years old: number one cut; naked, of course, except for flip-flops, and swimming trunks which were made of about five square centimetres of green lycra. He had about five piercings in each ear and what appeared to be a metal bolt, the kind discharged by a medieval weapon of war, through each eyebrow. The septum of his nose bore a ring big enough for a bull and his face looked as innocent of thought as a child's at the cinema. But then a voice caused his face to light up with a smile, a smile of pure love.

'Hello, matey,' he said.

Down by them now was a small boy who was patently the man's son.

'You all right?'

'Yeah.'

'Where's your sister?'

'She's coming.'

The line moved again, getting faster as they reached the summit, and now Dr Sweet and everyone around him could see the little traffic light that regulated entry to the flume-mouth: red, green, red, green. Next to it there was a CCTV monitor, checked by the flume attendant in addition to the traffic light, relaying pictures from the bottom of the slide – milky child-like figures tumbling from the tube with a splosh into the shallow pool, miraculously unharmed. Each and every one of them, in defiance of the no running notice, ran away from the splashdown site. They could slip, Dr Sweet silently observed. They could fall backwards and strike the base of their skulls against the unyielding floor cover. And that would be that. Bailed To Return. Bailed To Return. And on the CCTV monitor, he seemed to see again the man with the bottle, the little girl flashing across the frame like a ghost.

Bailed To Return. Had anyone else in this line any experience of being in a police cell? The answer, he considered, was probably yes, but the presence of a discreet fellowship of crime was no comfort. Dr Sweet felt himself become light-headed.

Curtly, the pool attendant at the head of the line gestured him towards the flume's entry hole, lubricant water gushing in at all sides. The structure surrounding the aperture gleamed and sweated with water; its blank paint looked like puffy, unhealthy flesh. Was Dr Sweet imagining it or did the rush of water lining the flume's entry tube slow to a trickle? It was drying into a sticky, spongy, resisting sort of circle.

Dr Sweet looked round at the line of faces of all ages and they looked dully back. He couldn't turn round now and do the walk of shame back down the steps. He couldn't back out of doing the flume; it was an unheard of act of swimming pool cowardice.

He stepped forward and placed his fingers squeakily on the bottom rim. The attendant brusquely indicated that going in head-first was against the rules, so Dr Sweet moved his hands to the top, assumed a seated position – and tried to descend.

As his bottom dragged along the dampish surface, it made a sound like rubbing a balloon with your thumb. Dr Sweet remembered a lost feeling from childhood: trying haltingly to go down a children's slide just after it had been raining. He stopped and a low murmur of consternation began behind him.

Dr Sweet tried to propel himself forward by bracing the soles of his feet against the sides and walking himself down, the way canal-bargers are supposed to get themselves through tunnels. Minimal ground was gained until, mortifyingly, he felt a small foot on his back, a foot he guessed must belong to one of the children behind him. With surprising strength, it gave a mighty shove between his shoulder blades and Dr Sweet, the great middle-aged obstacle, was slitheringly dislodged. He began to pick up speed and, without thinking, leant back almost prone, feet first: the flume equivalent of a downhill skier crouching, elbows in, knees bent.

Christ, this was like a bobsleigh run! His body swung torpedo-like up round to the left as the tube veered off to the right, and up to the right as it veered off to the left. The tube was a U-shaped cross-section now, open at the top, and there was no obvious reassurance that he wouldn't simply be flung out at a tight bend and shatter both femurs on the concrete surface below. He could see the corrugated plastic sheeting that formed the central part of the ceiling, adjoining what looked like great metal plates, interconnected with rusting poles that delineated the triangular steeple at the summit. He was close enough to touch them.

And all the time he was picking up speed, shooting suddenly into an enclosed portion of the tube which was quite black with rippling streams of neon light, like the hyperspace scene in 2001. Oh Christ, moaned Dr Sweet silently. Why in the name of merciful God hadn't he remembered how unpleasant all forms of sporting activity were? All things done outside? All things with a changing room? He was picking up speed like a train with a dead driver. Bailed To Return. Bailed To Return.

Then the home straight arrived, still in a closed part of the tube but in a calmer, undeviated path which seemed to release, fractionally, the paralysing grip on his brain. He realized that by sitting up he should be able to slow himself down. Tensing what passed for his abdominal muscles, long withered and submerged under a pool of fat, Dr Sweet desperately jack-knifed his sagging upper body into a notional perpendicular formation and did indeed decelerate. From here he should be able to see the light at the end of the tunnel.

What he saw was very strange. As if looking into a telescope from the wrong end, he saw Cordie inside a circle of white light, surrounded by black, holding up her hand to him. Was he having a near-death experience? Had he had a heart attack in the last eighty seconds?

Soundlessly, he got closer and Cordie got larger and clearer in the circle of white light. He could make out her little orange bathing cap and Popeye armbands. She was giggling and holding something up. What was that noise?

Dr Sweet was beginning to veer crazily from side to side as the tube began to broaden and fan out. *Cordie*, he wanted to shout, *get out of the way*. I'm going to bash into you. For God's sake, Cordie, get out of the way. Cordie. But Cordie was laughing out loud as she waved the object in her hand, which was black and oblong.

As Dr Sweet shot out into the splashdown zone he realized two things at once: what Cordie was holding was his cellphone, which was ringing; and he wasn't going to hit her because at that point in the route, there was a powerful decelerative retro-current to immobilize emerging bodies almost entirely. More important than that, the water here was actually quite deep, so Dr Sweet was dunked into a pool, swallowing the equivalent of a biggish coffee mug of chlorinated water, a mortifying experience which bookended the whole fiasco nicely.

Spluttering to the surface, he saw that Cordie was now helpless with laughter, and it was only through some effort that Alice and the handsome man weren't doing the same.

'Daddy, your phone! Phone, phone, phone! I haven't answered it; I was waiting for you to answer it, but you were on the flume,' said Cordie. She pressed the green 'answer' button and handed it to him.

Dr Sweet coughed convulsively and unable to think of anything else to do, spoke into the phone.

'Mr Sweet? Mr Sweet!'

'Is that the police?'

'No, Mr Sweet,' There was a little, tinny laugh. 'My name is Rory Studholme and I'm a journalist from the North West London News Agency. I've had a bit of difficulty tracking you down actually; there seemed to be no reply from your home number. Is now a good time to talk?'

Dr Sweet was positive he knew what this would be about: the Ruzowitsky's big Christmas campaign to increase prostate cancer awareness. How effective had it been? And how close had the Ruzowitsky research teams come to any viable treatment? He had been briefed by the press office months ago in how to answer questions like this, but naturally preferred to do so from his office, with all the facts and statistics to hand.

Cordie was pulling at his left calf with both hands linked around it, as if measuring the extent of her grip. He could feel her plucking painfully at the little hairs there.

'Mr Studholme,' he said, with a mirthless little professional laugh of his own. 'It really isn't very convenient at the moment, I'm at the swimming pool! Could you call the Ruzowitsky Institute press office to fix up an appointment to see me?'

'I called the press office and they said to speak to you personally,' said the voice, which had now become strangely urgent. 'Mr Sweet, I am writing a story about your attack on the child abuser in the PriceBest supermarket.'

A wind-buzz of silent consternation sounded in Dr Sweet's phone and his head.

'Mr Sweet, are you still there?'

'Yes.'

'I'm writing a story about how you grappled with the child abuser as he menaced a small girl in the store, and now how you are under arrest for murder.'

He looked back down. Cordie had disappeared; suddenly she was hundreds of yards away. Alice and the handsome man seemed to be having an intimate tall latte. They were laughing, talking. Wait. The handsome man was turning his head away from her. He was showing her his ponytail and she was fingering his elastic band. More laughing.

'What child abuser? What are you talking about?'

'The man you tackled, Mr Sweet. The man you tackled was a registered sex offender.' There was a silence and then Rory took a different tack. 'Mr Sweet, are you upset about the way the police have treated you?'

'Yes, well, I . . . look, what exactly do you know about this?'

'Did it take courage, Mr Sweet, to do what you did?'

'No. Listen, who are you?'

'I've told you, Mr Sweet, my name is Rory Studholme, and I am from the—'

And here Dr Sweet's phone lost its signal. His ears retuned to the incessant shriek and bottled roar of the pool. A klaxon sounded, of the sort that warns of fire or imminent nuclear attack. Cordie ran up.

'Daddy, the wave machine! The wave machine's starting! Can I play in the waves?'

'Yes, darling, if your mother goes in, too.'

He went over to the café table where Alice and *her* new friend were finishing their drinks. They looked up together, in easy symmetry, as he approached.

'Alice, could you look after Cordie in the water?' he asked, not allowing himself to be introduced to her new acquaintance. 'I need to go outside for a bit.' Dr Sweet headed off to the family changing room.

In the pool building forecourt, just by the little slip-road that led to the car park, he dug his hands into his jacket pockets, the letter crinkling in his left fist, and fancied he could still hear the groan and heave of the pool wave-maker, like an obsolete piece of agricultural machinery, lifting and lowering immobile buoyant swim-mers, despatching great slaps of water against the tiled walls of the leisure complex. It was cold out here and not all that light; it might even be starting to rain. He was at that stage in his life when time was beginning to pass in a corrosive drizzle, a dull blizzard of minutes, each tiny impact wearing his skin into a coarse, tired grain. Opening his eyelids often felt like removing the weather tarpaulin at Wimbledon.

Should he try calling the man back? His cellphone disclosed the number without difficulty. Or would the man ring him back? Instead of feeling galvanized, Dr Sweet had never felt more like letting it all wash over him, allowing this flood tide to carry him along the shore, or irrevocably away from it.

The passing cars had their headlights on and, as they streamed up the hill, a speed camera positioned just near the fork in the road gave a periodic warning flash, hardly visible in the sugary daylight. Dr Sweet thought this explained what he saw next: a flash that came just after an unfamiliar voice hailed him. Dr Sweet turned, his hands still bunched into his jacket, bulging and bulking it out, his still-damp hair caught in straggling wisps over his ears, but his face instinctively set in a cautious, diplomatic half smile. And it was in this posture that the nation would come to see him: his face and body momentarily lit like a crime scene in a stark, metallic white-blue, hands in pockets, swivelling towards the camera from the hips, the little half smile in bud.

13

Of all Dr Sweet's research team, it was Hattie who discovered the story first. Michiko, Heinrich, Bela and Olwen sat in the coffee room in London, sipping their Nescafés from the machine and blithely ignoring the newspapers fanned out for their convenience on the mahogany side-table placed under the big portrait of the institute's founder. Hattie, in a hotel room on the other side of the world, was brought up to speed on her group leader's new pre-eminence before any of them.

Actually, the 'hiking' part of their honeymoon had not materialized. Hattie's parents had paid for a hotel suite in Sydney for two nights, and the plan was that the tougher, outdoorsy part of their holiday would begin after that. But once the two days was up, the pair of them decided they were happier moving from the suite into a regular double room and simply relaxing for a few more days. When Hattie telephoned her parents to let them know of this change of plan, they cheerfully, but tacitly, assumed their daughter and son-in-law were intoxicated with sensual pleasure, ardently pursuing the business of providing them with grandchildren. But nothing could be further from the truth. The fact was that the sexual part of their honeymoon was turning into a fiasco. Hattie and

Arlen were staying on at the hotel with one increasingly grim aim in view: to achieve at least one bona fide sexual act as a married couple before venturing out into the wilderness.

When they had arrived in the suite after the wedding, both were a little tipsy, yet frantic with desire after the almost unbearably sexual experience of waiting while all their guests departed. They were hardly virgins, and yet for Arlen there was something intensely erotic about seeing Hattie disappear halfway through the reception in her wedding dress and reappear in her trim, chic little going-away outfit: an old-fashioned idea and yet happily chosen. Arlen repeatedly muttered into her ear that he couldn't wait to see that outfit in a crumpled heap on their hotel-suite floor. But when it was, and Arlen's similarly old-fashioned morning suit next to it, Arlen disconcerted his young bride with the ardour, and indeed the volume, with which he demanded one specific sexual practice. It was something in which he had never before shown any interest, in the course of what Hattie considered their respectably bold and adventurous lovemaking.

When Hattie hesitated, Arlen said nothing, but reached into his travel bag, from which he extracted a sheaf of images downloaded from the Internet, putting his interest and connoisseurship of this practice beyond question. Hattie was not a prude, but there was something less than lovable in the furtive way Arlen had hidden it all from her until now, and his evident assumption that the married state made this a conjugal right.

'Ah, c'mon, Hat, be a sport,' he slurred.

'I don't know, Arl. Why d'you want to do it like this? Can't we just have sex in the normal way?'

A testy discussion of the word 'normal' commenced, and their wedding night then descended into an ill-tempered argument about the willingness to compromise being the foundation stone of any long-term relationship. Eventually, and in a thoroughly bad mood, bride and groom prepared to settle down for a night of chaste restraint, but Hattie unbent sufficiently to agree to giving Arlen hand relief, to which he submitted as if to a necessary if slightly painful medical procedure.

The next night, after a languid day of facials in the spa and relaxation in the steam room, Arlen again raised the issue of his special interest and Hattie this time gamely agreed, going so far as to drink seven large bottles of Evian after dinner. The outcome, however, was still unsatisfactory; Hattie was too selfconscious, and the second night of their married life concluded in the same fraught and frustrated way.

Once in the ordinary double room, on night number three, Arlen did not dare ask for anything more than normal congress. But now even that seemed to elude them and, following some desultory caresses, Arlen fell asleep, as if after a night of monumental exertion. Hattie stared at the ceiling, and occasionally at the bedside clock: it was 11.40 p.m.

Was this what married life was all about? Hattie's eyes brimmed with self-pity, and she felt the tears begin to cascade sideways, trickling absurdly into her ears, an experience she hadn't had since she was fifteen and living in her parents' house in Queensland. All at once, Hattie became very afraid of the abyss of failure and unhappiness that was opening up under her; she must pull herself together. Whisking the duvet briskly aside, she got up and walked over to their backpacks, their maps and equipment, all propped against the walls, and all unlikely to be used ever again. Still in her nightie, Hattie got herself an Evian from the minibar, dutifully ticking it off the hotel's checklist, and then sat at the desk at the other end of the room. For no real reason, she clicked on the Internet icon at the computer monitor provided. Inevitably, her thoughts strayed to Dr Sweet. What was he doing now? She felt little or no affection for him, considering his ridiculous and spiteful behaviour at their last meeting, but she couldn't help but think about what could possibly have happened to him since the arrest. She was convinced it had to be some sort of mistake, and Hattie had left for Australia before she could hear or participate in the torrent of rumour that must be sweeping the building.

Idly, she entered his name, 'Dr David Sweet' in the Google search engine, the way she often had in the first infatuated days of their affair, and expected to see only the academic references and publications this search usually produced. But this time there was something else: a reference to the website of a major British newspaper.

She clicked on it, and after fifteen seconds or so, the news page was constructed, and then the text of a story about Dr Sweet. The headline read, HAVE-A-GO HERO DOC HELD BY POLICE, and the story was attributed to the 'Crime Staff'.

> A courageous cancer research doctor, who intervened to stop a six-year-old girl being menaced by a registered paedophile, has been arrested for murder, it was revealed last night.
>
> David Sweet, 41, was in a late-night convenience

store in Hornsey, North London two days before Christmas when he saw the little girl, Zalihe Yildiz, being abused by the man, who was holding a broken bottle.

Witnesses say Dr Sweet instantly squared up to the man and told him to leave the terrified little girl alone. The man, John O'Rourke, was a convicted sex offender, required to register his place of residence with the local police. He turned on Dr Sweet and a struggle ensued that one witness called 'Terrifying'.

This struggle concluded with O'Rourke sustaining a blow to the head which resulted in a permanent loss of consciousness, and Dr Sweet arrested for murder, although no charges have been formally brought.

Little Zalihe is shaken up, but safe and sound, thanks to Dr Sweet. One local said last night, 'It simply beggars belief that the police will do nothing to help ordinary citizens being harassed by criminals and burglars, and yet they arrest Dr Sweet. That man is just a hero.'

Dr Sweet is a senior scientist at the Ruzowitsky Institute for Cancer Research in London. He is currently released on bail. The Crown Prosecution Service refused to comment.

After a few moments more, a photograph of Dr Sweet appeared in the square box next to the story, the one taken of him outside the swimming pool: it had been cropped down so that it just showed his face, and it wasn't clear that it had been taken outside, or that its subject was in any way caught by surprise. A humorous, quizzical, smiling face.

Stunned, Hattie re-read the story, and then re-read it again. *That* was why Dr Sweet was so tense and unhappy the last time they'd met. Suddenly, Hattie thought about Jaime, her little eight-year-old cousin who'd been their bridesmaid, and who had been as good as gold throughout the service, never once crying or being naughty. Hattie imagined Jaime in danger from a violent pervert – at the mental mention of the word 'pervert' she shuddered with anger – and then imagined a man with the courage to stand up to the evildoer. A man who risked physical assault himself, or a blow that might leave him in a wheel-chair, a quadriplegic, risking incarceration and disgrace, but who set it all aside to see that a little girl was safe. And this man needed love and companionship and friend-ship from her, but at the very moment he'd needed it most she had spurned him and broken his heart into a thousand pieces.

There was a grunt and she turned around to see Arlen stirring in his sleep. One tanned leg, covered with blond downy hair, poked from the duvet as Arlen turned over, whinnying gently and hugging the pillow. Hattie went over and looked at him. Her husband did have kind of a long head; a head that went out a very great deal at the back. Was it a forceps birth, she wondered? Did the doctor, way back in the 1970s, grab that head of his with a pair of medical pliers and just heave?

Hattie looked at Arlen's sleeping face. (She had often read that loving couples did this kind of thing all the time, and yet she had never done it with Arlen, probably because she usually slept so much more soundly than he did.) Hold on. Arlen was saying something. He was talking in his sleep. Aware of carrying out an intimately intrusive, even disloyal act, Hattie placed her ear very close to Arlen's mouth. When she was a little girl on seaside holidays, she was told that holding a shell up to her ear would allow her to hear the sea; yet doing so blocked out the sound of the sea that she could hear perfectly well anyway, and replaced it with an odd, hollow rushing noise. Hattie expected to get a hotline into Arlen's unconscious mind, but heard only a kind of inchoate floppy noise, like a seal stirring inside a cave.

Hattie pulled her head away from Arlen's mouth and thought about the miserable expression on Dr Sweet's face the last time she'd seen him. Her whole body started to shake with emotion; she positively vibrated with self-reproach. And then she found herself consumed and swept away by a different emotion, an emotion she realized was utterly new to her. She felt the most passionate love and admiration for Dr Sweet. Whatever sleepiness she had was gone. The urgency, the sheer crackling excitement of it all was now dawning on her. She could almost feel her pancreas, her spleen, her kidneys, her brain, every organ in her body re-attuning itself to British time, eleven hours in the past. What was Dr Sweet doing right now? At this very moment? Hattie had never given him any love letters or love tokens, except for a strip of three photo-booth pictures, with the fourth snipped off for her Ruzow-itsky ID card. Was Dr Sweet looking at these unsmiling photos now, bent and smeared in his sweaty fingers? She went back over to the computer screen and gently put her fingers on the picture of his face.

With a stab that made the backs of her hands prickle, Hattie realized she could e-mail Michiko to find out what was going on. Michiko, the quiet, sweet-natured post-doc who Hattie had always got on so well with: well enough to confess to her the beginnings of her affair with Dr Sweet, when they had both been to a conference together in Ware. Michiko had been alarmed and disapproving but obviously fascinated and excited at the same time. After that initial confidence, Hattie had not cared to talk to Michiko about it any more, for fear it should become common gossip, but she was sure Michiko would understand why she needed to talk to someone about it now.

Hattie logged on to her Hotmail account, and found her in-tray of thirty-two messages. She trawled through the e-mails promising viagra through the post, a way of re-mortgaging her house and XXXX hot porn, but nothing from Michiko. However, there amongst all the junk, was a message from Dr Sweet with the words 'mad about you' in the subject field. Hattie felt her pulse hammer in her neck as she double-clicked it open.

The message was dated 21 Dec, time 11.06, so before their last tryst in the Rylands, before his arrest. What was it he'd wanted to say in a message, but couldn't say in person? Hattie read on:

> hattie, hi. how are you? i'm a bit low. do you remember that guy I said was going out with alice, the one from new york. well, it looks like she's going to be living out there, and she may well get custody of cordie while she's in america: or re-apply if I contest it anyway. and there's something else . . .

That's where it ended. Dr Sweet must have sent it accidentally, but there was no follow-up. The 'something else' – was that his attack on the pervert? Hattie exhaled and

Arlen stirred again, this time mumbling audibly, his great long cigar-shaped head nuzzling and rumpling the pillow. Was he waking up?

Hattie tapped out a message to Michiko:

michi, what's happening to sweetie?

And within about a minute she had a reply:

you're not going to believe it . . .

14

Cordie thought all the photographers outside the front door on her first day back at school were brilliant. They were there from really early in the morning when it was cold and dark and rainy, and they'd been there the previous night as well. One of them had a little step ladder, like the one her dad fell off once when he was trying to get into the attic and her mum had told him not to, and she wasn't at all sympathetic when he fell off and there was a big clang. Her grandma said Cordie wasn't to open the curtains in her bedroom in case they took a photograph. Cordie pondered a moment and, just for fun, reached up and pulled back the curtain; there was a lot of clicking and flashing, then she tugged it back and it stopped. Then she pulled it open and there was more clicking and flashing, so she pulled it back and it stopped again! She quickly whipped it open, whipped it back, and heard a click and a very rude word. Cordie supposed she'd better stop.

When she was washed and dressed and came down for breakfast, all the curtains were drawn in the kitchen as well and the blinds in the other room, even though it was getting light by now. Cordie wanted a cup of tea like all the grown-ups, but with lots of sugar and milk, and she was allowed to have one. Grandad and Grandma and her mum and dad were really quiet.

Then her mum asked her dad if he was sure he wanted to take Cordie to school and Dad said he was. Grandad and Grandma didn't say anything, but they couldn't take her to school because they didn't have a car. Cordie had Cheerios for breakfast, which Grandma poured hot milk on, heated in the microwave, and Cordie said she didn't like it and almost cried, so her mum quickly took it away and poured it down the waste-disposal and gave her some new Cheerios with cold milk without a single word said.

Mum asked Cordie if she needed a wee before going out and she nodded and went off, and when she came back her dad had his coat on and was holding up hers, and her *Jungle Book* lunch case and book bag were standing next to the front door.

The door opened and everyone started flashing, taking pictures again, and then they all started running backwards while she and her dad moved towards his car. Cordie smiled and put her hand up and waved the way she did when people took pictures on holiday, but Dad put his arm right across her and pushed her hand down, and she felt the material of his coat sleeve brush her face and pull down her lower lip as it went past in a nasty blubbery way.

Then her dad did a strange thing: he picked her up and walked along more quickly. Cordie didn't mind being picked up like this by her mum, even though she was now a big girl, but her dad didn't know how to do it. He would walk along with his body straight and Cordie would just slide down, so he would hold her extra hard and it would hurt. When her mum did it she pushed her hip out so that she could sort of rest on that, and she once said her dad had never, ever, ever, got the hang of moving his hips properly in carrying Cordie, or dancing, or anything else.

When the photographers saw she looked sad, they just stopped taking pictures. It was just like on holiday. But when she did another little smile just before reaching the car, they did some more flashes.

Cordie went in the front and put her seat belt on and Dad got in the driver's seat but he didn't put his seat belt on and then Cordie told him he had to because it was against the law. They went off and Cordie saw that her dad was looking at the crowd of photographers in the rear-view mirror.

Only when he couldn't see them any more did he start acting normally again.

He said, 'How are you, Miss Cordie?'

Cordie said, 'OK.' She looked at her book bag and her *Jungle Book* lunchbox, picture-side up, and saw Baloo dancing in the clearing of the King's part of the jungle, with his great left paw round Kaa's neck and his right paw in her hand. They danced around for a bit with Bagheera looking on, for once actually approving, and the King himself looked pleased, about to slap his great brown hairy palms on the flagstone floor. This went on until the car stopped outside Cordie's school. There weren't any photographers there.

Dr Sweet reached across, and pushed open the door so Cordie could get out. Cordie had missed the main assembly; she didn't know why. He leaned in for his kiss, saying, 'How much do you love me, Cordie? How much do you love your poor old dad?'

Cordie said, 'Too much', which is what she always said, and got out, and then she went into school, with her bags and her dinner money in an envelope.

The first period was literacy hour, and all the others were really weird. Cordie was on the Kangaroos table and they were practising writing out the letter *n*. All *n*s over and over again. *nnnnnnnnnnnnnnnn*. Even her best friend Sally was quiet and didn't say much while they were writing out the *n*s. Then Sally said that at register everyone had been told that her dad had got into trouble with the police but that it wasn't his fault and everyone had to be nice to her.

There was a horrible boy called Gary Long over on the Hippos table practising writing out *o*s – *oooooooooo*. He shouted that, Ooooo, he was scared of Cordie's dad, and people started laughing, so Cordie got in really quick and said yes he probably WILL get you all!

She said it very loudly and she was really pleased at the way it shut them all up. Some of the others pushed Mark and said, '*Yeah, Mark. Yeah, Mark,*' and she was even more pleased and Sally even tried holding her hand, right there in the lesson but Cordie wouldn't let her; she just went on writing out *n*s.

When Cordie had finished writing her *n*s, she was allowed to sit on her own and read. She took the books out of her book bag. One of them was a school book called *There's A Moth That Eats Books At Our House*, but the other one was a book that belonged to her daddy, which she'd found at home, and noticed because it had a big picture of the Eiffel Tower on the front. They were doing national costumes at school – there was a big poster on the wall – and she liked the French national costumes and all the other things on the wall about France. She had asked her mummy if she could go to France and her mummy had said, 'Yes, one day.'

She would show the book to Sally. She looked inside and saw that her daddy had written something in it.

Then they had to go to assembly and Mrs Curzons said they were all to close their eyes and think about something important to them. Cordie scrunched her eyes up tight and thought about how her daddy had punched a man in a shop and got into trouble, but everyone knew that he'd soon get out of trouble. Her mummy said it wouldn't be long before everything would be normal again, but Cordie hoped it wouldn't because it was interesting, and it kept Mummy staying at her daddy's house and it kept her grandma and grandad there, too.

Just before playtime, Cordie got out her book bag and took out the book with the Eiffel Tower on it. She studied her daddy's writing for a bit.

At playtime everyone wanted to be her friend and that had never, ever happened before, but Cordie just walked around the edge of the playground with Sally and they looked at the ornamental garden, and the other girls did a really loud clapping game:

> Not last night but the night before
> Twenty-four robbers came knocking at my door
> I went out to let them in
> And this is what they said to me:

Cordie and Sally could hear an ice-cream van in the side road, but Cordie wasn't allowed hardly any sweets because her mummy said they had a bad effect on her.

Chinese lady touch the GROUND
Chinese lady turn a-ROUND
Chinese lady do the SPLITS
Chinese lady do the KICKS

Just then an older girl and boy went and bought her some crisps and she and Sally ate them; it was nice and Cordie thought some more about Baloo.

Then Gary Long came over, trying to make friends. He tried giving her a picture of Batman saying it was like her dad. Cordie said Batman can't fly and he's got a stupid belt, and then she and Sally both ran off skipping with their ropes at the same time, almost as fast as normal running. She and Sally and some other girls did skipping and then Gary Long kicked a tennis ball over and it put Sally off, so Cordie grabbed the ball and threw it on top of the school roof, and everyone laughed and then they did hopscotch until it was the end of break.

They all went back inside and Cordie went and found her book bag again and got the Eiffel Tower book out. She asked Sally if she wanted it, and Sally said yes she would because she liked France as well. So Sally put it away in her book bag.

Everyone was looking and smiling at Cordie and Sally on the way in; they let them have their crisps, wanted to stand next to them. And Cordie could see her teacher looking at her, and talking to the headteacher.

Gary Long came up and tried to offer her some white chocolate buttons but she said she only liked brown chocolate buttons. The teacher said he wasn't allowed to eat sweets in the lesson and took them off him and he almost cried.

Their teacher Mrs Curzons said they were having a concert later on in the term and they would be singing in a big choir, but some of them could sing in threes and fours if they liked. She asked if anyone wanted to do that, and no-one put their hand up. Then Cordie raised her hand, and lots of people put their hands up, too. Then Mrs Curzons asked if anyone wanted to do a solo and only Cordie put her hand up, although Sally asked if she could do a solo with Cordie. But Mrs Curzons said no because then that would be a duet.

After that they had numeracy, and they sat down at the tables doing take-aways and adds. But Cordie and Sally were giggling and they got told off by Mrs Curzons. Then there was a loud bang at the long window by the door to the playground and they all looked round; there was a man with a camera which made a flash, then the man turned around and ran away. Mrs Curzons ran out to chase him and so did the caretaker, Mr Golby, and the whole class ran over to the window to look.

Mrs Curzons couldn't run very fast, but Mr Golby sprinted, and it was shocking for the class to see a grown-up running and being very angry at the same time. He caught up with the man just as he was trying to get on a motor scooter by the class gates. Mr Golby grabbed the man's anorak; the man pulled away, and the class couldn't quite see what was happening because the wall was in the way, but they heard the sound of the scooter's engine, and then Mr Golby reappeared, looking gloomy and cross.

Cordie was watching what was going on, but she was also thinking of what she was going to sing. Mrs Curzons had offered to accompany anyone who wanted to do a solo on her guitar, or get Mr Curzons to come in and accompany her on the piano. Cordie didn't want any accompaniment. She was going to sing on the karaoke machine she had got for Christmas, with its tape machine and little microphone.

Mr Golby was talking to Mrs Curzons as they came back in. Cordie turned round and saw that every single person in the class was looking at her. Gary Long held out a bag of brown chocolate buttons.

15

As he looked out of his lab window, Dr Sweet got an inkling, a batsqueak, of the emotions that were on their way. A crowd of photographers – bigger than yesterday's – had gathered round both the front and back entrances to the building, and the Director had put everyone on animal rights Yellow Alert.

This was an emergency procedure he had drawn up five years ago when animal rights activists had picketed the institute for five consecutive days, necessitating a large police presence. Every other protester had a placard showing a photograph of an orang-utan wearing what appeared to be a shallow chrome helmet with wires hanging from it – a sensational provocation all the more terrifying because, as it happened, there was no primate research at the Ruzowitsky, or any animal experimentation in that sense. The demonstration had arisen because of a very incautious interview the Director had given on the radio in his capacity as Secretary of the Research Defence Society, defending animal research in the fiercest possible terms. The result was an uproar.

The Director had taken a far lower profile ever since then, but there were all sorts of rumours about emergency evacuation provisions, secret bunkers and passageways and a worst-case-scenario procedure in the event that the protesters got close to the Director himself.

He certainly hadn't told Dr Sweet any of the details. They stood side by side, looking at the photographers and reporters on the pavement many floors below, and the Director allowed a heavy palm to fall on his subordinate's shoulder, a bluff manly gesture from which Dr Sweet flinched, as if from a falling tree.

'Quite a crowd, eh?' The Director was evidently holding him utterly responsible for them, but in what spirit exactly Dr Sweet could not be sure. 'Have you seen that outplacement counsellor yet?'

Dr Sweet sagged, under the weight of the Director's palm, at the thought of the outplacement counsellor and his impending unemployment.

'Not yet, actually, no; I've been meaning to get round to it,' he said weakly. The Director kept looking out of the window, with his great meaty hand in place. Then he turned back to Dr Sweet with an odd little moue of resignation. He agitated the palm into a shake and then removed it. 'No rush,' he said, flicking his eyebrows up, and then left. Dr Sweet saw that the skin on top of his head wasn't taut at all.

Once he'd gone, Dr Sweet returned to his swivel chair by the big Mac computer screen, and stealthily removed the press clippings that bulged in a big cardboard-backed envelope.

He could hardly believe it. Just looking at all of it made his insides race. Reading last night's coverage he thought he'd heard a low moan from somewhere, like the wind, or the ghost of a murdered Victorian child. It was his own entrails, under exceptional nervous pressure.

Dr Sweet was a hero; there was no doubt about it. Middlebrow columnists, editorial writers, reporters and pundits of every stripe – they all sided with him, based on the fantastic version of the facts originally published and never investigated, still less corrected, by any media outlet. The inquest's open verdict and the fact that the Crown Prosecution Service still hadn't decided whether or not to press murder charges all but paralysed his mind. His Bailed To Return letter still crinkled in his pocket, worn almost to pieces.

But there was no doubt that this possible murder charge had electrified everyone. Dr Sweet had sent a memo to the Director immediately on his return to the lab, explaining that the newspapers and media had got it all wrong, and that his lawyers were currently explaining all this while the police were having to re-interview Mr Yildiz. The Director had composed an urbane reply to the effect that he naturally understood and that Dr Sweet should not give it another thought.

If Dr Sweet was honest with himself, however, there was a terrible, secret thrill in being thought of as a murderer – in a good cause. Everyone he met was slightly intoxicated by their proximity to a killer who had acted to save a child. It was the perfect mix of danger and righteousness. Dr Sweet felt people react to his mere presence, really *react*, for the very first time in his life. He thought: this is what being beautiful must be like.

Just to try it out, to flex this steely new muscle, Dr Sweet casually and even lightly swung out of his office for a loose-limbed directionless ramble. Everyone, but everyone, in his lab got to their feet for no good reason. These were the sullen mutinous types who could hardly be bothered to return his polite good morning last year. Now they made to look busy, and not just that; they made eye-contact, they paid him respect.

Dr Sweet smiled and walked on down the corridor. Now, who would he drop in on? How about Sam Pumfrey, an appalling new lab head just in from the National Institute of Health in Washington, who had looked down his nose at Dr Sweet's work?

Dr Sweet peeped in through his glass door to see that Dr Pumfrey was talking to his group in a huddle. Obviously he needed to speak to them all about something important and didn't wish to be interrupted. Excellent.

He knocked on the door and breezed in. They all jumped up, and even Pumfrey straightened a little; it was as if he had jabbed them all with an electric goad.

'Jane,' he said cheerfully, speaking directly to one of Pumfrey's post-graduate students, and ignoring the lab head entirely, an unthinkable breach of etiquette. 'Do you still need that antibody we were talking about?'

'Oh, er, yes, Dr Sweet. David,' said Jane, blushing.

'Fine,' said Dr Sweet. 'We can have a chat about it later on.' He then treated himself to another piece of delicious effrontery, nodding casually at Pumfrey without apologizing for the interruption, then breezing out without closing the door.

They didn't know *how* to react to him! Everyone had known his career was on the skids; God alone knew he had nothing left to lose in that department, but now everyone knew why all the photographers were outside. Dr Sweet, timid, silly Dr Sweet, had turned out to be a – Dr Sweet giggled audibly at the thought – a *killer*. Not an adulterer, not a tax-evader, not a banal falsifier of scientific results. Dr Sweet was a killer. And a killer that everyone not so secretly sympathized with! If Frank and Jesse James had decided to start up a cancer research lab, and walk around the scientific corridors in flapping white coats, their six-guns clanking at their hips, they couldn't have felt better than this. Without realizing it, Dr Sweet started to walk more quickly, breaking into a jog, then a run. He was running! The double-doors at the end of the corridor loomed up and he clattered through them, skipping down the staircase two steps at a time.

With a thud, he landed at the bottom, twisted an ankle ever so slightly, and felt his fatuous euphoria pop like a soap bubble. The paint on the walls reminded him of the police interview cell, the single lavatory, the hideous throne in a tiny state room of shame. The feeling flooded back into his head so completely he felt dizzy and sick.

Fucking hell. Jesus Christ. Oh, merciful Jesus. Dr Sweet's repertoire of blasphemy and obscenity was entirely obsolete. Swearing, even with 'motherfucker' – an expletive that had become absolutely commonplace with every class and age of Briton – was not merely inadequate, but incorrect. What was happening felt more like as a boy when he was told of his father's stroke: a great and terrible thing that required a heightened response.

He had gone to visit John in hospital once, and only once. He and Rosemary had taken the bus to the neurological ward on a Saturday lunchtime: he still in his school uniform – Cordie would listen saucer-eyed to tales of when children had to get up on Saturday morning to go to school – his mother wearing a coat and skirt *suit* he had never seen before, a heavy tweed in a kind of Irish-stew-brown and dark red. She had a handbag too, the kind of stout capacious bag all women had in the English mid-Sixties, with two brass clasps that snapped shut at the top.

Dr Sweet's loathing of hospitals dated from then; he had been an in-patient himself for the compulsory removal of tonsils and thought it not at all bad, but now there was a presentiment of seriousness and death. He was oppressed by the columns of direction signs – opthalmology, radiology – with their unhelpful pointing arrows and the distinctive sans-serif lettering, a part of hospital design which was not to change for decades. As Dr Sweet and his mother walked hand in hand to the ward, he looked down at his reflection in the vivid burgundy linoleum, leaning forward a little so he could see his face, plumply peering up over his trotting, swaying torso.

He'd expected the ward they were about to enter to look like the children's ward: all patients the same age, in candy-stripe pyjamas, the metal beds and their surrounding areas, customized with drawings, cards, flowers. But this was an adult ward. They were all old and still and silent, all accompanied by a tense crescent moon of miserable relatives.

He didn't immediately recognize his father. Something about this setting denuded John of his individuality. He and his mother were immobile at the ward's threshold, and many years later, he suspected his mother had been stumped as well – and how much more mortifying must that have been for her? Or perhaps her hesitation was a gathering of courage, a gulping back of stage fright.

'John, Darling. What a *wait* we had for the wretched, wretched *bus*!' It was a greeting delivered with explosive, musical gaiety, like the last line of a Gilbert and Sullivan chorus.

But John was crying. Crying in a mopey, speechless, self-pitying way that had earned Dr Sweet an old-fashioned clip round the ear from *him* many a time. Well, maybe not crying but allowing tears to leak uninterruptedly. Rosemary sat on the chair opposite John and continued to talk; Dr Sweet lowered himself onto a chair at the end of the bed by the charts.

'The consultant says you'll be home by the end of the week! *Won't* that be nice?'

The sound of his mother's jollying-along voice being used on his father, and in front of him, was more disturbing than he could ever have thought possible. It was like a bad dream. What was the matter? Why was he so sad?

'And look what David's got! Look what his housemaster found in a second-hand bookshop in London.'

This had been a moment he had been looking forward to on the way here, but now he didn't know what to think. Cautiously, like a captured felon removing a pistol from his coat pocket with finger and thumb, under the gaze of armed police, Dr Sweet removed a slim hardback book from a marbled paper bag. It was a first edition of *Mathematical Mysteries: Problems and Solutions For the Curious Reader* by John Sweet, published by Victor Gollancz at twelve shillings and sixpence, and brought out when Dr Sweet's father was still an undergraduate at Manchester University.

Each short chapter was an algebraic or geometric teaser, allegedly accessible to the 'well-educated general reader' and soluble by means of the complex equations proposed at the end of each part, but playfully premised with jokey situations by which the author sugared the pill of difficulty. A cheeky boy might have to calculate the angle for laying a ladder against a wall for the purposes of scrumping apples from an orchard, and in all cases where a cheeky boy was needed, the author had called him David – the name he would later give to his son. Each part was accompanied with Ronald Searle-ish cartoons and the introduction contained an uproarious account of the high-spirited games of Fizzbuzz that would occur in his rooms with other maths students after some glasses of the landlady's medium sherry.

John had lost his copy, and the only others were in libraries, so this was a find. Gingerly, at his mother's fiercely bright beckoning, Dr Sweet came into John's field of vision.

He was lying on his side, face resting on the mattress by the pillow. It was now that he could see that one half of his father's face was immobile, blank; the eye had a kind of poached egg look. The tears streamed down his face and stayed there with a rippling glycerine fixity, like lava, fed continuously somehow from below.

'Da – ad.' He had the childish way of importuning the word, a two-tone break in the single syllable, but said quietly. 'Mr Perry at school found a copy of your book in a second-hand shop in London, and it's a sort of get-well soon present to you but he didn't have time to wrap it.' He had expected every component of that last sentence to be spaced out with delighted whoops and congratulatory laughter from his father, not to mention supportive interjections from his mother. It was a communication he'd thought would take minutes to get through: a precious store of conversational ammunition that he'd run through in a few seconds. He looked away to Rosemary, who did nothing but smile encouragingly at him. Apparently, the burden of making conversation still rested entirely with him.

Smiling weakly, he placed the book next to John on the bed, on the sheet, nodding, as if to say: take it, take a look.

John looked down at it. The active side of his face began to tremble. The book was starting to make him very angry, or very upset, or both.

'John,' said Rosemary, in a quiet, falling tone, as if hoping her cadence would suppress this unquiet emotion. Dr Sweet said nothing and John continued to shake. Rosemary scanned the ward for the sister. Like a head waiter, her eye was not to be caught. Actually calling for help, making a fuss, would probably worsen the situation, Rosemary calculated, and what a painful expertise in this sort of decision-making she had had to amass in the past eight days.

In any case, however, John did something that distracted her: he moved his arm towards the book. This was precisely the sort of positive coordinated impulse they had been hoping for. John's pale fingers reached the cover. Transfixed, both Dr Sweet and Rosemary looked at this little still life, then a little thin keening or whinnying made them both look up at John's face. Now he was smiling, and it was at this happily chosen moment that the ward sister appeared on some supervisory pretext, but possibly also to enforce a tactful break in the visiting period.

'Goodbye, John, I'll see you tomorrow,' said Rosemary.

'Goodbye, Dad,' said Dr Sweet.

In no time, they were back out in the corridor again, with the red linoleum and the signs, having decided to stow the book in John's locker. Unpredictably, his mother whirled around on her heel and knelt in front of him, forcing him to stop, and then plucked at his school tie, implying with a genial *tsk* that it was crooked when it was nothing of the kind. The crazy-TV pattern of her jacket again, close up, filaments of gold and burgundy emerging tinily from the rough tweed. Her face was set in a hard, tough smile; her eyes glazed and blazing with emotion.

'Oh *look*,' she said. Now she had got him on something: His shirt-tail was out. Keeping his shirt-tail in was something he was never to get the hang of; no matter how capacious his shirts, they would end up billowing out behind him, spinnaker-like. She reached round and Dr Sweet felt the tweed under his chin as she tucked the shirt all the way round his back with a practised slice of her hand. And then she just stayed that way for some minutes, kneeling and embracing him, while Dr Sweet submissively remained in position, smelling the varnish-paint-chemical-hospital smell that years later he would associate with imprisonment in East Holloway Police Station.

He could be charged with murder. The duty solicitor had explained to him what that meant. A trial, during which he could certainly expect more of this sort of treatment from the media, but a possible conviction nevertheless. A 'London bang-up'. A stay in Belmarsh Prison in south London – one of the most horrible places in the world – then, maybe, a transfer to a lower grade prison in the country somewhere. Visitation rights? Sure.

Your parents. Your mum and dad, their faces creased with shame and grief. Alice and Cordie would be far, far away – in the United States of America with Alice's new partner, maybe fiancé by then. And as for complaining about the infringement of visitation rights informally agreed upon, as for *contesting* that *in court*. Good luck! Good luck explaining to a judge in the Family Division that your ex-wife should be compelled to relinquish an important career advancement, not so you can visit your daughter, but so that she can visit you, a convicted murderer, in prison.

Now Dr Sweet felt sick. He felt metal in his throat again; he smelt the paint and the disinfectant. He tasted the long-stay institution. Twisting his shirt front in his hand, he ducked into the men's toilets and went straight for the washbasins to run cold water over his hands. His reflected face, cast in the brownish glow of the lavatory's twilit bower, discomfited him. Dr Sweet shut off the water and looked at his upturned palms, water trickling through the fingers – the hands of a killer. He dried his hands and tucked his shirt in.

Outside, in the corridor, the Director was talking to Professor Sir Hendryck Klost, an elderly Nobel laureate who had been director of research at the Ruzowitsky in the early Eighties. They both affected a Kennedyesque arms-folded posture, leaning into each other; the Director looked abashed and alarmed by what Sir Hendryck was telling him. Dr Sweet really had to be getting back to his lab now, and the only way was to walk or scuttle past them. He straightened his shoulders and started.

To his astonishment, his presence had a cattle-prod effect on Sir Hendryck. The great man stood up a little straighter as Dr Sweet attempted to walk between the two men.

'Dr Sweet? Dr Sweet. David,' he said without looking at the Director, or attempting to get any kind of formal introduction – Dr Sweet was not so far gone that he didn't recognize an echo of how he had treated Dr Pumfrey just ten minutes before.

'Sir Hendryck,' said Dr Sweet on a falling note, coolly failing to inject into his voice the expectant tone of a lower-ranking scientist. He smiled politely and absently raised one of his killer's hands to smooth down his tie – the killer's hand that could, say, have grasped Sir Hendryck by the throat and slammed his empurpled head back against the wall. 'How are you?' he continued. 'It's good to see you again.'

Sir Hendryck raised an eyebrow, still smiling, and still without any conversational reference to the Director.

'We met at Lisbon: the apoptosis conference.'

'Yes. *Yes*. Yes, of course.' Sir Hendryck clearly did not remember, but was delighted that this contact bolstered the legitimacy of their encounter now. 'And how are you . . . bearing up?' He ventured this question with the nearest semblance of humility that a man of his age, seniority and profound belief in his own social and intellectual superiority could manage; a hesitation bordering on diffidence without any appreciable incursion.

'Oh, work is always difficult at this time of year,' Dr Sweet deadpanned, 'and we have so much experimental work along with preparing various publications. And I am trying to organize a little holiday for my family later in the spring.' This last sentence was a barefaced lie, but an indispensable part of the coded message he was sending to Sir Hendryck: he did not care to discuss his current difficulties explicitly, he was saying, his scientific work was far more important. But make no mistake, protecting family and children was his first priority. It was a superb, steely performance, and Sir Hendryck acknowledged it with a minute Teutonic nod of respect. Dr Sweet smiled and continued on his way, after giving the Director a mute little greeting.

It was all he could do to stop himself running again. Where did he get this kind of chutzpah? What was this feeling that buzzed in his bones, cartilage, his skin? Back in his lab, everyone saluted him with a jump. Dr Sweet ran a little check inside his head. Had that stopped feeling good? No, that had not stopped feeling good. His little fiefdom, his principality was now showing its unelected ruler undreamt-of levels of obeisance. What matter that it was soon to be overrun by his enemies and partitioned and annulled in a dozen different ways? This period of loving submission from his subjects was all the sweeter, all the more exquisite for their monarch's impending exile.

Looking preoccupied, Dr Sweet swam into his office and refreshed himself by checking on the continued presence of the media encampment outside. They were still there; if anything, there were more of them. They had all heard the story of how he had been led out of the front door by two policemen and none of them wanted to miss the spectacle of his re-arrest, although they imagined the coppers in uniform, and Dr Sweet in cuffs and a white coat.

Hattie knocked on the door, and made so bold as to come in and close it behind her. She looked girlishly shy and obviously wanted to say something important.

Dr Sweet had been dreading this moment. It hurt his heart to look at her, and it hurt his heart to think about her, which he did quite a few times every day, always with a fishhook-tweak. Did she want to say something understanding and gentle about their last, terrible meeting?

'David, I think we should go to the zebrafish room.'

The zebrafish room? The scene of their assignations in happier times? This was seriously bringing him down, but he went anyway. And when they were right by the zebrafish tanks, Hattie smiled as if in the middle of some frozen discourse, her hand arrested in mid-gesture, about to slap her forehead with her palm.

'We have bred zebrafish without *BAD*, which is proapoptotic, yeah? And apoptosis, *cell death*, is vital for the prevention of cancers, yeah?'

'Yes,' said Dr Sweet with baffled coldness. Already extensively accustomed to his prestige, he was displeased by this tone of casual familiarity on the part of one of his subjects, particularly this one.

'And so if *BAD* is important, these fish should all have cancer, but they don't.'

'No. No, they don't.' Dr Sweet could feel the chill of professional failure return, mingled with his sexual rejection.

'But apoptosis is needed through all stages of development, so shouldn't our mutant fish look really *fucked up* by now?'

There was a silence while they both looked down into the cold, dark tank.

'Yes,' he said thoughtfully, 'yes I suppose they should.'

'David,' said Hattie. 'What has happened is this. Gene

duplication is common in zebrafish, isn't it? So there will just be another *BAD* gene, mostly similar to the one we've got rid of, ninety per cent similar. When we get the sequence of the zebrafish genome, we'll find another *BAD* gene. That's why our mutants look so healthy, isn't it?'

Dr Sweet conceded her point. It was smart work and it clarified things. But it took them all the way back to square one so he was disinclined to celebrate. It was time to change the subject.

'So, how was your trip?' He couldn't say 'honeymoon'; the confectionery word stuck to his palate. 'How's Arlen?'

'Oh David,' said Hattie, wretched with unhappiness and longing to put her arms around him as in the naughty, conspiratorial old days. Her honeymoon had, of course, been an unmitigated disaster. Their sexual problems had hardly been solved by Hattie's obsessing over Dr Sweet's crisis, and she couldn't bring herself to tell Arlen what this new complication was. The trip had been cut short: no hiking, no wilderness, no romantic adventure, no nothing. They had parted company at the airport in a sour, glowering silence. Their marriage was effectively over, and their terrible, expensive mistake stunned them both. 'David, I want to . . . I wanted to—'

'It's OK, Hattie, I wanted to say something actually. I wanted to apologize for the way I behaved.' These last sentences slipped out of his mouth, part of the autopilot self-assurance to which he now had mysterious access. And did he sense that Hattie wanted to rekindle their relationship?

Of course he did. But wilfully, cruelly obtuse, he behaved as if all Hattie wanted to do was talk about the difficult circumstances of their break-up, wanting to let him down gently. He kept up the front of tragic, yet magnificently dignified loneliness, *apologizing* for his ill-natured jibes, implicitly humble and even tacitly congratulatory in the face of Hattie's happy young life.

And all the time he knew, he guessed, he felt what pain was in Hattie's heart. At the very least he knew she wanted comfort, wanted – heaven help her – a hug, after the calamity of her non-marriage.

'Oh, David—'

'No, Hattie, that's all right. I'm all right. I behaved very badly. It was very stupid of me. You don't have to say anything. I'm glad you and Arlen' – getting the name right – 'have found happiness together.'

As Dr Sweet hiked up to the moral high ground he was euphoric with lack of oxygen.

'David, Arlen and I . . .' Hattie found that she couldn't tell Dr Sweet what had happened, despite his disingenuous little nudge in talking about their 'happiness'.

Dr Sweet gave her his bravest, most sexy, saintly smile possible. 'Hattie, dearest, I told you.' He reached out and stroked her arm, downwards from the shoulder to the elbow, cupping it briefly. 'I'll be all right. I've got to go now.'

The buzzing agitation in his body had subsided now, or rather, it had normalized in some way, regulating its existence so that he was aware only of a pleasant continuous hum. Walking was easier, power-assisted; it felt like moving on an airport travelator. Dr Sweet gathered up his files and put them in his bag with the superb agility of a young Nureyev. He swivelled and positively danced on the balls of his feet.

Five thirty: time to leave the lab. With the Director's

permission, he had ordered a car on the Ruzowitsky account. A needlessly large people carrier now idled at the front entrance, and the photographers, guessing who it was for, had cleared a path to the passenger door.

Dr Sweet did his semi-weightless travelator stride out of the lift, into the lobby and past Arthur, who now had only solicitous smiles for the office hero. The cameras massed, a lens mosaic.

Emerging from the double doors, and honoured with a twenty-one flashgun salute, Dr Sweet remembered what it was that had looked so strange about his appearance in the men's room mirror. Was he imagining it or did he have fewer grey hairs? Did he, in fact, have *more* hair altogether?

16

Half a mile from home, Dr Sweet had the car drop him off so he could walk the rest of the way. The traffic wasn't bad, and the classical light music station on the radio was soothing, but he wanted to get out and walk. He wanted to try out this new feeling.

Dr Sweet was on the Holloway Road, London's most Soviet avenue, wide, yet clenched with gridlocked traffic, between whose immobile columns shivering entrepreneurs attempted to sell the drivers cellophaned single roses or copies of the evening paper. On the pavements, trestle tables displayed capsule calculator batteries, rolls of black plastic rubbish bags pinched tight in the middle with elastic bands, zippo lighters that flashed shimmeringly when chinked open, posters of Tupac Shakur, and miniatures of Padre Pio. On the other side, by the bus stop, a man declaimed the gospel according to St Matthew through a megaphone. At regular intervals, yellow metal Metropolitan Police signs, mounted like easels, constituted an alternative, sensationalist local news outlet. Murder, sexual assault. At 3.45a.m. last Monday a man was knifed by two others in the course of an altercation. Had Dr Sweet seen anything? Did he wish to telephone the Crime-stoppers anonymous information line?

He was well enough used to the heavy tread of the Holloway Road, but it had no effect on him now. Walking along, he almost felt as if his steps must not be too vigorous or enthusiastic lest he jounce floatingly up into the air.

Was this what being *young* was like? Was this how he'd felt twenty, twenty-five years ago? Dr Sweet realized the answer all at once: hell, no. When he was young, chivvied by his parents, tense and worried at school and university, no money to do anything or go anywhere, he didn't feel like this.

'Oy!'

Dr Sweet flinched and turned. Like everyone else on the Holloway Road, he was hyper-aware of when an 'Oy!' was aimed at him and no one else. This one was loud enough to make the backs of his hands prickle.

'Oy! Mr Sweet!'

It was a man and his wife, or maybe his girlfriend, with a small child. They were waving and giving him the thumbs-up. A few more people stopped to see who they were shouting at, then they too turned to Dr Sweet and cheered and waved, giving him a thumbs-up. A few cars in the short-stay drop-off area outside the supermarket honked adoringly, and from the driver's side of one, a forearm and fist came out and punched the air in salute, like a single, twanging antenna.

His admirers couldn't see Dr Sweet blushing; how long had it been since he'd blushed with pleasure? He had blushed with mortification and dismay often enough recently, maybe *flushed* was closer to it. But blushing?

Dr Sweet waved back with a rueful, lopsided smile that said, You know and I know I shouldn't be deriving pleasure from this. Then he travelatored forward, hurdling the *oys* and honks and grins.

It was just outside the Diadem, a colossal fun pub converted from a disused cinema, that the fan worship stopped him in his tracks. Two young men in leather bomber jackets and pale Gap chinos gasped with pleasure at the sight of him. 'David,' one said.

Did he know them? They looked familiar. One had an odd fringe and a moustache. 'David, David,' said the other, grinning so that his front row of teeth clamped chipmunkishly over his lower lip, hopping from foot to foot, holding the end of each too-long sleeve in his fist.

'Yes?' said Dr Sweet uncertainly.

'Don't you recognize us?' he beamed. His bomber jacket had a tartan lining. 'It's us, Barry and Colin. Barry *Cole* and Colin *McCready*.'

His arresting officers.

'Oh Jesus,' said Dr Sweet, unable at that moment to keep the horror out of his voice. Why was it they looked so young?

'It's all right,' said Barry, as if Dr Sweet had apologized for something. 'Come and have a drink.' He was chewing a fresh stick of gum, and there were little breaths of sweetness coming from him. From the hand of a passerby, a strip of discarded cigarette packet cellophane helicoptered glistening to the pavement.

Dr Sweet followed the two of them into the giant pub, a deafening Vegas-style trading floor of leisure. Towards the far corner – and the bar took some minutes to traverse – was the family area where Barry and Colin's wives and children were waiting. Dr Sweet's appearance generated double-taking ripples of celebrity recognition and awe, like an Edwardian Prince moving along a crowded railway station with two equerries.

Colin's partner, Jean, was with her two daughters, Myfanwy and Frances; Barry's wife, Kathryn, had their young son, Conor. The children had Cokes and Sprites and bags of fluorescent cheesy snacks, which they were currently neglecting in favour of a lacrosse-style game with nets on sticks and big fluffy purple balls which occasionally bounced over to their table, though with insufficient mass to upset any drinks. Jean and Kathryn were about the only people in the pub to have no great respect for Dr Sweet's fame, and merely smiled. All around them the Diadem boomed.

Dr Sweet had asked for a beer, amateurishly neglecting to specify the brand, and Colin came back from the bar with a pint of bitter – warm, soapy treacly beer he hadn't tasted since his student days.

'Listen, David,' said Barry grandly when the round was all sorted out. 'You really shouldn't worry. To be honest, we all thought this little piece of nonsense would have been dropped by now.' Looking him directly in the eye, Barry then pursed his lips so intensely Dr Sweet thought he was indulging in some sort of homoerotic no-hands kiss-blowing, but without relinquishing his gaze, Barry merely brought his brimming drink up and sipped.

'Listen,' Dr Sweet said at last. 'Isn't it improper for you to be buying me drinks like this?'

'It would be improper, if we were police officers, certainly,' said Barry, 'but we're not.'

'No,' said Colin, 'we're not.'

The Diadem roared. Dr Sweet struggled to make sense of what he'd been told.

'You're not?'

'Ho no. We're not.'

'Then what are you?'

'*Retired!*'

Colin and Barry said it both together, and then brought their glasses up for a tandem swallow, like Swiss clock figures.

'Retired?' asked Dr Sweet weakly as a big purple ball bounced amiably off the side of his head.

'We've retired. Ill health,' said Colin briskly. 'Stress. Thirteen years in, and the stress was unreal.'

'It was doing your head in,' said Barry supportively.

'Yours, too,' was Colin's comradely response.

'So we've got a very nice retirement package with benefits. And do you know what?' A strange, dreamy sadness clouded Barry's face. 'It's good to get your retirement in while the kids are still toddlers.'

They all turned and looked at the children. Myfanwy, Frances and Conor, playing their lacrosse game in the play pit. Many other drinkers were looking at their children, too.

'To be quite honest, David,' said Barry at last. 'It was what you did that inspired me. Your achievement.'

Dr Sweet felt the syrupy beer stealthily unbutton the waistcoat of his alert state.

'There was no achievement,' he said, but with less finality than strict candour demanded.

'Don't be so modest, David,' said Colin. 'You saw a child in danger and you acted, at considerable hazard to yourself. The man you confronted, it turns out he was on the Register because of exposing himself in a children's playground some years ago. But who knows where that behaviour might have led?'

At that instant, Dr Sweet tried to remember the events of that night in PriceBest, but found that he couldn't order them into a narrative. Cause and effect were uncoupled; consecutive acts were disordered. The shop, the man, Kamil, his little girl – the images allowed themselves to be shuffled and reshuffled. What *had* he actually done?

'What have *I* actually done?' demanded Barry rhetorically. 'When have I showed any courage like that?'

Colin wasn't having this. 'Now come on, Barry. Come on, Barrington, my son. I've seen you go steaming in.' Barry smiled modestly. The tense hierarchical division between the two of them, and indeed their professional antipathy to Dr Sweet, so obvious when they were interviewing him at the station, seemed to have dissolved in the spirit of good fellowship.

'The thing is, though,' Barry continued, 'I've never had a bad one. I've never done a real riot or a real picket line duty, the way our forefathers did. It's just, I don't know. The technology does the job now. CS pepper spray, CCTV. When did we get the chance to take someone on the way David did? Did I tell you my grandfather was evacuated at Dieppe?'

'Yes you did,' said Kathryn acidly, speaking for the first time.

The Diadem made a sound like surf retreating over pebbles. A ragged cheer from the children greeted the arrival in the kids' play area of Uncle Chuff, a tall thin-faced man in a multi-coloured suit and jester's medieval hat who the Diadem's licensee had hired to amuse the children.

'I know what you're going to ask, David.' Barry was more expansive now. David sagged a little; the heavy bitter had unhooked the hawser wires that kept his torso vertical. 'You're going to ask what I'm going to do in my retirement. Well, the truth is that I'm not sure. One option, of course, is to help Colin with his survivalist website.'

As Barry talked, Dr Sweet re-established his internal, intestinal monitoring. Did he still feel good? Did he still feel young? Was getting drunk a different experience? Was getting drunk, being drunk, more enjoyable in his new state of grace? When he'd first got drunk he was twenty years old, a student – very late to lose your drunk virginity. What had impressed him most at the time was the sudden shift from feeling great to feeling like he needed to be sick. What was it ex-Detective-Sergeant Cole was saying about his case?

'Basically, this guy, this proprietor is changing his story. Back and forth, back and forth. First he said he was there, saw it all. Then he says he wasn't; he was in the stockroom, just like you said. But then he says he was sort of in between, close enough to see what was going on. The CPS is reluctant to press it, and frankly I think they would have dropped it by now, had it not been for all your coverage in the media.'

A branching, hairline crack appeared in Dr Sweet's well-being.

'What do you mean?'

'Well,' said Barry, exhaling, 'they don't want to be seen to be giving aid and comfort to some sort of vigilante.'

'But I'm *not*. That's not what happened. It's *not*.' Conviction came back into his voice, together with an unbecoming squeak of panic.

'Yes, well, I understand that,' said Barry, closing off the discussion with an opaque form of words that reminded Dr Sweet of his old policeman's demeanour. How very much Dr Sweet now regretted coming into the Diadem.

Uncle Chuff was strapping strange bulletproof-type vests, made of a prickly black material, onto each of the shrieking children in his care. Soon they were all kitted out like this – lacking only black peaked caps and rifles. The attention of Barry, Colin, Kathryn and Jean, along with all the other parent-drinkers, was wholly engaged as Conor, Myfanwy and Frances grouped expectantly around Uncle Chuff. Spotlights picked out a part of the wall covered in a green fuzzy felt, and decorated with big cartoon cows and zebras, hippos and horses, like colossal fridge magnets.

Colin grabbed Dr Sweet's upper arm and shook it in an excess of friendliness. He grinned. 'David, mate,' he said, positively beaming, 'you've got such fucking *respect*. This is what it's all about.' Colin gestured with his head at Uncle Chuff and the children, and turned round to watch.

A tape-recorded drum roll spilt from the speakers. Then, for once, the Diadem went quiet, expectant. Uncle Chuff strode out to address them in a broad Lancashire accent through a headset mike. He had a gangly, daddy-long-legs stride, as if he were walking on stilts.

> *Me name's Uncle Chuff*
> *And I know me stuff*
> *But the question I hear*
> *Is 'Why's this bloke here?'*

Dr Sweet and his daughter

Well ponder no more,
Get ready to roar,
The secret that's hid is
I'm here to throw kiddies!

Now the noise and cheering was deafening. Uncle Chuff swooped down and picked up little Myfanwy by what looked like the scruff of her neck and the small of her back (but was actually two small handles sewn into her jacket) and threw her with a great hoisting motion, like heaving sacks of potatoes into the back of a truck. Myfanwy hit the fuzzy felt wall and stuck there, on her back, attached like Velcro. She screamed and giggled with pure joy. Uncle Chuff did a jubilant prancing dance, legs splayed, lifting each knee in turn, and with arms bent at the elbows, he punched the air above each rising knee. All the little black-jacketed children mimicked him.

Uncle Chuff!
Uncle Chuff!
Uncle Chuff!

They gathered around him, clamouring to be thrown. One by one, Uncle Chuff grabbed the tiny supplicants and hurled them against the wall. Splat! Splat! Splat! Soon there were about five or six screaming children, pupils dilated with over-excitement, wriggling and scattered over the green fuzzy wall like bugs on a windscreen. The Diadem erupted. Smaller, slighter adults clambered into the kids area, begging to be thrown themselves.

Dr Sweet rose to his feet, and Barry, Colin and the other drinkers looked over at him, instantly assessing his frame as slighter than the other patrons. A cheer began to erupt, but Dr Sweet had turned round, hunching his bag against his side, and was beginning to jog for the far distant exit.

17

Cordie knew the holiday spirit was over the minute her mum started telling her off. While they were living in her dad's little house, she thought she could be pretty sure of never getting told off, but now she was.

'Oh, Cordie, what have you *done?*'

She had used the backs of some of her mum's letters from work to paint on. She had done it before and her mum had never got cross. But come to think of it, those had been letters that her mummy had thrown away in the waste-paper basket. These were letters she had found in Mummy's brown leather briefcase, and one of them was a letter she had opened on the doormat. She had drawn the sea on all of them, the bluey-grey sea, the sea that goes on for ever. She'd had an idea she could Sellotape them all together, then she'd got out her poster paints – a tin with shallow circular pots in them that had mostly gone crackly and dry. She'd muddied them up with some water from the tap, and then painted the sea on the backs of the letters; blue-grey sea that went over the edges of the paper and onto the table because she hadn't put any newspaper down.

'Oh *no*! Oh, *Cordie*! What *is* all this? What's all this

terrible *mess*? Oh, Cordie you're going to have to clear all this up.'

Cordie's face crumpled and she was just going to cry when they heard the front-door bell.

'Well, I can't believe that's your father,' said Cordie's mum, sounding just as cross with him as she was with her. 'He's very early.' Alice stomped out into the hall, and Cordie started to cry, expecting her dad to come in any second so she could run to him.

But it wasn't her dad. It was a man. A man came into the kitchen with her mummy, who was wearing a funny sort of smile and looking nervous.

'Cordie,' she said, 'you remember Lyle, don't you? He's popped in to see us.'

The man smiled and turned his head a bit; he had a ponytail tied up with a red elastic band.

Oh, yes. It was the man from the swimming pool. Cordie remembered bumping into him at the pool when she got water in her eyes and it stung. He looked different.

'Hello, Cordie!' said Lyle, and stuck out his hand, the way her grandad did sometimes, and Cordie knew that she was expected to hold it with her hand and waggle it up and down.

'I've got something for you, Cordie,' said Lyle.

'It's not my birthday yet,' said Cordie smartly, which made Lyle and her mummy giggle in a funny nervous way.

'Well, I know,' said Lyle. 'Well, I suppose I *didn't* know. Ha! I don't know when your birthday is, so this is a sort of an un-birthday present. Here it is!' Lyle took out a pair of child-size pool goggles, tinted blue. 'I didn't have time to wrap them or anything.'

Cordie took them wordlessly and her mum said, '*What* do you say Cordie?'

'Thank you.' Cordie put them on and the whole room was blue. The kitchen table was blue, the garden out of the window was blue, her mummy was blue and Lyle was blue. They were both smiling at her.

'I think she looks like you,' said Lyle.

'I think she looks like her father,' said her mum, and Cordie thought that just because she had gone quiet and was wearing goggles, they must think she couldn't hear them or something.

'So,' she could clearly hear Lyle saying to her mum, 'this problem you're having with the heating in this house. I'm sure it's just a question of bleeding the upstairs radiators. I've got a key with me.'

Bleeding? With a key? Cordie didn't know what the man was talking about.

'Can I try out my goggles in the sink?'

'Yes, of course, darling, only try not to get your hair too wet.'

Cordie filled up the kitchen sink and put her head under. She looked around at the completely blue undersea sink world. There was the plug with its little chain, all blue. She fished about and brought a teacup down into the deep blue sea, and then a spoon and she made them swim about together until she got bored and, with a great splashy whoosh, brought her head up out of the sink.

Both the adults were gone. She looked around. They weren't in the blue kitchen or the blue garden. She heard noises and footsteps overhead. They must be in her mum's bedroom making the radiators bleed. When would they be coming down?

Cordie dabbed her forehead with a towel and went for a little wander around the entirely blue house. She opened a cupboard door and then the washing machine, and felt around with her finger in the rubbery seal. She found a 5p coin down there and kept it. When would Mum and Lyle be coming down? She could hear a funny sort of scratchy-slithery noise.

Cordie resolved to go upstairs and ask if she could have fish fingers on toast tonight. She walked up the blue stairs, slowly, dawdlingly, one at a time, counting the steps. She hung on the handrail a bit, then sat on the stairs and rubbed her finger along the woolly carpety texture and its brass edging. Then she got up and walked a bit further to her mum's bedroom. Her forehead still felt cold and damp from the sink. She would ask about using her big towel as well as the fish fingers.

There were definitely funny sounds coming from the room. She walked onto the landing and looked out of the window into the blue undersea street with cars and people swimming along – there were the photographers floating around opposite the house. She saw one notice her at the window and ducked back. Then she turned round and looked at herself in the landing mirror. Her blue hoopy T-shirt and jeans, hair in bunches, eyes like a funny blue goggly-eyed insect.

Funny sounds were still coming from her mum's room. Radiators. Blood everywhere. Maybe Lyle and her mummy were doing an operation on the radiators, like the one she saw on television at school once, only for some reason they were using a key instead of a scalpel blade.

Now she had her hand on the highly polished blue

doorknob, and for a moment looked at her bulgy reflection in it. She twisted the knob a bit; it squeaked and the funny noises suddenly stopped altogether; she started to open the door.

Then she remembered Barbie lying on the floor just inside the doorway of her bedroom. What about making Barbie swim underwater in the sink with the spoon and teacup? Cordie let the doorknob go, and went to pick up Barbie and thoughtfully stroked her blue hair. She went into her room and changed Barbie into a swimming costume. Then she went out onto the landing again and held Barbie up to the window so she could see what was happening out in the street. Together, they looked out at the silent aquamarine world, a world in which Dr Sweet was just beginning to appear, walking round the corner from the next street. He really *was* early.

Cordie and Barbie looked around, wondering if Lyle and her mum had finished their operation yet or if they would want Dr Sweet to help. Decisively, Cordie swung Barbie's arm up so that she could tap sharply on Mummy's door.

'Daddy's coming up the road,' she called out smartly, and quickly went back to check on his progress. She knew that it was only ever her dad that the photographers were interested in. Then she jogged back down the stairs to the kitchen with Barbie. With a plunge, and undaunted by the icy cold, Barbie jumped into the sink and swam around in the translucent inky water next to Cordie's great moon-like submerged face, bobbing about with the teacup and spoon and swimming, mermaid-like, in and out of the grater.

Cordie withdrew her head when she felt something

brush by her back. It was Lyle, with her mum behind him, apparently in a great hurry.

'I can go out of the back way, can I?' he said, with a sidelong glance at Cordie.

'Mmm, yes,' said her mum, biting her lip with her arms folded. 'That'll be a quicker way for you to go home anyway, won't it?'

'Yes, right, that's right.'

'Goodbye, Lyle,' said Cordie politely, holding out her hand.

'What? Oh yes, right, bye,' said Lyle, waving vaguely at her as he tried to unfasten the garden door.

'Mum, can we have fish fingers on toast tonight?' asked Cordie.

'Yes, yes, you can,' she said, helping Lyle out of the door into the garden, where he scurried down the path and out of the back gate. Cordie could see his ponytail bobbing away urgently in the back alley.

'Cordie, it's probably best if . . . It's best if you didn't—'

Then they heard Dr Sweet's key in the lock.

18

'Hello!' said Dr Sweet from the hallway. 'Hello?'

No-one answered him. Dr Sweet unslung his shoulder bag and put it on the floor, then casually draped his jacket over the banisters.

'Hello?' He went through into the kitchen, where Alice and Cordie both looked at him blankly, their foreheads apparently slick with sweat. No, Cordie's forehead actually had water on it.

'What's been going on here?' asked Dr Sweet equably.

'Cordie's been putting her face in a sinkful of water, haven't you, Cordie?' said Alice quickly.

'Why?'

'To try out my goggles,' replied Cordie.

That was when Dr Sweet noticed Cordie's goggles, which she had pulled down to her neck.

'Goggles,' he said genially. 'And who got you those, then?'

'I'm sorry about this awful mess, David,' said Alice with suddenness and contrition. 'Cordie's been painting on the kitchen table without putting newspapers down.'

'Oh well, not to worry,' said Dr Sweet easily, looking at her pictures among the debris. 'Cordie, you are naughty to make a mess, especially when your poor mother's actually got you a present!'

'What do you mean?' asked Alice.

'The goggles,' he said, looking up.

'Cordie, do you want to use my big towel to dry your forehead?' asked Alice. 'You don't want to get a chill.'

Cordie scampered off upstairs. 'Mum and Dad not back yet?' he asked.

'Rosemary said they were going to a concert at the Wigmore Hall,' said Alice.

'What's she been doing these paintings on?' asked Dr Sweet with a little indulgent laugh.

'On the backs of letters, letters we haven't even read yet. It's too bad of her.' Alice frowned.

At that moment, Dr Sweet saw something that made him stop, like a hiccup or a jab in the ribs. An envelope, addressed to himself from Dartmouth Media, an envelope that had been ripped open. Very slowly, he turned Cordie's painting over and read:

Dear Dr Sweet,

I am very pleased to inform you, on behalf of Dartmouth Media, that you have won one of this year's Heart of Gold awards, to reward exceptional courage shown by ordinary people, this to be presented at the Dorchester Hotel on Thursday 27th March this year.

I am further empowered to inform you that you have won the '32-carat distinction' prize awarded to that person who, in the opinion of the judges, has shown the most remarkable act of bravery.

I would be obliged if you could complete the details form enclosed, and confirm that you will be available on the awards date, and that you will, within reason, make yourself available for relevant promotional duties.

Congratulations!

With every good wish,

Yours sincerely,

Angie Meredith
Media Relations

A brief handwritten note had been appended under the signature:

Speaking as a mum, can I say how glad I am you got the prize?!

Alice and Dr Sweet re-read the letter in silence and took in the names of Dartmouth Media's advisory council, printed on the letterhead, that had deliberated over this year's award list. The council was composed of life peers, former Cabinet ministers, a Reform rabbi, a conservative Catholic theologian, a distinguished therapist and the editor of the newspaper in whose publication the results of the ceremony would occupy twelve or fifteen pages.

'Well,' said Dr Sweet, feeling buoyant. '*Someone's* on my side.'

Alice snorted.

'What?' he asked.

'David, it's a transparent attempt to flush you out.'

'Flush me out?'

'Yes. Who do you think has been pestering you for the past month? Badgering you for details about *our* private life? Exactly these people. How is this award any different?'

'Well, I don't know, Alice,' said Dr Sweet with a bland little smile. 'It *is* the Heart of Gold awards.'

Everybody knew about these awards; they were given to teenage girls who'd pulled pensioners from overturned buses and toddlers who'd telephoned the hospital when their mothers had collapsed with asthma attacks. Their tales of untrained, civilian courage were a rare, almost uniquely redemptive moment in the tabloid year of voyeurism, envy and bad feeling. But this was the first time the award had gone to someone like Dr Sweet, someone who had taken such direct action.

'And anyway,' scoffed Alice, 'you've already told the police that this whole thing is a misunderstanding. And how on earth can they give it to someone with . . . with *all this* hanging over them? It's not on.'

Dr Sweet had never won anything in his life. He'd never won any of the awards and medals that various European scientific organizations had founded, and as for a Fellowship of the Royal Society, he could whistle for it.

The very first time he'd used an Apple Macintosh computer in the 1980s, a small but heavy grey box with a screen the size of his current rewritable CD-drive, he had printed the name Dr DLK Sweet FRS on the lab's new laser writer, just to see how it looked.

It looked good. He liked the symmetry of three letters either side. Before anyone could see it, Dr Sweet crumpled the paper up and threw it away. Very often, in the years that followed, he measured achievements and progress against that imaginary title. It was only with this letter in his hand that he realized the FRS was now out of reach – on tiptoe, at the fullest extent of his fingers, it was just out of reach, and getting higher every minute.

Outside he could hear the photographers rustling. The pair of them listened to the press in the street with the same intimidated connoisseurship that colonial army officers attended to restless native movements. Next door, they could hear the sounds of *The Jungle Book*'s music and final credits. There was a soft inhaling hissing noise from the disc and then nothing. Dr Sweet waited for Cordie to run into the kitchen and say hello to him properly, but nothing happened.

At that moment, Alice's voice sounded crisper and cleaner to Dr Sweet than it had for a long time, as if it had been remixed through some impossibly sophisticated digital remastering system, or as if she were speaking on the top of an alp, through air of crystalline purity.

'David,' she said, 'please tell me that you are not going to accept the Heart of Gold award.'

PART THREE

19

The months passed; the clocks went forward and bright, cold, changeable winter became ambiguous spring. In the parks, flowers and shrubs were coming into bloom earlier than ever, and all along north and west London, travellers on the top of double-decker buses found that the thump of overhanging branches on the roof was muffled by leaves. Zippered fleeces, cashmere topcoats, padded reversible ski jackets and collapsible umbrellas were left behind as Londoners found themselves outside in pleasant walking weather; taxi drivers found custom less easy to come by and as the weeks ticked past the streetscapes were frequently framed by a fierce blue sky. The weather was London's friend that spring: there were no floods to destroy uninsured property, no freeze to trap the unwary pensioner or motorist, and hospitals and mortuaries took a breather after the winter's annual frenzy of activity. And in the centre of London itself, in one of the city's grandest streets, a boulevard of elegance and amplitude, the state broadcaster was beginning a new series of its popular radio current affairs programme, *And This Concerns Me How?*

And This Concerns Me How? had been on the air for three years and was one of the most listened-to discussion shows on the radio, with a lively and popular website. The show's presenter, Sho Prynne, chaired a weekly discussion on some hot topic, but without the consensual detachment traditionally expected. She would often weigh in on someone's side, shamelessly exploiting her position to trash and dismiss the views of an invited contributor, an insult compounded by failing to despatch that person's fee for some months. Sho was a fan of dissent and discord and an aficionado of irony.

Before the first programme in the new series began, each contributor had been asked to say something 'for level' by the sound engineers behind the glass. It was a ritual that always discomfited the newcomers. These technical niceties were, in any case, rendered irrelevant by the end of this show, when the bellowing would be loud enough to trigger feedback on a par with a Jimi Hendrix guitar solo.

She had begun with a scripted introduction.

Welcome to *And This Concerns Me How?* with me, Sho Prynne. Today we are looking at the question of courage and the individual's moral responsibility to intervene and take action. Is such action irrelevant, even irresponsible? Should we ever 'have a go'? With me is Dr David Sweet, the man who as many of you know is the winner, the *controversial* winner, I should say . . .

Sho had added this *faux* spontaneous moment in advance.

. . . of this year's Heart of Gold distinction award, for his bravery in physically taking on a registered sex offender who was threatening a young girl. But of course Dr Sweet was also arrested in connection with this act, and a charge of some sort is now expected to be brought within days. With me also is Barry Cole, the former police officer who arrested Dr Sweet, now retired and currently Executive Director of the Moral Action project, inspired, it is understood, by his contact with Dr Sweet. And lastly, we have Chris Fareham, a north London community leader and churchman.

Dr Sweet, can I ask you first how you feel about being offered this award, and indeed how you feel about accepting it?

Dr Sweet began by smiling, an obsolete gesture on the radio, and Sho motioned him to speak with an impatient circular hand movement.

'Well, Sho,' he said, 'I must say first of all that the media coverage of the events leading up to my arrest has been woefully inaccurate and I fully expect, incidentally, to be vindicated.'

Nothing nettled Sho more than a supercilious and diversionary remark by a member of the public about the media.

'Vindicated, Dr Sweet?' she snapped. 'You mean you expect to be found *not guilty*? You expect a jury will acquit you?'

Dr Sweet had not expected such a fierce and specific question, coupled with a disconcertingly non-specific air of hostility.

'I expect to be vindicated by whatever outcome,' he replied, 'but as for your question about the Heart of Gold. I am very happy to accept it.'

'And why is that, Dr Sweet?' said Sho impatiently.

'Because for one thing I am flattered to be honoured like this, and for another I think it's right that individual acts of courage should be rewarded in a society where individuals are encouraged to think that a peaceful, comfortable, entirely risk-free life is a kind of civil liberty.'

'But surely this is a very *controversial* award, Dr Sweet?'

'That may well be, Sho,' he said, 'if people have disagreed about it; if they have controverted on the subject, then yes I agree it is controversial. Presumably, however, what you're suggesting is that it's questionable or wrong?'

'Well, isn't it?' asked Sho, nettled again and reluctant to give Dr Sweet the satisfaction of upholding his pedantic objection.

'No. No, it's not wrong. I don't believe it is wrong.'

'Dr Sweet,' said Sho, leaning back and signalling to Chris Fareham that she was about to bring him into the discussion, 'you must be aware that to give the Heart of Gold to someone for killing another human being with his bare hands, albeit accidentally and with the highest possible motives, is tantamount to asking the public to take the law into their own hands.' Dr Sweet made as if to answer this, but Sho cut him off with one of her most annoying hand movements, a police-style stop signal, raising the palm of one hand, while with the other she indicated Fareham.

'Chris Fareham, you have written and lectured widely on the boundaries of public rights and responsibilities – what do you think?'

'I think it's a disgraceful award,' said Chris in a low,

resentful drone, his gaze cast piously down, eyelids fluttering slightly. 'It's thoroughly irresponsible.'

'And why is that, Chris?' Sho's expression was now urgently attentive and supportive, like a midwife at the beginning of what promised to be a difficult labour.

'Because it sends completely the wrong message to communities in the UK,' was Chris's response. 'It suggests that killing registered sex offenders is in some way acceptable.'

Dr Sweet made a feint, a physical movement at Sho's palm, which was still raised in his direction. He wanted to say that he was not aware of the victim's status in this regard at the time of the incident, but, media novice that he was, felt he could not just shout his objection without the chairperson's permission.

'Well,' said Sho, adding a sceptical head-shaking laugh which suggested she couldn't let that remark pass unchallenged. But instead of allowing Dr Sweet to speak again, she made a tiny boxing-referee break movement with her hands, indicating that both men must hush, and then cued in Barry.

'Barry Cole,' she said severely, 'no matter how revolted and frightened we are by certain lawbreakers in our society, surely it is our duty not to 'have a go' ourselves? Surely we have to sit back and allow the properly constituted authorities to do the job?'

No-one knew better than Sho that using the word 'surely' was code for saying that you were in fact not entirely sure about a widely accepted truism, and were soliciting dispute. That and the phrase 'sit back' got the required response from Barry, who sat forward with an expression like setting cement.

'Sho, can I say something in all sincerity?' he rumbled. 'The greatness of this country was built on actions like the one that David Sweet . . .' He searched for the *mot juste*. 'Like the one David Sweet executed on the twenty-second of December last.' It was all too obvious that the last time he had spoken in public was in court. Chris Fareham gave a mutinous, impertinent snort. Sho considered it, and took a different tack.

'Barry, you're the executive director of the Moral Action Project, a pro-individual organization, and you *support* Dr Sweet.' Caveats like these were essential to remind contributors of the roles in which Sho had cast them. 'You arrested this man on the original charge of murder before your retirement due to stress, and now you've gone through a Damascus-style dark night of the soul. How did that make you *feel*?'

'The feeling was extraordinary, Sho,' replied Barry with a seraphic smile, his concrete face suddenly and completely melting. 'All my life I've been involved with policing the community' – the word 'community' elicited a slight, unconscious nod from everyone present – 'but now I feel as if my *thirteen* years on the force have been on the wrong track. What I should have been doing is acting as an enabler. An enabler who in a real sense enables.' There was another snort from Chris Fareham. 'An enabler who liberates the individual to police him or herself.'

There was a third snort from Chris and Sho allowed him in.

'This is just mob law,' he jeered. 'I've had a look at Mr Cole's Moral Action website and it's just photographs of Mr Sweet here and highly questionable right-wing rabble-rousing. It's pure Fascism.'

'Now look,' Dr Sweet blundered in. 'I'm not responsible for that and I'm not condoning vigilantism, but that man was attacking a young girl.'

'That's not quite what you told the police, David,' said Sho sweetly, and Dr Sweet almost bit his tongue. It wasn't what he'd told the police, was it? No, the man was *menacing* the young girl, a concept somewhere between attacking and threatening to attack. Wasn't he? Is that what happened? Dazed, Dr Sweet tried to remember in the milliseconds available to him. Before he could rally, his highly unwelcome ally Barry Cole had barged in again.

'Listen, David Sweet did what was right, he used his common sense, and the overwhelming majority of people agree.' This was correct, as opinion polls commissioned by Dartmouth Media – who were coincidentally the independent producers of this programme – had established.

'Right? *Right?*' Chris Fareham's voice had gone up about an octave. 'How on earth are we supposed to believe that he knows what's right?'

'Chris,' said Barry, audaciously addressing a remark directly to another contributor without going via the chair, 'nobody's impressed with your flaccid moral relativism. If a child of yours was being threatened like that, you'd do the same thing. So would Sho, so would I, and Dr Sweet we know about. So why pretend otherwise?'

In spite of himself, Dr Sweet said, 'Yes' and Chris Fareham sat forward, white with anger. 'That's a typical arrogant *scientist* attitude.'

For the very first time, Dr Sweet found himself seriously engaged in the discussion. He emerged from his shell of tension and clenched preoccupation with managing the situation. 'Just what do you mean by that?' he said.

Sho sensed that they were now off the point but that a first-class argument was on the way.

'You scientists,' sneered Chris Fareham. 'You really think you've got hold of the objective truth.'

'We have,' said Dr Sweet simply. 'We have got hold of the objective truth. About the physical world, that is precisely what we have objective hold of.'

'Bollocks,' jeered Chris. 'Science is just another belief system. It's incredibly naïve of you not to see that.'

'You're the one being naïve,' said Dr Sweet coldly. 'That's the biggest, most fatuous piece of intellectual pusillanimity I've ever heard.'

'Science is just another religion,' said Chris, more patiently, with a sad, pitying smile.

'Science is not a "belief system", it is *the*, definite article, *truth system*.'

'That's pure authoritarianism. You're so *blind*. Can't you see how blind and arrogant you're being?'

'Can't you see how blind and arrogant *you're* bloody well being?' shouted Dr Sweet, the first time he had raised his voice in intellectual argument since he was a student. 'Here we are in a bloody electrically lit studio transmitting radio waves. Science allowed us to do that, science and the discovery of truth. Do you think if there was a Muslim, a Catholic and a Rastafarian in the room now, on the panel, on this programme, do you think electricity and radio waves would operate differently for each of them, depending on what place those things had in their belief system?'

'That's a cheap shot,' said Chris.

'Look,' hissed Dr Sweet, and in the next moment Sho realized that the idiot meant this expression literally: he was asking them to look at the carafe he'd lifted off the table. He was doing something visual on the radio. 'Look.'

Sho interjected lamely, 'Dr Sweet has lifted a carafe of still mineral water off the table.'

'Science has given us an understanding of the cognitive and physiological processes whereby we can grasp something like this.' Still holding the carafe, Dr Sweet leaned over towards Fareham with a lurch, banging Sho painfully on the shoulder with it. He then held it over Fareham's head and said, 'And science has given us an understanding of what happens if I let it go, unless your separate but equal belief system dictates that it's going to float up to the ceiling.'

'Waaurggh!' said Fareham, convulsively thrashing his arms over his head, as if a giant wasp had settled on his nose. He knocked the carafe out of Dr Sweet's hand and it landed with a heavy *chink* on the table, the contents glugging out audibly.

'I wasn't going to drop it on your stupid fat head, don't be such a drama queen,' said Dr Sweet indignantly, appealing to Sho.

'That's water you can hear, everyone, not blood,' said Sho with an uneasy attempt at humour.

'How dare you do that to me?' squealed Chris Fareham, shoving Dr Sweet's lapel and hitting the central microphone with a *thunk* that made the technician behind the glass wince while the producer smiled happily.

Barry Cole saw that the moment had come for action, the sort of bold action he had been espousing.

'Stand back please, Sho,' he said, removing something from his jacket pocket, 'I am going to incapacitate the assailant.'

For Chris Fareham the next few seconds were a bit of a blur. One moment he was remonstrating with an arrogant and emotionally unstable scientist, the next he was face down, burying his face in the studio's hard green floor matting, nuzzling it like a pillow, smelling it, tasting it, experiencing it more intimately than anyone ever had or ever would, while his wrists were secured behind his back and Barry's boot was on his neck.

'I think we're out of time,' said Sho.

20

'No, we've got five more minutes,' said the producer through her earpiece.

'We're *out* of *time*,' said Sho with a savage gesture at him, as Chris wriggled soundlessly on the floor, and so the programme concluded with an unprecedented few minutes of classical piano.

Such was Dr Sweet's popularity, or rather such was the remarkable media consensus that the embattled Dr Sweet deserved support, that his reputation was not to suffer on account of this programme. Almost all of his friends and acquaintances listened to it, and one of these was Kamil, proprietor of Archway Road's PriceBest supermarket, who turned off the television in order to tune in on his little transistor radio.

The photographers had bothered them a bit as well – for a while. But there was no doubt that the prosperous Anglo-Saxons down the hill were what the papers were looking for. It wasn't *his* daughter they bothered; Kamil was glad and never read any of the press coverage.

He had given up smoking since the incident, and drinking was something he didn't do anyway. He did a little running, some swimming. He kept his sentry position in the shop, but without the arm behind his back.

He listened to the programme with some detachment, and indeed it was perfectly possible to believe that it had nothing to do with him. When it was over, he switched the radio off and the television back on. He felt what he always felt at five in the afternoon, or indeed two in the afternoon, or even eleven in the morning: Kamil felt tired. The back-breaking work of running the store had never got easier. Up at five thirty, unlocking the heavy steel security shutters over the door – the ones over the other plate-glass windows stayed permanently in place. Taking deliveries of bread, the rolls and croissants that assumed a rock-like texture by early afternoon. Keeping control of the vast stock – the vegetables and fruit displayed moulderingly outside; the shrinkage and pilferage of these perishables theoretically offset by the vast amount of non-time-specific goods like dishwasher salt, which could be kept for ever. And then there was PriceBest's other unique selling point; its only selling point: convenience. They were open from dawn until late. They worked and worked and worked; they worked until there was a pain in their backs and sides and feet. The turnover was enormous but they only just kept their heads above water.

Kamil had thought at first that Dr Sweet liked him; they had had chats. But then one day he paid for his paper and milk without a word and left. Without any explanation he cancelled his home deliveries. Kamil was just another shopkeeper to him, he saw that now. And when he gave Dr Sweet his change, and felt how soft his palm was, the taunting difference was trailed across his senses like a silk banner. That had hurt his feelings, more than Dr Sweet could ever have imagined.

But Kamil's cousin and his cousin's father were scholars in Ankara. His family were distinguished, far more distinguished than the British ignoramuses and louts that hassled and robbed him all the livelong day.

He had come to this country back in 1995; his family came from Kemer in southern Turkey, a blank place which about a decade and a half before had been turned into a giant building site by German and Canadian construction interests, and then into a kind of package-holiday zone. Kamil had worked in one of the hotels as a waiter – lucrative work, too – watching a succession of German, Dutch and British holidaymakers get stunned, traumatized and viscerally upset by the hottest weather they had ever known, trying to behave as if they were in Brittany, attempting to lie on shadeless beaches whose gravelly surface was sun-blasted white, like the scene of a nuclear strike.

But while his brothers went to Germany to work in the service sector, Kamil had come to dark, cold, unforgiving Britain to get married to Sevinç, a second-generation Turkish woman in the UK whom he hardly knew. The idea was that they buy the lease on PriceBest from an elderly Italian couple and sell a whole lot of things the previous people hadn't wished to: cigarettes, newspapers, continental foods.

But hours and hours could go by without anyone ever coming in. It felt dusty behind the security grille, like an Egyptian tomb, walled up with washing powder, aerosol cheese, luxury cat food, shoe-creme applicators and Chicken Tonight.

Even the police had come very, very slowly after the incident. That was the norm. For every racist daubing, every disorder, every burning piece of paper shoved through the letterbox grille, he had phoned the police, and he was wasting his time.

It was only when Kamil actually told them there was a *dead body* in his shop that they came round, and even then not for eighty minutes. Did they think he was making it up?

When the two policemen, Cole and McCready, finally arrived, like unwilling explorers penetrating the tomb, Kamil had looked at his stock, his business concern, as if for the first time, through their eyes. The three of them stood there, looking round at the bulging, teetering goods.

Then they looked again at the dead body lying between them, face up, not squinting or flinching at the ceiling neon strip lights the way anyone else would, the gnarled outdoor face slack and blank, the greasy brown-black jacket flung up behind his head in his last, fatal slide forward.

The dead body. In these British times of peace, the number of ordinary people who had seen a dead body was diminishing rapidly. The police officers had seen plenty, though generally people like Mr O'Rourke here hadn't. Kamil had seen a corpse before, a man who had fallen from the scaffolding in Kemer, and was dead, quite dead, when he hit the ground.

Curtly, the policemen had asked him what had happened. Kamil didn't know, but he had heard the argument between Dr Sweet and this man from outside. He assumed that Dr Sweet had attacked him in some way. Part of him, some obscure part, *wanted* there to be trouble in his shop, real trouble. But trouble that, for once, wasn't directed at him, or for which he could not be held tacitly responsible by the racists and bigots he had encountered these six years in London. He wanted the luxury of witnessing trouble, the way his customers did.

Kamil wished Dr Sweet no harm, but apart from everything else, he knew that with anything less dramatic than what he claimed to have happened, with anything less than *murder*, the event would be deemed some sort of 'accident', and the ultimate culpability in the matter would somehow inevitably revert to him.

So with his eyes on his daughter, the only witness of the event, Kamil had recited what he thought must have happened, apparently inviting her to corroborate and taking her abashed silence as confirmation:

'This man, Mr Sweet, a regular customer, came in and started arguing with this other gentleman; I have not seen him before at any time. There is the bottle.'

They had all looked at the cracked bottle of olive oil.

Then, while waiting for the pathology staff to come and remove the body, there had begun the tiresome business of reviewing the security video tapes, which were inconclusive. Perplexingly, the tapes showed the principals appearing in and out of various screens; they showed their encounter at the till but not the event itself. What they did show was Dr Sweet backing away with O'Rourke holding the bottle, which Kamil had implied, without actually saying, was the murder weapon.

'So are you saying that Mr Sweet managed to get hold of the bottle?' asked Barry Cole, at last, in a manner he knew would be repudiated in court as a leading question. It was best to get the witness's story straightened out here and now.

'That is the bottle,' Kamil had replied, pointing again.

At this stage, Kamil told Zalihe that she should go to

her mother who had remained upstairs and with whom the police did not wish to speak. Finally, once the body had been removed, Kamil gave the police the last delivery address he had for Dr Sweet and they went.

He swabbed and scrubbed where the body had been: there were no particular instructions from the authorities in this respect, even though he had died near food. He almost expected there to be a glowing, radioactive chalk line around where it lay. In fact, he virtually created one with the vigour of his scrubbing.

In the weeks that followed, Kamil saw nothing of Dr Sweet in his shop, and heard from the police only that the body had not been cremated, but was being held in the morgue in the event of a possible inquest or a murder charge. Gazing at the radio now, he couldn't recognize this squalid, disreputable mess. A sheen of myth and news had been varnished over it, the dictates of significance had rounded off its edges. Even now, Kamil couldn't be sure that it wasn't *something else* they were talking about, some later and far more vividly real event which, by a strange coincidence, resembled the scrappy, unpleasant nonsense that had been played out in his store.

Somebody was coming in. Customers? No. It was his daughter Zalihe home from school; she'd brought a friend back with her to play. They scampered in and Zalihe kissed her father as he said hello to her friend, quite distantly and wearily. They put their little backpacks down behind the till, near the little wooden stool that Zalihe sat on when she was with him in the shop, together with a little book that belonged to her friend. His brother Adil had picked them up, and Adil, the driver, would be taking Zalihe's friend home afterwards.

Zalihe's face looked different now; it had changed subtly in the last few months, and Kamil often found himself wondering if witnessing the death of this man had had anything to do with it. Her eyes were sadder and more watchful, the line of her cheeks and chin softer, as if she had put on weight, although this could hardly be true. Sometimes, when she was bent over a book, Kamil could see the planes and folds of her face in a dramatically foreshortened way, and it accentuated how much older she sometimes seemed. Kamil knew that in other circumstances, in other families, Zalihe might be encouraged to have therapy, but the idea horrified him. He believed in letting this chaotic, unformed event wash away into oblivion; bolting it to the struts and supports of meaning and personal significance could only keep its pain alive longer. And in any case, he knew enough about therapy to know that the only form it could possibly take would involve family discussions and Sevinç would not hear of that.

His wife was modest and retiring to a fault; praying many times a day, she hardly, if ever, ventured into the store itself, contenting herself with superintending the passing of its VAT accounts to her father, whose capital had made it all possible in the first place. She and Kamil lived in the two-floor flat above the store with her parents, who mercifully were in Turkey at the time of the killing and were still to return. The couple had never once alluded to the event since it had happened. The only words that had passed between them were when the police had left with the body and Sevinç appeared in the stockroom doorway. Their eyes met and Kamil had said, 'There has been an accident; a customer got into a scuffle with another customer. The police have taken him away.' Thus, with the implication that the officers were discharging a janitorial function in disposing of the ugly corporeal mess, Kamil disposed of the stigma of a visit from the forces of the law. Sevinç watched, gently, as Kamil bent down with a bucket and scrubbing brush to wash the floor, then she went back upstairs to the flat and sat beside Zalihe, stroking her hair as they watched cartoons on TV.

Kamil had never said anything about it to Zalihe and she had never said anything about it to him. She had never been particularly close to her father and Kamil did not know if he was pained or relieved about this. He himself had never been close to his father, and both his parents were now dead.

He went over and looked at the book Zalihe's friend had placed on top of the two backpacks. It was a long, thin paperback, or rather some sort of perfect-bound catalogue or booklet. It had a very large picture of the Eiffel Tower on the front, with the twinkling lights of Paris down below, but the title was simply incredible, *The European Academy of Molecular Biology, Tenth Symposium: Beyond The Genome – Paris, École Normale Supérieure, 18–25 Août*. Inside were incomprehensible descriptions of . . . well, what? Kamil riffled through, perplexed. Scientific experiments? Scientific staff? Laboratories? *Cancer?*

Kamil winced at the subject and turned back to the title page. Here he saw the initials DLKS and HMcB united in a biro'd heart shape. And then, on another page, he saw that Zalihe had written her name, but in the English version that he and Sevinç loathed – SALLY SALLY SALLY – in big red letters. And just above he saw that her friend had written her name in even bigger letters: CORDIE CORDIE CORDIE.

What on earth was this? If only Zalihe hadn't been so silent since the death of that man, he might have some clue as to what she was thinking about. But now she was really silent with him. Was it the killing that was to blame? She was talkative enough with her mother; at least, he assumed so. Was she, and the thought almost made Kamil break out in a cold sweat, quiet with him because he had been present at that horrible event, and her mother hadn't? Did he now just remind her of something unpleasant? How could he break this association? They must do more things together. She must learn to think of him and Sevinç as a single mother-and-father entity. They must go out more, to visit their relatives in Southgate, say.

Kamil walked out into the stockroom, through to the hall and looked up the stairs to the flat, then squinted out into the yard where Zalihe and her friend were playing. He listened to the television, the traffic; then the new dissonant two-note alarm he had attached to the door to warn of an approaching customer sounded, and he resumed his post.

21

Cordie was looking through a microscope; all she could see was a lot of milky glop. She turned the metal knob and could still only see a lot of milky glop.

'I can only see a lot of milky glop,' she said. Her dad put his hands on her shoulders, very lightly, to move her out of the way, then he shifted the slide a bit and turned the knob again, and got Cordie to put her eyes back to the microscope. Now she could see a triangular shape with a thing like a raisin in the middle.

'Oh yeah,' she said quietly.

'That's a cell,' said her dad.

'It's very, very small,' said Cordie wonderingly.

'Yes.'

'Were you scared when the police put you in the cell?' Her daddy's mouth opened, but he didn't answer at first, and then a Japanese lady came in, wearing a white coat like her dad's.

'Hi, Michi,' he said to her.

'Hi,' she said and then smiled extra wide at Cordie. 'Hello, and who are you?'

'I'm Cordie,' she said, getting that mouth-twisty feeling at saying her own name.

'I'm Michiko; is this your first time in the lab?'

Cordie nodded and shyly grabbed her father's calf, burying her face in his trouser leg. Both the grown-ups laughed at her, the way she knew they would. She didn't listen to what they said, and then the Japanese lady went away and Cordie went for a little walk on her own. There were lots of shelves and glass tubes. There was a blue metal box on one of the benches with a rubbery sort of cup on it. Cordie pushed her finger into it and it started to spin, just as her father had told her it would. She put the flat of her hand on it and it spun. She leaned over and put her forehead on it, and it spun and made her whole face buzz.

She went into her daddy's little office and spun around a lot on his swivel chair until it stopped spinning and she had to spin the other way. She was a bit bored now. She was really waiting for Grandma and Grandad to pick her up and take her home for tea.

Someone came in: she was really pretty with short hair and a short T-shirt and a ring in her belly button.

'I bet you're Cordie,' she said and Cordie didn't reply. 'Hi, I'm Hattie,' she went on.

'Hello,' said Cordie, and went on swivelling.

Hattie watched her for a bit and said, 'You must be awfully proud of your daddy.' Cordie swivelled, looking at the floor. It was a bit like the roundabout in the playground.

'We're all really proud of your daddy. *I'm* especially proud of him.' Hattie looked at Cordie, but Cordie made no reply. She could see her daddy vaguely in the other corner of the lab doing something, then he moved and she couldn't see him any more.

'I expect your daddy's mentioned my name a bit, has

he?' asked Hattie quietly, and Cordie played with the big desk calculator, entering the number 07734 that spelt 'hello' when you turned it upside down.

'Can I have a sweet?' Cordie asked, spotting the pack of Starbursts that Hattie was holding along with a clipboard.

'Yes, of course,' said Hattie, and Cordie took a strawberry one, unwrapped it and put it in her mouth. Hattie did the same and they both chewed together, then Hattie said, 'So has he? Mentioned me, I mean.'

Cordie swivelled round to her daddy's computer and called up the Bob the Builder website game. 'Do you want to play?' she asked Hattie.

'Oh, yes, OK,' said Hattie, and together they played, helping Bob put together things that a careless little dog had broken around the house. They did well. Cordie felt like another Starburst, even though she knew she wasn't really allowed to have them as sweets made her feel over-tired and over-anxious.

'He's talked about you to Mummy,' she said to Hattie and watched how Hattie went all tense and pale and tried to pretend she hadn't.

'Oh really?' she asked. 'What does he say?'

'Can I have another Starburst?' asked Cordie.

'Yes, sure.' Cordie took two and settled down to another game on the Bob the Builder site, this time helping to drive Bob's van around the village streets so he didn't crash into anyone.

'So, Cordie, what does he say?'

'He says you're nice.' Cordie watched Hattie blush and then try to pretend she wasn't by looking at the papers on her clipboard.

'Can I see your desk?' asked Cordie.

'Yes, Cordie, of course you can!' They went over to Hattie's desk, which was really just a little bay between the work benches. Cordie looked at the postcards and photos that Hattie had stuck around her computer screen. She looked at a group photo with her daddy and all the people in his lab. He was standing next to Hattie in the picture.

'Mummy said something about you,' she said, and Cordie could see Hattie swallowing. She reached over and took another Starburst without asking and it made her feel giggly. 'Mummy said something about youuuuu,' she dragged out the last word and giggled, and Hattie giggled too, but not as much.

'So what does she say?'

'She . . . said . . .' Cordie dragged it out like a guessing game, tilting her head and grinning.

'What? What?' said Hattie, gently poking her in the tummy and giggling herself.

Then Cordie noticed something on the desk. It was Hattie's hole-puncher and it had some letters on it: HMcB. She saw the same letters on the glass bottles on the shelf over her desk and on a big styrofoam container with crushed ice in it. HMcB everywhere. HMcB. HMcB.

'Are those your initials?' asked Cordie.

'Yes, they are,' said Hattie.

'I've got a present for you,' said Cordie, jumping up. 'It's a present. I've got you a present.'

Cordie watched Hattie's face go suddenly puzzled and serious, then she rushed back into her daddy's office and started to rummage about in her little rucksack.

Hattie looked around the lab and Cordie knew that she was looking for her daddy.

'Found it,' she said, and pulled it out.

'Oh, Cordie,' said Hattie with a frown, 'you don't have to get me a present. *Have* you got me a present?'

Cordie brought it over. It was a small booklet with a picture of the Eiffel Tower on the front and the words *The European Academy of Molecular Biology, Tenth Symposium: Beyond The Genome – Paris, École Normale Supérieure, 18–25 Août*. Then there was a big biro heart shape and the initials DLKS and HMcB inside.

'There,' said Cordie, pointing excitedly at the second set of initials. 'That's you. This is yours. You've got to have it!'

Hattie went very pale, which only made Cordie giggle even more, just as the door swung open and Grandad and Grandma came in wearing their big coats, ready to take Cordie home. Hattie didn't know whether to take it or not, so Cordie shoved it into her hand.

'That's your present.'

22

While Hattie was talking to Cordie, Dr Sweet was in the men's room, looking at his reflection in the mirror, something he now did several times a day. There was no question about it, he had fewer grey hairs, and even the ones he had looked pale, sort of sun-bleached, rather than grey. His hairline at his forehead and temples had come down a bit and his skin looked tauter and brighter. Dr Sweet fanned his hand out on his solar plexus in a flamenco-type gesture, thumb extending to the sternum, little finger towards the belt. He was thinner as well. He felt younger and stronger. He felt like he could do, oh, fifty press-ups.

With a quick, lively step he pirouetted out into the corridor and said hello and goodbye to John and Rosemary, who were taking Cordie home, then he whisked into the lab where Hattie appeared to be slipping a booklet of some sort into her folder.

'Everything all right?' he asked. 'Did you get on all right with Cordie?'

'Oh yes,' said Hattie wonderingly, 'she's a very unusual, uh, child.'

Dr Sweet noticed the Starburst pack. 'You didn't give

her any sweets, did you? She's not really allowed to have any.'

'Oh no. Nope. Not at all.'

There was a silence and Dr Sweet asked, 'What's the matter?'

'Come with me,' Hattie replied curtly and led him out to room 408, his experimental annexe.

'What's going on?' he asked.

'David, don't be cross,' she said. Dr Sweet seethed, waiting for her to continue. So she was collaborating with someone else. Fooling around. Cheating on him. 'You remember Steve Chatwin, the guy at our apoptosis meeting in Lisbon last year, who works at BCL Pharmaceuticals?'

Dr Sweet nodded.

'Well, it turns out that he did a screen for small molecules that would promote *BAD* activity and it . . . well, it turns out that they got some pretty good hits. He contacted me to test them in our assays, and I've been trying them out in tumour cells in culture. Now look.' She gestured towards the microscope.

Dr Sweet was at first too astonished to reply. His subordinate had been making decisions, collaborating, all on his budget, without any authorization from him. If it wasn't for the fact that his lab was going to be swept away like so much dust he would have been really annoyed. As it was, he ducked down and looked through the microscope at the plates Hattie gave him.

Now he really was astonished. The tumour cells had been killed. The tumour cells had been targeted, taken on and wiped out. They had gone. He straightened up so quickly that he banged the bridge of his nose, and looked

speechlessly at Hattie. Then he looked through the microscope and stood up again.

'Who have you told about this?' he said at last.

'No-one,' said Hattie. 'No-one in the lab. No-one at
BCL. No-one. But that's not all. Come over here.'

Hattie took Dr Sweet by the hand and led him downstairs. They entered one of the closed compartments and
she pointed at the cages at the end of the room. There,
in a writhing, wriggling pink mass, were a consignment
of 'nude mice', genetically designed animals with no hair
and no immune system, state-of-the-art biotech rodents,
brought into being for the express purpose of cancer
research. Yet another unauthorized incursion into his
budget. But again he was completely calm.

'I think *BAD* is going to work *in vivo*, David,' she said,
secretively, almost whispering. 'I've applied carcinogens to
our nude mice and got some nice tumours on the go.
Look.'

It was true, they had lumps on their backs and necks.
The diagnosis was very clear. These mice had *cancer.*

'We can zap them with the compounds from BCL,
can't we? The ones that look good in the cell assays?' Dr
Sweet was silent. Hattie tugged at his sleeve, shaking it.
'Can't we, David? Shall I go ahead?'

They both looked at their wriggling nude, cancerous
mice. Could this be true? Could it really be true that here
at the Ruzowitsky they were onto something that no-one
in Washington, Harvard or UCLA had any idea about?
He couldn't believe it. He *didn't* believe it. This must be
some stupid thing she and Arlen had discussed.

'All right,' he said quietly. 'Do it if you like.'

At that instant there was a hesitant cough from the doorway and an unfamiliar voice said, 'David.'

They jumped apart guiltily, and turned to face the voice, which turned out to belong to Sir Hendryck Klost. His old, collapsed, liver-spotted face was set in a curious, knowing smile. Oh my God, they both thought, had the old boy somehow divined what they were up to?

'Sir Hendryck,' gulped Dr Sweet, in his alarm pronouncing the name with a glottal Afrikaans accent, as if he'd just glimpsed him in the veldt.

'David, have you got time for a little chat in the Director's office?'

Of course he had time. Without a single word to Hattie, Dr Sweet turned away and followed the older man down the corridor in a silence punctuated only by elaborate expressions of thanks as Sir Hendryck held various doors open for him.

It was only when they arrived at the Director's office that Dr Sweet sensed how odd this conference was. Dr Sweet was mutely bidden to take his ease in one little armchair opposite the sofa; the Director himself did not appear to be present, but his assistant, Jenny, was, and she was briskly asked to fetch coffee. Nor was that all: two other people were there, on the sofa, evidently at Sir Hendryck's request. One he recognized from the Human Resources photo-gallery in the ground-floor corridor: Roger Dalton, the outplacement consultant, whom in all the excitement he had clean forgotten to consult – a small man with squarish steel-rimmed glasses and a luxuriant mop of grey-blond hair whose individual filaments glinted in the sunlight. The other was Zoe Kingfisher, head of

Media Relations at the Ruzowitsky, who had rejoined the organization having just had a baby.

Sir Hendryck joined them, stretching urbanely on his matching cream armchair. He directed his enigmatic smile to each of the three in turn, finishing with Dr Sweet.

'So David,' he said. 'Quite a business.'

'Quite a distraction,' Dr Sweet stonewalled back.

'Mmm,' agreed Sir Hendryck, stalemated. 'You know Roger and Zoe, of course?'

'Oh yes,' said Dr Sweet reaching over for a belated, smiling handshake. There was another pause in which the reality of his last conversation with the Director in this room put a decisive halt to the euphoria in his head. Was he going to have to discuss his imminent move to the University of Douglas in the Isle of Man? But where was the Director?

'Roger,' he said, 'I can't apologize enough for not having got in touch before now.'

'Don't give it another thought,' chortled Sir Hendryck, as if this had been addressed to him. The four of them sat in silence for a while, Sir Hendryck continuing to smile, and Dr Sweet tried delicately to engage Roger and Zoe in eye contact, hoping they would explain, unprompted, why he was there. Finally he broke the ice himself.

'Will the Director be joining us, Sir Hendryck?' he asked faintly, feeling like a character in a costume drama.

'No, he will not,' said Sir Hendryck, the smile vanishing. 'He will not be joining us.'

'And why . . . why is that?' Dr Sweet asked.

'Because he has been dismissed,' said Sir Hendryck. 'I, as the chairman of the Ruzowitsky board of trustees, and with, I may say, their unanimous support, have dismissed him.'

Again Dr Sweet looked around for enlightenment. With their subtle grimaces and elevated eyebrows, Zoe and Roger signalled that they were *au courant* but could say no more.

Dr Sweet turned once again to Sir Hendryck who fixed him with a stare of impenetrable severity. He couldn't tell if he was expected to know or to guess, or what. Eventually he spoke again in a tiny little voice, 'Why has he been dismissed, Sir Hendryck?'

The older man replied, in a tone of infinite sadness, 'Because he had, without authorization, been spending the institute's money on building a panic-room-style bunker to protect himself against a possible animal rights protest situation. But it was not merely that,' he went on. 'He had been storing Metropolitan Police uniforms for favoured senior staff to dress up in so that the protesters would think they were officers sent to control the demonstration. Impersonating a policeman is, of course, entirely illegal.'

'Ah,' said Dr Sweet unhappily.

'I'm afraid that is not the sum of it,' said Sir Hendryck. 'The Director had his own costume disguise prepared.' At this Zoe and Roger looked around vaguely, out of the window and at various corners of the ceiling. 'I myself only became aware of this when Arthur notified the trustees with a formal complaint that he had been asked to handle this costume and that the fur was giving him a rash.'

Another quiet settled on the room. 'Anyway, David,' he said, brightening, 'Zoe has something to say to you.'

Zoe nodded, and cleared her throat with a little *krk* sound.

'David, we think that your work on *BAD*, and its implications for cell death and apoptosis, could form the centrepiece for a promotion we want to do in the autumn.'

Dr Sweet was nonplussed. Jesus. Had Hattie blabbed about her secret little mice project? Did they know something? He was expected to reply here, but didn't know how. 'Well, that's . . . that's great. But I do hope I can be involved in some way.'

Sir Hendryck spluttered with laughter at this absurd display of inappropriate humility. 'Involved? In some way? But, my dear fellow, you'll be involved in every *possible* way!'

'But won't I be at the University of Douglas in the Isle of Man by then?' Dr Sweet asked it without bitterness, but with a pale grim smile directed at the floor just in front of the sofa.

'No, David, you won't. At least, I very much hope you will not wish to be,' said Sir Hendryck.

'You mean . . . I can continue my lab?' Dr Sweet had entirely abandoned any pretence of cool detachment.

'David, didn't you just hear what Zoe said?' said Sir Hendryck. 'You, and the work being done by your group, will form the centrepiece of the research being done here. And yes, you can continue with your lab! But I do hope not simply as a lab head.'

'Not just as lab head?' said Dr Sweet.

'No,' said Sir Hendryck, chucklingly shaking his head. 'You are the new Director of the Ruzowitsky! Jenny!'

The Director's assistant – that is to say Dr Sweet's assistant – entered smiling with a still foaming bottle of champagne which she placed on the low glass table between them and then backed away while Sir Hendryck proprietorially did the honours.

Drinking on Ruzowitsky property was something expressly forbidden, and though this was a licensed exception, the festivity was slightly stilted.

'David, congratulations on your new preferment,' said Sir Hendryck, savouring the archaism, 'assuming, that is, that you wish to accept it?'

'Oh yes,' said Dr Sweet, his assent drowned in another wave of polite laughter from Zoe and Roger.

'I think I can say that your compensation package will be fully commensurate with your new status,' he added smoothly, and Dr Sweet just blinked, as he realized they knew nothing of Hattie's discoveries. They simply wanted to keep him on, and with more money. 'This is a very good day for the Ruzowitsky, David, a very good day indeed. And I think I can say that the founder himself would have approved.' The four of them glanced over to the portrait of Max Ruzowitsky, half expecting him to nod and mouth the word 'yes'. But Ruzowitsky just stood there, with one hand on his wife's shoulder and the other on his younger son's.

Would he have approved? It was with a small frisson that Dr Sweet realized the answer was yes, and that among those present, he alone had read the relevant passage from Ruzowitsky's memoir, *The Way I Succeeded* in its original 1979 edition:

You can't *call yourself* rich if you work for anyone. You'll never *be* rich if you work for anyone. You'll certainly never get rich through raises and salary hikes, because no matter how substantial these may seem, they will always be only a *fraction* of what the really rich people who employ you are making. But there is one real entrepreneurial buzz to be had from working for someone else, and that's manoeuvring your bosses into giving you a raise because they think you're going to quit, and because you have convinced them that your *prestige* and *market value* somehow exceeds that of your notional superiors in the chain of command. Now you're getting your raise from a position of strength, not weakness. Now you're winning money, not just earning it like some no-account little suck-ass salaryman. I remember when I started out in retirement facilities, I told my bosses at Seniors Green Pastures in Florida that the boys at Grey Refuge in Grosse Pointe had made me a mouth-watering offer. My cringing little boss doubled my salary right away. And when I opened my paycheck it felt like there were my boss's freshly cut balls in there, hot, moist and steaming. That had to feel good.

23

Alice fastidiously replaced the cup of home-made cappuccino, fitting it into the saucer, and felt the tiny line of froth expire on her upper lip like a line of surf on the sand. This was another regression, another deplorable concession made to the events of the last month and a half. She was supposed to have given up coffee; it made her too manic. She had herbal tea instead, or better yet water. She had read somewhere that you were supposed to drink the equivalent of eight glasses of water every day, and used to make an effort to drink a whole bottle of mineral water, but it was just ridiculous; she felt bloated and had to keep running to the lavatory, and anyway who has *time* to drink a whole bottle of water? But she badly missed her coffee, and thought the circumstances were enough for a dispensation. And her ex-husband's cappuccino machine was another inducement.

She was the only one drinking coffee, though. John and Rosemary were drinking tea from a large brown, properly warmed pot covered in a woollen dress. There was another cup set out for Dr Sweet, who had yet to come down for breakfast, and there was a cup of microwaved warm milk for Cordie, who sat there with a livid plump frown, unable to open any of her birthday presents until the family group was fully quorate.

'Come on, Daddy, come *on*!' she shouted.

Cordie had gaily coloured packages and a fanned stack of cards next to her plate. And, as this was her birthday and an extra special day, a fun-sized bar of chocolate. Her mother had allowed her this teaspoonful of rocket fuel and hoped the results would not be too catastrophic.

Alice had cards as well. It was a quirk of their family life that Alice's birthday happened to be on the same day, a coincidence that bonded mother and daughter at first, but now was significant for the opportunity it gave Dr Sweet to insert himself back into her life, for he could hardly be denied access to his daughter's big birthday moment, and Cordie could hardly be denied her requests to have this in tandem with Alice's. So for five successive years, Cordie and Alice had had their breakfast present-and-card-opening together, and this was to be the first post-divorce dual event.

Dr Sweet finally came downstairs. He *did* look different. He had been asking her if he looked different for ages, apparently fishing for compliments; he clearly thought he looked better, as he kept going on and on about how much better he *felt*. Alice had blandly told him she couldn't see any difference, but she could.

He looked younger and it didn't suit him. He looked like the *molto agitato* post-doctoral academic she had met so many years before, with all youth's gaucherie, and none of its charm. He was the sort of man who needed some years; he needed to get a bit plumper and more subdued. It wasn't that middle age suited him exactly, it was more that youth didn't; it was a casting problem.

'Hello everyone. Hi.'

Everyone. Alice flinched at this general address, as if they were some sort of cheerleading team. John and Rosemary gave genteel hellos and Dr Sweet swooped down and attempted to kiss Cordie on the crown of her head, a grotesque condescension she calmly ignored.

'*Now,*' she said. 'Now can we open our presents?'

'Not yet, not yet,' said Dr Sweet twinklingly, adding, 'Now, now then, wait' – this last to drown out the siren-wail of Cordie's '*Oh . . .*' as it climbed an octave and a half. He trotted into the next-door room and brought back two parcels, one about twice the size of the other. With his back to them all, he unwrapped them quickly on a tray on the countertop, took out a cigarette lighter – but he didn't smoke? – whirled it in a kind of circular stirring motion and then turned to reveal the secret, saying, 'Tad-daa!'

Of course. Cakes. Cordie's had six candles. Hers had thirty-four, all of them somehow lit. Dr Sweet brought them over on a tray, a tactless penny-farthing diagram of the mother–daughter relationship, and it was like the old joke: she really was driven back by the heat. Then unforgivably he started to sing, and raggedly, unsteadily, John and Rosemary politely joined in.

Alice had always hated 'Happy Birthday'; she hated its uninteresting, funereal progressions, the kind of thing best accompanied by a wheezing organ, like a sombre Victorian hymn. She hated the two sudden high notes in the third line, with their ruthless parody of gaiety, the line ending with a mock-spontaneous collision of her name with her daughter's, shoehorned into two syllables, and then the heavy pull of the final rallentando. But most of all she thought it was a hateful song to have sung to you while you had to maintain a good-sport grin for what seemed like forty minutes, your mouth pulled into a rictus of ironic enjoyment, but unconsciously mouthing the words and following the line of the song. And, apart from everything else, she felt she should be singing it to Cordie.

Dr Sweet should have known that cakes and candles ought to be for later, not now, at breakfast on a school day when there were things to do, and even then it had to be a special cake with the lowest amount of sugar possible. What was he thinking of? Cordie herself maintained an attitude of benign happiness, her eyes gleaming, something else which caused Alice anxiety. Was she to be allowed some of this cake before going to school? What was in the cake? Her irresponsible ex-husband must know that there could be implications for her behavioural condition, and it was *so* important for her to stay calm as she was taking part in the school concert that afternoon, something in which he had taken no interest whatsoever. Did he want her to go off the rails again? And if they stop her having cake, won't that create the most appalling row? And if John and Rosemary thoughtlessly offer cake, taking their cue from their son, will she have to stop them and upset his parents as well?

All these thoughts raced through her mind as the fourth and final line ground inexorably to its conclusion, and she found anxiety and anger welling up. With fierce internal discipline, she mastered the situation by rising on the cries of 'speech' and so silencing John and Rosemary's feeble, dutiful segue into 'For She's A Jolly Good Fellow'.

'Thank you *so* much for that, and *wasn't* it nice of Daddy to show you the cake that we're going to have at your party later on?' Cordie's eyes flickered with puzzlement at this misdirection, but she was won over by Alice's next question, 'Do you want to open your presents first, or wait for me to open mine?'

There was no mystery about that. As Alice cleared away the cakes with a bit of a look at Dr Sweet, Cordie ripped open an extensive addition to her Barbie and beanie canon, as well as giant story books, pre-pubescent make-up and glittery hair accessories. Then Alice unwrapped some CDs of world music from Havana and Malawi and a wooden device with rolling balls in it, like castors, designed as a back-rubber, to massage one's aching lumbar region.

This present, from Dr Sweet, was presumably for Richard to use on her. Alice was not sure quite how to take it, especially as Richard didn't seem to have sent a present, at least not to this address.

'*What* a nice Barbie,' said Rosemary to Cordie, her voice becoming dangerously loud. 'And who is that from? Is it from your mummy?'

Cordie shook her head, while inspecting her Barbie with the rapt yet inscrutable air of a top-flight surgeon deciding not to amputate.

'Well, it's not from us,' she smiled. 'So it must be from your *daddy*.' Rosemary turned to Dr Sweet, who was busying himself clearing away, giving him a strange hard look, a look that Alice saw, but then averted her eyes just as Rosemary glanced in her direction.

Where was Richard's card? Where was Richard's present? Alice realized she didn't care. She was astonished when she got cards or notes from people saying they hoped she'd 'have a great day' on her birthday. Have a great day? Well, often in the past she and David had made plans to go out for a meal or the theatre with friends, a sitter organized for Cordie. She'd hoped and expected to have a nice time, sure. But a *great day*?

'Is my bag anywhere?' Her ex-husband was now fussing around self-importantly. He had a jacket on, and Alice realized that he was wearing a suit. A suit to go to the lab. She thought he hated suits. She thought the last time he'd worn one was to be invested with his D.Phil.

Today was Cordie's big day. She really was expected to have a great day. Not merely was this her birthday, but she was due to sing at the musical concert organized by her teacher, Mrs Curzons. It started at 2.30 p.m. and they were all going to go: Alice, John, Rosemary and Dr Sweet. She had been practising it an awful lot at school, but at home Alice had hardly heard it. Mrs Curzons had, however, assured her that it was going to be splendid.

Was the concert why Dr Sweet had a suit on? Somehow Alice thought not.

'*There's* the wretched thing.' Dr Sweet found his bag and started rummaging in it.

'David,' Rosemary called out to him in an oddly serious voice, 'remind me again what the plan is for this afternoon.'

Dr Sweet looked quite blank.

'Cordie's concert,' said Rosemary reproachfully, 'don't tell me you'd forgotten?'

'Of . . . of course I hadn't forgotten,' he said, placing himself between Cordie and Rosemary and lowering his voice to a hiss. 'Mum, please don't be silly. Of course I hadn't forgotten, had I, Miss Cordie?'

But Cordie didn't reply, busying herself with brushing

Barbie's blonde mane entirely over her face and then turning her round to look at her neck, a process which she had once confided to Alice was so that she could imagine what Barbie would look like with no face and a very low forehead.

It was time for the divorced parents to go to their workplaces and for the grandparents to take Cordie to school. Alice had her coat on, and looked back at her presents: the CDs, sleek upscale paperbacks and the massager. She looked at Cordie's: the Barbie, the beanies, the big books – and the wrapping paper for both sets, which John had collected and folded up for (possible) re-use.

'Bye-bye Cordie,' said Dr Sweet loudly. Cordie said nothing. Holding Rosemary's hand, she prepared to leave through the back door. Dr Sweet put his bag down, rushed round and headed Cordie off. He knelt down in front of her.

'Cordie? Bye-bye, Miss Cordie?' Nothing. 'Are you all right, Cordie?' Nothing. He looked up at Alice, questioningly.

'She's fine. She's a bit nervous about the concert today, aren't you, love?' said Rosemary, 'but you're going to be smashing, aren't you?'

Dr Sweet looked back. He, too, was quite certain Cordie was going to be smashing. He put his bag down, did up one of her coat buttons that was half undone, and held her hands between the finger and thumb of his own.

'Jolly good luck today, Miss Cordie. We'll all be there! Cheering you on! I mean, you know, break a leg and everything. Not really, it's just an expression. I suppose

it's for acting, not singing really. How much do you love
me, Miss Cordie?' he asked. 'How much do you love your
poor old dad?' Cordie turned to look up at Rosemary,
waiting to go.

24

This really was more like it. Dr Sweet had been moved into the Director's office. He could look out at Queen Square, bathed in a little fresh spring sunshine, and at his knot of photographers outside the building, a crowd only slightly diminished in size. And he still had his old office, what he mentally termed his 'little working office' or '*in situ* office', next to the lab. He could pop in there any time he felt like it.

It felt good. There was really nothing in his office yet, the former Director's belongings had been removed, and all he'd put out was his old photo of Cordie, Alice and himself on the Suffolk coast. Taken years ago now. Alice was crouching next to him on the sand, and he was holding Cordie under the armpits; she was very little, so her fat little legs with their dimpled knees were hanging down, feet resting on the sand so that she was theoretically standing up. Alice was pointing at the camera; Cordie was looking up at his chin and smiling.

Who had taken the picture? They must have asked a stranger. No, wait, he must have set his camera on a timer. He couldn't remember. In theory, every photo taken of him should have a visual-sense-memory superimposed on it: the memory of the person in front of him taking the photo, a camera obscuring their face. But he couldn't ever remember that. The photo, the image itself, supplanted the real memory; it became the memory. Only recently, Dr Sweet had seen an old Super-8 home movie that his father had taken of him and his mother on holiday in Dorset in 1972, playing cricket, tennis, swimming, waving at the camera. Looking at it, he vividly remembered every-thing – everything except the image of his father pointing an alien, borrowed home-movie camera at him, something that would have been very unusual, something that John was never comfortable with and never repeated on any subsequent holiday. His father holding a buzzing camera, looking through the viewfinder. It must have happened and yet he had no memory of it whatsoever.

Dr Sweet wondered about getting a new photo of Cordie, with maybe a separate one of Alice, now that the *en famille* shot was so obviously inappropriate. But he had lots of footage of the pair of them on his camcorder. He could download some freeze-frames onto his Mac, print them out. That would be a nice little project for him. And yet he couldn't help remembering how cold Cordie had been with him this morning. He'd thought she would be thrilled with the Barbie he'd got her. And she seemed to be – until she realized it was from him.

He looked at her smiling in the photograph. Maybe she smiled like that at Alice now when he wasn't there. Maybe she smiled at John and Rosemary when they took her out. But she didn't smile at him. Still. Still.

With an effort, Dr Sweet dispelled this unwelcome train of thought. Here he was. His new office. He clicked on his e-mail icon and discovered two new messages. One was from Sir Hendryck, welcoming him to his new perch.

The other was from Angie Meredith at the Dartmouth Media Heart of Gold office, asking him to make himself available for a rehearsal at the Dorchester on the morning of 27 April, before the lunch ceremony itself, and that they would have a suite reserved for Dr Sweet and his family all day.

Dr Sweet luxuriated in these two pieces of intelligence and their combined effect. He had a chair that allowed him, encouraged him, to lean back expansively.

'David?'

Dr Sweet jolted back up to the perpendicular, never having learned the manager's art of not responding immediately to the call of a subordinate.

Hattie was in the doorway, looking flushed, twitchy and excited.

'Hattie, how are you? I haven't looked in on you today; I got in late. What's happening?'

'I need you to see this,' was all she said, and disappeared out of the frame. Dr Sweet leaned back a little again, and then pushed forward to get the necessary momentum, and got up to his feet, his knees cracking.

'What is it? Hattie? What is it?'

But Hattie had gone. His heart rate starting to climb, Dr Sweet stepped out into the corridor and Hattie was there, walking backwards, gesturing to him to follow with her left hand, suppressing a grin. He broke into a little trot, and it was all Hattie could do not to run herself. They trotted and ran as far as the door to his lab, and then went past it. Dr Sweet knew where they were headed; they were going to see the mice.

Once there, Hattie punched in the security access code with sharp little sweaty-slippery stabs that almost snapped her forefinger back at the first knuckle. She got it wrong and was repulsed with a thin warning honk and a red light from the control console. Both of them knew that getting it wrong again would trigger the emergency alarm, immobilize all the doors and bring the security staff up. Hattie and Dr Sweet would have to calm down.

She repeated the code, absurdly slowly, as if picking out an arpeggio on a piano keyboard. This time the console emitted a trill and, with a green light, they were in. With jittery little steps, Hattie brought him round to the last closed compartment on the left, then she veered away and stood back, hopping up and down with agitation. In each fist he could see she was gripping the red material of her sweater below her lab-coat sleeve. She was waiting for him to open up and take a look.

When he did so, it was with two brisk movements of his hands – open, look, close – and then he turned back to Hattie.

'These the same mice?' he asked, and Hattie just nodded, biting her lower lip so it stretched out white.

He turned back and looked again. Yes, these were the same mice, the same nude mice, wriggling and entwining, little sniffing noses, minute whiskers quivering, sealed up slit-eyes. But with one difference: the tumours had disappeared.

Great God almighty, the special genetically bred nude mice were cured. They were cured. They had cancer, and they were cured. And *BAD*, their project, his project, had done it. Dr Sweet turned back to Hattie, whose lips were parted now; the impress of her teeth on her lower lip had left a sharp little L-shape. She was smiling. Dr Sweet didn't know what to do.

Hattie held out her hands to him and he did the same to her. They grasped each other by the elbows, shaking them a little, still not speaking. Then Hattie pulled the door back herself and looked at her little babies – their little babies – snaking her arm around her companion's waist. Dr Sweet pulled the door closed again and brought his face very close to hers.

'Do you know what this means?' he asked.

'Mmm,' she said.

'We should go to a clinical trial straight away,' Dr Sweet went on, breaking the gaze into each other's eyes for a moment and looking away. 'Straight away.'

'Yes,' she said at the edge of her breath. Then the big LCD beeper she had clipped to her lab coat pocket went off. She'd left something on the timer.

'Listen,' she whispered, as if with a lover's confidence, 'stay here. I'll be right back.'

She went. Never before had Dr Sweet understood the phrase 'weak at the knees', but now his knees had turned to jelly. He sat down on the little stool by the opposite wall and settled his palms on his thighs.

The cure. It was something he had thought didn't exist. It wasn't merely that, like scientists of an earlier generation, he didn't expect to see it in his own lifetime, it was that over decades, the definition of what a cure could be had been eroded by agnosticism. His job was to analyse, infinitesimally, what cancer was: its structure, its function, its origin. In molecular biological terms, he had retreated into the first half of Marx's dictum about philosophers wishing to understand the world while the point was to change it. He was trying to *understand* cancer, the painful, horrifying disease that claims one in three, you, or someone you love. It was the last intellectual frontier in the anxious, prosperous West. His were what Bacon called the experiments of light. As for the experiments of fruit, well, he had never seen himself doing those experiments; they were performed by a mistily imagined collection of others, and even then he saw them as managing cancer, containing it, controlling it. A definitive cure for cancer – well, you might as well find a cure for death. We were all in remission, weren't we?

He looked in again at the nude mice. They weren't in remission; they had been cured. He had cured them. Dr Sweet staggered back and sat down once more. Could it really be true? Had he actually . . . but Dr Sweet could not say it; he could not enunciate, even to himself, the final two c-words.

Minutes passed and Dr Sweet's breathing gradually calmed. Why didn't he believe it could be true? Wasn't it just a symptom of his defeatism, his low self-esteem, his contemptible pusillanimity? When did he stop believing anyway? What right had he to abandon, by stealth, the prime objective, an objective the laity believed in? An ideal on the basis of which they had bankrolled his career and hundreds like him?

Was it because he didn't believe that he personally could be important? Was it because he thought in his heart that he was just a functionary, filling up his days and paying off his mortgage with science-like activities, with no more importance than raffia-weaving in a psychiatric hospital? If that was so, then he really ought to be ashamed of himself. The fates had sent him a sign, a blessing, that he didn't deserve. All the indications were that he had actually achieved something useful for humankind. And why not? Science proceeded across a broad front: the breakthrough has to come somewhere, the first breach in the wall has to come some time, why not from him? Why not from Dr Sweet? Why not?

So little by little, with a distinctively experimental excitement he hadn't felt in two decades of scientific work, Dr Sweet allowed himself to believe it.

'Jesus,' he breathed, breaking out into a broad grin and then smothering it quickly, not wishing to tempt the gods. Then three delirious, wonderful words crept unbidden into his head, delicious and terrifying in their import, their mighty backlash of possibility.

'The Nobel Prize,' he whispered, and the phrase eddied about the dull featureless room like a mantra that might unlock a cabinet of treasure in *The Arabian Nights*. The Nobel Prize. The Nobel Prize for Medicine. Nobel laureate. Its modifications and variations reverberated in his head like an exquisite piece of music. Men and women hardly ten years older than Dr Sweet had been distinguished in this way, so he asked himself again, why not him?

The announcement. His appearance on the news. On websites all over the world. His parents' reaction, Alice's reaction. It all rippled across his mind like movie pictures. The message of congratulation from Downing Street: the brief but warm handwritten note on heavy, official paper, expressing profound congratulations on this achievement for British science. The invitation to chair myriad prestigious committees. And then the journey to Stockholm – he would generously allow Alice and his daughter to come with him – the gloriously arcane traditions performed in that foreign tongue in austere, grand blondwood halls.

Perhaps there would be some translation service, some humble Scandinavian amanuensis would murmur an English rendering of the superlatives about his work and career that were echoing around the room. Then his own speech, prefaced with an adorable admission that it would have to be in English, the little ripple of respectful laughter that would greet his self-deprecation. And all this on top of his recent courageous action; it really was too much.

The pent-up excitement and shock were beginning to discharge themselves in a film of sweat, thrilling, athletic, three-minute-mile sweat. Dr Sweet just sat there glowing, happily wriggling and squirming, just like his on-top-of-the-world, never-felt-better nude mice, the proud new stars of his classroom, putting the sullen underachieving zebrafish in the shade. All this, he considered, would have another knock-on effect. Alice could hardly refuse his request for access to his daughter now, no matter where she was living. Could she? A popular hero, a distinguished scientist, wishes for access to his daughter, perhaps two months in the year? Or three months? Or maybe he would be living in New York himself by then, department chairman at Columbia or the Albert Einstein School of Medicine. He could have a fantastic apartment in Manhattan. No judge in the world would refuse him, surely?

But there was something else. Would Cordie want to see him? Unwillingly, he reviewed the scene in the kitchen. Cordie unwrapping the Barbie, liking it – but then going cold the minute his mother told her who it was from. And then not speaking to him when he said goodbye and good luck. Not saying a word, not a *word*. Sending him to Coventry. No-one had never done that to him before in his life, not even at school.

The security console outside went bip, bip, bip, bip, trrrrrr, and Hattie was back in.

'Hi,' he said softly.

'Hi,' she breathed back. Why were they whispering?

'Everything OK?'

'Yeah.'

They looked at each other again, dead straight. Then Hattie and Dr Sweet took hold of each other by the elbows and started to jiggle, giggle and laugh out loud.

'Shh!'

'Shh!'

They just grinned.

'We go to a clinical trial right away.'

'Right away, chief.' Hattie did a little salute and then grabbed his arms again. They moved closer.

'Hattie,' he asked, 'is Arlen . . .?'

'Arlen's at home. I mean, he's gone back home to Australia. It was a mistake. It didn't work out.'

Dr Sweet pursed his lips in a smirk and ran his tongue over them. Then he said, 'In that case, do you think there's any rooms free at the Rylands for a long lunch hour?'

Hattie and Dr Sweet kissed and then Hattie went out to fetch her bag.

25

Getting out of the building to the Rylands wasn't at all the straightforward business it used to be. It wasn't simply a matter of deceiving Arthur on the door. Now they had the press to deal with as well. Going out the front way, past Arthur, was out of the question, so they had to take the lift down to the second floor, separately, then they ran down the fire-escape stairwell to the lower ground floor and took the staff entrance directly into the cafeteria kitchen, then in full swing serving lunch, risking being glimpsed by staff lining up for food. Mouthing 'sorry' to the cooks and kitchen porters, waving genially and holding a piece of paper that implied he was in the middle of official business, Dr Sweet walked casually through, followed by Hattie, out to the delivery entrance and up the car-park ramp into the streets behind the Ruzowitsky.

No-one was there. No press, no photographers. They'd done it! Elation was now added to excitement, and they all but ran to the Rylands. Pantingly, brazenly, cheerfully, Dr Sweet asked if there was a room free. There was. His credit card swiped, he got the key and ignored the receptionist's facetious question about luggage.

It was a smaller, darker room than they were used to, but that didn't matter. It didn't matter times ten to the power of ten, as his father used to say in more innocent circumstances.

Dr Sweet and Hattie kissed swooningly and collapsed sideways onto the bed. She pushed his jacket off his shoulders. He undid her shirt buttons and got her top off. She was wearing a *purple* bra! Dr Sweet greedily smoothed his hands over her breasts while kissing her. He kicked off his shoes, and she got down to her underwear and pulled his trousers off, so they reversed inside out, and trailed from his feet for the next few seconds of groping and pawing.

They stopped and laughed for a bit, and then kissed again. Hattie unhooked her bra and let him nuzzle her for some minutes while she sighed. Then she pulled his head up so they were face to face.

'There's no rush,' she murmured. 'We can make it a long lunch.'

'Mmm,' he said, and they kissed some more.

'You know what?' she asked.

'No. What?'

'You look different. You really do.'

'How do you mean?' he asked.

'Well, your hair. It used to have a little grey. Didn't it? I mean, I'm not making this up, am I? Did you colour it or something?'

'No.' He smiled. 'Really, no.'

She ran her fingers through it wonderingly. 'It's thicker, too. There's more of it, more than when I first met you.' She gave him a baffled sort of grimace-grin. 'What have you been doing?'

He shrugged, shaking his head. 'Nothing. I mean I really don't know.'

'It's not just that. You seem . . . different. Your face looks less lined; you look younger.'

'Hah!'

'No, and your upper arms, your chest. Hey, have you been working out?'

He had to laugh, suspecting a tease. 'No, really no. I know what you mean, though. I have felt much better since . . . well, since this whole thing. I feel physically lighter.'

'David?'

'Yeah?'

'Will we have co-credit on this? You know, our experiment, the nude mice?'

Dr Sweet looked serious. 'Of *course*. No problem. It was your . . . I mean, I couldn't have done it without . . . we couldn't have done it. You did a fantastic job.'

'David, darling, that's fine. You know, you're the lab head; I just want a credit.'

'No problem.'

They stroked and kissed a little.

'You know, *you* look a bit different,' said Dr Sweet at last.

Hattie burst out laughing. 'At last he notices.'

'What? I don't get it?'

'I've had *my* hair coloured!'

'You have? I mean, yes, I see it.'

'The hell you see it. What is it you see?'

'You've had your hair coloured,' said Dr Sweet in a small voice after a pause. Hattie sighed.

'Yes, I've had it tinted. It's kind of reddish. What do you think?'

'It's bloody marvellous,' said Dr Sweet dreamily, sincerely.

They kissed again.

'You know, Hattie,' said Dr Sweet, 'when all this is over, you and I, we could sort of, go away somewhere. The Caribbean, Mauritius.'

'Mmm, that sounds great. We could just lounge around on the beach.'

'By the pool.'

'In our room.'

Dr Sweet started kissing her neck and then worked his way round her collarbone.

'My hair feels weird at the moment, actually,' Hattie sighed complacently. 'Sort of nylony. Something in the conditioning. Kind of like a Barbie doll's hair.'

After a second or two, she felt Dr Sweet's lips cease to truffle wetly; they stopped stock-still, pressed into the fleshy skin by her left shoulder.

'Ohgh fucghk,' she heard him say tensely. He looked up. 'What time is it?'

26

The clock in the school assembly hall had stopped. It wasn't half past two, it was actually closer to quarter to three. They had been sitting there for about twenty minutes: John, Rosemary and Alice, with a seat saved for Dr Sweet – a vacant place they'd had to defend with increasing vehemence and strained politeness as the beginning of the concert approached.

Alice had taken time away from the office to be there and her ex-husband had promised faithfully that he would do the same. Well, she supposed it must be something important, although what could be more important than this? Everyone had been so proud of Cordie wanting to do a song – she was proud, Mrs Curzons at the school was proud – and her father, supposedly, was proud. This was so important to little Cordie. Alice felt a cold wave of anger and scorn for her ex-husband, his thoughtlessness, his arrogance. He can't even get it together to come to a school concert.

It was three o'clock. The children were seated cross-legged on the little raised-dais stage. Their various instruments were laid out neatly on a trestle table, stage left. To the right was an upright piano. Alice, John and Rosemary could see Cordie, impassive, cross-legged like the rest, hardly talking to those on either side of her. John and Rosemary had waved to her an awful lot, like lots of the mums, dads and grandparents, but Cordie hadn't waved back, or frowned to show she was embarrassed like some of the other children; she'd just looked blank. What was she thinking?

Alice took out Dr Sweet's little video camera, trained the lens on Cordie and, without filming, zoomed in for a close-up. Her daughter's plump face filled the little flip-out screen, an image transmitted and reconfigured as hundreds of thousands of pixels.

Cordie looked perfectly calm, much calmer than any of her relatives. For comparison's sake, Alice swivelled the camera round and, zooming back out, took in the strained attentiveness of Rosemary and John's church-parade self-possession, rendered impassive by the fact that she saw only his stroke profile. Then back to Cordie, sphinx-like.

Two minutes past three. Alice had the palm of her free hand pressed down on Dr Sweet's empty seat, which required a posture of subtle discomfort. In addition, she now had to repulse people who wanted the place by sporting an almost continuous head-shaking teeth-clenched smile, the opposite of a nodding dog.

Five minutes past. Alice took her hand away in order to stow the camera carefully in her bag. A grandparent instantly appeared in the aisle, holding a tiny silent child in his arms, miming a request, unanswerable in its moral force, that the seat could not remain unoccupied while he was standing and, furthermore, that he proposed to use it for two people. Dr Sweet clearly wasn't turning up and Alice could defend her position no longer. The man sat with a small, gruff *hmph*, and at that moment Mrs Curzons got up to speak.

'Hello, everyone, thank you so much for coming to this special musical concert. Before we start, can I ask everyone to make sure that their telephones are all switched off? The first item is the whole choir singing "All Things Bright And Beautiful"!'

*

There was a rustling as all the children got up; their school uniform sweatshirts presented a broad, chocolate-brown stripe across the stage. Mrs Curzons played a drawn-out, clattering introductory chord on the piano to establish what key they were in, the way John and Rosemary remembered the national anthem being introduced at school concerts of their own youth.

Cordie sang like the rest of them, her mouth opening and closing in an earnest, winking O, her face and gaze focused ahead into the middle distance. Alice knew she was supposed to be vividly, exclusively aware of her daughter's presence in the throng, but always felt that it was submerged and subdued when Cordie was in a school group. She looked strangely like all the rest, and for a moment Alice could hardly distinguish her from all the other chocolate-sweatshirted children.

Rosemary could remember singing this hymn as a child and was mildly amazed it still had such currency. But she had sung it when she was older – twelve, thirteen – and facing the dais, the way she was now, at school prayers in full uniform – blouse, skirt, tie, with, heaven help her, a straw boater hung up with all the others in the school cloakroom, but which had to be worn outside in the school precincts or on the train to and from school. Rose-mary had hoped that stiff, uncomfortable straw boaters would be a thing of the past; but she knew Alice and Dr Sweet were brooding about sending Cordie to a private prep school where precisely this sort of archaism was flaunted as a guarantee of quality. She looked at Cordie's little singing face, imagined a straw boater on it, and felt a wave of sadness.

John now wanted nothing but to leave Dr Sweet's cramped house and go back to his own home and garden, which he was sure would be running to ruin without his care. He had been wondering if he and Rosemary, or even just he on his own, could make a day trip there to look after things. They had been delaying this in case the police made an arrest and their help was needed immediately. But now this possibility had receded. John didn't really believe the catastrophe would happen, and even the crowd of reporters outside the house – at first so astonishing, so intolerable – did not disturb him any more. While the threat of the police hovered over them, he and Rosemary had thought it right to carry on regardless with things like this, a duty to civilian morale, the way he remembered his own father cheerily organizing rugby matches and outings in the phoney war of 1939. This, however, was simply becoming irksome. What were they *doing* here?

Alice was trying not to think about her attempt to talk to Richard on the phone that day. She had not, in fact, spoken to him at all. He had already told her many times, in breezy e-mails, that he had a supremely important mergers and acquisitions meeting all day, a meeting that was expected to continue into the evening by virtue of having to take 'this bunch of boring people from Rotterdam out to dinner'. Nevertheless, Alice had put in a couple of calls. The first was fielded by his genial assistant Elaine, with whom she laughingly exchanged badinage about Richard's 'impossible' schedule. The next time her call had gone directly to voicemail – Elaine's voicemail. Alice brooded about this, working the incident in her mind as if on a potter's wheel, trying to establish its sense, its symmetry. The first time she had spoken directly to Elaine, she considered, she had ended the conversation by asking how the 'bores from Rotterdam' were behaving themselves. Elaine had paused for a fraction of a second and said, 'Oh, we're not looking forward to them!' Not *looking forward* to them? But weren't they there at that very moment? Wasn't Richard busy with them now? Wasn't that why he couldn't speak to her?

'All Things Bright And Beautiful' came to an end, and Alice applauded in the special parents-school-concert way she had developed: sharp claps, spaced out. Don't clap madly right off the bat, she knew, pace yourself, you're going to be doing so much clapping your palms will run with blood, so save it for Cordie's solo effort later on.

The next item was an ensemble of descant recorders, six children holding their instruments tightly in two hands, eyes cast down as if about to enact a religious mystery in front of a secular audience. Mrs Curzons spoke to them very quietly: 'Ready?' They nodded and she turned round to the audience.

'Ladies and gentlemen,' she said brightly, 'our recorder players are now going to do an instrumental, but do please feel free to join in singing the words.'

The audience smiled murmuringly at this invitation

and Mrs Curzons turned round and cued in her instrumentalists: 'Three, four . . .'

The group launched into a remarkably loud atonal
wailing, notes fluctuating wildly across octaves. It was like
a very challenging sort of progressive jazz, made more
mysterious still by the demonstrative way some players
would wave the shafts of their recorders around while
puffing into them, purple-faced, while others would
remain stock-still, their mouthpieces hanging negligently
from their lips as if in some sort of trance.

Presently Rosemary recognized the tricky, stuttering,
dotted rhythm. 'Da-da-*dum*-dum-*dum*.' She smiled and
then spoke: 'Fare thee *well*, fare thee *well*, da-da-*dum*-
dum-*dum*-dum-dum. For I'm off to Lou'si-*an*-a for to see
my Susy-*an*-na, / Singing Polly Wolly Doodle all the day!'
Triumphantly, encouragingly, she burst into this chorus
again; loyally Alice joined in, and John smilingly muttered
away. It wasn't long before a relieved audience burst into a
full-throated chorus of 'Polly Wolly Doodle'. Their singing
almost drowned out the instrumentalists, who redoubled
their efforts, getting the kind of volume from their decant
recorders similar to car horns or air-raid sirens. Boister-
ously, the audience stepped up their own performance,
even adding a bit of percussion, clapping and stamping at
key moments:

> *Fare thee well!*
> *Clap, Clap!*
> *Fare thee well!*
> *Stamp, Stamp!*

Eventually the players ceased, raggedly, discontinuously,
like an infantry division in disorderly retreat, with one or

two of them on the verge of tears. The audience felt their ears buzzing and their throats parched.

Grim-faced, Mrs Curzons mounted the dais again in the echoing quiet.

'Thank you to our recorder players for their rendition of "D'ye Ken John Peel".' She quietly turned over a page in her notes.

'Now we have a solo performance from one of our youngest musicians. Ladies and gentlemen, will you please welcome Miss Cordie Sweet.'

Alice leaned forward, every tendon in her body twangingly taut. This was it. Her solo piece. Cordie had never let Alice hear it. She had merely had Mrs Curzons' repeated assurances that it was an interesting performance and very accomplished. But the title was supposed to be a big surprise, 'a big birthday surprise', that's what Cordie had said to her.

Anyway, Cordie's father wasn't there to see it. Alice looked around at the grandparent with the child in his lap. With a start, she remembered her archival duties, removed the video camera and got ready to record.

Cordie got up from the cross-legged line and calmly walked over to the side table, where she was joined by her friend Sally. The pair of them got to work assembling what was evidently a substantial collection of instruments and props. Two chairs were placed downstage about eight feet apart. Cordie then produced what Alice recognized as the karaoke box she had got for Christmas. This was placed next to the chair stage right. They then produced a patchwork quilt of A4 sheets of paper, sturdily taped together, on which was painted a grey, expansive sea. The two girls briefly held it up for the audience to see and then laid it down between the chairs, using the legs of each to prevent it from rolling back up.

It was time for the last piece of stage furniture. Solemnly, Cordie's friend passed it to Cordie and she put it on the chair stage left.

It was a doll, Cordie's Barbie. The audience were now starting to murmur restively; when would the show start? Was this part of the show? All eyes swivelled to Mrs Curzons, who was obviously not going to intervene. All was apparently just as it should be.

Sally retired and Cordie switched on her karaoke box and held the microphone tightly against her chest, not too close to her mouth. The tinny music started up and, with a theatrical gesture, Cordie pointed at the doll, propped up against the chair-back on the other side of the painted sea, and began to sing in a clear treble voice:

> *My Barbie lies over the ocean,*
> *My Barbie lies over the sea,*
> *My Barbie lies over the ocean,*
> *So bring back my Barbie to me.*

Alice felt her vertebrae melt and slide into each other. She felt her tightening scalp pull skin up from between her shoulder blades. She thought: is this what parental pride feels like? Because it was the most powerful emotion she'd ever felt in her life. Cordie was singing on her own, a song that she had sort of made up herself. In front of a whole crowd of grown-ups. Had Alice ever done anything similar at that age? Had she done anything similar at any age at all? Cordie went into the chorus:

Bring back, oh bring back,
Oh bring back my Barbie to me, to me.
Bring back, oh bring back,
Oh bring back my Barbie to me.

Alice zoomed in on Cordie's face and looked at it on the screen for a long time. She was singing with absolute concentration, even passion. Her forehead was puckered in a frown, a line next to her left eyebrow. It was a frown-line she had inherited from her father.

Cordie went into the second verse, a repeat of the first, and her voice became yet more plangent, even keening. And it was here that Alice noticed a strange mood come over the audience as they watched Cordie yearningly gesture to the Barbie, who stayed, Stuart-like, over the water.

They were all growing sad. Cordie's sweet, attenu-ated voice settled over them like a web of melancholy. She wanted her Barbie and for all they knew, her Barbie wanted her. But they were separated by a cruel, unforgiv-ing fate, placed on distant shores. Who knew what emotions seethed within Barbie's hard plastic torso, what anguish was concealed by her perky smile? Was Cordie actually ventriloquizing exactly those emotions? The corners of every mouth began to turn down as the parents, grand-parents and godparents all began to remember their own toys: the teddies, footballs, tin soldiers and box games, all destroyed and gone, dismembered, deflated, up in attics and out at jumble sales.

Now, at a signal from Cordie, Sally came forward, picked up Barbie and carefully held her horizontal, flying above the heaving grey ocean, and carried her across, a few centimetres above the waves. Then she placed her in Cordie's left hand and Cordie clutched her to her chest and started singing again:

> *My Barbie's flown over the ocean,*
> *My Barbie's flown over the sea,*
> *My Barbie's flown over the ocean*
> *My Barbie's come right back to me.*

The audience became faintly delirious with relief and almost applauded when Cordie went into a chorus:

> *She's come back; she's come back*
> *She's come back (my Barbie) to me, to me . . .*

Tentatively, they even tried joining in, but were at once interrupted by an earsplitting crash from one side of the hall. There was utter silence except for a thin, wheezing musical accompaniment of the karaoke box. The fire-exit door had banged open, swinging round and knocking over a papier-mâché display of a farmhouse and barn-yard animals. A sweaty, dishevelled man staggered in, and realized with a gasp of dismay that he wasn't at the rear of the auditorium but in plain view of everyone.

He looked round and saw Mrs Curzons and all the chocolate-sweatshirted children looking at him with shocked disapproval, except for Cordie who remained quite impassive. They appeared to be waiting for him to say something, and he in turn seemed mutely to anticipate some rebuke or instruction from them. Many parents had swivelled their video cameras towards him, half expecting his entrance to be part of the show, and his flushed, clueless face popped up in miniature in a dozen different flip-out screens.

Dr Sweet tried a smile.

'Am I too late?'

27

Dr Sweet had flagged down a taxi, eventually. Once out of the Rylands, it had started to rain, as on his last visit, and all the cabs had mysteriously vanished or coldly extinguished their yellow livery of light. He had hopefully windmilled his arms at one or two, just in case, in the way of despised tourists or out-of-towners. When he finally found one it was dropping off, and he hung about menacingly while it expelled its passengers, proprietorially holding the door open for them and scowling at anyone else who might dare to claim it.

His frenzied offer to the driver to add five pounds to the fare if he could 'step on it' was coldly rebuffed with a lecture on the overwhelming need for safe driving and, as the journey wore on, the unspoken thought that five pounds was only slightly more than the regular tip anyway.

Dr Sweet had looked at his watch, and the meter, at the meter and his watch in obsessive turn. Three o'clock came and went as they stalled and crawled up the Seven Sisters Road. A quarter past came and went as they rounded into Hornsey Road. The climacteric of half past went by as they crept in a caravan of seething vehicles up Crouch Hill.

Jesus. He was going to miss it. He was going to miss Cordie's big birthday concert. He couldn't believe it. Every muscle in his legs and arms was taut and clenched, as if he could propel the taxi to its destination by physical effort. He had missed it. Hadn't he? Shouldn't he just relax?

No. There was still a chance he wasn't late. He had to keep going, so pointlessly his muscles were all tensed up. By the time he saw the infants' school he felt as if he had been snowboarding all afternoon. As the taxi wheeled round to the entrance, Dr Sweet pushed a note through the little window.

'OK, there you go. Keep the change!'

'You owe me another one pound seventy-five.'

'Oh *Christ*.'

He jogged up to the front entrance, but the door was closed – and locked. Of course! They must be using the side entrance.

Yes, it was open. Dr Sweet could hear music from somewhere, as he ran down corridors lined with notices and drawings, running in a way he hadn't for years. Where was he? Where were they? The music sometimes sounded closer, then mysteriously further away, as if he were scurrying up the staircase in an Escher drawing. Where was the hall? Where was he going? What was the time now? At last the music was so loud he knew he must be there, and this was the door!

Cordie had not wished to resume her song after he had shamefacedly made his way to a seat, and neither Alice nor his parents had even looked at him. Mrs Curzons had introduced a few more musical events, but within ten minutes the concert was over.

If only he'd had his own car, he could have gone home separately, or better, invented some excuse to get back to the lab. Instead he had to sit in the passenger seat while Alice drove, with John and Rosemary in the back, Cordie sitting blankly on her grandmother's lap.

'You were *wonderful*, Cordie,' said Alice. 'Easily the best.'

'You were marvellous,' said Rosemary.

'Top-hole!' chimed in John.

Dr Sweet churlishly remained silent. He could not, in all good conscience, praise a performance he hadn't seen, and apologizing again for having missed it would have been out of place, especially as he had been gabblingly contrite for the past twenty minutes to Cordie, Alice, his parents and Mrs Curzons for destroying the barnyard-animal display the children had spent months making.

Should he tell them about his discovery now? Should he tell them he had made what was arguably the most important medical discovery of modern times? Should he tell them, yes, all right, he was late, but that was because he had been busy working on something supremely wonderful for mankind, something that would make them all proud of him.

There seemed no easy way to do it. The time wasn't right, so he just sat there in grumpy silence, which merged into a quiet that settled on the car's passengers once all the congratulations had died away.

Back at the house, Dr Sweet found the two cakes in their penny-farthing formation in the kitchen. The sight of them suddenly made his mouth water.

'Cordie! Mum! Dad!' he shouted as they took off their

coats in the corridor. 'Let's have some *cake*! I'll put the kettle on and we'll have some *cake*!'

John came into the kitchen to speak with him alone, without Rosemary, a sure sign, ever since his earliest boyhood, that something was seriously wrong.

'I don't think so, old boy,' he said sadly, 'your mother and I are a bit tired. I think we'll go upstairs and read and perhaps have a bit of a nap.'

John went out and Alice came in. Dr Sweet knew better than to offer her cake.

'Alice,' he said, 'I really am so sorry about this afternoon.'

But Alice didn't sound angry.

'No, David,' she said with a thin smile, 'that's all right. You were held up at the lab, you couldn't get a taxi, I understand. I really do. It's all right. It could happen to any of us. Really.' She smiled again and placed her hand briefly on his forearm. Dr Sweet couldn't believe that she wasn't angry.

'You're not angry?'

'Angry? No, no, don't be silly. It's a shame, but you didn't do it on purpose, so there we are.'

'Would you like a cup of tea?'

Alice thought about this for a moment and then exhaled heavily.

'Do you know what, David, I'd better go out again and shop for tonight's dinner, so really I've got to go now.'

'You don't want me to do it?'

'No, no,' she smiled, 'it's my turn. I'd better go now.'

She went. Dr Sweet looked again at the cakes, which had 'Alice' and 'Cordie' iced in genteel piped letters. He wondered if it was dark enough to turn on the lights in the kitchen. Then Cordie came in. He guessed, unhappily, that she had been upstairs putting Barbie and the rolled-up sea away in her room. Cordie looked out of the window into the garden.

'You can have some cake now, Cordie, if you want. It's OK. You've done your concert and it's your birthday. You love cake. Have a slice of cake.'

Cordie ignored him.

'I'm going to have some cake. Should I have a slice of your cake or Mummy's cake?'

Silence.

'Cordie, you know I really am sorry about missing your song. Everyone says it was really brilliant. Perhaps you can sing it for us again tonight, after supper?'

Cordie bent her face down and laid her cheek against the cool countertop, just by the bread board with its sunburst design. Dr Sweet went up to her and tried to position his face opposite hers, but she turned her head over to look in the other direction.

'Cordie,' said Dr Sweet carefully, after another silent standoff, 'there was a reason why I was late, you know. I think I might have made an important discovery at work.' He looked steadily at the back of her head, the blank mop of hair. 'That was why. I mean, I wouldn't have been late if it wasn't very, very important, would I? You see,' Dr Sweet brought his head very close to hers, 'I think I might have discovered the cure for a very bad illness. Or something that could lead to the cure. The terrible disease that killed your granny and grandad on Mummy's side. That was before you were born, so you didn't know anything about it. But it was terrible and very sad, and I think I might have found a way of curing it. I haven't told *anyone* yet, not even Mummy. You're the only one I've told. Isn't that good? What do you think of that?'

Cordie lifted her head up and looked out of the window, still without saying anything.

'Please say something, Cordie. Just a few words for your dad. How much do you love me, Cordie? How much do you love your poor old dad?'

Cordie said nothing, just turned and left the kitchen. Her father didn't attempt to follow her. It was getting dark, but he didn't switch the light on. With his knife hovering, he tried choosing which of the cakes to cut. Then he laid the knife down, and sat at the table, both palms laid flat.

He remembered when he and Alice first brought Cordie home from the hospital, tucked up in her little Moses basket. They had put her on their kitchen table, one just like this, and looked at her, two little fists drawn up to her face like a tiny pugilist. And Dr Sweet had systematically gone through in his head all the terrible things that could happen to her: illness, car accident, disaster. He reasoned that the odds against each thing happening were millions to one, but the odds against each specific thing happening after being specifically mentally anticipated were clearly much greater. So by imagining each individual catastrophe he was scientifically decreasing the chances of it happening. It made perfect sense. Throughout the succeeding years, Dr Sweet had watched Cordie and wondered what she was seeing, what she was thinking, what she was remembering. When he thought back to his own earliest memory, he thought it was his fifth birthday party, or perhaps what he remembered was his sixth birthday party. Everything before that was a blank. So when he looked at Cordie crying, Cordie playing, Cordie sleeping and Cordie being fed, he realized that this was her pre-history of selfhood. She would remember nothing of this, but any second now, any moment, something would happen that would stick to the photographic plate of her remembering mind and never get erased. It would be her first memory and her life would begin.

What would it be? Singing that song? Seeing her father stumble into the concert hall midway through? Seeing her father come back from the convenience store before Christmas in a state? Or something less dramatic? Her pushchair from years ago? Baloo and Mowgli? The view from her window onto the garden, with its dank lawn and freezing red-and-yellow plastic Wendy house? Her mother taking her swimming? Or none of these things?

But now all that was in the past. It was a memory, his last memory, of her. There was no point in thinking about it. Why didn't he just face it now? His daughter was going to be more attached to his ex-wife than to him. The way Cordie was behaving now was an indication of how she would behave around him from now on, when she was twelve, eighteen, twenty-one, thirty-five. A withdrawn young girl; an angry teen; a defiant young woman, a self-contained professional adult with a private life almost entirely hidden from her ageing father. All this was a straw in the wind. Why should he use up his energy fighting the inevitable? Wasn't it time to move on? After all, hadn't it come at the right time? He was finally making something of his life, his career. All divorced fathers had to accept the fact that there was no point trying to maintain the relationship with your children that you had in the family home. All that was gone now.

He thought, I shall turn my back on her. I shall turn my back and go my own way. I shan't destroy myself searching for a love to which I am no longer entitled. I shall turn my back on her.

All at once, Dr Sweet thought about some lines of a poem, something he'd had to read in a General Studies class that all university entrance scientists were forced to take. It was Milton's *Paradise Lost*, book nine. The serpent is telling Eve not to be afraid of God, because a frightening God is not a fair, beneficent God and so not an authentic God:

> *God therefore cannot hurt ye, and be just;*
> *Not just, not God; not feared then, nor obeyed:*
> *Your fear itself of death removes the fear.*

He could remember his old teacher reading it out as if it were yesterday, and telling the sullen, prototypical physicists and chemists and mathematicians that these lines had a simple power no-one could match. Were they a wicked sophistry or, he daringly asked, an inspiring call to arms for humanism and atheism? For how could an innocent person in an innocent world be *afraid*? Wasn't the serpent right? Isn't there something heroic and thrilling about taking your fear and using it as a weapon?

I shall turn my back. I shall have a new life and a new family and new children, too. This has all been a mistake. It didn't work out. Why spend the rest of your life becalmed in a mistake? Why double and triple the pain by staying there, especially as the other participant in the mistake is moving away? The untenability of the situation is obvious, and so is the way out. Why be loyal to unhappiness? Your fear itself of death removes the fear.

When all this was over, Dr Sweet thought, he would sell this house and find somewhere else, somewhere different, somewhere new. He would move in with Hattie. Maybe she would get pregnant, maybe they would both move abroad: Europe, the States. He would start again, and get it *right* this time. All it needed was courage and clear-sightedness. All it took was the clarity of mind to rise above your immediate situation and see what it was, where it was going and how it could be changed. Dr Sweet had decades of adult work and life ahead of him. He didn't have to keep ploughing the same furrow. He didn't have to keep doggedly picking the same unlucky lottery numbers. He could choose some different lottery numbers. He could do something else, something that might radically improve his life. It was all there for the *taking*.

So why was he just sitting here in this dark kitchen? Dr Sweet slapped his thighs with an air of energy and decision, got up and switched on the lights at last. He listened for the sounds of Cordie playing, heard nothing, and assumed she was reading and that his parents were having their nap. Alice would be back from shopping in about twenty minutes, which meant dinner wouldn't be ready for another hour and a half.

Something was nagging at his mind, and it was only now that he realized what it was. It was the girl who was standing next to Cordie when he'd blundered in. She seemed to be part of Cordie's song, although no-one had mentioned a duet and he had been too mortified to ask. He had a snapshot memory of her giving a Barbie to Cordie. She had been looking directly at him at the same time as Cordie, the same cool blank look – a slight, dark-eyed, olive-skinned girl whose chocolate sweatshirt hung looser on her than on Cordie. Dr Sweet wondered if *her* parents were in the audience, and why that thought was so obscurely troubling to him.

Then there was the sound of the key turning slickly in the lock, and the rustle of plastic shopping bags crumpling heavily on the mat. Alice would need some help.

28

It was clearly going to be the most exciting ceremony in the history of the Heart of Gold awards.

The main dining room of the Dorchester looked magnificent, lit with a dozen chandeliers, and with the powerful arc lights trained on the stage positioned at one end of the room where the presentations were to take place. Wines were offered to those of an age to accept them. The many teenagers and young children present, imminent recipients of Heart Of Gold awards, had to refrain and content themselves with Diet Coke, squash, juice and Fruit Shoot.

Ros, assistant to Angie Meredith, head of media relations at Dartmouth Media and associate producer of this event, was having a far less enjoyable time, having brown-bagged her lunch at 11.45 a.m. before everything began. She wore a headset mike from which she was continually chivvied and blamed by Angie.

'Hi . . . yes . . . mmm . . .' she said. 'Yes, I've told her, Angie, but she's only ten years old and she doesn't really understand the concept of a running order . . . No, I didn't use that technical phrase to her; I didn't say "running order" . . . Of course not . . . No, she's stopped crying . . .

She's going to be fine . . . Her mother has calmed down an awful lot . . .'

Dr Sweet was calm, presiding over his table like some benign Sicilian don. Alice and Cordie were to his right, John and Rosemary to his left. With what he considered remarkable generosity, he had invited Alice to bring Richard along, but Alice had become cold and evasive at this suggestion, and said she didn't think it was appropriate any more, and that if it was all right with him, she wanted to bring someone else. This turned out to be a large, genial man with his blond hair tied back with an elastic band, a man whom Dr Sweet recognized from somewhere.

Cordie had a small child's portion of everything on a special little plate, as did the other children present. There was no distinction between the child prizewinners, the children of the adult prizewinners and the children helped by the prizewinners, adult and child.

Directly opposite him, at their round table for eight, were places set for the people *he* had saved, a happy pairing arrangement of rescuers and rescued that was duplicated on every table for whom the beneficiaries of the prizewinner's courage were not from the same family. They were for Kamil and his daughter Zalihe, Kamil's wife having elected to stay at home and look after Price-Best with Adil. They hadn't yet arrived; perhaps they'd got lost, perhaps they were held up in traffic. It was something else that Ros was worried about, as they hadn't yet videotaped Kamil and Zalihe's tribute to Dr Sweet for use in the edited version of the ceremony that was due to be broadcast that evening. They were going to have to tape it when they arrived, after the main course.

Dr Sweet felt a little unsure about how he would greet Kamil. Would he be irritated at being put in the position of the humble recipient of Dr Sweet's and the Dartmouth Media Group's bounty, a bounty that moreover drew attention to his own apparent failure to protect his daughter?

But in his mind, Dr Sweet had semi-consciously decided to smoothe away the potential embarrassment of their meeting by inflating in his mind the extent and warmth of their acquaintance *before* the great incident. The whole business of Dr Sweet having withdrawn a lot of his custom from PriceBest, his implied disapproval of the quality of their vegetables and the unreliability of the newspaper delivery, all that was airbrushed out of his mind. He and Kamil were neighbours and friends, with a breezy, chaffing relationship.

The first course was served: a quaint prawn cocktail, offered simply because the organizers had discovered that this was virtually the only dish that would be eaten by both adults and children. Dr Sweet thanked his waitress perfunctorily as she placed his prepared glass in front of him. John and Rosemary did so with a warmth that got a smile and a laugh from her, a snatch of conversation, a nodding of the head from the waitress and an 'oh yes' from all three of them. What had his parents said to her? Dr Sweet had never had that knack of being easy and friendly to strangers and now, he supposed, he never would.

Everyone ate but Cordie. She took her proportionately small silver-plate spoon and gently disturbed the shelled prawns' tips, as she might exotic seaweed or molluscs on some underwater reef. She still wasn't speaking to Dr

Sweet. He wondered if he might address a few words to his daughter again, solely for the purpose of monitoring the situation.

'How are you, Miss Cordie?' he called over to her.

Nothing. Alice gently smoothed her hair with her hand, an attention Cordie accepted calmly but wordlessly. Dr Sweet smiled at John, who smiled back instantly. His parents were more nervous than anyone, much more so than they had been at Cordie's concert. At least there they knew, or thought they knew, what was expected of them.

Still no Kamil and Zalihe. Ros was now rigid with tension as she spoke to Angie from her headset mike.

'No, no. There's no point, Angie . . . If they're coming on the underground, their phone wouldn't get a signal anyway. Oh! Angie, yes, she's here. No, no, not them. *Aggie's* here.'

There was a hen-coop flutter behind Dr Sweet, who had to crane his neck round 180 degrees to see Aggie Figgis, the presenter of *Aggie!*, a daytime television show and the author of a number of books on subjects such as parenting, drugs, wheat intolerance and coping with the terrible twos. Aggie was the host of the afternoon's proceedings; she had straw-coloured blonde hair which rose up translucently in a kind of angular widow's peak from her scalp, and was wearing a heavy two-piece suit of tweed-like material in a cartoonishly large houndstooth design. Everywhere, people reacted to her face with its enormous blue eyes and retroussé nose, a face like that of a stately juvenile lead of the pre-war stage. It was a compellingly urgent, searching face, which had solicited the most searing of testimonies and eloquently expressed mute disapproval of the undeserving, who so often appeared on her show to parade their emotional and sexual incontinence. Like a magnet under iron filings, Aggie's face caused the guests to stir and prickle. They half rose from their seats, their lunch neglected, hoping to be called upon, perhaps in unconscious imitation of Aggie's regular television guests, who were seated on a banked slope around which Aggie would roam with her microphone.

Dr Sweet realized that she was looking for *him*. When her eyes made contact with his, he shrank from their power. Aggie bore down on him with a smile that suggested the containment of passionate tears. He twisted his chair round and rose as the others had done, putting out his hand for a formal greeting. But Aggie was beyond such courtesies. She reacted to him as to a child she hadn't seen for twenty years. She was evidently on the point of placing both hands on his cheeks and cupping his face, but at the last moment contented herself with a hearty handshake.

'David,' she said. 'David, this is an honour for me. An *honour* for *me*,' she repeated with generous emphasis. Dr Sweet looked into her eyes and felt how small and frail she looked in the flesh, yet how attractive. It was impossible to say how old she was.

'I am so looking forward to introducing you in the 32-carat section, David. And this little lady must be . . .'

'This is my daughter, Cordie,' said Dr Sweet, falling easily into the subservient manner of a Lord Lieutenant introducing the monarch to local dignitaries.

But it wasn't. Aggie was looking at Kamil and Zalihe, who had just arrived, Kamil giving an opaque half smile and Zalihe absently looking about her.

'This must be Zalihe,' said Aggie, having consulted

her PA on the point. 'How lovely of you to come. Sit, sit, you're not late at all. Sit.'

Aggie swept on, and the back of her single-vented jacket with its vivid, jagged design, looked like a television set with bad reception bobbing away backwards through the crowd. Kamil and Zalihe did not sit, Kamil apparently considering that he also needed to be invited to do so by Dr Sweet as the head of the table; it was a hesitation that undoubtedly signalled a reserved, even cool relationship with him.

'Kamil. Hello again,' said Dr Sweet, shaking hands and summoning up the geniality he had decided upon earlier. 'And hello.' He turned to Kamil's daughter, who had plonked herself down next to Cordie, and the pair of them were gigglingly poking each other's prawn cocktails with their little spoons.

'Zalihe – Sally,' said Alice smilingly, giving both versions of her name in a kind of bilingual reflex. 'How are you?' Rosemary pleasantly began a conversation with Kamil on her left, which in a miraculously short space of time secured a broad smile from him and a chuckling exclamation of, 'Yes!'

Of course, Alice had known about Cordie being friends with Zalihe for quite some time. But Dr Sweet felt slightly dizzy and sat down. That was it; this was the little girl who had helped Cordie with her song; the little girl in the shop. She lived locally and she went to the same school as Cordie. Seeing her brought back that night with a terrible clarity and force, unmediated by prizes or interviews. How Cordie had been watching *The Jungle Book*; how he'd had testy words with his parents and Alice and how he'd wanted to get out of the house. And in the shop, the lady with her little girl in the pushchair leaving just as he came in. The man, John O'Rourke, with the bottle, and how he had wondered if he could just leave and pretend he hadn't seen anything. He looked at Kamil and realized that he, too, hadn't known who his daughter's best friend was.

The main course arrived: rump of lamb, little pasta dishes for the girls and a vegetarian option for Kamil. Dr Sweet was delighted to concentrate on the food, gulp down the heavy Australian claret that came with it and put his flashback behind him. His mind turned back to the sunny mood of satisfaction which had sustained him until now. This lunch was to be a little epoch, a secret farewell celebration consigning the old David Sweet, the professionally disappointed divorcee, to history. The new Dr Sweet was the Director of Research at a major scientific institution with an exciting new relationship and – dare he say it, even in the silent chamber of his skull? – a major medical breakthrough. He was on the verge of a monumental discovery that would be greeted with massive appreciation, And this award, well, it was a presentiment, a happy augury for future status and success. His *courage*. It took courage to put the past behind him and build a new future, didn't it?

The main course finished, it was time for the initial prize-giving. Aggie took up her position by a lectern on the left and her zigzag two-piece returned the stage light fiercely. Her face appeared on television monitors in an expression of transcendental calm. By twisting his neck, Dr Sweet could see the autocue from which she was reading.

'Ladies and gentlemen,' said Aggie, 'this is a very

special awards ceremony. Heaven knows, I've been present at a few, but this is the only one that really means anything to me, because the people that we are honouring today have achieved something far in excess of coming up with a new movie, or a new TV series or a new restaurant. They have distinguished themselves in acts of courage – real *courage* – courage that often required them to risk life and limb. When I look at these people, sometimes very young people, I feel humbled. Nothing I did in nursing my husband back to health after his heart attack comes close to this, in my opinion. Ladies and gentlemen, these are not ordinary people – they are *extra*ordinary people. But let's get on with the first Heart of Gold award, which goes to Rebecca Beasley, Ally Stahl and Kathy Dennison.'

There was a flourish of applause which was immediately muted by sharp, stabbing musical stings. The lights dimmed yet further to allow the audience to concentrate on the monitors, on which appeared a video presentation of what Rebecca, Ally and Kathy had done. They were three sixteen-year-old girls who had saved a seven-year-old from drowning in a canal: he had run away from his mother and fallen into the water chasing a balloon. Rebecca had jumped in to save him; Ally had used life-saving skills to expel water from his lungs and Kathy had called for help on her mobile and run along the towpath to find the boy's mother. The video was an interview with the three girls, who were modest, even self-deprecatory about their remarkable bravery and presence of mind.

The lights went up, to more music, and Rebecca, Ally and Kathy went up to the stage from their table – at which sat their parents, the little boy and *his* mother, who joined them a few moments later. They looked down shyly, and could hardly be prevailed upon to look up for the photograph of them receiving their award from Aggie. A roar of applause swept up from the assembly of television personalities, politicians, sports stars. On Dr Sweet's table, the enthusiasm was overwhelming, led by John, Rosemary and Kamil, who revealed his ability to whistle by putting thumb and forefinger in his mouth.

Rebecca, Ally, Kathy and their party resumed their seats and Aggie took up her place at the podium once again. If her face had been preternaturally serious at first, it now took on an aspect of extraordinary intensity: partly severe and partly seraphic. She held this expression while the audience settled down again.

'Ladies and gentlemen, I now want to talk to you about a lady called Jasmine.' The cameras picked out the broad, pleasant face of a middle-aged Jamaican lady who suddenly flinched and smiled as she saw that all eyes were on her. 'On a cold November afternoon last week, Jasmine did something very outstanding indeed.' Aggie made a broad, sweeping gesture to the monitor screens, and again the lights dimmed and the musical string repeated itself. Another video presentation told the story of how Jasmine, a hospital dinner lady, had discovered that a disturbed young female patient had got out onto a high ledge with her newborn baby in her arms, and was threatening to jump. There was no time to alert the relevant emergency services, so Jasmine knew that there was nothing else for it but to crawl out onto the ledge herself and talk the young woman down. She was threatening to jump and take anyone close enough down with her, but Jasmine kept looking into the woman's eyes, asked what her name was, what her baby's name was and, with no training of any kind in this sort of thing, persuaded her to come back inside.

The lights came back up and Jasmine shyly made her way to the stage amidst ecstatic cheering and whooping. And there was something else too: all around him, Dr Sweet could see people crying. John and Rosemary both had tears in their eyes and so did Kamil. Alice was openly sniffling and looking in her bag for a tissue. Zalihe and Cordie were shiny-eyed, but to his increasing chagrin, Dr Sweet realized that he couldn't feel anything at all, merely a strange, cold apprehension at his own impending distinction.

So the afternoon went on in what became a compelling rhythm. An introduction from Aggie, a television presentation on the monitor, detailing some astonishing act of selflessness and humanity, and then the irresistible discharge of emotion as the prizewinners made their way onstage to a stirring musical accompaniment. A little boy who saved his mother's life after an asthma attack, a young merchant seaman who had survived 70 per cent burns to become a physical therapist, an elderly gentleman and former amateur bantamweight boxer who had disarmed the robber holding up the off licence where he was buying his daily bottle of stout. All were greeted with a crescendo of group emotion as the person concerned threaded their way round the tables towards the front. People were crying openly. Clearly, in many cases, years of repressed emotion and sadness were being purged. Only the children were exempt from being lachrymose, but even they were rapt. Dr Sweet, on the other hand, felt as if everyone was now speaking a foreign language of which he understood only the barest smattering. He looked around and realized that his was the only face not covered in tears. What was *wrong* with him?

After an hour and a quarter, the main part of the event was over. Everyone on their table looked at each other with sad, complicit smiles. John honkingly blew his nose. Dr Sweet thought the only thing to do was fake it, so he blew his nose as well, then pursed his lips very hard and looked down sadly at the floor.

*

Ros bustled up. 'Kamil, Sally,' she said, 'we need you now to record that insert.' They remained immobile, Kamil perplexed by these technical terms. 'Come *along*, you two,' she repeated brightly, pulling down the mouthpiece of her headset with finger and thumb, in order to talk to them more emphatically. 'Follow me.' Kamil and Zalihe got up, and walked behind Ros, hand in hand, as if they were brother and sister, and not father and daughter. But then Ros stopped, wheeled around and returned to Dr Sweet.

'Oh, David,' she said, a little distantly. 'There's someone here to see you.' She spoke coldly because no one at Dartmouth Media approved of unannounced visitors asking to see the participants and possibly disrupting the proceedings.

'Who is it?' he asked.

Ros checked her clipboard. 'It's Ms Harriet Arkell; she's in the annexe over there. Please, David, don't be too long, we might need you at any time. Over there.'

'I won't be long,' Dr Sweet said to Alice, who arched her eyebrows at him.

'Miss Cordie,' he said to his daughter, 'I'm just off for

a bit. I won't be long. I'll be right back.' Cordie gave him a look of inexpressible blankness and turned back to Zalihe.

He stood, glad of the distraction, and made his way across the great mass of tables towards the side annexe. What did Hattie want? Did she just want to be close to him at this special time, he wondered complacently? Perhaps she just wanted to put her arms around the 32-Carat Heart of Gold winner and tell him she loved him. A spring entered Dr Sweet's step as he approached the annexe. Or perhaps there had been some new development in their great experiment. Until now, Dr Sweet had thought that secrecy was of the essence, but now, as with a secret affair, he desperately wanted it to be revealed; he wanted to be found out. He turned the gilt door handle.

'Hattie.'

Hattie was alone in the annexe and, as Dr Sweet had imagined, walked over to him and put her arms around his neck. But he hadn't pictured her bursting into tears.

'Hattie, what's the matter?'

'Oh David, I'm *sorry*. I probably shouldn't have come, but I thought I had to tell you. And I needed someone to talk to anyway.' Hattie's lower lip was trembling – in a very different way from all the others at the prizegiving.

'What *is* it?'

'Well, I've got some good news and some bad news. Which do you want first?'

This question had always exasperated Dr Sweet. 'The . . . the good news.'

'Well,' said Hattie, 'your solicitor called the lab. He said he'd been leaving messages all over the place, but you've all got your cellphones switched off.'

'What did he say?' asked Dr Sweet sharply.

'He said the CPS aren't proceeding with the case. That's it. You're off the hook. Free and clear.'

Dr Sweet gasped with a little exhalation, then remembered the second part of the conversation.

'And the bad news?'

'It's the BLC compound, David,' she said, shaking her head and slumping down on a chair. 'It's *BAD*. We took it for a phase one clinical trial.'

'Yes, at Hammersmith Hospital. But I'm not expecting any results from that yet.'

Hattie looked up at him. 'No, nor was anyone. We were trying it on fifteen terminal cases. The first was a Mr Leadbetter, seventy-seven years old; he has pancreatic cancer, terminal case. He'd agreed to try anything we had. Nothing to lose.'

'Yes?' asked Dr Sweet in a very small voice.

'Well, it turns out these compounds are all very well in mice and other mammals, but they're as toxic as hell in humans. Mr Leadbetter died this morning, David. Some pretty nasty side effects, too.'

In silence, Dr Sweet and Hattie listened to the buzz from the other side of the door.

'Well,' he said at last, 'we must expect reversals like this. This is just the sort of thing we have to prepare ourselves for. We have to carry on. Thank you, Hattie. Thank you very much for telling me. You did the right thing.'

There was a knock and Ros put her head round the door.

'Gonna need you in *five*!' She spread five fingers out starfish-style, flashed a smile and was gone.

'OK, I'd best be going,' said Hattie, unhappily gathering up her coat.

'*Thanks* Hattie.'

'OK.'

'I'll see you tomorrow in the lab.'

'OK.'

'Thanks again.'

'Right.'

Hattie went, but Dr Sweet hesitated before following her out. He didn't feel like telling anyone about the CPS and perversely wanted to savour this terrible defeat. His cure, the great cure, had turned out to be as poisonous as hemlock. It was back to the drawing board. And all those Nobel dreams ... he winced, as if swallowing a thistle. The blondwood halls, the distinguished Swedish gentlemen, the scientific committees and governmental endorsements, all of them gone. And what did he have now?

'David, I really do need you this minute!' said Ros, popping her head round the door again.

'All right, Ros, just coming,' said Dr Sweet quietly.

'Everything all right?' asked Ros coolly.

'Yes, yes,' he replied, realizing that this withdrawn behaviour was in bad taste at such an occasion. 'Everything's fine.'

They went back out into the mêlée, where the noise had become deafening. Dr Sweet almost had to jog to keep up with Ros. They left the main hall, went through an enormous set of double doors, mirrored with a queasy tint of gold in which Dr Sweet's reflection looked hunted. They emerged into the main lobby of the hotel, or more particularly the handsome broad avenue that led up from the front entrance. It was here that gilt tables and chairs were laid out for people having afternoon tea. A pianist was trickling out 'Fly Me To The Moon', and Dr Sweet found himself humming along. He started humming just that little bit too loud, and caught Ros's eye, who frowned back – openly frowned, with no pretence at courtesy to an honoured guest. He had responsibilities as the star of this show and he seemed to be losing concentration, losing focus. Dr Sweet caught her drift and shut up, instantly feeling his mood become grimmer.

They went into a suite atop a shallow flight of stairs on a mezzanine where a crew was taping Kamil and Zalihe's testimony in the tasteful surroundings of an intercontinental hotel room. Ros splayed her fingertips on the door and pushed it open very quietly, in case they were recording. Dr Sweet found himself wondering if he should go to Mr Leadbetter's funeral.

'I really don't think that's a good idea, darling.' Nige, the director, was arguing with Neil, his cameraman, as to the merits of using the interview they had just filmed. Kamil had committed to record his own tribute to Dr Sweet: a notably restrained, almost neutral account, in which he had been absent in the stockroom for hardly more than a moment and had re-entered to find the man sprawling on the floor. Crucially, he would commit himself to no more than saying that Zalihe was frightened and Dr Sweet was 'a good man'. They were supposed to edit this segment at top speed and get it into the video presentation now, cleaning it up for transmission later that evening. But as far as the production team were concerned, this was really an unmitigated disaster. Nothing in Kamil's bland and unenthusiastic statement was usable. Nothing.

And the director had been quite unable to coax anything more out of him.

So they turned to Zalihe.

Kamil's daughter was due to figure just in the shots of Kamil, who was supposed to shower praise on their award-winner while his little girl snuggled up to him heartwarmingly. But as if in parallel to Kamil's bafflingly cold deposition, she had sat bolt upright, silent and unsmiling. After a tense, whispered consultation with Ros, Nige turned and said, 'Sally? We think it would be great if we could just have a chat with you on your own. Would you like that?'

'No,' Kamil said sharply, not on her behalf exactly, but to assert his affronted sense of protocol: that these people had presumed to address this to his daughter and not to him. A flash of fear ignited behind Ros's eyes. An interviewee cutting up rough was all in a day's work on another sort of programme, but on Hearts of Gold? When they were running out of time?

'Kamil,' she said, uncoiling a steely display of professional emollience, 'it would be so lovely if we could have some shots of Sally on her own. It would be so lovely for us.'

Kamil calmed a little, but his essential misgiving remained untouched. 'You see,' he smiled hesitantly, 'Zalihe has not spoken all that much about it yet, or anything much, to anyone at all.'

He smiled apologetically and a mood of suppressed panic and dismay settled on his three interlocutors. But then, as if by magic, the stalemate was lifted by Zalihe herself. After looking curiously at Dr Sweet for a moment, she announced, 'No, I want to talk about it.' Kamil looked at her with astonishment. Now she wants to talk? After all this time? But Ros and her colleague were thrilled. Little Sally was going to open up. Perhaps something could be salvaged from this after all.

Zalihe was arranged in a comfy chair with a little mike clipped to her dress. Wordlessly, they decided Ros would be a better interviewer than the director. Time was pressing, so she started straight in:

'Sally, what do you think of David? Do you think he was brave to save you?'

'No,' said Zalihe as sharply as her father had just done, in a beautifully clear voice, as resonant as a little silver bell. 'I think he was really scared.'

'Well,' said Ros, carrying on with a steady voice, 'lots of brave people do things when they are scared, don't they? That's partly why it's so brave.'

'I think he was just trying to get away. He didn't hit that man. I think he was just trying to get out of the shop. He kept saying "Oh shit oh shit." He was shitting himself.' And with that, Zalihe folded her arms and put her chin down a little, indicating with precocious confidence that the interview was at an end.

Ros stood up from her supplicatory crouch; Nige ran his tongue over his front teeth, distending his tightly pursed lips into a simian pout. Neil switched off his camera and light. They withdrew once again to a huddle at the other end of the room.

'I'm not sure we can use that,' said Nige.

'You *think*?'

Then Ros looked up at Dr Sweet, who seemed to be gazing at his reflection in the hall mirror and mouthing the word 'Leadbetter' to himself.

'All right,' she said curtly. 'We'll have to . . .' She turned to Kamil and Zalihe. 'Thanks *very* much, people, that's great. Can I ask you to get back to your table now?' Obediently they left. Then Ros looked at Dr Sweet and, now at the end of her tether, addressed him as she would a non-house-trained dog. 'Come on, you.'

29

When he came back, Cordie thought her dad looked totally different. It was like when she saw his passport photo once; he looked the same but different. He was pale and nervy and wouldn't look at anyone for very long. When he smiled it wasn't a real smile, but a funny sort of pushing up of the corners of his mouth. He looked like boys at school when they'd been told off. He hardly replied to her mummy when she asked him if he was all right and he didn't say anything at all to her mum's friend from the swimming pool who came round to bleed the radiators. He just plonked himself down and drank almost a whole glass of wine in one go.

She looked around at all the other tables, and quite a lot of the time they were all looking at her daddy and everyone on *their* table. Everyone was talking and it was very noisy. Cordie put her fingers in her ears and it all went muffled. She took them out and it was a big roar. In, out, in, out. Muffle, roar, muffle, roar. She did it in a little rhythm, as if everyone was roaring together. It was so loud she couldn't hear what everyone was saying. She told Sally to look up at the ceiling and they looked at the big chandeliers, big round chandeliers with thousands of jewels in them which shone with a yellowy rainbow light.

If she kept looking she could see the ordinary light bulbs behind them making the jewels shine.

'Atchoo!' she said and closed her eyes, and against the browny-red darkness there were splodges and globules of green and yellow in chandelier shapes.

Her mum asked her if she was going to finish her ice cream and she opened her eyes and looked at it. It wasn't proper ice cream: it was a sorbet, blackcurrant flavoured; it tasted all icy. Her mum said that if she was finished she should put her spoon on her plate, pointing upwards.

Cordie and Sally were wondering what was under the tablecloth, so they peeled it back and found another creamy cloth underneath. They peeled that back and it was just wood! Nothing but cracked-up brown wood, worse than the kitchen table at home. There were some words that looked like they'd been burned into the surface; it said SUPPLIER. Her mum was getting cross that she and Sally were flapping the tablecloths up over the edges of other people's plates. Cordie asked her to look at the brown wood, but she wouldn't and told her to put the cloth back. Then her dad said she could keep looking at the table if she wanted to. He was speaking in a funny, quiet voice and looking at her. Cordie put the cloth back, picked up her spoon and put a tiny sliver of blackcurrant sorbet on her tongue. Now her dad was saying something to her, asking her how much she loved him. She didn't say anything. He didn't seem like himself; he didn't seem like her dad.

A lady came and took everyone's plates away, then another lady came and brought great big bunches of grapes. Cordie asked her mum to peel her one, like Cleopatra in something they'd once watched on the Cartoon

Channel, and she made a sort of cross-funny face and said, 'You!' She and Sally ate a lot of grapes, spitting out the pips on their hands and dropping them on the floor. Then someone came round with cheese, thin biscuits and slices of brown bread. She and Sally cut themselves some pieces of squishy blue cheese, put it in their mouths and went 'Ugh!' clutching their throats and pretending to be sick, and Sally's dad told her off and Cordie's mum told her off too.

Now a man came round and offered more drinks, and everyone said no except her dad, who had a 'small brandy', and her mum made a face at him and he just grinned at her using the same forced smile. The lady with the earphones came over and told Cordie's mum that the prize-giving was about to start, and that she might want to get Cordie cleaned up a bit because the camera might be on her, so she wiped some of the cheese-mess off Cordie's face while Cordie wriggled and whinged, and Sally's dad did the same thing to her. The lady with the headphones went round to her dad and started talking to him but he looked like he wasn't really listening; he was just looking at Cordie and her mum in a strange way. He didn't look very well. Then an old man came round with a box of cigars. Everyone said they didn't want one, and her mum said he shouldn't offer them around with so many children there; the man just shrugged and said it was what they did at all the functions.

Then her dad said he wanted a cigar. Her mum told him not to be so silly, but no, he said he wanted a 'fine cigar' and that he hadn't had one since a couple of Christmases ago and he'd quite like one now. But they give you *cancer*, hissed her mum and her dad said he knew that, but a little of what you fancy does you good. Oh very bloody scientific, said her mum, and Grandma said could you please not swear in front of the children, and her mum said sorry.

The man went round to him, and he chose the biggest, fattest one he could, and the man took it and chopped the end off with a little silver cutter and gave it back to him. Then he said that would be seventeen pounds fifty and would he be paying by cash or with a credit card? Cordie knew straight away that her dad had thought it would be free, and she could see that her mum spotted the same thing because she spluttered and drank some water. Her dad slowly got two notes out and gave them to the man who said he would return at the end of the ceremony with his change, and that made Cordie's dad look even crosser. Then he lit his cigar, which gave off a blue smoke that Cordie didn't much like and neither did Grandma and Grandpa, but her dad just kept looking round at them all and drinking.

The cigar smoke was beginning to make her eyes sting and she wished she'd brought her goggles. She asked if she could have some water and her mum asked her dad to pass Cordie the bottle. But he wasn't listening. He was signing an autograph for a girl who had come across and was leaning over. When he'd finished and she'd gone, he looked, beaming, around the table again and called across to her, asking how much she loved him, calling himself her 'poor old dad'. But Cordie didn't answer because the prize-giving was going to start.

30

Everyone tensed as the lights went down, everyone but Dr Sweet, who felt only a spongy calm. He dropped his cigar into his empty glass and listened as from afar to its weak fizz.

Aggie was up on the podium again, her jaggedy jacket rippling in the distance like a mirage.

'Ladies and gentlemen, this is the most remarkable part of this remarkable ceremony. A special 32-carat Heart of Gold award has been formulated and designed for one outstanding individual. Naturally all our prizewinners are outstanding people, but this one was a little bit special. When we first announced this particular award, some found it startling, some found it controversial, but slowly but surely everyone has come round to our way of thinking: that the man we are about to honour is a wonderful individual who has shown courage and real action.'

With this, Aggie stood back a little, and the television monitors glowed into life for the final time that day. Instantly, the broad and smiling face of Barry Cole filled the screens.

'I used to be a policeman,' said Barry, 'and along with my colleague, Colin McCready, I was called to a crime scene at a convenience store in North London shortly before Christmas last year. It looked like an open-and-shut case. But as our investigations proceeded, things became complicated. The man who had been killed had been threatening a defenceless child, and the so-called *killer* had been standing up for her. In the light of all this, is not the law an arse?'

Barry let that rhetorical question ring in everyone's ears as the screen image dissolved to a montage of newspaper headlines, columnists' and editorial comments, magazine covers of Dr Sweet and snippets of lively discussion shows from radio and television. Then it was back to Barry.

'This man was Dr David Sweet, who when he isn't saving the lives of innocent children is finding a cure for cancer. My colleague and I became so moved by what Dr Sweet had done that we quit the police service there and then and devoted ourselves to promulgating the kind of selfless moral action he showed.'

The screen dissolved again to a still photograph, the old one of Cordie, Alice and himself on the Dorset coast. Dr Sweet vaguely remembered scanning and e-mailing it to Ros a few weeks ago. But really almost everything was vague now. The floating sensation was more acute than ever. Another face loomed up on the screen: it was the bald, round head of the Ruzowitsky's former Director, filmed in the windswept landscape of the Isle of Man.

'David Sweet is a great scientist and a lovely guy,' he said to the accompaniment of distant sheep. 'I'm proud to have worked with him.' His broad face disappeared, and was replaced by the long, sharp head of a young Australian, announced by the on-screen caption as 'Arlen

Forsyth, friend'. 'I love this guy!' he shouted and his face faded to blank.

'Ladies and gentlemen,' said Barry's voice, 'I give you – David Sweet!'

There was a tumultuous roar. Everyone stood and applauded. Dr Sweet looked around at the faces at his table: John, Rosemary and Alice, clapping and grinning, Kamil and Zalihe clapping, Cordie just looking at him. For a moment, he didn't think his legs were going to work, then Alice caught him under the armpit, as if trying to hoist him to his feet.

The next minute he found himself walking, threading his way around the tables and instinctively looking down, just as everyone else had done. He saw his shoes padding along the ground, brightly polished, one lace starting to lag. He felt people thump him on the back. He looked up occasionally and saw Aggie smiling, with her head tilted to one side, applauding very slowly, loosely and surely noiselessly, clasping and unclasping her hands.

Then he was at the very brink of the stage. Dr Sweet negotiated the shallow little run of steps with caution – how awful to trip up now – and found himself on the platform, Aggie coming towards him with deliberate steps and holding out his award: his Heart of Gold, a large gold heart attached to a heavy rosewood base by thin gold stalks, the base fringed with a platinum edge and with the number '32' etched onto the heart's right-hand ventricle. He saw that his name, David Sweet, had been engraved into the pewtery surround. He accepted it and juggled it a little in his hand, as if testing its weight, and this got a little *woof* of laughter amid the acclaim. Aggie said something to him and he said something back, although he could hear neither side of the conversation. Then she gestured at the microphone and backed away from him in the same choreographed way, her hands clasping and unclasping. Dr Sweet went up to the microphone and, with a great echoey *ahem*, enforced utter quiet on the proceedings.

His first thought was that he had gone blind. The lights were all shining directly into his eyes and he could see nothing at all.

Dr Sweet said: 'I . . .'

The light seemed to shimmer and swarm in front of him, like the concave interior of a vast burnished container turned this way and that, but he found that he could see through it by shifting his weight and standing a few centimetres to one side, away from the microphone. Then he could see faces looking up at him, ovoid discs with facial expressions showing respectful interest, shading off into discomfort and concern. Dr Sweet was hardly a newcomer to public speaking; he had given talks about his work at conferences in capital cities all over the world. He had spoken to audiences two or three times the size of this; dashingly plugging his laptop computer into the stage projector and using his PowerPoint software to project graphs, images and movie sequences showing cell growth. He wasn't like all these other tongue-tied Hearts of Gold award-winners. He was a *middle-class professional*. It was in Paris, he now remembered fondly, at just this sort of event, where he had first slept with Hattie. They had kept the catalogue programme as a kind of sentimental souvenir. Where *had* that gone? Where had Hattie gone, come to that? Gone back to the lab, he supposed, to work as best she could.

There was a distinct rustling of impatience from the crowd. From the corner of his eye, he could see Aggie make tense little get-on-with-it movements with her head, her mouth stretched into a thin line whose infinitesimal upward curvature only just qualified as a smile.

Dr Sweet looked back at the audience, who were now entirely visible, though still bathed in a heavy sunset wash of light. And there was his family: his old mum and dad, and Alice, who he noticed looking at him with a certain leniency, even tenderness, just like when they were married.

And there was Cordie, gazing at him with piercing directness. He could discern her very clearly in her best little party dress and mop of hair. That was how she used to look at him when she was in her high chair. He would be washing up in their little kitchen, humming or singing to himself, and then remember she was there, look up, and find her facing him in her chair, having obviously been silently inspecting him all the time. And there she was now, her face utterly calm and immobile, entirely free of the metamorphosis from congratulatory euphoria to discomfort and concern that was being played out on the faces of everyone else. Her wide, clear eyes looked into his, ignoring his Heart of Gold. Everything he knew, Dr Sweet considered, his daughter knew as well.

'I can't . . . I can't accept this,' said Dr Sweet at last, and many present sighed with relief. This kind of dis-avowal was wholly traditional. Many Hearts of Gold felt that their award should go to the *entire* paramedic team, the *entire* staff of the inner-city remedial reading initiative, and in fact the proceedings had been considerably delayed by getting these other groups to troop up and join the winner.

But it then became horribly clear that this was not what Dr Sweet meant. He was looking about vaguely, holding the Heart of Gold not with a firm proprietorial grip, but gingerly cupping it in both hands, as if looking for someone to take it from him. Dr Sweet turned to some executives of Dartmouth Media and the commercial sponsors ranged on his left, and held it out to them, ever so slightly. Their faces were those of a masked Greek chorus. Dr Sweet turned round to face Aggie, and gently held it out to her. Her mouth was stretched more thinly than ever, and with a curvature unquestionably pointing downwards. Dr Sweet held it out for her a little more, but Aggie shook her head with a ferocious little quivering motion.

He turned back to face front once more. Dr Sweet now held his award not at the bottom, but by one of the thin gold stalks connecting the heart to the heavy base, and immediately he felt the strut snap. Very slowly, he started to sag at the knees, bending down, keeping his back straight. He was trying to place his Heart of Gold on the floor as discreetly as possible. Suddenly, he felt Aggie's fierce grip on his elbow and his Heart. The roofing-felt roughness of Aggie's vivid tweed abraded his skin as she embraced him fiercely, bringing his torso and head up to the mike with a single wrenching hug, while not allowing him to relinquish his award.

'Ladies and gentlemen, David's a little overwhelmed,' she said into the microphone, her face close enough to his for him to get a tiny pepperminty breath. 'I know how he feels, I'm a little overwhelmed myself. In fact, I think we're all just a little overwhelmed. But let's give him another round of applause!'

They did so. Aggie relaxed her grip and Dr Sweet leant forward involuntarily, like a ventriloquist's dummy bowing. He was then ushered off the stage under cover of another musical interlude. Ros directed him to place his other hand under his Heart to prevent it coming to grief, and Aggie followed, catching her subordinate's eye with the tough, self-satisfied air of a professional who has been extinguishing fires like this on live television for almost twenty years. Not that it *was* live, of course, and this near fiasco would have to be heavily edited.

When Dr Sweet returned to his table, his party could hardly catch his eye, being fully aware of his mortifying failure to either graciously accept the award or repudiate it convincingly. Dr Sweet put it down with a heavy *thump* on the table, where its loose stalk twanged.

'Well done!' said Kamil brightly at last, and everyone else echoed this, John and Rosemary most forcefully. Alice's guest clapped him on the back, from which Dr Sweet flinched as if he had sunburn. He tried to smile by forcing the corners of his mouth against gravity. Zalihe and Cordie just looked at each other.

There was movement in the room now that the house lights had gone up. People were milling about, going to each other's tables. Everyone in Dr Sweet's group stirred, too. Alice spoke. 'Well, I suppose we'd better make a move. We don't want the children to get overtired.'

But just as everyone was standing up, Ros came over to Dr Sweet.

'David,' she said sharply, and then into her headset mike: 'Yes, I've got him, Aggie. He's right here. Did you want to say anything to him?' Ros then winced as if from a loud bang. 'No, all right. Mmm. Yes, I'll . . . Mmm.'

'Yes, Ros?' asked Dr Sweet, utterly cowed.

'David,' said Ros. 'The photo? The group photo? You know.'

Dr Sweet did not know, but Ros stepped aside and gestured at the group that was assembling on the stage he had just ignominiously left. They were the winners, and all of them were sitting on rows of chairs facing a camera, as if for a sports-team picture, each with their Heart on their lap. Dr Sweet took a few steps closer and could see the privileged empty seat, reserved for him, in the middle of the front row. Aggie was standing there, now sporting a mike headset herself, looking at him crisply and cradling her right elbow in her left hand, right forefinger pressed to her lips. Numbly, Dr Sweet allowed himself to be led forward by the arm – his party drifting behind him, unsure whether they too might be required – and submitted equally timidly when Ros suddenly pulled him back.

'Where's your thingy?' she groaned. 'Your award?'

They turned back for it. Dr Sweet almost pushed past the family group to get his Heart. He looked for it on the table. Within a second or two, everyone was looking for it: Alice, John, Rosemary, Kamil, Zalihe, Lyle all looking for the Heart of Gold on the table, under the table, under the tablecloth. It was gone. Ros's face went the colour of Milk of Magnesia. Then Alice's head made two convulsive turns, one to look at the exit behind the table and one to look back at the stage.

'David,' she said. 'Where's Cordie?'

31

In the corridor she'd reached from the first staircase, Cordie stopped and looked at it again. She looked really closely. She thought her face looked funny in the gold Heart. She put her face right up next to it and her reflection looked all fat and bulgy and gold. Her nose was squashy and fat like a pig's. She was a monster.

'Bleargh!' she said softly to herself, like a big growling monster. 'Bleargh!'

She walked on, imagining the big gold bulgy monster chasing her. She ran for a bit, the loose stalk on the Heart twanging and pinging against the Heart itself. Some of the doors of the corridor were open and cleaning ladies in smocks were coming out with trolleys. She peeped inside and saw the grandest, cleanest room she had ever seen, with a television high up on the wall. She asked the cleaning lady if she could ride on her trolley and the lady said no, but nicely, and she asked where her mum and dad were and she said they were coming. Then the lady saw the Heart and she went really serious.

'Did you win that?' she asked, and Cordie fibbed and said yes and the lady said nothing at all, and Cordie said she'd better go.

When she got to the end of the corridor there was

another big staircase with an enormous polished handrail. Cordie remembered when she used to slide down the banisters at Granny's house and almost broke them. She couldn't have got up on these banisters even if she'd wanted to; they were too big and brown and wide and shining. Cordie put the Heart down and put her head through the white wooden railings and looked down: two storeys to the ground. Then she turned onto her back and looked up – the handrail looped round and round and round lots of times all the way up to the ceiling. She could see tiny hands trailing along it. She thought about walking on the ceiling and seeing the same thing looking down. It made her feel dizzy but excited at the same time.

She pulled her head out, picked up the Heart and went up another flight. There had been some people in the round curly bit of the stairs, but in the corridors she had the place to herself. Cordie looked at the Heart again. For the first time she saw it had her dad's name on it, David Sweet. Cordie supposed that David was her dad's first name because they both began with D.

Cordie looked at the radiators and wondered if they'd been bleeding. They were long and low, but otherwise looked the same as the ones at home. She knelt down and looked at them more closely. They were black, but there were bits where the black paint had come off, and there was shiny metal underneath which made her face looked bulgy like the Heart. She examined the hole in the wiry grey carpet where the pipe from the radiator went down into the floor. It was damp and gungy and smelly; something wet had made the carpet go black. Cordie remembered when she'd had a nosebleed on holiday and her T-shirt had got stained black, not red. Her grandad had tried to press a cold key on the back of her neck without warning her and she had wriggled and it had fallen down the back of her jeans and her dad had got cross with both her *and* Grandad.

Cordie didn't know why she'd taken the Heart away from the table, but it was partly because seeing her dad with it made her sad and cross at the same time. She thought she would take it, go as far away from him as possible, go to the very top of the hotel, to the very farthest corner, away from the big, crowded room with all its noise that she could still hear in her head. She had tried shutting her eyes, she had tried putting her hands over her ears, but she could still hear it. She put the Heart down and tried doing both again, but she could still see the faces and clapping hands. It was like the feeling she used to get when she was little just before going to sleep; a rushing feeling as if she was whizzing along on a fairground ride when she was actually completely still in bed, trying to go to sleep. This was like that and she didn't like it one bit.

Cordie could hear someone running up the stairs and she ducked into an alcove. She pushed the door and it opened.

32

Having received the concierge's assurances that his staff were on the lookout and there was no way her daughter could have left the hotel and got anywhere near the busy main road that divided the hotel from the park, and having further secured an undertaking that he would detain any unaccompanied child who tried to leave, Alice had instructed everyone to split up and search. John and Rosemary were to check the ballroom at the back; Kamil and Zalihe volunteered to go back down the lobby and check the main hall and its adjoining rooms; Alice was going to look in the restaurant and the bistro next to it, and Dr Sweet said he would check the remaining rooms on the ground floor and the corridors upstairs.

He started galloping down various passageways. He went into the bar, and distracted guests by saying, 'Cordie? Are you there? Come out now, Cordie!' Then he ran out and found himself in the lobby again, getting double-takes from people who had no idea about his Heart of Gold. He looked deathly pale and sweaty, with his shirt-tail hanging out.

Where to now? Surely any second Alice, surefooted, capable Alice, would appear with Cordie? But she didn't. There were only other guests: Americans, Germans, Swiss, checking in and out, trailing suitcases on wheels. Everybody would be roaming around other parts of the building, probably expecting *him* to find her. They were relying on *him*. Dr Sweet galloped down a second corridor, leading to the cloakrooms and the hotel's newsstand. He went past lighted cabinets, containing vastly expensive handbags, swathes of luxurious silk in the form of handkerchiefs and scarves, tiny, gleaming chrome personal stereos, all with impossible price tags. He shambled to a halt outside the newsstand with its smart, worldly display rack of the *International Herald Tribune*, *Der Spiegel*, *Le Monde* and *The Economist*, and ducked inside moaning, 'Cordie?'

No. Dr Sweet ducked back out, *literally* ducking now, every physical movement accompanied by a hunch of tension. He looked down the passage from where he'd come. Nothing. He wheeled back round, trotted on past the cloakrooms, yelped like a madman into the men's and women's lavatories and then continued on down the stairs to the spa. He came to a halt by the cool, trickling fountain centrepiece, which stood just by the massage and aromatherapy studios, and twisted his head this way and that like a submarine periscope.

'Can I help you?' asked the frosty white-smocked assistant behind the desk, bringing to the question its fullest traditional subtext that what was being offered was not help but a request to go away.

'I've lost my daughter,' he said with brutal clarity. 'Have you seen a little girl?'

'No, I . . . no, we haven't,' said the assistant, exchanging glances with a colleague who had just joined her, an older lady wearing glasses with a thin silver chain around her neck.

'You're quite sure?' asked Dr Sweet, guessing correctly that curtness not apologetic supplication was going to elicit the clearest response.

'Quite,' said the older lady seriously.

Satisfying himself that there were no rooms further along past the spa, Dr Sweet abruptly turned tail and went back upstairs. Puffing now, in fact almost completely out of breath, Dr Sweet cleared the main lobby area and pressed one of the call buttons by the bank of lifts. His seething, ferocious impatience transmitted itself to the frankly terrified guests through the clenching and unclenching of his fists, his constant stepping back to monitor the lifts' glacial progress, and breathing heavily and fiercely through his nose. Then, with a convulsive start, he wrenched himself away from the lifts and galloped up the stairs to the first-floor corridor.

Nothing but some cleaners coming out of rooms. Dr Sweet did a strange little pigeon-toed jog down the passageway, glancing into the rooms whose doors were jammed open by the cleaners' trolleys.

He almost cannoned into one of them as she reversed out of a doorway pulling her cart, while uncomfortably holding a mop in one hand. She turned and looked at him with startled affront. Fifteen years in the restaurant and hotel cleaning business and an annual talk from the managing group's head of security had taught her that only one type of person runs in the corridor of a five-star establishment like this: someone who has been discovered stealing from the rooms.

Dr Sweet veered around to his right and, without

thinking, the cleaner tried blocking his path with her cart, jerking it back far enough to catch Dr Sweet on the hip. 'Ow,' he squealed with an unbecoming lack of adult stoicism, clutching his hip as if to staunch the blood from a gunshot wound, at the same time as the cleaner barked, 'What are you doing?'

Dr Sweet straightened, loosening his grip on his injured side. With an effort, he remembered why he was here. 'I'm looking for my daughter, my little daughter. Have you seen a little girl, about so high, mop of fair hair?'

'Was she carrying one of those Heart awards?'

'Yes. *Yes*.'

The cleaner softened, giving him a radiant smile.

'You must be so proud of her.'

33

Standing on the table was fun. Standing on the table was great. It was the sort of thing she wasn't allowed to do either at her mum's house *or* her dad's house. But she was doing it now all right. Cordie knew they would be worried about her and that they'd be cross, so she thought she might as well do some extra naughty things while she was here.

When she got into the room at first, Cordie didn't know what to make of it; it was huge, much bigger than the others. There were no televisions and no bed, just this big brown polished table with loads of chairs round it. And at every chair there was a place setting, like at home, but there were no place mats or knives and forks, just little pads of paper, tiny little pads, smaller than any pads she had ever seen, but no-one had done any drawing on them. Next to the pads were blue pens. She had put the Heart down on the table, clicked a pen and drawn some lines. Then she had tried drawing the Superman 'S', but it wouldn't come out right. You sort of had to draw the gaps the 'S' made inside the shield, and not the 'S' itself. She'd tried it about two or three times and then given up. Then she'd gone over to a metal contraption which had a sort of glass plate and a big arm with another metal thing on it. It had a switch on the side, so Cordie had turned it on. Right away there was a kind of air-blowing noise, like a fan, and the machine projected a big square of light up onto a screen from the glass plate. Cordie looked into the light and sneezed, 'A-choo!' Then she put her hands on the plate and they made big outlines on the screen. She made a rabbit and a donkey with her hands, the way her dad had taught her how to do once, but then thinking about her dad made her feel sad again so she stopped.

And that was when she climbed on one of the chairs and then up onto the table. The tabletop was so polished that it was actually quite slippery; she had to get her balance, feeling how to plant her feet. But once she'd done that, it was great; it was easy. Cordie was so high up, sort of like being on stage, higher up than when she'd sung her song at school. She walked from one end of the table to the other and it took ages, loads longer than if she'd tried walking across the tables in either her mum's or her dad's house. Of course, she wouldn't be allowed to there.

From one end of the table she saw the Heart at the other. She thought about how her dad had been different ever since this whole thing started. She couldn't really talk to him any more, and her mum didn't talk to him the same way either. When Cordie thought about all this, the funny rushing sensation in her head came back, so she measured the length of the table in paces, heel-to-toe. Thirty-five paces!

She picked up the Heart, turned around and took thirty-five paces back to the other end of the table where, for the first time, Cordie noticed the big window, entirely open to the street; there was a little breeze coming in. Cordie could see some treetops from where she was, but thought she could get a better view by going up to the open window.

She climbed down and reached the window ledge by standing on another of the chairs. The ledge was just level with her feet and she could see a big park with lots of trees and a busy main road, almost a motorway, below her. She could see a wonderful big blue sky, and clouds and birds were flying around almost level with where she was. Clutching onto the window frame with one hand and keeping hold of the Heart with the other, Cordie climbed out on to the balcony and looked down.

The breeze ruffled her hair, but she didn't feel in the least dizzy. She saw the tops of people's heads, like little pebbles moving along. Cordie looked at the greens and browns of the trees and thought it was like the jungle, when Baloo had picked her up and taken her up high in the safety of his paws. The sun had just gone behind a cloud.

Cordie felt as if she wanted to be over on the other side of the trees somehow. She felt the way her Barbie had felt in her song, on the other side of the ocean. The bushes and the road and the cars along the near side of the park looked close; close enough to reach out and touch. Confidently, Cordie relinquished her hold on the window frame and, smiling at a sudden encouraging thought, felt in her pocket for something and took it out: her Superman badge.

34

Dr Sweet had gone past the conference room twice in the course of his galloping up and down the second-floor corridor. He had run along the empty passageway once, pushing speculatively at each bedroom door to ensure they were locked, and then back again to the stairwell to consider his options. It was only when he looked at the double doors of the conference suite, close by on his left, that he saw a thin chink of light.

He pushed them both open and blundered in, gasping the word, 'Cordie,' too out of breath to shout anything. His clothes stuck sweatily to his body.

'Cordie. Cordie?'

There seemed to be nothing there; it was just a conference room with a big mahogany boardroom-style table. But someone had been here. There was a strange whirring sound, and Dr Sweet saw that it came from an old-fashioned overhead projector which was plugged in, switched on and beaming a square of light onto the screen above. He switched it off and the projector sighingly relapsed into silence.

It was now that Dr Sweet saw that one of the little pads on the table was out of alignment with the rest and its pen had been placed crookedly on top. Something had been drawn there: a series of diamond-shapes with blunted, flattened tops. No, that wasn't right, they were kind of heraldic, like shields. They had curious outline shapes drawn inside them. Dr Sweet felt a terrible intestinal coldness as he realized they were supposed to represent the letter 'S'. He turned towards the empty, open window, half obscured by a partly drawn curtain.

'Cordie.'

Dr Sweet approached the window slowly, all but holding his breath, grandmother's-footsteps style. The breeze cooled his forehead. He heard the Park Lane traffic, far away below.

Dr Sweet put his head out of the window, looked around to the left and there Cordie was, out on the small balcony, holding the Heart, looking right at him, nothing between her and the open air but a single black rail, which for an adult would be about waist level, but which for Cordie was chest-height. Neither of them said anything for a moment, and neither looked down.

Dr Sweet knew he shouldn't move towards her, and heard his voice approach a kind of bomb-disposal-expert level of calm.

'Cordie?'

Cordie nodded her head imperceptibly, compressing her lips.

'Why don't you come in now? Be very careful, keep hold of the rail, and just move very slowly towards me, love.'

Cordie didn't move, and an instinct told Dr Sweet to keep talking as if he wasn't insisting or repeating himself.

'Time to come in now. Nice and easy. Stay very close to the window. Nice and slowly towards me now.'

And so, with obediently slow, incremental little steps, Cordie began to move towards Dr Sweet. Her father allowed himself to glance down for a second, and saw Cordie's feet in red sandals and cream socks on the grey stone ledge with its tiny cracks and holes. He didn't look at the sheer blank of air and light, five inches or so to the right.

She was almost within reach of his outstretched hand. What Dr Sweet felt like doing was making a sudden swipe, grasping her wrist tight enough to make his knuckles the colour of snow. But he knew he mustn't do that. Because pulling Cordie was the way to make her freeze; she was like a seat-belt in that regard. So he just let her keep coming, not losing eye contact, gently smiling and murmuring.

Cordie placed her hand in his. Gently, and without panic or any rushed movement, Dr Sweet brought his other hand round to encircle her waist and lifted her back inside the room. It was only here that Cordie offered any resistance at all. She leant back towards the window and, with a single movement of her arm, hardly more than a sharp straightening of the elbow, threw the Heart out. After a beat, they put their heads out of the window together and watched the glistening gold organ plunge down and scrape the edge of the wall which deflected it into a shimmering spin. Then it hit a ledge, at which point Dr Sweet's award shattered into three distinct pieces: the Heart itself on its base and the two thin stalks or struts, all of them landed in the awning extended over the main entrance to the hotel. One of the pieces rolled over to the right, and looked for a moment as if it was going to tumble out and down onto the pavement. But no, the three now quite dull and metallic-looking fragments remained quite still.

Father and daughter sat on the chairs by the conference table in silence, Cordie's feet dangling. They looked around at the panelled walls with their colourful abstracts illuminated by concealed lighting, that had been activated when they came into the room. Dr Sweet breathed heavily through his nostrils, looking sideways at Cordie whose lower lip was now trembling ominously. He embraced her until she was quiet.

'You're all right, aren't you, Cordie?' said Dr Sweet. Cordie nodded.

'Would you like to come downstairs with me now?' 'Yes,' said Cordie simply.

Getting down, Cordie put her small hand in Dr Sweet's big hand, and together they walked down the stairs, towards the lifts and the lobby. Her hand was still too small to interlock with his thumbs properly; it was more a case of holding her hand in his palm. As Dr Sweet and his daughter walked together back down the stairs, they both imagined the group that would be waiting: Alice, Alice's friend Lyle, John, Rosemary, Kamil and Zalihe – all in a group, smiling, relieved, pleased to see them. Just a few moments more walking and they would come into view.

But just at the bottom of the stairs, Cordie stopped. She put her arms up and shook them. Dr Sweet picked her up and hugged her to his side. Cordie tapped his hip with her hand, so he stuck it out to stop her sliding down. Then he strode round the corner, while Cordie gently and experimentally folded his ear back and forth.

ACKNOWLEDGEMENTS

Heartfelt thanks are due to David Miller, Peter Straus, Melanie Jackson, David Baddiel, Catherine Blyth, Mike Baker, Anna Chapple, Charlotte Raven, Andrew Kidd, Becky Senior, Sam Humphreys and Ted. And for her help, her support, her advice, and for her love of both the tough and tender kind, my extra special thanks to Caroline Hill.